"THIS MOST BEAUTIFUL SITE IN BOSTON DOES NOT BELONG TO THE JUDGES, IT DOES NOT BELONG TO THE LAWYERS, IT DOES NOT BELONG TO THE FEDERAL GOVERNMENT. IT BELONGS TO THE PUBLIC" … STEPHEN G. BRYER.

"OUR GOVERNMENT IS THE POTENT, THE OMNIPOTENT TEACHER, FOR GOOD OR FOR ILL, IT TEACHES THE WHOLE PEOPLE BY ITS EXAMPLE" … LOUIS D. BRANDEIS, 1928.

"JUSTICE IS BUT TRUTH IN ACTION" … LOUIS D. BRANDEIS, 1914.

"THE LAW IS THE WITNESS AND EXTERNAL DEPOSIT OF OUR MORAL LIFE. ITS HISTORY IS THE MORAL DEVELOPMENT OF THE RACE" … OLIVER WENDELL HOLMES, 1897.

"THE LIFE OF THE LAW HAS NOT BEEN LOGIC: IT HAS BEEN EXPERIENCE" … OLIVER WENDELL HOLMES, 1881.

BOOK ONE OF THREE-BOOK TRILOGY:

HORRORS OF THE MIND ENTERTAINMENT, LLC

This novel is a work of "creative" fiction. All characters in this novel are fictitious. Any resemblance to actual events or locales or persons, living or dead, is entirely coincidental. This book contains sexually explicit scenes and is intended for mature audiences only.

Becky Lawrence waited impatiently in Judge Charles Woodbury's office. She stared out through the wall-length glass conoid wall into the Fort Point Channel squinting, watching the Liberty Fleet of Tall Ships cruise by; her attention momentarily diverted to the old, decrepit shack on stilts where it is rumored the Boston Tea Party occurred. The light was blinding and Becky could no longer focus. A beam of sunlight formed a rainbow prism, and her eyes followed its course hitting the far left wall of his chambers.

Becky slowly walked toward the array of golden-framed memorabilia. The first gold-embossed mounted frame was Woodbury's Bachelor's of Art from Yale University dated June 1, 1975. Next in queue the Judge's 1978 Harvard Law School Maxima Cum Laude Juris Doctorate. Her eyes meandered to an enlarged 15 x 20 photograph of Woodbury shaking Ronald Reagan's hand.

Becky was nervous and began to pace. She'd been anxious since receiving the Judge's email at 8:35 a.m. requesting her presence at 1:00 in his chambers. Her hands were shaking and her heart racing as she continued to pace as the food arrived.

"Hi, Ms. Lawrence," Juanita Ramirez said as she parked the food cart in front of the Judge's Victorian mahogany desk.

"Hi, Juanita," Becky said as the Judge approached smiling. "Thank you, Juanita," Woodbury said with a smile as he shook Becky's right hand, and their eyes locked in mutual admiration.

"Good day, Judge," Juanita said with a grin while exiting.

"Please have a seat, Becky," the Judge said as he scooped salad into a bowl, topping it off with a heaping scoop of tuna. Becky's stomach rumbled as she watched him pour the raspberry vinaigrette over his heaping mound.

"Becky," Woodbury said as he sat in his leather chair which squeaked under his weight, "eat."

Becky hadn't eaten breakfast and although her stomach growled, she was nauseous as her nerves were frayed. She scooped salad into a bowl, topped it with a small scoop of tuna, dousing it with red wine vinegar dressing.

The Judge ate his salad voraciously intermittently smiling at Becky. She picked at her bowl eating the tuna off the top. "Becky, I asked you to join me for lunch today to talk about your future. How long have you been clerking for me now?" Woodbury asked as he grinned and stabbed the romaine.

"Um," Becky said nervously as she played with her salad, "well, since my second year at Harvard Law, and, um, well, you know, I graduated last June so it's almost two years, your Honor."

Woodbury smiled as he scooped more salad into his bowl. "You still want to be an Assistant U.S. Attorney I am assuming?"

"Yes, sir," Becky said as she chewed a cucumber slice.

Woodbury grabbed a manila file folder and handed it to Becky before sitting back down and devouring his lunch. Becky opened it and held the finely engrained paper with Judge Woodbury's emblem scrawled across the top. Her hands began to shake as she read the addressee: "Ms. Angela Perez, United States Attorney for The District of Massachusetts, U.S. Department of Justice."

“Dear Angela,” Becky read as her hands trembled and the Judge winked: “I am writing this letter of recommendation for Ms. Rebecca D. Lawrence. After graduating magna cum laude at the top of her class at Harvard Law, Becky Lawrence has become my most treasured law clerk. Her superior intellect and her sharply-honed legal mind in conjunction with her criminal justice acumen continues to impress and astonish me daily. There is no better judicial candidate for Assistant U.S. Attorney in this district or any other than Ms. Rebecca D. Lawrence … kindest regards, Justice Charles P. Woodbury, Federal Judge, John J. Moakley U.S. Courthouse, 1 Courthouse Way, Boston, Mass.”

Becky looked up and into the Judge’s warm blue eyes. “I don’t know what to say, your Honor,” she whispered as her fork stabbed a cucumber wedge.

“Your face speaks a thousand words, Ms. Lawrence,” Woodbury said as he grinned.

“Thank you, Judge,” Becky said as she doused the wedge in dressing.

“I will look forward to watching you in awe as you try cases before me,” Woodbury said as he stood and walked around the desk. He stood in front of Becky; and as Becky rose, Woodbury grabbed her into a bear hug whispering: “I’m gonna miss you in the meantime.” A single tear rolled down Becky’s left cheek.

Woodbury sat at the edge of his desk holding a document in his right hand as Becky sat down in her chair. “Listen, I hope you don’t mind, but I sent this letter to Ms. Perez last Tuesday. Here’s her email response.”

“Dear Judge Woodbury, I have had the personal pleasure of meeting your current law clerk, Ms. Rebecca Lawrence, and I am prepared to waive the customary formal interview process within the United States Attorney’s Office. With gratitude and appreciation, I am prepared to offer her a full-time position within the United States Judiciary.”

Becky looked into Woodbury's eyes; he smiled without his lips moving. "Congratulations, Becky," he said as she placed her right hand into his open left palm.

"I don't know how to thank you, your Honor," she said as tears began to dampen her pretty face except to say: "Thank you, Judge."

As Becky walked through the maze in the "back of the house," accessible only to judiciary personnel, her mind reeled backwards in time to her Harvard graduation and then flashed back to dancing around her grandmother's living room at nine as her Grammy twirled her around and around as she sang: "I am woman watch me grow … I am strong, I am invincible, I am woman," and Becky's smile faded into a frown. "God, if only Grammy could see me now" she thought, "I miss her."

Becky waved her Judiciary ID in front of the scanner, and the door slowly automatically pivoted. She walked past Woodbury's courtroom, Courtroom No. 1, and walked toward the balcony in front of the 88-foot-high, 372-foot wide arched-glass conoid wall, staring into the panoramic view of the Boston Harbor.

"I miss my grandmother," she thought as she walked toward the brick wall to glance at the court calendar for the next day. "Courtroom No. 1, Judge Charles Woodbury, 9:00 a.m. CR-13:40221, United States v. Eric Ramon, Final Pretrial Conference" she read as her iPhone began to buzz nestled in the right front pocket of her blazer.

"Ms. Lawrence?" a woman's voice inquired.

"Yes?" Becky said as her voice cracked.

"This is Angela Perez, Ms. Lawrence."

Becky held the phone in front of her face and stared at the touchscreen dumbfounded.

“Ms. Lawrence?” Perez asked wondering if the call had dropped.

“Yes, I’m here,” Becky said mouthing, “Oh, my God!”

“I’d like to meet with you. I’m leaving tonight for Washington to meet with Holder and was wondering if by any chance you’re free this afternoon? I checked Judge Woodbury’s calendar, and there’s nothing on the docket.”

“Sure, yes, of course,” Becky said excitedly.

“Let’s say half an hour,” Perez said with a grin, “you know where we are … ninth floor.”

“Yes, sure,” Becky replied as she began nervously twisting her hair.

Becky walked into Courtroom No. 1 and slowly walked toward the clerk’s bench. The courtroom was empty and eerily quiet; yet, Becky could feel eyes upon her. The ghost sat in the witness box and smiled as she looked around nervously. There was no one there. Becky smiled as she peered around the periphery of the empty courtroom: “There’s something so serene and tranquil when the courtroom clears,” she thought and grinned.

The ghost stood and walked toward her, his black eyes inquisitively staring into her petite pretty face. The ghost lunged forward and passed through her; and as he appeared behind her and turned around to face her, she mumbled: “Charlie?” as a freezing mist enveloped her silhouette and the stench of sulphur filled her mucous membranes. Becky gagged and mumbled: “What’s that smell?” as goosebumps covered her body. She yawned and stared at her cell: “22 minutes,” she said out loud under her breath.

Becky took the elevator down to the lobby as her body warmed causing her to spasmodically twitch. She walked into the coffee shop. “Hi, Alan,” she said with a grin.

“Hi, Becky,” Alan replied as he grabbed a large styrofoam cup and poured the Dunkin’ Donuts blend in, capping it with a splash of light cream. “So how are you, Becky?” Alan asked with a smile.

Becky tried to avoid eye contact as Alan was legally blind and his eyes darted in opposing directions. “He can’t see you,” she said to herself, “dummy.”

“I’m good, Alan,” Becky said smiling, “and you?”

“Oh, good. I’m good,” Alan said as he placed her large regular on the glass countertop. Becky placed three one-dollar bills into Alan’s open left palm. He passed the money back to her saying: “It’s on me today. Have a good one, Becky.”

Becky walked toward the rear door of the Moakley and walked outside saying “hi” to John and Peter who stood guard. She strolled down toward the water, the fragrant savor of saltwater roses, Rosa Rugosa, permeating the air. She sipped her coffee as she knelt and sniffed and sighed: “Aw.”

She downed half the coffee inhaling the landscape … “11 minutes,” she thought as she picked a handful of blueberries, staining her right palm as she swallowed. “Nine minutes,” she mumbled as she walked up the concrete walk and licked her lips tasting the salt of the Atlantic and throwing her empty styrofoam into the trash receptacle.

As Becky stepped off the elevator on the ninth floor and stumbled toward reception, Angela Perez approached with an outstretched hand: “Hi, Becky,” she said as she clenched her right hand. “Follow me.”

Becky followed the U.S. Attorney for the District into her office as Becky whispered in her mind: “Wow, this is amazing … easily rivals the Judge’s chambers.”

“Have a seat, please,” Angela said with a smile as she sat at her desk.

“This is beautiful,” Becky said looking around the office as she placed her hand on the old antique English oak dropfront desk.

“Thanks,” Perez said as she grinned. “I want to welcome you to the United States Attorney’s Office.” Perez handed Becky two thick blue binders stuffed to the max. The first binder was labeled: “Protocols,” the second: “Rules and Regs.”

Please familiarize yourself with these in the next few days. You will be tested on your knowledge.” Becky frowned as Perez said with a smile: “I’m kidding, Becky.”

“Oh, yeah, yeah,” Becky said as she nervously giggled.

“Listen, as all new Assistant United States Attorneys, you will be assigned to a senior prosecutor. You will aid and assist in all of his/her current prosecutions. I have temporarily assigned you to Zachery Woods as his caseload is voluminous, shall we say; and as I’m sure you know, he is one of this district’s most prominent and influential AUSAs.”

Becky smiled and said: “psyched” in her mind. She loved Zach and his courtroom dramatics ... “Ain’t no one who can sway a jury like Zach,” she thought as she continued to grin, “And besides,” her mind reeled, “he’s hot.”

“I’ve given Mr. Woods all of your contact information. He is very much looking forward to working with you, Becky, as I am.” Angela stood and walked toward Becky with her right arm extended. Angela shook Becky’s hand vigorously as Becky thought: “Oh, vice grip.”

“Follow me, please,” Angela said as she walked out of her office and treaded down a long hallway. She passed Zach’s office and two doors down, the name plaque read: “Rebecca D. Lawrence, AUSA.” As Becky reached up with her right hand to touch the plaque, it fell to the ground.

“Hmmm,” Perez said, “we’ll have to fix that … so what do you think?”

Becky smiled as she cased her periphery: “I think it’s perfect,” she said as she looked around her new office facing the Boston Harbor. Her eyes followed the glass wall toward the ceiling as her face contorted.

"Yeah, blind's broken; this will be fixed by the end of the day," Perez said as their eyes locked. "I know… you'll never get any work done with this view, right?" Angela said as Becky nodded and walked toward her small desk staring at the array of file folders covering the desktop.

"Welcome to the United States Attorney's Office," Angela said with a smile as she walked out into the hallway. I sent you an email with my contact info," Angela said as she winked as her voice faded, and Becky stared out into the harbor as her father's voice resonated in her mind:
"Girls like you need to concentrate on their intellect." The ten-year-old looked into her father's eyes: "Girls like me, Daddy?" Her father patted her head: "Yes, Becky, you know, chubby girls," and a single tear fell from the corner of her right eye as Becky's body twitched.

"Excuse me?" said Jeremy Lyons with a lisp. "Oh, hi, B-b-b-ecky," he stammered as he wheeled in her belongings from the Judge's chambers.

"Hi, Jeremy," Becky mumbled as she thought, "God, he gives me the creeps. I know he's retarded, but there's something off about him."

"Need any help?" Lyons stuttered.

"Um, yeah," Becky said as she unloaded her Northwestern B.S. diploma and her Harvard J.D.

"I'll be right back," Jeremy said stuttering, "gotta get s-s-s-s-u-plies." Becky felt goosebumps exploding on her arms and the tiny cilia-like hairs on the back of her neck stood erect: "Oooh, he's creepy," she thought as her body spasmodically jerked.

Becky unpacked both huge cardboard crates and laid everything on the floor in front of her desk. Jeremy hung her plaques with a savant's meticulous precision as Becky watched rolling her eyes: "Wow, this is gonna take two days," she thought as she smiled at him. "Good job, Jeremy," she said as he nervously chuckled: "Th-th-th-th-thank you," as he giggled.

Becky loaded her wooden bookshelves with assorted legalese and had everything in its place as Jeremy hung her Harvard plaque. She looked at her cell; it was 4:45. "Jeremy, listen, why don't you leave me this little box?" she said as she pointed to a small cardboard box containing a hammer, nails, glue, and an array of miscellaneous items.

"You s-s-s-sure?" Jeremy asked as he stared at her shoes. "I like your shoes," he mumbled as he chuckled.

"Creep," Becky thought as her face took on an intense snare: "I'm sure, Jeremy," she said as her mind pondered: "What's with him and shoes … hmmm, fetish," she answered as he stared at her feet.

"I really like your s-h-h-h-oes," he said as he nervously giggled.

"Thank you, Jeremy," Becky said as Lyons walked toward the open door and into the hallway. She followed and closed the door behind him: "Creep" as he said out loud: "nice shoes, B-b-b-ecky."

As Becky hung the rest of her memorabilia and temporarily stood in the doorjamb admiring her unique artistry, she thought of Jeremy staring at her shoes as he gawked, and Becky said out loud "creep," as she began to sing softly:

"So I creep, yeah, just keep it on the down low, said nobody is supposed to know" … her body convulsed as her mind focused on the way Lyons stared at her shoes and she said out loud: "Gross."

He's a creep all right as she sang: "So I creep, yeah, 'cause he doesn't know what I do and no attention goes to show, so I creep." Becky booted her PC down and closed her office door at six o'clock as she mumbled under her breath: "Outta here."

Becky tossed and turned and by 4:55 decided she couldn't watch her alarm clock anymore. She showered and straightened her hair and sat down in front of her PC at 6:15 to check email. Her eyes widened as she counted: one, two, three, four, five -- five emails from Zach today. "Jesus, does he sleep?" she said out loud as she grinned and opened the first email timestamped 5:55 a.m.: "Hi, Becky, could you please meet me in my office at 8? Need to prep for nine o'clock pretrial … thanks "Z" … "Z" Becky repeated as she smiled and opened the second:

"Hi Becky, need you to attend proffer in U.S. v. Hill, et al @ noon, 'k' … thanks, Z. (ps. Please print Officer Mackey's report.)"

Becky sipped her coffee and opened the third: "Hi Becky, change in time … proffer at 11:00 now, okay … thanks, Z."

"Oy," Becky said out loud as she took another sip of her Green Mountain Columbian. "Hi, Becky, U.S. v. Ramon Final Pretrial, please bring file with … thanks, Z."

"Wow," Becky said as she finished her mug, "I'm tired already," and she smiled and opened the last email timestamped 6:52: "Welcome aboard … Z."

Becky arrived at the John J. Moakley U.S. Courthouse at 7:35, grabbed a large regular from Alan, and began searching for the Ramon file as she queued to print Mackey's police report. She couldn't find the Ramon file and soon became exasperated and didn't notice Amanda Jenkins standing behind her.

"Excuse me?" Amanda whispered in a high-pitched tone as Becky jumped as her body twitched as her heart ferociously pounded causing her pulse to escalate rapidly as the adrenaline rushed.

"I'm sorry," Amanda said as Becky attempted to compose. "You scared the crap out of me," Becky said as she giggled and outstretched her right hand, "Becky Lawrence."

“Amanda Jenkins, your assistant and Zach’s paralegal,” Amanda said as she giggled and shook Becky’s hand.

“Oh, thank God,” Becky said as she vigorously shook her hand, “nice to meet you.”

Amanda looked around at the disarray on her desk. Becky followed her eyes and said: “Can’t find the Ramon file, grrr.”

“I’ve got it,” Amanda said with a smile, also printed the Mackey report and everything Zach needs for the proffer.”

Becky sighed “aw” as Amanda continued: “Listen, Zach forgets to cc me so from now on just send me his emails or cc me on your replies, okay?”

“You are a walking miracle, you know that?” Becky whispered as Amanda smiled.

“No worries,” Amanda said as she walked out of Becky’s office: “See you at 8,” she mumbled as she smiled. Becky looked out into the harbor and the Lion King freeze-framed in her mind: she was sitting with Grammy in the dark theater smiling, staring into her grandmother’s light green eyes. She watched as Simba grew from a cub into a handsome lion with a full orange mane as Timon, Pumbaa, and Simba began to sing as did Becky: “Hakuna Matata, what a wonderful phrase … Hakuna Matata, ain’t no passing craze. It means no worries for the rest of your days; it’s our problem-free philosophy, Hakuna Matata.”

Becky sat at her desk and sipped from her coffee humming “Hakuna Matata, what a wonderful phrase,” and downing her coffee, “ain’t no passing craze.” Her head bounced as she brought it up a slight octave: “It means no worries for the rest of your days”… she walked towards Zach’s office and stood in the archway still humming: “It’s our problem-free philosophy, Hakuna Matata.”

Zach was on the phone smiling and waved Becky in. Amanda mouthed: “hi” and motioned for Becky to sit next to her directly across from Zach's desk.

"Okay, sweetie," Zach said smiling: "See ya later, alligator," as he placed the phone onto the receiver. "My daughter, she's five," Zach said as he stood and rounded his desk extending his right hand. Becky stood and Zach grabbed her into a hug: "Welcome," he said as Amanda giggled. "I was so psyched when Angela told me you'd be working with me," Zach said as he returned to his chair: "Now, let's get to work. First up: Ramon."

Zach put his dark-rimmed frames on his nose and read from his lap. He lifted his glasses with his left hand and said: "Becky, have you had a chance to familiarize yourself with this one?"

"Briefly, this morning," Becky said as she grinned … "um, looks like a simple cocaine base distribution: no?"

"Exactly," Zach said grinning, "slight hiccup, though."

Amanda rummaged through her file folder in her lap and handed Becky a ten-page typed report entitled: "Statement of Radio."

"Radio, huh?" Becky asked as she looked into Zach's magnetic brown eyes and felt a polarized sexual attraction as Zach smiled at her as he licked his bottom lip.

"Yeah, um, Radio, our cooperating witness. Take a look at this." Zach flung a stapled bundle toward Becky which she caught just before it hit the floor.

Becky perused the CW's CORI: "CW 'Radio a/k/a William Worthington,' date of birth: August 30, 1965: 1992, aggravated assault and battery, nolo contendere, served 18 months, Barnstable; 1993, 1 kilo heroin, possession with intent to distribute, not guilty; 1994, 2 kilos cocaine base, possession with intent to distribute, plead guilty, served 43 months released for "good time"; 1994, domestic abuse, nolo contendere, served 27 months, released "good time"; 1995, assault and battery with a dangerous weapon, continued without a finding; 1997, 5.5 gram cocaine base, possession, intent to at her and licked his bottom lip.

"Shit, time to go," Zach said as he walked toward the hallway continuing to hum: "Mmm mmm, mmm-mmm-mmm-mmm, mmm mmm, mmm-mmm-mmm-mmm-mmm-mmm," as Becky smiling glanced at her iPhone: "8:42."

"I'll meet you downstairs," Zach said as he answered his cell and walked down the hallway.

"Amanda, the CW's such a scumbag," Becky whispered.

"Tell me about it …tried to talk to Zach about this a couple of weeks ago and he slammed me hard so I" --

"Shut up, huh?" Becky said as she winked. "This should be interesting," Becky mumbled under her breath as she followed Amanda toward the elevator.

At 8:55 Woodbury's clerk, Joshua Levy, approached the bench: "Hi, Becky," he said with a smile, "congrats."

"Hi, Josh," Becky said as she looked at her cell. Becky sat down and whispered to Amanda: "Where's Zach?"

Amanda raised her eyebrows: "He'll be here," as Becky stared at her cell: "8:57." The defendant was brought into the courtroom, his ankles shackled and his wrists handcuffed behind his back. He wore a bright orange jumpsuit and struggled to walk as the chains twisted and resisted every motion forward.

Becky leaned in toward Amanda: "baby," she said as she stared at the young defendant who was seated next to the federal defender. His counsel rose and approached Becky: "Hi, Tim O'Brien," he said as he outstretched his right hand.

Becky rose and shook his hand firmly: "Rebecca Lawrence."

"Oh, sure … I knew I recognized you; you clerked for the Judge,"

Timmy said as Joshua said: "Excuse me. Becky, where's Zach? Judge wants the case called."

Becky shrugged her shoulders as Zach entered the courtroom.

"Fashionably late, Zach?" Josh said as Becky and Amanda smiled as their eyes met.

"Yeah," Zach said taking his seat as he coyly smiled at Becky as she squirmed uncomfortably in her seat.

Josh stood as the Judge entered: "All rise." As Woodbury sat behind the bench, Josh continued: "This Honorable Court is now in session. This is the matter of the United States versus Eric Ramon, Criminal No. 13-40221. Would counsel please identify themselves for the record?"

Zach and Becky stood. "Good morning, your Honor. Zach Woods and Rebecca Lawrence for the Government."

"Good morning, your Honor. Tim O'Brien, Federal Public Defender's Office for the Defendant who is present and seated at counsel table."

"Good morning, everyone," Woodbury said with a grin as he placed his John Lennon glasses on his nose. "Mr. Woods, as a preliminary matter and an intriguing sidenote: why is it that every AUSA is late to my proceedings when you're in the building up on the ninth floor?"

Zach stood and nervously adjusted his tie as the ghost threw him a menacing snare: "I'm sorry, your Honor, but"--

The courtroom filled with the pungent stench of rotten eggs, and the Judge whispered to his clerk: "Josh, what's that smell?" Joshua shrugged his shoulders as Becky whispered to Amanda: "Smell that?"

"No excuses please, Mr. Woods," Woodbury said as Josh covered his face with his left hand and gagged. "This is the final pretrial in this matter, counsel. I have ruled on the government's motion to suppress the cooperating witness' prior criminal record. The motion is denied."

"Your Honor, if I could briefly address the Court," Zach interjected as his eyes began to tear.

"Mr. Woods, the government's motion, Docket No. 192, is denied. I will not entertain oral arguments. I read your brief in its entirety. The jury has a right to know about 'Radio's' criminal past and his perhaps selfish motivation to cooperate with the government in this case."

"Excuse me," Woodbury said as he gagged: "Josh, call someone up here, will you?" The Judge squeezed a gob of hand sanitizer into his palms and raised his hands to his face momentarily quelling the stink.

Charlie's black eyes fixated on Becky; and as he puckered his lips, a fine mist steamed from the witness box, where the ghost sat smiling, and meandered through the courtroom filling the air with the fragrant distinctive aroma of lilacs, Becky's favorite flowering scent. Woodbury raised his eyebrows and lifted his lenses.

Zach inhaled the lilac dust and thought: "What the f-?" as he smiled at Becky and then Amanda. "You smell that?" he whispered.

"Hmmm," Becky said feeling black eyes upon her. Her eyes darted toward the vacant witness box, and Charlie giggled as she stared perplexed.

"Counsel," Woodbury said as Zach sat next to Becky. "Counsel, Docket No. 191, the defendant's motion to suppress his prior drug-related convictions is granted."

"Your Honor," Zach said exasperated as he stood as Timmy O'Brien smiled at the young defendant, "May I be heard?"

“Mr. Woods, I will not entertain oral arguments this morning. I will not have our jury tainted by allowing the defendant’s past drug convictions to convict this young man before evidence is presented in this courtroom.”

“But, your Honor,” Zach said as sulphur permeated the courtroom. Zach began to gag as Charlie giggled insanely from the witness stand. Becky temporarily closed her lids and heard: “Charlie, Charlie, Charlie” …

“Josh,” Woodbury whispered, “you call someone?”

Joshua Levy stood and put his right arm on the Judge’s bench as the Judge leaned in to hear him. “Judge, maintenance and IT are on their way... stinks in here.”

“Maybe a sewerage leak from the pier?” the Judge whispered as Joshua shrugged his shoulders and scrunched his nose. “Hmmm, maybe,” Josh said as he nodded his head: “You want to suspend?”

“No, I’ll just wrap it up. Watch this.” Josh grinned widely as he sat down.

“Counsel, aside from the pending motions I’ve already ruled on, are there any other preliminary matters for the Court to take up at this time?”

Tim O’Brien stood: “Not from the defendant, your Honor.”

“Your Honor,” Zach said as he fumbled with his tie, “I would really like the opportunity to address my” --

“Mr. Woods, I will not entertain oral arguments on the preceding motions I’ve already ruled upon.”

“Then, no, your Honor,” Zach said as Becky continued to stare into Charlie’s black eyes. Charlie blew her a kiss, and once again the courtroom filled with the unique aroma of sweet lilacs in bloom.

Amanda smiled at Becky noticing how angry Zach appeared. As he pouted and grunted, Amanda and Becky spoke to each other with their eyes.

The Judge placed his glasses on his bench as his mucous membranes filled with evanescence of lilac. “Excuse me, counsel,” Woodbury said as he raised his eyebrows symmetrically, “does anyone smell flowers?”

Charlie smiled as Becky continued to blankly stare into the witness box. Becky rose and without premeditation shouted: “Yes, your Honor” she said as she smiled, “lilacs.” Woodbury smiled and winked at Becky as she sat back down. Zach was angry and staring at the floor.

“Since we’ve already gone over empanelment and peremptory challenges, counsel, if there are no further matters to come before the Court, then” --

Zach stood; and as he leaned toward the microphone, it squeaked loudly and reverberated throughout the large high-domed courtroom. “Your Honor, I would really like the opportunity to address Docket No. 192 and” --

“Mr. Woods,” Woodbury said as his face contorted in anger, “I have already ruled on the government’s motion. I have made it quite clear that I will not entertain further legal argument on this matter. Now, are there any other matters you would like to” --

“No, your Honor,” Zach said as he growled, throwing an angry facial gesture toward the young defendant.

“Then we are adjourned on this matter; I look forward to seeing all of you three weeks from Monday. Please be here, Mr. Woods, by 8:45.”

Joshua stood: “All rise,” he said as the Judge left the courtroom. “Becky, Becky,” Josh whispered.

Becky rose and walked toward the clerk's bench as Charlie followed her with his large engaging jet-black eyes. "Hey," she whispered.

"Hey," Josh said with a grin, "Judge wants to see you for a minute. You know, not for nothing, I'm gonna miss ya," he said as he shuffled the papers on the bench.

Becky put her right hand on his left forearm focusing his attention: "I'm gonna miss you too, Josh," she said as he smiled, "but something tells me I'll be here a lot."

The phone rang and Josh whispered: "You can go back now," he said as he dialed "1, 2, 3, 4" into the panel mounted inside the clerk's bench on the far right wall. Becky walked toward Amanda noticing Zach was gone.

Amanda raised her brows. "Gonna see the Judge for a minute," Becky whispered.

"Sure," Amanda said, "want me to wait?"

"Na," Becky whispered, "I'll see you upstairs." Amanda leaned in and whispered into Becky's left ear: "Boy, he was kind of hard on Zach today, huh?" Becky shook her head up and down and smiled before disappearing into the Judge's robing room.

Woodbury stood and walked toward Becky. "Hi, Judge," Becky said with a smile. The Judge hugged her and she stood nervously with her arms at her sides.

"Have a seat, Becky," Woodbury said as he sat next to her. "Listen, have you read through this case?"

"Hmmm," Becky replied inquisitively staring into the Judge's eyes.

"Look, the cooperating witness is a career criminal; maybe you could talk to Zach about, you know, a potential plea here?"

Becky began nervously twirling the bottom of her French braid. "I tried, your Honor, but" --

"I understand, Becky. Listen, try again because your only witness aside from the DEA agent is 'Radio' and" --

"Yeah, I know," Becky said as she shook her head up and down spasmodically.

"Don't have much pull upstairs, huh?" Woodbury said with a grin.

"Understatement of the year, Judge," Becky said continuing to twirl her hair.

"Everyone good to you up on the ninth?" Woodbury asked as he raised his left eyebrow.

Becky nodded affirmatively as the Judge whispered: "Try and talk some sense into him before Monday?" He smiled at Becky as he exited. As he stood at the entrance to the hallway, he turned around and said loudly: "See you Monday morning, Ms. Lawrence."

"Judge?" Becky said with a question in her tone. The Judge stared at her as she rose. She walked toward Woodbury; and as she met him in the archway, she whispered: "Judge, I don't know how to thank you for" --

Woodbury pulled her into a bear hug, and Becky's arms hugged his back as her body went limp. "My pleasure," he whispered as she mumbled: "thank you," and tears streamed down her pink cheeks.

"See you Monday, Ms. Lawrence, that is, unless you can work a miracle here," Woodbury said as he turned around and walked down the hallway. With his back toward her, he said loudly: "It's good having you in my courtroom again, Ms. Lawrence." Becky smiled as she used her Federal Judiciary ID to gain access back into Courtroom No. 1.

The courtroom was empty by all appearances. Charlie sat in the witness box watching intently as Becky stared through him. He puckered and Becky smiled as the overpowering savor of lilacs infused into the air. She walked toward the exit feeling a presence she couldn't quantitate. She turned around and Charlie smiled as he vanished, and she quietly sang: "If I could talk, I'd tell you; if I could smile, I'd let you know; you are far and away, my most imaginary friend."

As Becky walked toward the rail humming and stood peering into the harbor, she turned on her iPhone 5S. She watched as it read: "One new voicemail." She pressed "voicemail" but the signal was lost. "Crappy reception in this building," she mumbled to herself as she continued to hum: "You are far and away, my most imaginary friend."

Becky walked out the back entrance of the Moakley smiling at Peter who was drinking coffee from a small styrofoam cup. "Hi Becky," he whispered as she walked out onto the concrete walk. She pressed "voicemail" but still "no signal" flashed across the touchscreen and no bars appeared visible. She walked toward the harbor; and as she approached the saltwater roses and the distinctive luscious aroma filled her nostrils, her voicemail connected:

"Hi Becky, it's Zach. Wow, that was fun with Woodbury, huh? Listen, maybe you could talk to him … um, after all, 'he likes you.' Meet me at quarter of 11:00 my office, thanks."

Becky smiled as she knelt before the roses inhaling their sweet fragrance. Two teenage boys on motorized scooters whizzed by her as she said out loud: "Wow, those things are fast," as she walked back toward the courthouse. As Alan poured Becky's coffee, she glanced at her cell: "10:27."

Thanks, Alan," Becky said as she put a Hershey bar with almonds on the counter and her stomach grumbled.

"Hungry, Becky?" Alan said with a smile, "I'm sorry, is this" --

"Oh, I'm sorry, Alan," Becky said as she avoided his eyes, "it's a 5."

Alan handed her $1.45 and Becky smiled as she opened the coffee and took a sip. She walked out of the coffee shop sipping her coffee as she hummed: "If I could talk, I'd tell you; if I could smile, I'd let you know; you are far and away, my most imaginary friend."

As she stepped into the elevator still humming, she thought to herself as she shook her head: "Can't get that song out of my mind." She got off on the ninth floor and walked into her office. She closed the door and inhaled her candy bar feeling guilty and ashamed. She wiped the chocolate from the corners of her mouth and downed half her coffee. She turned on her PC and went directly to ECF to look into the up-and-coming proffer at 11. She continued to hum: "If I could talk, I'd tell you"... she queued in the docket number and hit "docket report."

She hummed: "my most imaginary friend" as she set the indictment and memoranda of the parties in queue. She sipped her coffee as the printer jammed. As Becky struggled trying to remove the paper jammed into the laser cartridge, she hummed as she smiled: "You are far and away, my most imaginary friend."

She downed the rest of her large coffee just as the printer finished its hum. She grabbed the papers and placed them into a file folder. It was 10:45 and Becky left her office still humming: "You are far and away, my most imaginary friend."

Becky spotted Amanda walking toward her as she approached Zach's office. She looked in. Zach wasn't in. As they stood in the hallway, Amanda whispered: "Wow, so weird this morning, huh?"

Becky shook her head: "Yeah, I was like totally gagging … smelled so bad in there."

Amanda nodded: "And then out of nowhere the courtroom fills with the heavenly scent of" --

"Lilacs," they both whispered as they giggled.

"You happen to read the indictment in this case by any chance?" Amanda said as she leaned her head against the wall.

"Looks like a simple drug case, no?" Becky said as Amanda's face pouted.

"What?" Becky asked.

"Another one of Zach's now infamous deals," Amanda said as she passed Becky the "Recorded Statement of the Cooperating Witness: 'Foo'."

"Foo?" Becky said with a smile.

"Yeah, also known as 'Foo-Foo," Amanda said as they giggled. Becky and Amanda were cracking up as Zach approached.

"What's so funny?" he asked as he strolled past them into his office.

"Nothing," Becky said as she smiled at Amanda whispering, "Foo-Foo"?

Zach's face took on a serious tone. "Becky," Zach said as he sat at the edge of his desk facing her, "what's with Woodbury, huh?"

"Zach," Becky said as Amanda stared at the floor, "Judge asked me to talk to you."

"Oh?" Zach said with a grin.

"Yeah, he thinks this case is a loser, wants you to think about dropping it down to a lesser" --

"Seriously?" Zach said as he slid off his desk and walked toward his wall-length view of the inner harbor. "Now, he's going to dictate to the government how to try a case?"

Zach's attention was focused on a small sailing ship navigating against the current. Amanda looked up at Becky as she mouthed: "Be careful."

"Zach," Becky said as she stood and walked toward the glass, "the cooperating's such a scumbag."

"Your point, Ms. Lawrence?" Zach said exasperated as he faced her and licked his bottom lip.

"You might want to think about it is all," Becky said as she walked back toward Amanda noticing her sullen expression.

"Okay. This proffer should be interesting, ladies. Defendant knows he's bagged. We've got audio. We've got video. Hopefully, he'll just be candid, and we can hammer out a cooperation agreement."

"Hmmm," Becky moaned as she sifted through the indictment. "The Grand Jury charges: Count One: (Title 21, United States Code, Section 841(a)(1): Possession with intent to distribute and distribution of cocaine base; Title 18, United States Code, Section 2: Aiding and abetting; (Title 21, United States Code, Section 846 (b): Conspiracy to (Distribute)."

Amanda handed Becky a typewritten document entitled: "Defendant's Memorandum In Support of Motion in Limine to Exclude Informant Testimony and Request for a Liability Hearing."

Becky looked up at Amanda. "This was filed Friday."

"Hmmm," Becky said as she began to digest its contents: "Defendant Marvin Hill is faced with a government witness, Jeremiah Washington, a/k/a "Foo" a/k/a "Foo-Foo," Becky smiled as she said "Foo-Foo" as Amanda giggled, "who has been told repeatedly by an FBI agent who has been supervising his informant activities that the payments he will receive in exchange for his cooperation and testimony are contingent on the outcome of the trial. The testimony of such a witness threatens Hill's right to a fair trial:

"Just as a payment may provide witnesses an incentive to come forward and testify at some risk to themselves, so too can the same payment provide an incentive to witnesses to come forward and lie simply for the purpose of receiving the payment. Even so, as long as there are adequate safeguards, the potential corruption should not condemn the practice. But because of the vulnerability of such contingent-payment arrangements to corruption, they may be approved only rarely and under the highest scrutiny.

In recognition of the substantial risk that financial incentives can corrupt, either through an aggressive prosecutor seeking testimony inconsistent with the truth or a witness testifying untruthfully to satisfy the government's objectives, testimony given under an arrangement involving the payment of a 'fee,' 'salary,' or 'bonus,' whether contingent on the content of the testimony or not, may be received in court only within a structure of procedural safeguards"…

"Wow, this is good," Becky thought as she read: "In an argument that reminds us that the love of money is the root of all evil, the defendant herein asserts that the government's quondam financial arrangement with 'Foo' aka 'Foo-Foo' – 'dollars for convictions' – have so tainted his testimony as to work a violation of the Due Process Clause, U.S. Constitution Amendment V.

The relevant facts are not disputed. 'Foo' did not agree to serve as a government cooperator for love of country but, rather, because the government promised to compensate him.

A cooperator whose eyes are fixed on such a prize might well be tempted to wander from the path of candor and, thus, unduly prejudice the criminal defendant. Benefits made contingent upon subsequent indictments or convictions skate very close to, if indeed they do not cross, the limits imposed by the due process clause.

Defendant Hill hereby moves in limine to exclude Informant 'Foo's' testimony as such testimony is irrevocably corrupted by the original bounty arrangement."

Becky looked up as Zach cleared his throat. Amanda handed Becky Foo's CORI: Jeremiah Washington a/k/a "Foo" a/k/a "Foo-Foo." Becky smiled as she whispered to Amanda: "Foo-Foo": "1992, true name violation, guilty, served five months Suffolk County House of Corrections; 1995, aggravated domestic abuse, assault and battery, guilty, served 17 months Suffolk, released "good time credit"; 1998, 5 kilos cocaine base, possession with intent to distribute, nolo contendere, 46 months, Suffolk House of Corrections; 2001, 2 kilos cocaine base, Federal Jurisdiction, possession with intent and conspiracy (U.S.C. 841 (a) & (b), U.S.C. 846 (a) (b), subsequent offense, guilty, 120 months, released pursuant to cooperation agreement DEA & FBI: September 9, 2005."

Becky thought to herself: "aggravated domestic abuse, assault and battery, what a scumbag," as she sucked the end of her pen. "Upstanding citizen, huh, Zach?" Becky said loudly as Zach sat at his desk and licked his bottom lip as Becky fidgeted in her seat.

"Yeah, real nice guy, but, you know, in all fairness he's been extremely helpful in several cases. He's really trying to turn the cheek, you know." Zach looked deeply into Becky's expression attempting to decipher what side of the fence she meandered.

"Zach, exactly what is defense alluding to by "dollars for convictions"?

Zach stared intently at Amanda whose eyes shifted to the floor. "Ridiculous defense maneuver really," Zach said with a grin.

"Zach, um, how much exactly has 'Foo-Foo' received for his, um, professional services?" Becky asked avoiding Zach's intense stare.

"Why is this relevant, Ms. Lawrence?" Zach asked as he contemplated: "whose side you on anyway?"

"Zach, it's relevant," Becky replied as she continued to mutilate her pen. "How much money are we talking?"

Zach began rummaging through the Hill file … "Let's see, there was 16,000 for relocation to Massachusetts. Um, then there was the car accident and child support; hmmm, that was 11,000 … about $47,000," Zach said as he continued to feel Becky out as he licked his bottom lip.

“47,000 dollars?” Becky asked as she continued to peruse the file folder.

“Mmm,” Zach groaned.

“Um, who exactly has been promising ‘Foo’ a/k/a ‘Foo-Foo’ that his cooperation agreement hinges upon convictions?” Amanda giggled and stared at the floor.

Zach handed her a document entitled: “Exhibit A, Report of Special Agent Jeffrey Mazza, DEA.” Becky quickly skimmed the eight-page report as Zach continued: “I pulled the plug on this as soon as it was discovered. Told the agent it was inappropriate but”…

“Uh-huh, but the damage was done, huh?” Becky groaned as she continued to read. “You know, Zach, this taints this case. No matter what the verdict, this is a strong appellate argument to vacate judgment” --

“Becky,” Zach said as his face contorted in anger, “this guy’s a Blood. He’s small fry; it’s Veloz I’m after, a real piece of shit. You know of Veloz?”

Becky nodded: “Yeah, head of the Boston 93 Bloods, right?” Zach nodded as Becky grilled Zach with her eyes as she continued to read the egregious statements proffered by the DEA agent in charge of the Hill case. Her eyes fixated upon the last two questions on Page 4:

Q. Okay. So you told him he'd get paid for his services?
A. Yes.
Q. But at one point you told him that his payment would be contingent upon a certain number of convictions, is that correct?
A. Correct, sir.

“Becky,” Zach said as he cleared his throat, “I need to know that I can count on you.”

“Sure,” Becky said as she thought: “wow, this case is a loser; what kinds of deals you making behind closed doors, Mr. Woods?”

Becky stood and walked toward Zach: “Rat is an interesting colloquialism, Mr. Hill. Are you a ‘rat’ if you turn in your next-door neighbor who’s molesting his six-year-old daughter every night when the wife goes to bed? Are you a ‘rat,’ Mr. Hill, if you turn in a guidance counselor who is sleeping with his 14-year-old student? Are you a ‘rat,’ Mr. Hill, if you turn in a priest who’s molesting altar boys at his parish?”

Marvin Hill began shaking his head up and down. “You’re right, Ms.” --

“Lawrence” Mazza interjected.

“No. Call me Becky, Marvin.”

“Becky,” Marvin said as he grinned, “Becky.”

“Mr. Hill,” Zach began, “you are under no obligation to participate in this proffer session. You are free to leave any time you’d like.”

The agents’ and the attorneys’ eyes fixated on the young defendant squirming in his chair. Marvin nervously gazed into Zach’s eyes in focus.

“No,” Marvin said as he stared at the floor, “I want to cooperate.”

Becky approached Zach and whispered: “He’s scared.”

Marvin’s hands began to tremble: “It’s just where I come from, Mr. Woods, I won’t live long enough to testify against anyone if I turn rat.”

“I can assure you that you will have the full strength of the United States Government protecting you. I can’t promise you anything, but I can guarantee you that we will protect you. We will begin by placing you into the Federal United States Witness Protection Program or WITSEC. We will provide you and your family new identities with the appropriate authentic documentation.

Housing, subsistence for basic living expenses, and medical care will also be provided; job training and employment assistance may also be provided in the future. The U.S. Marshals provide 24-hour protection to all of our witnesses while they are in a high-threat environment including but not limited to: pretrial conferences, trial testimonials, and other court appearances."

"Uh-huh," Hill mumbled as he stared at Becky and smiled.

"Now, I know that you have a long-time affiliation with the Bloods," Zach said as he stared the defendant down.

Hill rolled up his left sleeve to display his inner forearm bearing a black upside-down pitchfork holding a red five-pointed crown upwards. Inside of this tattoo the number "5" was boldly highlighted.

Becky's eyes met Zach's and they began to converse without speaking; "Sorry I misjudged you," she dialogued with her eyes as Zach licked his bottom lip as Becky watched.

Hill opened his left palm displaying in handwritten red bold letters: "B-L-O-O-D." Again, Becky's eyes locked into Zach's intense gape. He grinned at Becky reassuringly sensing her fear as he continued:

Q. How old are you, Mr. Hill?
A. Um, 19.
Q. How far did you go in school?
A. Tenth.
Q. Tenth grade?
A. Mmm.
Q. Please verbalize your responses audibly.
A. Yep, 10th grade.
Q. Can you tell me when you joined the Bloods?

Hill became anxious. He began to cough and nervously his fingers played with the top button of his plaid shirt.

"Mr. Hill" Zach said. Hill continued to avert eye contact and stared at the floor.

"Mr. Hill?" Zach repeated as Marvin trembling continued:

A. Um, joined the Bloods in 9th grade after my father was murdered.
Q. I'm sorry.
A. Yeah, right.
Q. So you've been a member of the Bloods ever since?
A. Yeah.
Q. The Bloods are involved in trafficking heroin, cocaine, and guns in the Boston area; is that correct?

Hill stared at the floor unresponsive.

"Mr. Hill?" Zach said as Mazza nudged Hill's right arm.

A. Yeah?
Q. The Bloods are involved in trafficking heroin, cocaine, and guns in the Boston area; is that correct, Mr. Hill?
A. Yeah.
Q. Have you yourself personally been involved in trafficking heroin?
A. Yep.
Q. Cocaine?
A. Yep, mostly base.
Q. Uh-huh. How about weapons?
A. Na, not really.
Q. Weapons not your forte, Mr. Hill?
A. Huh?
Q. You don't get involved in guns?
A. Na, mostly dope.
Q. How long, Mr. Hill, have you been trafficking narcotics for the Bloods?
A. Um, since I was 15.

Becky's eyes met Amanda's as Amanda sat in Becky's vacant seat. Becky slowly walked toward the rear of Zach's office feeling all eyes glaring at her from behind. Amanda mouthed: "baby" as Becky nodded her head.

Q. Mr. Hill, last December there was an unsavory exchange of

gunfire in the North End where ten innocent victims were shot; they were caught between The Bloods and a rival gang known as The Latin Kings. Were you involved in this altercation?
A. Huh?
Q. I'm sorry, Mr. Hill ... were you involved in this gang warfare?
A. Nope.
Q. How about the other defendants charged in this conspiracy?

Marvin stared at the floor unresponsive. "Mr. Hill?" Zach asked as Becky rose and walked towards Zach.

"Mr. Hill," Becky said, "I know this is hard. These are your brothers." Marvin's eyes filled with tears as he spoke:

A. Yeah, some of 'em.
Q. Mr. Hill, of the other five named co-defendants in this case: Julio Ramirez, Chico Hernandez, Eric Jones, Eddie Hubbard, and Jose Veloz, to your knowledge who was involved in the altercation in the North End?
A. All of 'em except me.
Q. Mr. Hill, how is it you know that Defendants Ramirez, Hernandez, Jones, Hubbard, and Veloz were involved?
A. They talk 'bout it.
Q. Uh-huh, they talk about it. Do they feel bad about it?
A. (No response.)
Q. Mr. Hill?
A. I don't know how they feel.
Q. Do they joke about it?
A. Sometimes.
Q. Uh-huh. Mr. Hill, are you aware that four-year-old Timothy Watkins was caught in the line of fire?
A. Nope.
Q. Are you aware that he died on the scene?
A. (Witness shakes head.)
Q. Mr. Hill, are you aware that Timothy Watkins was gunned down by the Bloods as they shot into a busy North End neighborhood in the middle of the day firing at The Latin Kings?
A. Nope.
Q. How does this make you feel?

smile as Zach licked his bottom lip.

Zach looked puzzled and stared at her inquisitively. Becky said: "Zach, I know you don't want to hear this but this case is" --

"Difficult?" Zach interjected.

"Yeah, um, difficult, Zach," Becky said as Zach yelled: "Shit. Totally forgot the time: got a meeting with my kid's teacher. Crap, it'll be a miracle if I make it if I leave now." Zach ruffled through several file folders pulling individual reports and documents out before ultimately deciding to throw all of them into his briefcase which he struggled to close.

He walked toward the hallway not noticing Becky following a foot behind. Zach abruptly turned around in the archway; Becky was six inches from his face. Zach jumped and screamed: "Shit" placing his left hand over his throbbing heart. "You scared the hell out of me," Zach said out of breath as they stared at each other intently.

"Sorry," Becky replied with a grin.

"Thanks for helping me with Hill," he said as he placed his left hand onto her right shoulder and leaned in toward her whispering: "Good job, counselor. See ya manana." Becky's body swayed as she inhaled his pheromonal scent as he smiled and licked his bottom lip.

Zach ran down the hallway toward the elevator, stopped and turned around watching Becky walking slowly toward him smiling. "Thanks, Becky," Zach said with a coy smile.

"Hmmm, he's a babe," Becky said in the funnels of her mind, "total babe … too bad he's married." Becky felt a surge of heat as her cheeks pinkened, and she thought: "I'm lonely," as she walked into her office and closed the door.

At 5:15 Becky waited impatiently for her train at the Silver Line underground. Her cell vibrated and immediately went to voicemail. She recognized the number. It was Zach. She arrived at South

Station fifteen minutes later and listened to her new voicemail: "Hey Becky," Zach said as his voice cracked, "it's me, Zach. Listen, had a lightbulb notion of clarity this afternoon. Call me when you get the message."

Becky thought: "I can only imagine, Mr. Woods" … "a lightbulb notion of clarity," she repeated out loud as her face contorted. Becky hit "connect" on her iPhone and she heard: "Hi, Becky," as traffic whizzed by distorting his voice.

"Hello, Zach?" Becky shouted. She glanced at the screen and knew they were still connected.

"Becky?" Zach shrieked. "Becky?"

Becky placed her left hand over her left ear and was catching every three to four words Zach stammered in echo before she screamed: "Zach, I'll call you back," as horns began a blazing symphony on Congress Street. Becky walked into South Station mumbling to herself under her breath: "a lightbulb notion of clarity" … "who does he think he is: Emerson?"

Becky hopped on the Red Line to Braintree. The train was packed full of irritated, tired, and sweaty bodies packed in so tightly that as the train approached each station stop 15 to 20 people needed to step out onto the platform in order to allow others to exit. The train emptied by Quincy Center, and Becky was finally able to catch her breath and take a seat. She redialed Zach.

"Hi, Becky," Zach said as he chewed his gum.

"Hi, Zach," Becky said feeling her heart beating in her neck as it throbbed with each pulse.

"Wow, that's better … I can hear you now," Zach said as he continued to chew.

"Sorry about that," Becky said as her heart slowed, and she crossed her legs nervously.

“Listen, got a brainstorm this afternoon.” The subway train pulled into Braintree station, and Zach was disconnected.

Becky waited until she pulled into her apartment complex before hitting redial. She sat in her little yellow Bug yawning.

“Hi, Becky,” Zach said as his daughter sang incoherently in the background.

“Hi, Zach,” Becky replied as she leaned into the headrest yawning. “So what’s this, um, ‘lightbulb notion of clarity’?” she said as she smiled.

Zach giggled hearing his words repeated: “Um, well, it was fairly apparent that, um, Hill liked you, and, um, well” -- Becky grinned -- “um, well, it’s also crystal clear that he hates my f’n guts,” Zach said as his five-year-old daughter Emily screamed: “Daddy!”

“Shit. Becky, I gotta go. I’ll call you back.” Becky shut off the ignition and sat behind the wheel, her mind fixating on Hill screaming: “Fuck you,” as he spit in Zach’s direction. “Fuck you,” he screamed as he glared at Zach with dark, menacing eyes.

She opened her eyes as her mind repeated: “You can’t use what he said in the proffer.” She opened the car door and stood as Zach said with an enigmatic look: “Oh, yeah … watch me.”

Becky ate a Lean Cuisine Santa Fe Rice concoction and passed out on the couch watching Shark Tank. She woke at 2:05 a.m.; and with her eyes half-closed, passed out on her bed fully clothed on top of her Laura Ashley comforter. She awoke ten minutes before her alarm blazed, yawned and opened her eyes widely. “He’s making deals with the devil,” she thought as she turned on the shower.

Becky approached Courthouse Way at 7:15 a.m. Her cell rang as she entered the Moakley. She looked at her iPhone which displayed: “one missed call.” She recognized the number and moaned: “Oy … mmm, coffee.”

Becky got off at the ninth floor at the U.S. Attorney's Office and walked directly into Zach's office. Zach smiled as Becky stood in the doorway and motioned her forward.

"Just the person I want to see," Zach said as he flirted with his eyes and licked his bottom lip.

"Hi, Zach," Becky said as she opened her coffee and sat down across from his desk. Becky sipped her lukewarm coffee as Zach grinned.

"Becky, do you know why I wanted to make the deal with Hill?" Becky shook her head affirmatively as she continued to sip. She swallowed and whispered: "He's the small fry?"

Zach stood up holding a document in his right hand and walked around his desk. He sat on the edge of his desk two feet from Becky and watched as she swallowed. "Exactly, Becky," Zach said as his eyebrows raised, "but he holds the golden ticket."

Becky's mind flashed to Grandpa Joe in Willy Wonka as he sang: "I never thought my life could be anything but catastrophe but suddenly I begin to see a bit of good luck for me 'cause I've got a golden ticket, I've got a golden twinkle in my eye" … Becky placed her coffee on the desk next to Zach's right thigh as Zach handed her a document entitled: "FBI Organized Crime Drug Enforcement Task Force (OCDETF), Boston Division."

Becky quickly perused the first page before Zach interjected: "Go to Page 3." Becky struggled as the pages were crisp and stuck together; she wet the end of her pointer finger to lift the page as Zach moaned: "Hmmm." Becky crossed her legs as he watched.

In the center of the page in bold italics read: "*JOSE VELOZ*, Suspected leader of the Boston 93 Bloods in federal custody."

Becky grabbed her styrofoam cup and grinned as she said: "Hmmm, the big fish?"

"And you're married," she whispered as her cheeks reddened. Zach adjusted his tie and walked toward the wall-length glass facing the harbor. "You smell good, Ms. Lawrence," he said as he peered out into the water.

"Take a cold shower, Mr. Woods," Becky said as she grinned and turned around to exit.

"Hey!" Zach said as he turned to face her as she stood motionless in the doorjamb, her eyes fixated into his stare.

Zach pouted and moaned "Hmmm," as Becky's eyes met his: "10:00 status conference Courtroom No. 1" Zach said as he half-grinned.

"I'll be there, Mr. Woods," Becky whispered as she closed his door. Zach walked over to his door and turned the lock. He turned off the light and sat in his chair and pleasured himself as he continued to inhale Becky's scent. He closed his eyes seeing her enormous perfectly-formed nipple standing erect just inches from his oral grasp and felt her body hump him as he ejaculated.

Simultaneously Becky locked her office door. She closed her new blind. She pulled her pantyhose down to her knees and leaned back in her uncomfortable chair which creaked. She shuffled her pantyhose down to her ankles as she teased herself. She took off her left shoe and slid her pantyhose off. She leaned both ankles upwards straddling her desk. She closed her eyes feeling Zach's enormous bulge pressing into her as she fingered herself to the brink of orgasm continuing to inhale his pheromones which lingered on her clothes.

Nervously Becky looked around her office feeling "eyes" she couldn't see upon her. "Charlie" smiled as Becky thought: "I'm lonely. Oh, God," she said out loud softly: "he's such a babe," as she soaked her chair and the room filled with the savory essence of freshly-cut lilacs.

Becky pulled her pantyhose up ripping her left knee with her fingernail. "Shit" she mumbled as she applied a thin layer of sheer nail polish over the small tear. She grabbed her vanilla body spray and doused her neck, sprayed her armpits and her groin. Her cell began to vibrate in her blazer's inner side pocket straddling the hook on the back of her office door. She fumbled to retrieve it and missed Zach's call.

"Now what, Mr.Woods?" she thought as she hit "connect."

"Hi Becky," Zach said, "how you doing?" Becky closed her eyes and felt his hand squeezing her left nipple in her mind.

"Fine, Zach. What's up?" Becky whispered as she adjusted her skirt.

"Um, listen, I'm sorry about … well, you know," Zach said as his left hand cupped himself.

After a long uncomfortable pause, Becky whispered: "Oh, it's okay, Zach," she said softly as her voice cracked and she began to nervously twirl the end of her braid.

"It was totally my fault and completely inappropriate, and I'm sorry," Zach said as he smiled and became erect again.

"Hey, let's just forget it ever happened, okay?" Becky whispered as her right hand slipped into her bra and tantalized her now erect left nipple.

"So we're okay?" Zach said as he began to masturbate.

"Hakuna matata" Becky said with a smile as she twirled her nipple between her thumb and pointer finger.

"See you at 10, Becky," Zach said as he unzippered his pants.

"Zach?" Becky said with an inquisitive tone.

"Yeah?" Zach moaned as he grabbed his massive erect rim.

"Thanks, Zach." Becky said as she licked her lips.

“Thanks, Ms. Lawrence,” Zach said as he placed the receiver back on the hook and thought: “I’m gonna fuck her. I don’t give a shit ... probably gonna lose my job. I don’t care; I’m gonna fuck her,” he repeated as he came.

“Charlie” watched as Becky peeled her skirt upwards, pressing her iPhone into her chest. His eyes widened as she placed her phone on her desk and struggled to shed her black pantyhose down to her ankles. She stood in the center of the room and lifted her skirt up onto her stomach. Charlie approached her, his icicle hands lightly cupping her buttocks as she twitched and her skin filled with goosebumps further stimulating her.

As she touched herself, she moaned: “Oh God, Zach … oh God, he smells good;” and as liquid oozed down her inner thighs, meandering toward her knees, she inundated the floor at her feet, and the room filled with the sweet zesty balm of lilac as Becky closed her eyes and heard: “Charlie, Charlie, Charlie.”

Amanda knocked on Becky’s locked office door: “Becky?”

“Shit,” Becky thought as she noticed her pantyhose scrunched up in between her feet ... “um, on the phone, Amanda, okay …give me a minute?”

“Oh, sure. Hey, I’ll meet you in Courtroom 1 in 20, okay?” Amanda yelled as her voice faded.

Becky glanced at her cell phone: “9:40, crap” she said as she turned around. As a freezing cold mist descended upon her, she thought: “Wow, it’s freezing in here,” as she bent down and picked up her scrunched hose. She sat in her chair as she gently pulled her hose up each leg. Charlie watched as she buttoned her shirt and tucked it in.

He followed a foot behind her, stepping into the elevator just as the doors began to close. Charlie followed Becky, watching her shapely silhouette from behind. As she stopped to open the courtroom doors, Charlie’s freezing cold right hand touched her ass and Becky jumped and turned around to see Zach standing behind her.

"What?" Zach said as Becky snared. "What?"

"You know what, Zach," Becky mumbled as she walked into the courtroom with Charlie following close behind, occasionally turning around to look at Zach in angered contortion.

Charlie drifted into the witness box as Zach whispered into Becky's right ear: "What?"

"Nothing," Becky said as she slammed her file folder on the table.

"Look, I was thinking," Zach stammered as Becky interjected: "oh-oh, that's dangerous." Zach smiled and retorted: "Funny, Ms. Lawrence ... very funny."

Zach placed his right hand on Becky's left forearm as he whispered: "Look, let's have lunch. We've got to talk." Becky nodded her head in agreement as Joshua entered the courtroom.

"Hi, Becky," he said with a smile.

"Hi, Josh," Becky replied feeling Zach's eyes fixated on her ass.

"Everyone ready?" Josh asked as he stared at Timmy O'Brien at the defendant's table. Counsel nodded affirmatively in unison as Josh bent down and buzzed in the Judge.

"All rise," Josh said as Woodbury entered the courtroom. "You may be seated," Woodbury said as he smiled at Becky and winked with his right eye.

Timmy stared at Becky and as their eyes met, he smiled.

"This Honorable Court is now in session. This is the matter of the United States versus Marvin Hill, et al, Criminal Docket No. 12-30225. Would counsel please identify themselves for the record?" Josh said as he sat and coughed.

“Admonishing this practice, sir, and informing the agent of the inappropriate”--

“I have heard enough, Mr. Woods. I called this status conference to gain enlightenment into this issue which I have now sufficiently gleaned. The defendant’s motion in limine to exclude the cooperating witness’/informant’s Jeremiah Washington, a/k/a “Foo” a/k/a “Foo-Foo,” biased testimony is granted. The request for a liability hearing is heretofore denied.”

Timmy O’Brien’s mouth hung open, his tongue protruding; he smiled as Becky grinned and their eyes locked.

“Your Honor!” Zach shouted as the courtroom filled with lilac mist, “may I be heard, please?”

“No, Mr. Woods, you may not. The motion is granted. I will not entertain oral argument at this time. I will say this, Mr. Woods: this case is laden with appellate issues. No matter what the outcome or verdict, it is ripe for appeal.”

Woodbury looked at Timmy as he spoke: “Mr. O’Brien” --

Timmy stood as Becky continued to grin: “Yes, your Honor?”

The Judge scratched his right cheek: “A compelling and well-constructed brief, Mr. O’Brien.”

“Thank you, your Honor,” Timmy whispered as he looked at Zach, who threw daggers with his snare as Tim shrugged his shoulders.

“Your Honor, may I be heard?” Zach shouted. Charlie stared at Woodbury and smiled as Woodbury inhaled the lilac dust and sneezed.

“No, Mr. Woods, you may not. I will not entertain oral argument at this time. However, if you wish to file a rebuttal brief, I will read it, but this matter is adjourned. Good day, counsel.”As the Judge walked from behind the bench, Zach slammed his right hand onto the table causing a thump which startled Woodbury.

“All rise,” Joshua said coughing as the Judge stopped short in front of the exit door and turned around to face counsel. “Is there a problem, Mr. Woods?”

“No, sir, no problem,” Zach said as his face winced in pain and he rubbed the back of his right hand with his left. Woodbury grinned at Becky who smiled at the Judge in awe. Charlie watched their visual exchange as Becky closed her eyes and heard: “Charlie, Charlie, Charlie.”

Joshua remained standing: “You guys smell that?”

Becky began to giggle as Timmy said: “Um, yeah.”

Zach sat angrily in his chair pouting, calculating his next strategic move as Timmy said: “Nice to see you, Becky,” as he reached for her right hand. As they shook hands and smiled, Becky’s attention was drawn to Charlie. He stared at her inhaling her inner beauty from within as lilac mist enveloped them.

Becky watched standing as Timmy walked toward the back of the courtroom. As the CSO opened the door for him smiling, whispering: “Good job today, counsel; Mr. Hill is a lucky man,” Timmy turned around and smiled at Becky. She waved with her right hand as he left the courtroom thinking: “I adore her.”

Amanda quickly gathered the file folder contents as she communicated with Becky silently: “He’s pissed,” she said without speaking: “I’m outta here.” Amanda placed her left hand on Zach’s right arm. As his eyes lifted, she said: “I’ll see ya later.”

“Hmmm,” Zach moaned as Amanda left the courtroom. Zach stared at Becky as she sat down next to him: “What the hell happened?” Zach whispered as his face contorted in anger.

Becky wanted to shout: “I told you this case was a loser;” instead, she sat silently as Zach began to vent: “I told you he hates me. He wouldn't even let me speak." Becky nodded as Zach placed his right hand on her left knee. He whispered: "We've got to talk," as his hand caressed her knee and he licked his bottom lip.

Becky stood up slamming her knee into the underside of the table screaming: "Ow," as Zach grinned and thought: "Hmmm" as he stared at her ass. As she sat down Zach began to gently rub her knee as the tang of sulphur reeked throughout the courtroom. "Stop it, will you!" Becky said angrily as she slapped the back of his reddened hand. Zach stared into her eyes as he grew uncomfortable, repeating: "we've got to talk now … come on, Becky; let's get some breakfast, huh?" Zach said coyly, reeling her in.

"Okay," Becky replied as she stood deliberately backing away from him. Joshua entered the courtroom grinning: "Still here, huh?"

Zach threw him an angry piercing glare as Becky said: "Yeah, just leaving, Josh."

"Okay," Joshua said as he grabbed his Poland Springs bottle coughing, "See ya, Becky," he said smiling as he left the courtroom.

"See you, Josh," Becky retorted as she walked down the main aisle toward the exit with Zach following three feet behind, his eyes glued to her swag.

"Thanks, Mike," Becky said as the CSO held open the door for her. "Thanks," Zach said as he passed Mike by.

Zach whispered to Becky outside Courtroom No. 1: "Listen, I'll go get us some muffins and coffee … what's your pleasure, babe?" he said as he stared at her breasts.

"Blueberry," she said as she angrily placed her folder on the waste receptacle. She slid her right hand under Zach's chin and manually lifted his head so his eyes focused upwards into her face. He smiled raising only the right corner of his mouth as he whispered: "Meet me in my office in ten, okay?" Becky watched as Zach walked away from her toward the elevators. As he turned the corner, he looked back and smiled knowing full well Becky's eyes had followed; he'd felt her gaze upon his gait.

Becky walked into the ladies room and stared at her reflection feeling embarrassed and ashamed. "End this," she said in her mind. "He's your boss; he's married," she mumbled out loud as she exited. "You can't do this," she said to herself as the elevator door opened on the ninth. "Stop this," she mumbled under her breath as she walked into Zach's office. "Don't do it, Becky," she said out loud as she placed the Hill folder on his desk.

Zach walked in holding a tray of two large coffees and a small bag of miniature muffins centered between them. "Just tell him no," she said to herself as Zach placed the tray on his desk. "End this," she said in the funnels of her mind as she watched Zach lock his door. "Stop this," she thought as he lowered the blind. "Leave now," she mumbled in her mind as he kissed her. "Don't do this, Becky," she thought as he knelt down on the carpet in front of her and slipped both hands under her skirt, sliding her pantyhose down to her ankles.

"Oh, my God," her mind reeled as he rolled down her thong to her knees. "Zach," she sighed as his tongue licked her vulva as she swayed.

"Sit," Zach said as he pulled an armed chair toward her. Becky sat, her naked skin squeaking against the leather. Zach sat Indian-style in front of her bare knees, his head buried in her lap, her right hand pressing his head in deeper. As Becky became wet, Zach pulled his tongue out and watched as her clit engorged. He stood, his eyes fixated on her internal rose, as he unzippered his pants which fell toward his ankles.

Becky leaned forward and swallowed him. Zach gently pushed her head inwards as sweat dripped from his temples. She bit down on him and suctioned him, her teeth scraping against his queue. "Oh, God," he whispered, "That's good. I like that, use your teeth, baby."

Within three minutes as he felt the ejaculate rising within, he groaned "ah-ah" as he pulled out of her mouth and pulled her up into a stance. He sat in her wet chair inhaling her pheromones and suckled her right nipple as she sat in his lap.

“Don’t do this,” Becky heard echoing in her mind as she mounted him. “I don’t care,” she thought as she rode him, and he ejaculated deep within her as Zach’s office filled with the asphyxiating essence of sulphur. Zach gagged as Charlie sat on the radiator watching in disgust as Becky dressed.

“Whew,” Zach said grinning, “I need a shower,” as he wiped the back of his right hand across his wet forehead. He watched, his tongue licking his bottom lip, as Becky struggled to roll her pantyhose up her wet thighs. She fell backwards into the wet chair as Zach mumbled: “Problem, Ms. Lawrence?”

Becky smirked as she thought: “Shit, what just happened?” as her internal juice cascaded down her inner left thigh. Zach grabbed a coffee and sat back in his swivel chair. He opened the rim and took a sip as he watched Becky button her blouse as her bra disappeared from view.

Becky leaned over his desk and grabbed the large styrofoam cup, struggling to retrieve it from its cardboard prison. Zach held the tray down with his right hand as Becky lifted it.

“Thanks” she whispered as she avoided his eyes. She sat down in front of his desk and began to sip her coffee as Zach watched her intrinsic facial cues.

“Come here,” he whispered as he placed his coffee on the desk. Becky nodded her head back and forth and stared at the desktop. Zach stood and walked around the desk, grabbed the armed chair next to her, and pulled her chair in toward him.

“Zach,” Becky said with tears swelling behind her lids.

“Shhh,” Zach said as he placed his right pointer finger against her closed lips. She sipped her coffee as he stroked her bangs from her eyes.

"Zach," she said as he hushed her with a kiss.

"Look it. I'm your boss; I could lose my job for this; I deserve it" he said softly as he kissed her neck.

"Zach," Becky whispered as her body swayed to his touch.

"Shhh," Zach whispered. "I take full responsibility for this. This was like Sexual Harassment 101, no?"

Tears streamed down Becky's cheeks. Zach wiped them away with his right hand gently stroking each cheek dry with his fingertips.

"What do you want to do?" he whispered as she grabbed her coffee and downed it, instantly feeling the caffeine jolt to her brain.

"I don't know," Becky said as she finished her coffee and the empty styrofoam fell to the floor. She leaned forward to pick it up as Zach kissed her neck and the smell of decaying rotted flesh filled the air as Zach raised his voice an octave: "What's that smell?"

Becky gagged as Zach took Becky's right hand and held it loosely between his palms, his right hand gently massaging her fingers. "Tell me what you want," he whispered.

Becky pulled her hand out and rose, walked toward the glass conoid wall, and raised the blind. She stood, arms folded, staring blanketly into the harbor searching her mind: "What do I want … hmmm, what do I want?" … she turned her head back as Zach pushed into her from behind, his arms wrapping about her waist.

"Oh, my God," she thought as her body swayed, and she felt his erection pressing into her ass as she unconsciously mumbled out loud: "I think I want you." He held her tightly, his hands reaching upwards cupping her breasts. He kissed the back of her neck lightly as tears filled her eyes: "Now I'm his mistress?" she thought: "Oh, my God; he smells good," as tears streaked down her cheeks.

A double knock echoed as Amanda's distinctive high-pitched voice squeaked: "Zach?" Zach abruptly pulled away from Becky as she wiped the tears from her face. He looked down and noticed his zipper undone. Becky turned around and grinned with her eyes as he yelled: "Yep, give me a minute, please" as he tucked in his now wrinkled blue shirt and struggled to pull his zipper up.

Amanda yelled: "Okay, I'll be back," as her voice trailed. Becky reached forward and adjusted Zach's tie as he pulled her in toward him, his right hand gently massaging her buttocks.

She whispered: "We have to talk, Zach," as he kissed her and nodded whispering: "Any time, babe." She walked toward the door and unlatched the lock.

"Where you going, Becky?" Zach said as he winked.

"Ladies room," she said as she spotted her purse and briefcase next to his desk. Zach sat in his chair behind his desk and cocked his head back finishing his coffee as Becky grabbed her purse and briefcase and opened the door.

"Becky?" Zach whispered as she stood in the doorjamb. Becky turned around in the archway as Zach grinned with his eyes, "You're coming back, right?"

She nodded affirmatively and coyly smirked as she turned around and walked quickly toward the restroom. "I'm an asshole," she said in her mind as she swung open the door and entered the bathroom. "What the hell am I doing?" she said as she locked the stall … "seven years of college, I have like half a million in federal student loan debt, two years interning here, and, what, you moron, you just threw it all away."

As she opened her compact and stared at her pale reflection, her mind drifted to the sound of Zach's five-year-old daughter Emily, her voice singing incoherently … "he has a family," she said to herself as she reapplied her foundation, soaking up the shine on her forehead and chin. "Daddy!" she heard in her mind as she wiped the black mascara gently from under her eyes causing her skin to redden. She opened her liquid concealer and applied one tiny droplet under each eye.

As she gently camouflaged her reddened skin, she thought: "End this. You tell him: This can never happen again and walk away. You gave him your power," she thought as she smirked in the mirror, "now take it back." Her iPhone began to vibrate her purse on the countertop. She glanced at the makeup smeared across her fingertips and washed her hands.

As she wiped her hands dry, she picked up her cell: "one missed call" it said. She looked at the number, and she closed her eyes as Zach licked her from behind in her mind's eye.

"What the hell is wrong with you?" Becky said to herself as she walked out into the hallway and toward the balcony overlooking the harbor until the bars of signal returned. "One new voicemail," her iPhone vibrated as she pressed "connect."

"Hi," Zach said whispering, "it's me. Listen, we need to talk about the proffer. Amanda's here and, um, we're, um, kind of brainstorming you could say. Can you come back, please?"

Becky slid her iPhone into her purse and walked into the U.S. Attorney's Office. She walked with her head down, a sullen expression pictorially delineating her demeanor.

"Hi, Becky," the receptionist said as Becky looked up and mouthed: "Hi, Jenny."

"Hi, Becky," MaryAnn Adams and John Lovett, fellow AUSAs, former law clerks, chanted in unison as Becky walked by. She lifted her head only slightly, mouthing: "Hi."

"Hmmm," John whispered: "Something's eating her."

"Yeah," MaryAnn whispered back: "You hear what happened this morning ... whole courthouse's a buzz: heard Woodbury chewed

Zach up and spit him out."

"Oooh, do tell, do tell," John said smiling as Becky turned around and threw them a menacing glare as Becky's mind repeated: "Something's eating her, something's eating her" … Becky smiled as she thought: "Oh, yeah, something's eating me all right," as she blushed and devilishly grinned.

"Sorry," MaryAnn mouthed as Becky continued to walk with her head down, her purse digging into her hip.

Becky stopped short in the hallway just before reaching Zach's office. She leaned her back against the wall listening to Amanda: "Zach, let it go. I told you from the beginning, this case is a loser. It's a no-win. It's over."

Becky closed her eyes and watched as Hill screamed "Fuck you" and lunged at Zach. Her mind drifted to the questioning at hand which precipitated his outburst:

Q. Mr. Hill, are you aware that Timothy Watkins was gunned down by the Bloods as they shot into a busy North End neighborhood in the middle of the day firing at The Latin Kings?
A. Nope.
Q. How does this make you feel, Mr. Hill?

Becky thought: "How do you think it'd make him feel, Zach?" She closed her eyes:

A. Um, makes me feel bad.
Q. Are you aware that Christopher Russo, ten years old, was caught in the crossfire, shot in the back, and is now a quadriplegic?
A. Nope.
Q. And if I told you that Chris Russo will spend the rest of his life in a wheelchair and will need 24-hour medical assistance, how would you feel?
A. Um, like shit.

Becky said to herself: "And how would you feel, Zach?"

Q. Uh-huh. Do you feel personally responsible being a member of the Bloods?
A. Fuck you.
Q. Excuse me, Mr. Hill?
A. You heard me, you cretin.

Becky adjusted her skirt and stood in the doorjamb as Zach yelled: "Get off my back, Amanda, will you?" Amanda walked toward Becky and grabbed her right sleeve whispering into her left ear: "Maybe you can talk some sense into him?" as she stormed out.

Zach smiled as Becky walked toward his desk. "Hi, beautiful," he said softly as Becky sat across from him.

"Hi," Becky replied as she stared at her feet, "Zach, we need to talk." Becky nervously twirled her Harvard ring which needed to be resized and dangled loosely from her middle finger of her right hand. Whenever she was anxious, she would spin it as an unconscious obsessive compulsion. Becky spun her ring: "Zach."

"Yes, Ms. Lawrence?" Zach said as he tilted his head to the right.

Becky continued to spin her ring while fixating on the empty styrofoam container on his desk. "This was a mistake, Zach."

Zach's face took on a serious somber expression, his eyes inhaling her physical nervous mannerisms. "Becky," Zach said as she continued to twirl her ring. Becky momentarily looked into Zach's piercing brown eyes and stopped fidgeting.

"Zach, please let me speak. This is hard" --

Zach stared at his double-sided monitor flashing photos of Emily's birthday party bash. His eyes darted between Emily riding a donkey smiling and Becky's seemingly perfect white front teeth.

"I'm sorry, Becky," Zach said as he picked up a pen and began twirling it between his thumb and pointer finger and then tapping it nervously on the desk as he licked his bottom lip and watched her fidget.

"What just happened," Becky said as she averted his eyes, "it was, it was" --

"Mmm," Zach moaned and smiled focusing his eyes on Becky's blouse.

-- "it was incredible." Becky's eyes refocused on the empty coffee cup. "Best sex I've ever had," she said as he smiled and moaned "Mmm" as she thought, "And the only sex I've ever had ... God, I'm totally pathetic."

Zach grinned widely and slid his left hand under his desk and cupped himself. He grew more uncomfortable as she spoke: "Zach … you know this was a mistake," Becky said as her eyes met his. Zach scrunched his nose and his eyebrows formed an arch as he pouted.

Becky crossed her legs: "Listen, I won't tell anyone. You don't tell anyone. This never happened, okay?"

Zach stood and slowly walked around his desk. He sat in the chair next to her. He reached for her right hand and he caressed it as he spoke: "I don't think I can do that, Ms. Lawrence," he said as he kissed the back of her hand and his right hand began to slowly creep toward her inner thigh. He touched her so lightly it tickled, and she squirmed and smiled as she blushed.

"Zach," she said sternly as she stopped his hand in motion from progressing forward, "you're not listening," Becky said as she closed her eyes and watched his tongue lick her in her mind as she began to sweat profusely. "I can't do this," Becky said as Zach placed his hand on her knee and began gently massaging in small, deliberate circles slowly moving his hand up her inner thigh.

"You're married. You have a family," Becky whispered as Zach's hand continued upwards and began lightly stroking her vulva over her pantyhose. "You're my boss," Becky said as Zach forcefully inserted his pointer finger inside her through her hose under her skirt. “Stop” Becky demanded as Zach raised his finger to his nose and whiffed as he moaned.

Becky stood and stared down at him as he continued to lick his bottom lip staring at her groin. She stared into his eyes as she said: “You’re sick. You know that?” She walked over toward the glass wall and stood motionless, contemplating her impending exit maneuver. She didn’t hear Zach stand. She didn’t hear him walk across the room behind her. She didn’t see him lock the door.

Zach pressed into her from behind and whispered: “My marriage is a sham.” Becky whispered: “Please don’t do this,” as her body swayed, and her buttocks clenched his erection between her cheeks. He pressed into her as he whispered: “Wife and I haven’t had sex in years, since Emily was born.”

Becky turned around and faced Zach as she slowly backed away from him, backing toward the glass wall, the radiator pressing against the backs of her thighs. Zach walked forward, standing inches from her swaying body as Becky yelled: “Yeah, right. What do you think: I’m a moron?”

Zach cornered her; the back of her head leaned against the glass as the radiator pressed against the backs of her thighs. She attempted to run from him; and as she made a dash toward the right, he pushed forward and she fell back against the wall. His right hand began gently stroking her left breast over her blouse as he leaned in and kissed her. She cocked her head to the side and began to hump him wildly before opening her eyes.

“This is over,” she yelled as her right hand struck the left side of his face. He instinctively caught her forearm mid-air just after making contact. He held her wrist tightly with his left hand and began to kiss her forcibly. She pulled her face away and began to cry as her body swayed.

“Please don’t do this, Zach,” she cried as he gently took her down to the floor, still tightly grasping her right wrist with his left hand behind her back, causing her hand to go numb and her fingers to tingle.

As he kissed her neck and her body humped him as she moaned: "Oh, God," Zach whispered into her left ear: "Turn over, baby." He slowly lifted his weight off of her frame as his right hand reached up and pulled her pantyhose down to her thighs.

Tears streamed down her cheeks as she stood. "Take it off," Zach whispered as he pressed his face against her inner thighs and his tongue reached upwards and began wiggling her clit voraciously.

"Please stop," Becky cried as Zach rolled her black thong and pantyhose down to her ankles. Becky's face turned white and she tried to run from him. She stumbled against the side of his desk tripping on the hose and her thong now wrapped tightly bundled about her ankles serving as makeshift shackles.

Zach unzippered his pants and lunged toward her pinning her against his desk. He pressed into her from behind. "Please don't do this," Becky said as tears rolled down her cheeks. Zach dropped to his knees and began to lick her from behind. "Oh, God," she screamed as she continued to cry and laid her head and arms on his desk sighing in exasperation as she attempted to spread her legs apart.

Zach inserted his tongue deep inside her ass, and her juice flowed down her inner thighs as she pleaded: "Please don't do this." Zach took a step back and his left hand gently proceeded along the length of her inner thigh, down her calf; and as he encircled her ankle, he unhinged her hose. He stood behind her erect and leaned into her back. As he placed the tip of his cock in and out and swirled it gingerly against her clit, humping her without entering, he whispered: "You want me to stop?"

Cum splashed against his stomach as he giggled as Becky opened her eyes and shook her head up and down several times in quick succession. Zach backed up, arms raised, hands in the air. Becky peeled her body from his desk; and as she stood and turned around to face him, she wiped her wet cheeks with the backs of her hands.

Becky stared at Zach's immense erection as her juice flooded her thighs, and she licked her lips. Zach knelt on his knees and began licking her as she slowly undid each button of her blouse as Zach looked up into her eyes and smiled enigmatically.

"This can never happen again," she said as he stood before her. He unzippered her skirt; and as his right hand pulled her right erect nipple into his mouth, her skirt fell to her knees and dropped to the floor.

As he suckled her, Becky humped his right leg. He opened his eyes and released her breast. He dropped again to his knees and teased her with his tongue as she moaned and pressed his head inward. As he released his tongue and opened his eyes and stared up into her beautiful face, he whispered: "Turn over, baby."

Becky dropped to her knees in front of his desk, and Zach kissed her as his right hand caressed her left cheek. He whispered again: "Turn over, baby," as he forcefully flung his black leather chair across the room with his right hand.

Becky slowly turned around. With her knees on the carpet and her ass in the air, she said smiling with her head turned toward him: "Is this what you want, Mr. Woods?" as he forcefully thrust into her.

"Oh, God," Becky screamed as her lava pooled onto the floor. "What am I doing?" she thought as she experienced the most beautiful release she had ever known. Zach absorbed her inhibitions, stopped, and slid out. He held himself in his right hand and rubbed himself against her buttocks teasing her again to multifaceted cataclysmic orgasm.

"Oh, God," she whispered: "Put it in, Zach; please put it in." Zach grinned and giggled as he continued to tease her, rubbing the tip against her vulva as she humped him and soaked the floor.

"Say it, baby," he said smiling coyly as he put the tip into her just slightly. "Oh, God," Becky moaned. Zach whacked himself against her buttocks slowing wetting her anus with his tip: "Say it."

Becky reached her right hand under her ass and grabbed his balls tightly as he teased her and smiled. "Come inside me, Zach," she whispered as she cried as Zach said softly: "Shhh, that's not it. You're not ready, huh? Zach leaned down on his ankles and licked her anus, slowly dragging his tongue toward her clit. As he reached it, stretching his tongue and wrenching his neck, his middle finger wiggled inside her anus as she cried: "Put it in, Zach. Oh, God," as her pelvic floor contracted and cum sprayed across his face.

He giggled and whispered: Say it, baby. What do you want?"

Becky cried: "Fuck me," and Zach entered her slowly and gently, still teasing her clit with his fingertips. He humped her lightly as the fingers of his left hand played a harmonic symphony with her inner lips. Becky saturated the floor as she screamed: "Oh, God, Zach … harder."

"Shhh," Zach whispered as he plunged deeply inside and began to ride her. He smiled insanely as liquid jettisoned down his calves. As he felt his ejaculate imminent, he pulled out and whispered: "Say it," as he continued to tease her incessantly by gently putting his wet immense tip in, slowly letting it slip out of its own accord, while his pointer finger inserted gently and deeply inside her ass.

Her juice dripped onto the floor as Becky moaned: "Oh, God," as she doused his entire forearm. He smiled as the torrent ensued. She reached down behind her with her right hand and pulled her into him.

"Say it," Zach said as he rubbed the rim against her clit. Becky turned her head away from him as she climaxed and Zach smiled.

"Harder," she screamed as he forcefully penetrated her. She reached her left hand down and under and cupped his sack firmly as he whispered: "Ahhh" and ejaculated deep within her.

"Oh, God," she cried as she drenched the floor, and Zach collapsed on top of her, throwing her into her own juices, and the room infused with the pungent rotten stench of putrefying decayed flesh. Charlie sat on the radiator nodding his head in discontent and blew a fine mist of sulphur into Zach's face. Zach coughed turning his head onto Becky's back, choking on the foul odor as Charlie smiled and Zach whispered softly: "What's that smell?"

Zach slowly began to lift himself up and Becky whispered: "Don't leave me yet," as Zach smiled and collapsed on top of her back again, rubbing his face in between her clavicles. The aroma faded as Becky began to nervously giggle. Zach began licking her neck and tickling her, and they rolled over giggling as Amanda stood outside Zach's locked office door. As her hand reached up to knock, she heard laughter. She put her hand down at her side and pressed her ear against the door.

"Holy crap," Amanda said under her breath as she heard Becky giggle; she smiled and walked down the corridor toward reception. "Oh, my God," she mumbled out loud, "he's fucking her," Amanda said in her mind as her smile turned into a sullen pout, and she walked into her tiny cubicle.

"Oh, my God," she repeated out loud as she queued the answers to interrogatories in the civil case pending against Jose Veloz; her mind fixated on the headlines in the Boston Herald in bold italics reading: "*JOSE VELOZ*, Suspected leader of the Boston 93 Bloods in federal custody."

"Becky's a love," Amanda mumbled out lout as she stood by the HP as it read "processing" …

"Becky and Zach?" she mumbled: "Becky and Zach" … "Eeew, I need to talk to that girl," she said grimacing as she lifted the last page from the tray.

Ten minutes later Zach stood fully dressed adjusting his tie as he watched Becky attempting to roll her pantyhose up her damp legs. And as she pulled to tauten the nylon, the left leg shredded in her hands. He grinned as she threw her hose into his trash can next to his desk. Zach couldn't seem to manage his tie and sighed in exasperation as Becky smiled. "Come here," she whispered as he walked and stood a foot in front of her. Zach pressed into her and his hands reached around and cupped her buttocks as Becky fumbled.

As he pressed into her, he whispered: "Problem?" as Becky struggled with the fabric.

"Um, yeah," she said as she smiled and continued to fumble, "Zach, I can't concentrate." Zach smiled and dropped his hands to his sides as Becky fixed his tie in place. He pulled his leather chair into his desk and sat and watched as Becky tried to straighten the wrinkles out of her skirt with her palms.

Amanda approached Zach's door slowly and proceeded to knock in rhythmic calculated precision with the knuckle of her right index finger: rap-a-tap-tap, rap-a-tap-tap, rap-a-tap-tap. Her left hand turned the knob simultaneously finding it still locked in position. "Zach?" Amanda squeaked as Becky sat down.

"You ready?" Zach said as he stood and loosened his suffocating tie. His right hand reached deep within a box of Kleenex, and he tore the tissues out of the box and threw the massive swab on the puddle under his desk as Becky blushed. Becky nodded as she flirted unconsciously with her eyes and watched Zach's ass as he turned the lock and twisted the doorknob in his hand.

"Mmm," Becky moaned softly and Zach turned his head and smiled as she blushed.

Amanda walked into Zach's office staring into Becky's eyes: "What the hell are you doing?" she said with her eyes as her mind radiated through Becky's consciousness. Becky's eyes immediately gravitated toward the floor at her feet as Amanda smiled at Zach raising her brows curiously.

"Here," she mumbled as she flung the interrogatories onto his desk. Amanda's body language told a compelling story as she placed both fists against her sides and stared intently at Becky who continued to avert her stare and fixated on the tiny red stain imbedded in the blue carpet.

Zach was oblivious to Amanda's cues as he read through the Answers to Interrogatories in the accompanying civil action entitled: "Christopher Russo, Sr., in loco parentis, Christopher Russo, a minor child, et al, versus Jose Veloz, et al. His eyes fixated on the last question and answer on Page 8:

Q. Please state in full detail your knowledge of the events precipitating the gang violence in which Christopher Russo, among other minors, was injured on July 19, 2010, on Hanover Street in the North End?"
A. I have no such knowledge.

"Hmmm … yeah, right," Zach mumbled.

"Excuse me, Mr. Woods," Amanda replied as she threw daggers at him as her eyes darted between Becky staring at the floor and Zach reclining in his chair. Zach lifted his glasses: "Something bugging you, Mandy?" he asked as Becky raised her eyes toward his gape.

"No," Amanda said as her eyes met Becky's, her face scorn in contempt. As Zach's mouth searched for saliva, he opened his top drawer and unraveled a fresh pack of Wrigley's Doublemint. He held it up as Amanda and Becky nodded their heads side to side and Becky avoided Amanda's stare, again fixating on the tiny red blob in the carpet.

Zach stood and walked around his desk. He approached Becky cautiously and gently handed her the interrogatories. "I'll be right back," Zach whispered as his bladder warranted his attention.

Zach turned around and looked behind him as he exited. Once out of sight Amanda sat down next to Becky: "Look, this is none of my business" Amanda said as Becky's eyes met hers as the windows to Becky's soul unraveled before her. "You know he's married" Amanda whispered as Becky nodded.

Amanda placed her right hand on top of Becky's left hand, and Becky raised her eyes. "I really like you, Becky," Amanda said as Becky smiled: "I like you too, Amanda, a lot."

"End this," Amanda whispered, "before" --

"Before what?" Becky interjected, "before we get caught and I lose my job, before his wife finds out and divorces his sorry ass … before what: before I get hurt? Before what?" Becky repeated as she stole her hand back and nervously twisted the end of her now messy and disheveled braid.

"Before you get really hurt," Amanda whispered as their eyes locked. Becky placed her left hand on Amanda's right forearm and without speaking effectively communicated. Amanda whispered: "Too late, huh?" as a single tear dropped from the corner of Becky's left eye as Zach walked into his office, stood in front of his door, and said sternly: "Problem?" as he threw a menacing look at Amanda and inhaled the savory smell of lilacs permeating his mucous membranes.

"No," Amanda said as she stood.

"Mandy, get me the entire file folder on Veloz, will you?" Amanda nodded and walked out into the hallway as Zach closed the door and turned the lock. Becky watched and sighed as Zach knelt in front of her chair.

"You okay, babe?" he whispered.

"Mmm," Becky groaned as she wiped her tearing left eye.

"You didn't tell her, did you?" Zach said as he placed his knees on the carpet and put his right hand on her left bare knee. Becky didn't answer as he softly slid his hand up her thigh while clearing his throat.

"Didn't have to," Becky mumbled as Zach removed his hand and scratched the shadow under his chin: "Woman's intuition, huh?"

"Mmm," Becky groaned as Zach placed his head into her lap pressing his nose into her through her skirt. He whispered: "I just can't get enough," as Becky instinctively placed her right hand on the back of his head and gently pushed his face against her as her fingers began to play with his soft dark hair. He smiled as he inhaled her and pulled his face away smiling.

"Now, let's get back to work," he said as he stood in front of her as her eyes fixated on his enormous bulge and the backs of her thighs stuck to the vinyl as her juice dripped onto the chair.

"Problem, Ms. Lawrence?" Zach said as he pulled her standing to her feet and stared at the small puddle on the seat. He whispered as he grinned: "Turn around." He giggled as he felt her wet skirt. Becky stared at the floor as Zach pulled her into him whispering: "Look how wet you are for me, baby?"

He leaned forward and dipped his pointer finger of his left hand into her juice smeared on the seat and watched her body sway as she leaned against the desk as he sucked his fingertip dry, and she began backing up walking away from him toward the wall.

Zach placed his tongue on his lower lip and began slowly licking his lip as he approached her. Becky's right hand reached under her, and she began humping it wildly as Zach stared at her breasts through her white blouse. "I never stop thinking about you," he whispered as he lunged forward and pressed his erection against her as she groaned: "Oh, my God, Zach," as he fell to his knees and raised her skirt over her stomach and began licking the inside of her right thigh as he whispered: "Look how wet you are for me, baby," as cum oozed down her thighs in waves.

"I love you, Becky," he whispered as he grabbed her buttocks firmly, and she began backing up toward the wall as his hands fell at his sides, and he crawled on the floor toward her licking his bottom lip madly.

"You love me?" she said irritated. "What kind of game are you playing with me, Mr. Woods?" Zach stood and smiled at her. He took a step forward each time she stepped back. As her back hit the wall, he pressed firmly into her. Becky whispered as he unbuttoned her blouse: "You don't even know me," as Zach kissed her neck, and she smelled his savor as her body humped him as she began an intense conversation in her mind:

"Look at him; look how he looks at you, Becky … he's playing you, he's playing you," as he dropped to his knees and lifted his hands toward the small of her back and unhitched her skirt and began fumbling to release the zipper. Her skirt fell to her knees, and Becky wiggled her hips as it fell to the floor.

Zach slipped her thong down to her ankles and she stepped out of it as he sat on his ass and threw his back against the wall underneath her. Zach looked above his head and smiled as his tongue entered her; and as she ferociously humped, he whispered: "I know you better than you know yourself, Ms. Lawrence," as he ate her.

Becky closed her eyes as she released and Zach smiled as he watched streams running down her inner thighs and she thought: "Yeah, he's a player; yep, he's just playing me … Oh, God, I'm wet … damn, how many times can he go?"

Zach stood staring into her eyes; she unhitched the button of his slacks with her left hand, and he unzippered his pants which fell to his ankles as he nailed her to the wall and teased her vulva with his tip.

"Oh, my God," Becky screamed as Zach whispered "Shhh, I want you to sit on my face for a few hours, baby," he whispered as she lifted herself up against the wall and threw her legs around his back as he backed up. They kissed as he carried her across the room, and he laid her back gently across his desk.

As Becky lied naked on his desk, her ass overhanging the edge, Zach pulled his chair back into the desk. He sat down and watched her clit as he inserted his pointer finger deep within her. He watched as her juice dripped to the floor and onto his lap. He began licking her clit back and forth as he inserted his middle finger deep inside her ass and she orgasmed, inundating the floor as she screamed: “Oh, my God, Zach.”

Amanda stood listening at the door, her tongue licking her bottom lip as Zach whispered: “What do you want, baby?

“Oh, God,” Becky screamed as Zach wiggled her clit with his tongue and Amanda’s mouth fell open as her eyes bulged.

“Say it,” Zach whispered as Becky screamed: “Oh, God, Zach.”

Zach whispered: “Shhh … say it.” He stood up and threw the chair back against the wall with his left hand as he wiggled his tip against her clit, teasing her as she screamed: “Fuck me, Zach … oh, my God, fuck me.”

Zach giggled as he thrust deep inside her as she whispered: “Harder.” Zach thrust deeply inside her oral cavity; and as her pelvic floor contracted and her juice flooded the desk, he released as she whispered: “Oh, my God,” as her lava inundated him, and her juice dripped from the edge of his desk onto the floor.

Amanda stood at the door, her knuckle pressed against the wood, her mouth agape as she thought: “Oh, my God!” and walked down the hall toward reception as a sulphur vapor filled the interior of Zach’s office.

Zach walked naked to the far wall to retrieve his pants from the floor as Becky slid off the desk mumbling: “We can’t work together, Zach,” as she clenched her thighs together as cum infiltrated and flooded her down to her knees.

“Sure, we can,” Zach said smiling flirtatiously as he pulled his pants up and tucked his shirt in as he licked his bottom lip.

“Yeah?” Becky said as he handed her her wrinkled skirt. As she reached for her underwear, he put her twisted damp thong under his nose and inhaled exuberantly as he moaned: “Mmm.”

"How exactly is this going to work?" she shouted as she grabbed the thong from his grasp and slid her underwear over her ankles.

"I think maybe I should ask for an internal transfer," Becky said as Zach stood directly in front of her and pulled her toward him. "Don't do that," Zach whispered as he kissed her neck and hugged her as her body went limp in his arms. "We'll make this work," Zach whispered.

"How?" Becky asked as Zach sat down in his leather chair and Becky sat on his lap. Zach's right thigh instantly absorbed her excess fluid as he leaned his head into her breasts as he whispered: "I don't know, baby," as a rancid odor filled the room.

Zach lifted his head slowly and stared into her eyes: "What's that smell?" they said simultaneously as they giggled. Becky's head collapsed into Zach's neck; and as she kissed his earlobe and he twitched, he whispered: "Wow, I'm beat.

"I bet," she said as she smiled: "Wow, how many times can he go?" echoed in her mind as she sopped his lap and he groaned: "Hmmm."

"Zach," Becky whispered as she ran her fingers through his damp hair.

"Hmmm," Zach moaned as their eyes met.

"Listen, all we have on Hill and Veloz is Special Agent Mazza; and based on his 'dollars for convictions' promises … honestly, we have nothing."

Zach scratched his chin: "That's why we need to get Hill to turn against Veloz."

Becky stood up and glowered at Zach, her eyebrows fixated in an arch. She shook her head and began to pace as Zach watched her gait.

"Zach," Becky said as she began nervously twirling the end of her braid: "Zach, with 'Foo' excluded, why would Hill cooperate? He knows he's gonna walk. We have no witnesses, no evidence other than Mazza, and, quite honestly, he's a joke."

Zach stood noticing the myriad of wrinkles now deeply imbedded in his blue slacks. He tucked his shirt in and began fiddling with his disheveled tie.

"What exactly are you saying, Ms. Lawrence?" Zach said as he continued to struggle with his tie and she watched with her mouth agape as he licked his bottom lip.

Becky stood in front of Zach, her right hand gently touching his left cheek. Zach grabbed her hand and kissed her palm as she smiled. "I know you want Veloz ... Jesus, Zach, we all want him. He's like, um, you know, "gangsta" of the gangstas in Boston but" --

"But?" Zach said as he backed away giggling, repeating her spirited catch phrase: "'Gangsta of the gangstas,' huh?"

"But this is a no-win, baby. Who's representing Veloz?" Becky said as Zach returned to his desk and sat in his chair whispering as he wiped his forehead: "Whew, I'm wiped" as he grinned and Becky stared at him inquisitively.

"O'Connor, Michael O'Connor," Zach said as Becky sat in a clean dry chair and pulled it towards Zach's desk.

"He'll file a motion to dismiss today or tomorrow," Becky said as Zach stared dumbfoundedly at the ceiling. "You with me, Zach?" she whispered as his eyes focused toward her.

"Mmm," he mumbled, "tired … think you wore me out, babe." Becky grinned as he yawned ..."Becky, if we're gonna keep Veloz in custody, you gotta move on Hill. I'll feed you a great story, a compelling little tale. We'll tell him Ramirez talked; I offered him immunity to testify."

“Zach,” Becky said as she shook her head from side to side, yawned, and stared at the disarray of his desktop noticing a few long brown hairs stuck to a manila file folder in the center, “I don’t think I can do that.”

Zach stood up and walked around his desk and sat on the edge facing Becky. “So you’re gonna let this piece of shit walk?” he asked as he stared at her intently as Amanda knocked on his locked door: “Zach?”

Zach walked over to the door and just before he unlocked it, he turned his head and stared at Becky: “Ready?” he whispered. Becky grabbed some Kleenex off his desk and said: “Wait.” Zach turned around and smiled and grew erect as he leaned against the door and stared at her ass as she cleaned the seat next to her. She nodded and he unlocked the door. He walked around his desk and sat in his chair as Amanda slowly walked in, her eyes darting from Becky’s sullen face to Zach’s angry facial contortions.

“Everything okay?” she said as she stood next to Becky. Zach stared at Becky as she yawned and focused her attention on the tiny red stain in the carpet. Zach twirled a ballpoint pen in his left hand, occasionally stabbing it into the desk. Amanda’s eyes darted between Zach and Becky nervously.

“Okay,” Amanda said as she grinned at Zach, “what’s up, Zach?”

Zach stabbed his desktop calendar, and the pen stuck upright from his desk. “Get me all the raps and CORIs on all the defendants in the Veloz case, okay?”

“Okay,” Amanda said as she stood and turned around and began walking toward the door. “You’re not gonna let this go, are you?” she said with her right hand on her hip as Becky stared into her eyes. Amanda grinned and Becky’s eyes returned to the carpet. Amanda shook her head from side to side and sighed and walked into the hallway. Becky’s eyes slowly drifted upwards and stared intently into Zach’s face.

"I can't play these games," Becky whispered.

"Games?" Zach said as he smiled coyly. Becky stood from her chair as Zach swiveled his chair toward the window avoiding her eyes.

"You're making deals with the devil, Mr. Woods," Becky shouted as she turned and walked toward the door. As she stood in front of the open door, Zach scooted in front of her, his right hand closing the door into the jamb. Becky stared at the floor as Zach slowly lifted her chin with his left hand, forcing her eyes into his gaze.

"I'm not the bad guy here, Ms. Lawrence," he whispered. Becky stared at him, reached for the doorknob and left Zach stunned in the archway. He whispered "Becky!" as he watched her walk away licking his bottom lip as she turned out of sight. He picked up his office line and dialed "1" and connected to reception.

"Hi, Mr. Woods," Jenny said as she blew a bubble and it popped sticking to the underside of her nose. "Can I help you?" she asked as she attempted to peel the gum off, and it stuck to the phone.

"Yeah, Jenny, hi ... um, buzz Amanda for me please. Tell her to meet me in my office in 20." Zach stood gazing endlessly into the harbor. He watched as waves engulfed a small motor boat out by the first buoy. "I'm wiped," he thought as he scratched his head and giggled, "I'm fried," he said out loud as he cupped himself with his left hand.

Becky walked into the Clerk's office to check her mail bin. There was one letter inside of a manila envelope marked: "District Court Intraoffice Memo." She walked into the overflow jury room overlooking the harbor and opened it.

"Dear Becky," it read ... "The Judge," Becky said as she smiled and sighed in the same breath immediately recognizing his unique handwritten scrawl ... "I'd like to ask you to consult on a case presenting somewhat complex medical/legal issues. I know you're probably inundated upstairs but when you have a minute, please give me a call ... Warmest regards, CPW."

Becky smiled as her cell rang. She glanced at the touchscreen recognizing Zach's cell number. She let it go to voicemail as she stared out into the water in a fixated trance. She closed her eyes and felt Zach touch her. She watched as he carried her naked over to his desk in her mind. "End this," she thought as her cell rang again.

"Becky?," Zach whispered, "ignoring me?"

Becky nervously fumbled with her iPhone almost dropping it and catching it right before it hit the floor: "No, Zach, of course not. What's up?"

"Listen, 4:00 pretrial with Judge Sanford, Courtroom 19. I need you there," Zach said as he smiled and swiveled in his chair.

"Okay," Becky said as she looked at the time on her cell: "3:25."

"Can you come up here please?" Zach said as he continued to twirl, stopping only when he became dizzy and nauseous.

"Sure … want some coffee?" Becky said as she grinned.

"Yeah, that'd be great. Thanks, babe" Zach said as he adjusted himself. "Becky?"

"Yeah?" Becky replied as she stared at the floor thinking: "babe?"

"You okay?" Zach asked as he stood and held himself.

"Sure," Becky said as she pressed the elevator arrow down and the call disconnected.

Fifteen minutes later Becky walked into Zach's office. Zach's head was on his desk resting on his forearms with his eyes closed. Becky placed the cardboard tray containing two large regulars next to his head, and his body twitched as he opened his eyes slowly trying to focus.

"Tired, Mr. Woods?" Becky asked smiling.

"Hmmm," Zach groaned as he opened the rim and began to sip. "Thank God for you," he whispered, "hmmm, coffee" he said as he sipped and his eyes began to focus as Becky giggled.

Zach handed Becky a file folder entitled: "US v. James Curley." She opened it to the Sealed Affidavit of Julia M. Crowley, Special Agent, Federal Bureau of Investigation. Her mouth fell open as her eyes skimmed down to the fifth bullet point: "PHONE CALL FROM ATTORNEY JOHN GILL:

"On December 7, 2009, Attorney John Gill contacted the FBI and reported that a client, Joanna Clark, who later became a cooperating witness (CW), had been in Lawrence District Court trying to get a prostitution charge dismissed. According to Attorney Gill while they were in court, the CW pointed to the clerk magistrate and said: "I blew him in court yesterday."

Becky looked at Zach as he continued to sip his coffee: "Seriously?" she said as he smirked.

"Hmmm" Zach moaned in between sips.

Becky's eyes skimmed down to "(8) INTERVIEW WITH CW: On December 7, 2009, the FBI interviewed the CW. The CW advised that approximately three years ago in approximately August of 2006 she was arrested for prostitution. At that time while in lock-up at the Lawrence District Court the clerk magistrate known as "Jim" asked her if she was a "working girl," and told her that he would help her out if she helped him out."

Becky began to smile as Zach continued to sip.

"The magistrate took the CW out of the cell and into a room in the basement. The CW gave Curley oral sex, and he touched and sucked her breasts. The CW did not see Curley again until she was arrested for prostitution on December 6th, 2009. According to the CW, when she was arraigned, she saw Curley in the courtroom and waved to him. The magistrate took a recess and waved to the CW and took her to a small conference room. Curley then told the CW to go downstairs and wait for him on the bench. He told the CW that he wanted to see the CW's breasts and "eat her out."

"Tell me this idiot plead?" Becky said with a smile.

"Nope," Zach said as he took another sip, "bench trial coming right up, Ms. Lawrence."

Becky turned the page: "The CW indicated to Curley that she knew he helped her out 'last time,' and she would be willing to 'take care of him' if he helped her out again." Becky took the Affidavit and laid it on Zach's desk and her eyes focused on the "Deposition of Joanna Clark." Her eyes skimmed to the red highlighting on Page 3:

Q. All right. I'd like to direct your attention to August of 2006, specifically August 25th, 2006. Were you locked up in Lawrence District Court that day?
A. Yes, I was.
Q. And did you meet a man named James Curley that day?
A. Yes, I did.
Q. Had you ever met him before that day?
A. No.
Q. How did you come to meet him?
A. I was in lock-up downstairs in the Lawrence District Court, and he came down, approached me, and asked me if I was a working girl.
Q. All right. So he came down and what did he ask you?
A. If I was a working girl.
Q. And what did you understand that to mean?
A. If I was a prostitute, because that's what they call prostitutes: working girls.
Q. And, in fact, was that why you were in jail that day?
A. Yes.
Q. Okay. Now, the man who asked you if you were a working girl, would you recognize him if you saw him again?
A. Yes.
Q. Now, after he asked you if you were a 'working girl,' what did he say or do next?

A. He told me that if I helped him out and did a 'favor' for him, he would in exchange help me out with my case and get rid of my case.
Q. Did you think he had the power to do that?
A. Yes.
Q. So what happened next?
A. I got out of the cell. I got taken out of the cell, and he brought me through the hallway, brought me in the elevator, brought me upstairs through the courtroom, and behind the courtroom he brought me to a small room.
Q. All right. And when you went through the door that says "exit," what happened when you went through the door or what happens when you go through that door in the courtroom?
A. There's different rooms in different ways, and I went into the first room.
Q. The first room on the left?
A. Yeah.
Q. And what happened when you got into that room?
A. He locked the door and told me again to do something for him, and he started to take off his pants, unzipper his pants, and told me if I gave him a blow job that he would dismiss my case, get my case dismissed, and I did the deal.
Q. "The deal" being you performed oral sex?
A. Yes, I did.
Q. And why did you do that?
A. So he would dismiss my case.
Q. And, in fact, did you make bail that day?
A. Yeah, I got released. Yes.

Becky stared at Zach as Zach finished his coffee and yawned. She flipped through the deposition until her eyes scanned to the next highlight:

Q. So what happened?
A. So as he had his arms on the chair, after he said what he said he put his hands kind of like up under me and he guided me like up, and I was so nervous and I just didn't want to go to jail. So he basically led me up, lifted me, and he laid me onto the floor.
Q. And what happened then?
A. I was laying on the floor. He pulled down my skirt and underwear

and had me spread my legs. He ate me for awhile; it hurt actually, he sucked. He stood over me and -- he was standing over me and he said, he said, again he said: This will only take a second, he says, again, and he unbuttoned his pants. He zipped his pants down; you know, he pulled down his pants.
Q. And then what happened?
A. And then he had lie down and he kind of put his knees over me on the floor, you know, and he whacked it hard against my breasts. Then I closed my eyes. At one point I closed my eyes so I couldn't see what was happening, but I felt it; it felt like he was sitting on me, like going back and forth on me, you know what I mean.
Q. And so what happened next as he's going back and forth?
A. I felt semen on me like dripping, you know.
Q. Now, did you feel like you could resist him?
A. No.
Q. Why not?
A. Because number one, he was heavy, but I didn't want to go to jail.
Q. And so you said you felt semen, and what happened?
A. He ejaculated all over me. I just felt it.
Q. I'm sorry. After he ejaculated what happened?
A. He stood up quick and I opened my eyes and he zippered up his pants, pulled up his pants, and quickly he went towards the door.
Q. So what did you do? Did you clean yourself up?
A. Yeah, when he had gotten up, he opened the door. I just saw him get up. When he turned around, I had gotten up quick; it was my first instinct to just get up quick, and I looked at myself and I just had all this nasty stuff on me, like dripping from, you know, my tits. So I was looking around, I wanted something to just wipe it off of me, and the only thing that there was there, there was like a phone there and I saw a phonebook, so real quick I just ripped these pages from the phonebook; I was just trying to get it off of me, you know.

“Oh, my God,” Becky said as her face winced, “gross.” Tell me this isn’t a jury trial?”

“Nope, bench trial, Ms. Lawrence … I know,” Zach said as he pointed to her unopened coffee still in the cardboard, “coffee?”

“You can have it,” Becky said smiling, “looks like you need it more than I do right now, Mr. Woods.”

Zach licked his bottom lip as Becky watched, and he whispered: “You wore me out, babe,” as he smiled and struggled to pull the styrofoam from the tray. He opened the rim and began sipping.

“We can’t try this, Zach,” Becky said as Amanda walked into Zach’s office. As Amanda’s eyes met Becky’s, all three began to smile simultaneously: “Looking at Curley, huh?”

Once again Becky flipped through the deposition as Amanda pulled up a chair next to Becky. Becky’s eyes fixated on the next red highlight:

Q. All right, and back in August 2006 did you give him oral sex because you liked him?
A. No, because he promised to dismiss my case.
Q. Did you demand money from him?
A. No.
Q. So you were getting a legal favor in return?
A. Yes.
Q. Did you think you would get out of jail if you didn't do it?
A. No. I wouldn't, no.
Q. Why not?
A. Because I had a lot warrants and my record was pretty long.
Q. So you thought he had the power to let you out in exchange for sex?
A. Yes.
Q. What did Mr. Curley do with his hands during this meeting?
A. He was feeling his cock; it was hard.
Q. That would be his genital area?
A. Yes. He pulled down his pants. He was squeezing my breasts real hard, putting his penis in between, and, you know, he came all over me.
Q. Did you want to do that?
A. No, I did not want to do that. I had to do that.

"Gross!" Becky said as Amanda smiled at Zach. Becky placed the deposition on Zach's desk on top of the affidavit, and her eyes turned to the next document in queue: "Deposition of Sherry Jackson." Her eyes scanned to the first red highlight:

Q. This is another occasion; what occasion is this?
A. Another time he tried to get me to go down to the basement, but I told him no, but I don't remember -- I don't remember now, but, like I said, when I made the statements in the recording, it was right after the assault; and, of course, you remember more clearly right after something happens rather than two years after, but, yes, I remember, I remember saying that. I don't remember like what time. There were several times he approached me and said – well, so many different times, but, yes, this day that I got assaulted, yeah, he said that court doesn't begin until he says it begins.
Q. When you testified that he locked the door, pulled down his pants, had you on the floor, was squeezing your breasts hard, putting his penis in between your legs and ejaculated all over you, did you want to do that?
A. No, I did not want to do that.

"Okay, read enough of this case," Becky said as Amanda and Zach stared at her intently smiling.

Amanda whispered: "Time to go, guys," as Zach said: "Mandy, give me a minute with Becky." Amanda walked toward the door and turned around in the doorjamb throwing daggers at Zach.

"What?" Zach yelled.

"Nothing," Amanda retorted as she stared at Becky, shook her head back and forth, and walked down the hallway.

Zach whispered: "You okay?" Becky nodded her head up and down and rose from her chair.
"Sore?" Zach said with a grin.

"Shut up," Becky said as she walked toward the door. She turned around and smirked: "Coming, Mr. Woods?"

Becky spotted Amanda sitting on the bench just outside of Courtroom 19 at 3:55. "Where's" --

"Zach? Yeah, I know," she said with a grin as Becky held the heavy wooden door open for her.

"Hi, Mary," Becky said to the Judge's courtroom clerk as Amanda thumped her heavy file folders on the government's table.

"Hi Becky," Mary said with a grin, "how you doing?"

Becky smiled as Mary whispered: "Where's Zach, Becky?"

Becky looked at Amanda who stared at the clerk and smiled.

"Judge has to be out of here by 4:30. She wants this case called now" … Becky looked at Amanda who shrugged her shoulders and rested her head on her right shoulder.

Becky looked over at defense table, and Timmy O'Brien mouthed "hi." Becky stood with her right hand extended toward him as he met her in the aisle. "Hi, Becky," Timmy said, "nice to see you."

"You too, Timmy. Thanks. Listen, can we talk for a minute?"

"Sure," Tim said as he whispered, "take a walk with me." Becky followed Tim to the rear of the immense courtroom, and they sat down on the bench against the wall.

Mary stood and yelled: "Where are you two going?"

Timmy stood and adjusted his tie: "Mary, we might be able to settle this if we could have a minute?"

"Yeah, one minute; Judge is breathing down my back, people." The phone rang on the clerk's desk, and Amanda listened as Mary picked up: "Hi Judge," she whispered. "I know … counsel's talking, said they may be able to settle this ... yep, okay."

Timmy sat down and stared into Becky's eyes as he whispered: "Client's willing to plea."

"Oh, good," Becky said as she crossed her legs nervously as he smiled.

"I told Zach this a couple weeks ago."

"You did?" Becky asked as she uncrossed.

"Mmm, client will plea if he drops the counts involving 'aggravated sexual assault' … Zach refused."

"I'll talk to him," Becky said as she smiled, "so he'll plea to Counts One and Three if we drop Two, Four, Five, and Six?"

"Exactly" Timmy whispered. "Listen, if this goes to trial, how are you going to prove 'aggravated sexual assault' in this case anyway?"

"Seriously," Becky whispered as Tim smiled, and Mary stood: "Let's go, counsel." Zach opened the courtroom doors and spotted Becky and Timmy sitting in the last row. He adjusted his tie as he approached with his left hand extended: "Hey, Tim" Zach said as he shook defense counsel's hand.

"Hi, Zach," Tim said as he winked at Becky still seated.

Becky stood and whispered to Zach: "Can I talk to you?"

Mary yelled: "Zach, nice of you to make it. Let's go, counsel" as her phone rang ... "Hi, Judge."

"One minute, Mary," Zach yelled as Becky followed him to counsel table whispering: "Zach, he'll plead guilty to deprivation of law, he'll plead guilty to sexual assault, we just drop the 'aggravated' and this deal's done."

Zach sat down next to Amanda and motioned for Becky to sit to his right. As she sat down, he whispered: "So you think we should make this deal, counselor?"

"Um, yeah" Becky said as eyebrows formed an arch over her eyes.

"Okay, babe," Zach whispered in her left ear as he stood: "Mary, tell the Judge we have a deal."

"Too late. You tell her yourself," Mary said as she pressed "1, 2, 3, 4" and the door opened and the Judge entered.

"All rise," Mary said as she threw a dirty look at Zach as he smiled at her and she nodded her head.

"Good afternoon, counsel," the Judge said as she took the bench.

"Good afternoon, your Honor," echoed in harmony throughout the courtroom.

"Call the case, Mary, please, and you may be seated."

"This is the matter of the United States of America versus James Curley, Docket No. 09-10026. Would counsel please state their names for the record?"

"Good afternoon, your Honor," Zach said as he smiled: "Zach Woods and Rebecca Lawrence for the Government."

"Good afternoon, Mr. Woods, Ms. Lawrence … nice of you to make it on time, Mr. Woods."

"Sorry, your Honor," Zach said as he put his head down and stared at the floor.

Timmy smiled at Becky as he spoke: "Good afternoon, your Honor. Timothy O'Brien for the Defendant, James Curley, who is present."

"Good afternoon, Mr. O'Brien and Mr. Curley."

Zach slowly raised his eyes toward the Judge's: "Your Honor, it appears that we have struck a plea bargain in this case."

"Fantastic," the Judge said with a smile as she grinned at Becky.

"I have been informed by my colleague, Ms. Lawrence, that the defendant is prepared to plead guilty to Counts One and Three. The government will drop Counts Two, Four, Five, and Six involving 'aggravated sexual assault' in exchange.

"Best news I've heard all day, Mr. Woods" the Judge said as she whispered, "Mary, pick out a date for the Rule 11, please."

Mary whispered loud enough that everyone could hear: "Um, July 10th at 10?"

"Counsel?" The Judge said as she scratched her head and her black curly hair got caught in her diamond engagement ring. As she pulled the ring from her hair, she mouthed: "Ow" and Becky giggled as the Judge smiled at her.

"No problem for me, your Honor" Timmy said as he stood.

"Mr. Woods?" The Judge said as she gently rubbed her scalp.

"That's fine with the government, your Honor."

"Great. Then the Rule 11 will be July 10th at 10 a.m."

Mary stood: "All rise," she announced as the Judge walked off the bench staring at Zach and waving him toward her with her right hand.

"I'm in trouble," Zach whispered into Becky's left ear as her and Timmy's eyes locked in a smile.

"Yes, your Honor?"

"Listen, Zach. I like you. You know that."

“Yes, your Honor,” Zach said as he smiled enthusiastically.

“I’m a little sick and tired of waiting for you, though … understand?”

“I’m sorry, your Honor,” Zach whispered as she grabbed the left sleeve of his navy suit. “Glad you got rid of this case,” the Judge whispered. “You know I was a magistrate judge with the State for over 25 years, and this case is so embarrassing,” she whispered as she smiled and left the courtroom.

As Zach returned to the government’s table, Amanda patted him on the back: “Good job, Zach,” she said as she patted as Becky’s face took on a piercing snare.

“See ya, guys,” Amanda yelled as she picked up her folders and walked down the aisle. Zach leaned in toward Becky as Mary watched with a curious stare: “Jealous?” he whispered. Becky punched him in his left bicep, and Mary giggled as Zach yelled: “Ow! Watch it, Ms. Lawrence.”

“Bye Becky, see you Zach,” Mary said as she buzzed herself into the back of the house and exited their view. Zach yawned as his eyes watered.

“Tired, Mr. Woods?” Becky said flirtatiously.

“You wiped me out, baby,” Zach said as he yawned. “I’ve got to go home and crash,” he said with a smile. Nervously, he looked around the empty courtroom, leaned in toward Becky’s ear and whispered: “I love you,” as he placed his left hand on her knee under the table. Becky smiled with her eyes, her mind repeating: “Don’t say it,” as she stood and walked down the center aisle. She turned her head back to make sure Zach was watching and smiled as she exited as Zach grinned: “See you tomorrow, Ms. Lawrence.”

Three weeks later Becky walked into the Moakley at 7:05 a.m. “Hi John,” she said as she walked through the metal detector. “Hi, Ms.

Lawrence," John said as he winked.

"Becky, John … call me Becky."

John smiled: "Okay, Becky." Becky's mind moaned: "Coffee … coffee … coffee."

"Hi, Alan," she whispered as she sneezed.

"Hi, Becky. How are you?"

"Oh, good," she said as she sneezed again.

"Getting sick?" Alan asked as he poured her coffee into the large styrofoam cup.

"Hope not," Becky answered as simultaneously they shouted: "allergies?"

"Yeah, it's been bad this year," Becky said as she sneezed.

"Bless you," Alan said chuckling: "Yeah, tell me about it," Alan said as he smiled and placed her large regular on the glass countertop. "It gives me headaches," Alan said as Becky sneezed again.

"Thanks, Alan," Becky said with a smile as her iPhone buzzed in her right blazer pocket. She opened the rim and sipped while standing at the counter, one thought reiterating through her mind: "coffee, coffee, coffee."

Becky placed a 5 dollar bill into Alan's hand and said: "Keep the change, my good man," as she placed the coffee on the countertop and stared at her touchscreen: "One missed call" it said as she thought: "Yeah, wonder who?"

"Wow, it's only 10 past 7," she thought to herself as she walked out the rear entrance sipping her coffee and strolled down the concrete walk toward the harbor. "What the hell am I doing here so early?" she said out loud as she sipped and inhaled the saltwater roses infiltrating and overwhelming her olfactory senses.

She drank half her coffee as she sat on the bench overlooking the pier. She watched intensely as seagulls gathered at the dock to her left. She put her coffee down on the ground and pressed voicemail: "Hi Becky," Zach said energetically. "I know it's early but I've got to see you. Come see me when you get in, okay?"

"Thank God it's Friday," she said out loud as she sipped her coffee and placed the empty styrofoam into the trash as she walked into the rear of the Moakley. Just before entering she licked her bottom lip and tasted the salt of the ocean as she said: "Hi Pete," smiling at him as she passed by.

As the elevator doors opened on the ninth, Becky sneezed as she exited the elevator all over Zach's shirt. "Eeew" he moaned as he wiped the front of his blue shirt.

"I'm sorry," Becky said grinning as he stepped into the open elevator and nudged her back in. Zach pushed "1" and as the elevator began its descent, he pushed "stop."

"What are you doing?" Becky said as she began to feel the claustrophobia envelop and consume her. Zach pressed into her, pressing her back into the rear wall of the elevator. Her body went limp as she inhaled his pheromones and swayed.

"Miss me?" he whispered as he gently touched his left hand to her right cheek and kissed her. "Hmmm" she moaned as she began to pant and sweat.

"You okay?" Zach asked as he pushed "1" and the elevator began its descent once again.

"Oh, God," Becky said as her breathing stabilized, and she grabbed his left sleeve.

"How long you been claustrophobic, Ms. Lawrence?" Zach whispered as he kissed her left cheek.

“Um, all my life, I guess,” Becky said with a grin as the elevator opened on the third floor. Three people stepped in, and Becky and Zach leaned against the wall staring at each other smiling.

“Come,” Zach said as he walked into the coffee shop. Becky followed staring at his ass stimulated, trying to ignore his pheromonal tang as it engulfed her.

“Hi, Alan,” Zach said, “two large regulars please.”

“Hi, Mr. Woods … Becky?” Alan asked inquisitively.

“Hi, Alan,” Becky answered stunned thinking: “how?”

“Back again, huh? You like my coffee, huh?” Alan said smiling as Zach winked at Becky.

“Let me have a tray, please, Alan,” Zach said as his eyes wandered up and down Becky’s black pantsuit finally landing at her breasts as he grinned and she nudged his bicep as he screamed: “Ow.”

Becky followed Zach silently along the Harborwalk. The wind was voracious and whipping her long brown hair into salty knots as they walked and talked. “Where we going?” she whispered.

“Shhh,” Zach said as he smiled carrying the tray. They walked far down the pier, finally reaching a small vacant beachfront with an old wooden bench facing the inlet. Zach placed the coffee on the bench and pressed Becky into him. As they hugged, Zach whispered: “Feel this?”

“Stop, will you?” Becky said as her body swayed.

“Sit,” Zach said as he sat down on the bench and handed her a coffee. “Listen, there’s an evidentiary hearing on at 11 with Woodbury.”

“I know,” Becky said as she opened the coffee and took a sip.

“You research this?” Zach asked as he tiled his head back and poured the coffee down his trachea.

“Nope,” Becky said as Zach placed his left hand on her right thigh. She pushed his hand away: “Will you stop?” Zach giggled and she smiled as he whispered: “I love you.” Her mind repeated: “end this” as she mouthed: “I love you too.”

Zach smiled as he placed his left arm around her shoulders and whispered: “Evidentiary hearing, heroin distribution/ conspiracy, five defendants.”

“An evidentiary hearing this late in the game?” Becky whispered with her eyebrows arched as she drank.

“Yeah, I know … 20-year-old died from overdose so I” --

Becky interjected: “Filed for death resulting, huh?”

“You see,” Zach said as he snuggled close, “that’s why I love you.”

Becky shrugged her shoulders and spilled coffee onto his pants. “I’m sorry,” she said with a grin.

“Wow,” Zach smiled, “you hate this suit, don’t you?” Becky smiled as she sipped.

“O’Brien filed for this hearing a couple weeks back,” Zach said as he finished his coffee.

“Mmm,” Becky moaned as he kissed her. Her mind whispered: “end this” as she kissed him, and he placed his left hand into her blouse and inside her bra and twirled her erect nipple with mounting pressure between his forefingers. She inhaled his distinctive pheromonal blaze as her body fell limp into the bench. She cocked her head back to take another swig of coffee as Zach moved over two feet away from her and laid his head on her lap as his long legs dangled over the edge. Nervously Becky looked to the right, stared to the left; there was no there.

Zach sat up and squirmed in closer to her on the bench. He kissed her slowly and delicately as the fingers of his left hand played with her nipple, and she humped the bench and moaned: “Zach, what are you doing?”

Zach stood; and as he slid his cell phone out of his back pocket, his wallet fell to the ground. Becky picked it up as he grinned, and he pushed “5” on the touchscreen.

“Hi, Mandy ... listen, I’m with Becky; we’re in a meeting with defense in Veloz … we’ll meet you at 11 in Courtroom 1.”

“What are you doing?” Becky mouthed.

“Shhh,” Zach said as he pulled her standing in front of him, “I can’t concentrate ... come on.” Zach grabbed Becky’s right hand in his left, and they walked slowly toward the Marriott Longwharf.

“Are you for real?” she whispered as they stood just outside the main entrance.

Zach leaned his body against her, pinning her to the brick façade: “Feel this?” he whispered: “Come on.”

“What the hell are you doing, Becky?” she said under her breath as Zach handed his AmEx to the young girl in the front lobby as she hid behind a large marble column in the center. “Don’t do this,” she thought as they walked into the elevator. “End this,” her mind flashed as he closed and locked the door. “Oh, God,” her mind whispered as he pressed into her smiling: “Get naked.”

Becky hung her blazer meticulously on the hanger next to her shirt and slacks. She stood naked, scared, and wide-eyed, inhibited as she clutched her breasts with her hands and stared at his immense erection as he sat naked on the edge of the king-sized bed.

“Come here,” he said as she slowly walked toward him. “Sit,” he said as he slapped the mattress. Becky sat down as Zach sat on the floor at her feet. He placed both hands between her legs and spread them apart slowly as he licked his bottom lip. He placed the tip of his tongue against her clit and sucked it gingerly; and as her juice dribbled down her inner thighs, she mumbled: “Oh, God,” as she pressed his head in deeper.

“Put that ass on the edge here, baby,” he whispered as she leaned backward with her feet in the air. He got on his knees and raised his head as his tongue entered her and his middle finger thrust gently inserted inside her ass, and she screamed: “Oh, my God,” and came all over the floor.

An hour later Zach whispered: “Turn over, baby.” She slowly turned over lying on her stomach with her ass in his face. Gently Zach spread her legs apart with both hands pressed against her inner thighs; and as his tongue inserted inside her anus, she screamed: “Oh, my God,” as her magma sprayed through the air.

His tongue licked from her ass inward, and he ate her for over an hour until she began panting and screaming: “Oh, God,” as Zach struggled to swallow the copious deluge as her juice dripped down his thighs.

“Say it, Becky,” he whispered as he rose, his left hand placing his tip in and out of her teasing her incessantly as she moaned: “Oh, God, Zach.”

“Oh, God,” Becky screamed as her lava splurted against his stomach and he smiled as he whispered: “Say it, baby.”

Oh, God,” she moaned as he continued to rub himself against her inner lips, the middle finger of his left hand penetrating her deeply. “Put it in” she screamed as she humped his hand as he whispered: “What do you want, baby … say it” as his soggy pointer finger entered her anus.

“Fuck me,” she screamed as he entered her. As he thrusted deep within her, Becky began slowly creeping toward the headboard and the center of the bed.

“Where you going, baby?” Zach said still inside her, his body following her toward the headboard. Slowly he pulled out and began rubbing his tip in and out of her teasing her as she moaned: “Oh God, Zach,” she screamed as her torrent drenched the mattress.

“Spread your knees, baby,” he whispered as her arms leaned on top of the wooden headboard. He shimmied his head under her as she sat erect on his face, his tongue encircling her clit as her lava submerged his neck and chest. Fifteen minutes later as she fucked his tongue she screamed: “Oh, God, Zach; let me turn over.”

Zach smiled as she turned over and sat on the pillow, her engorged clit just above his head. He stared into her whispering: “You are so beautiful” as his tongue entered her, and she drowned the pillow. She spread her torso across his chest and firmly placed her teeth on him. As she swallowed him and teased him with her teeth repeatedly clenching down on him, he whispered as he licked her and she humped his mouth: “I like that … ahhh.”

He closed his eyes; and just as the last wave was about to crash onto the shore in his mind and he felt the ejaculate rise, he whispered: “I like that … ahhh, stop.”

“Stop?” her mind repeated as her mouth released him and her body humped his tongue as her juice flowed. Zach threw the wet pillow across the room. She lied down next to him with her head facing away from him gasping out of breath. Zach tilted her head toward him with his left hand under her chin and kissed her as the fingers of his right hand incessantly teased her to her zenith.

She spread her legs apart and humped his hand, her juice flowing down her thighs. Zach smiled as he kissed her and then softly whispered: “Say it,” as his entire right hand fit squarely inside of her.

Oh, God,” Becky screamed as he wiggled her clit and she soaked the mattress wilding thrusting her ass.

“Say it,” Zach whispered as he sat up and thrust his head down tantalizing her inner lips with his tongue. Slowly he slid his tongue into her anus and wiggled her clit repeatedly with the pointer finger of his left hand pressing it intermittently against the edge of his thumb.

She screamed: “Oh, my God,” as Zach smiled. As copious amounts of lava cascaded down her inner thighs toward her calves, he whispered: “Oooh, you like that, baby?” as he applied suction and temporarily gagged as he swallowed and moaned.

“Put it in,” she whimpered as she turned around and got on her knees in front of him. As he ejaculated deep inside her, his left pointer finger continually playing with her, her torrent cascaded and marinated the mattress, penetrating the box spring. Zach collapsed on top of her as she fell into the wet, sloppy mess. Sixty seconds later Becky said: “Oh, my God,” as he grew hard again inside her.

Zach stood up whispering: “Gotta pee,” and ran toward the bathroom. Becky giggled as she lifted her body off the sopping mattress. “Oh, gross,” she mumbled as she struggled to find a dry spot way down by the edge of the bed. Becky heard the shower turn on as she picked her thong up off the chair by the table next to the bible. “That’s ironic,” she said out loud as she pulled her thong over her wet thighs. “I need a shower,” Becky mumbled as she felt her damp body fill with goosebumps.

She sat at the edge of the king-sized bed in her Victoria Secret black bra and matching thong staring at the floor at her feet yawning. Zach approached her naked and wet, water dripping from his hair down his back and chest. He stood directly in front of her fully erect. She slid him into her mouth and bit down gently yet firmly. She closed her eyes and watched as Zach licked her repeatedly and thought: “Hope I’m doing this right?” as she rode him with her mouth, her teeth clenching him tightly. As he thrust in and out of her throat, she grabbed his balls with her right hand, and he came as he screamed: “Ahhh.”

Zach collapsed on the bed facedown cupping his sack and groaning:

"That was incredible. Listen, babe, we gotta get out of here. Go get ready, okay?" Becky stumbled into the bathroom. She filled the bathtub with three inches of lukewarm water and hopped in naked.

She sat in the water for a few minutes and got on her knees to clean herself with the soap when Zach walked in. He was wearing only his brief and knelt down on the floor next to the tub.

"Give me," he said as he stared at her breasts as he grabbed the Dial from her left hand. While on her knees leaning forward over the water, Zach cleaned her front to back. As she stood he wrapped a white terry towel around her shoulders.

"Sit," he whispered, motioning her to sit on the rim. She sat wiping her torso with the towel. Zach sat Indian style on the cold tile as Becky spread her legs, her ass teetering across the wet ledge. Zach licked her slowly, tantalizing her clit as his tongue wiggled it repeatedly while the middle finger of his left hand entered her ass. He smiled as he watched her juice drip down the side of the bathtub and onto the floor.

"Guess I need another bath," Becky said smiling as she hopped back into the now cold water. Zach stood and walked to the vanity splashing cold water on his face. Becky grinned as he remained hard and she couldn't peel her eyes from him.

"Crap," Zach said staring at his erection … "see what you do to me, baby" he said as he winked and left the bathroom mumbling: "Come on, Ms. Lawrence … it's 10:30, babe; gotta go."

"Jesus," Becky mumbled as she got out of the tub and wiped herself noticing she was sore, and it hurt to the touch. "10:30" she said aggravated as she slid her pantyhose on as Zach watched fully dressed in his navy suit fumbling with his tie.

"It's 10:30 already," she mumbled exasperated as she buttoned her short-sleeved white shirt. "Seriously, it's 10:30?" she shrieked as Zach giggled still fumbling with his tie. Becky slid her skirt up, tucking her shirt in, as she giggled watching Zach's ineptness. She walked over to him grinning: "Give me that" she said as she adjusted it. He pulled her in toward him, pressing into her. He kissed her gently on her lips as he grabbed her ass with his left hand and ran over her breast with his right. She whispered: "How many times can you go? Aren't you tired, Zach?"

Zach threw her one of his now legendary enigmatic looks and sat down on the wet bed. As his ass absorbed the fluid, he screamed: "Shit!" and stood up as she giggled. "Listen, I'm gonna leave now ... won't look good if anyone should see us strolling into the courthouse together at 10:30, you know." Becky shook her head affirmatively and grinned. She walked over to the hanger and grabbed her blazer off the hook throwing it over her right arm.

Zach walked toward her and hugged her. He whispered: "I love you … by the way, best blowjob ever" he said as he smiled and opened the door. "I don't know how you do that with your teeth, but, oh, my God," he said as he grabbed his cock with his left hand and smiled.

"Zach," Becky whispered as he turned into the hallway. He turned his head to see her as she approached the doorjamb: "I love you," she whispered as he grinned.

"I'll see you in Courtroom No. 1 in 20, babe," Zach whispered as he walked down the hallway toward the rows of elevators. Becky watched as he turned around the corner and smiled at her before disappearing from view.

Becky walked into the courtroom at 10:50. Tim O'Brien sat with the defendant at defense table. The room was full of spectators chit-chatting simultaneously. Becky slowly walked toward the clerk's bench as Joshua said: "Hi, Becky." Becky threw her file folders on the table and smiled: "Hi, Josh, how you doing?"

Josh blushed momentarily: "Good, good, and you, my friend?"

"Good … thanks, Josh" Becky said smiling as Amanda approached behind her silently from the back of the courtroom. Amanda tapped her right shoulder and Becky jumped and leaped around to face her.

“Jesus,” she said laughing, “you scared the shit out of me.”

Amanda smiled as Becky recomposed and Timmy smiled and then whispered to the defendant to his left. Amanda whispered into Becky’s right ear: “And where’s Zach?”

Becky shrugged her shoulders and grabbed the water jug and poured a glass of water. She downed it and then poured another. “Thirsty?” Amanda said with a grin as Becky guzzled her second. She poured another glass full and sat down as Josh whispered: “Where’s Zach, Becky?”

Becky raised both hands, elbows at her side, her palms fanning out from her inner body in a familiar gesture meaning: “I don’t know.” Josh smiled as Becky blushed. Amanda poured herself a glass of water as the medical examiner approached Becky.

“Hi, Steve Fields,” the doctor said as he extended his right hand for a shake. Becky shook his hand firmly: “Becky Lawrence, AUSA. Thanks so much for coming today” she whispered as she let go of his hand. “Should I sit in the stand” the doctor asked raising his brows.

“No, Doctor. Please sit behind me. The Judge doesn’t like that. I will press to make sure you’re the first witness up this morning as I know you need to get back to the crime lab.” Fields shook his head up and down and smiled and sat down behind the prosecution table nervously adjusting his tie. Becky smiled as she thought: “He doesn’t wear ties … look at him choke.”

Josh stood and whispered: “Becky, it is 10:55. Where is he?”

“I don’t know, Josh” she stammered as Zach stood behind her. He walked up to the clerk’s bench and shook Joshua’s right hand: “Sorry, buddy,” he whispered as Joshua smiled, “No problem.”

Joshua remained standing as he buzzed in the Judge: “All rise.” As Judge Woodbury sat behind the bench, Josh announced: “This is the matter of the United States versus Roland Martinez, Docket No.

1:10-cr-10068. Would counsel please introduce themselves for the record?"

"Good morning, your Honor. Zach Woods and Becky Lawrence on behalf of the United States."

"Good morning, Mr. Woods and Ms. Lawrence," Woodbury said as he poured a glass of water from his decanter.

"Good morning, your Honor. Timothy O'Brien for the defendant, who is actually standing next to me now, and I see that we have an interpreter but it's actually not necessary.

"All right. Mr. O'Brien, Mr. Martinez, good morning. We have an interpreter with us; I'll ask him to stay in the unlikely event that the defendant might need some help as I anticipate he may not understand the medical jargon. You may be seated, counsel … Mr. Woods, you may proceed."

"The government calls Dr. Stephen Fields.

"Doctor, would you please remain standing" Woodbury said with a smile.

Zach smiled at Becky: "With the Court's permission, may I stand here rather than standing at the podium?

Woodbury raised his glass in his right hand: "Yes, you may, Mr. Woods."

Zach stood next to Becky who remained seated at counsel table: "May I proceed, your Honor?

Woodbury took a sip of water: "Please, Mr. Woods -- Josh, swear in the doctor, please."

Q. Good morning, Dr. Fields."
A. Good morning.
Q. What do you do for work, sir?

A. I'm the Chief Medical Examiner for the Commonwealth of Massachusetts.
Q. And what is the title of your current position?
A. Currently, Chief Medical Examiner.
Q. How long have you held the position of Chief Medical Examiner?
A. I had my official appointment in October of 2009.
Q. When you say "official," were you the acting Chief Medical Examiner for a period of time before that?
A. Yes.
Q. And for what period were you acting Chief Medical Examiner?
A. Since the end of May in 2005.

Becky was exhausted and began yawning halfway through Zach's initial examination as he meticulously went through the Doctor's current curriculum vitae and published scientific abstracts. Woodbury began to yawn as he watched Becky's eyes glazed over.

Becky scratched her head and whispered to Amanda: "Get on with it, Zach."

"Seriously," Amanda giggled as she whispered: "boring."

Q. Just one moment, your Honor. I'm going to probe in a little bit more detail as to each of the components of the substances found in the victim's system at the time the samples were taken, but let me just ask you this, Doctor: at the time as a result of your external exam, internal exam, and the review of this toxicology report, Exhibit 17, did you form an opinion to a reasonable degree of medical certainty as to the cause of death of Chelsea Jones?
A. Yes, but also including the review of the police report, but after I reviewed all of that, I did, yes.
Q. By the "police report," you mean the initial data or information you received?
A. The initial data and we received later a formal report.
Q. Okay. So after doing all of the work that you did --
A. Yes.
Q. -- including the review of all of the information available to you including those things that you just mentioned, I think you just said yes to the question as to whether you formed an opinion to a

reasonable degree of medical certainty as to the cause of Chelsea's death?
A. Yes.
Q. And what is that opinion?
A. It was acute intoxication by the combined effects of ethanol, opiates, and citalopram.
Q. And did you form an opinion as to whether the opiates played a significant causal role in Ms. Jones' death?
A. Yes.
Q. And what is that opinion?
A. They played a significant role in the cause of her death.
Q. Okay. So another way of asking that question is: do you have an opinion as to whether the use of heroin resulted in the death of Chelsea Jones?
A. I believe it played a significant role in the cause of her death, yes.

Charlie floated in the air behind the witness box. He opened his mouth and a fine, invisible mist saturated the air as the distinctive aroma of rotten eggs penetrated the courtroom. The Doctor gagged and blocked his nose with his right hand as the Judge whispered: "Josh, Josh."

Josh stood and leaned over the Judge's bench. "What's that smell?" Woodbury asked as Josh shrugged his shoulders and blocked his nose. Becky plugged her nose with her right thumb and pointer finger as Amanda gagged.

Q. Let me just back up then. I want to go back to Exhibit 17. Let me ask you to focus on the ethanol. Based on the toxicology report, ethanol was found to be present at somewhat different but consistent levels in the vitreous humor and the blood; is that right?
A. Yes.
Q. And ethanol reflects the presence of alcohol --
A. Yes.
Q. -- at the time of her death? Based on the level that's reflected in Exhibit 17, is that level of alcohol in and of itself enough to cause the death of a woman of a similar size and age to Chelsea Jones?
A. I believe that would be unlikely.
Q. Unlikely you said?

A. Yes.
Q. And in this case you testified that there was an interval of three days between the date she was pronounced dead and the date of the autopsy?
A. Yes.
Q. How, if at all, did the passage of time, that is, the lapse of those three days, affect the level of ethanol in her body?
A. Well, when a body starts to decompose, one of the events that's going on is bacteria within the body begins to metabolize or break down parts of the body tissue, and one of the byproducts of that metabolism of the tissues is the production of ethanol so you can -- so the ethanol level that you measure post-mortem can be -- that can be higher than it was at the time of death because of this decomposition effect that can happen.
Q. Okay. So, I take it, that that means that at the time of her death the ethanol level may have been reported lower than what's reported in the toxicology report?
A. It may have been, yes.
Q. Is that something that you would have considered in your opinion?
A. Yes.
Q. Let me move on to the citalopram. The toxicology report reflects that citalopram was present; do you recall that?
A. Yes.
Q. What is citalopram?
A. It's a type of antidepressant.
Q. Is it a prescription medication?
A. Yes.
Q. Looking at the toxicology report, was the level of citalopram present in the body of Chelsea Jones in and of itself sufficient to cause the death of someone of a similar size and age?
A. That would be very unlikely, sir.
Q. Okay. Unlikely in the same way as the ethanol level, is that right?
A. Yes.
Q. And, finally, let's move to the opiates. You testified a little bit that opiates reflect the use of heroin?
A. It may. In this case it certainly does.
Q. Okay. What does the presence of opiates in her body indicate to you as the medical examiner when reviewing this report?

A. Well, she has one of the -- 6-acetylmorphine is one of the metabolites. That is the first metabolite of heroin, and then morphine, free morphine, is one of the others; it's the next step in the metabolism of heroin, so the presence of those two together indicates to me that the individual took heroin.
Q. Okay.
A. Does that answer your question?
Q. I don't know. Let me just sort of peel back the layers of that a little bit more?
A. Yes.
Q. You mentioned 6-acetylmorphine as being one component that was present in her body; is that always the case that you find those two as a pair, the free morphine --
A. No.
Q. -- and the 6-acetylmorphine?
A. No.
Q. And why is that?
A. Because the half-life of 6-acetylmorphine or the rate at which it is metabolized is relatively, relatively rapid; it's a matter of minutes.
Q. So if they're not both always present, what does the presence of 6-acetylmorphine in this case suggest to you?
A. Well, it suggests, first of all, that the individual took heroin but also that she most likely took it relatively, relatively close to the time of her death as opposed to if only the free morphine was present."

Becky whispered to Amanda: "boring!" as Amanda giggled and the Judge shook his head back and forth as Becky stared at the floor.

Q. The toxicology report reflects that there were certain other substances found at some level in her body; did any of those other substances have a significant bearing on your opinion in terms of the cause of death or was it really the three things we talked about?
A. Those three things.
Q. Let me ask you this then: in your opinion would the level of citalopram in combination with the alcohol present in her body at the time of her death, would they have together caused her death absent the heroin?
A. I think that is hard to say for sure. I think it's unlikely, but I can't be 100% sure. It's not what happened in this case, but I can't -- I

think it's unlikely, but I can't say for certain."

Amanda whispered to Becky: "Oh, my God. Thank God this case didn't go to a jury, huh?"

Q. Okay. So it's your expert opinion that but for the heroin being present those two substances, the citalopram and the ethanol, would not themselves have resulted in the death of Chelsea Jones; is that fair to say?
A. That's not exactly what I said, but I think it's unlikely that the ethanol and the citalopram by themselves would have caused her death, but what I meant to say was in this case she died from a combination of the three including the heroin. She did not die just from ethanol itself. What could have happened --
Q. Can you tell us --
A. You know, it's really hard to say. There are a lot of things that are possible, but that's not what happened here.
Q. Okay. Can you tell us why you believe that that was not what happened here?
A. Because of the level of -- I mean, you just can't discount the level of morphine or of the opiates that are present in her system. I just can't ignore that.
Q. Okay. And in your opinion how, if at all, did the opiates interact with those other two substances?
A. They interact as respiratory depressants.
Q. Okay. Can you just describe what you mean in a little more detail?
A. Yeah.
Q. When you say "respiratory depressants," which of those are respiratory depressants?
A. All of them can have that effect.
Q. All three of them?
A. Yes, particularly together.
Q. Okay. So the alcohol in and of itself --
A. Yes, it can. Yes.
Q. And the citalopram?
A. It can.
Q. And what effect would the addition of the opiates have to their effect on the body as respiratory depressants?

A. Again, it would increase respiratory depression.

Zach winked at Becky, as Woodbury raised his glasses, and said: "I have nothing further, your Honor."

"Cross-examination, Mr. O'Brien?" Woodbury said as he winked at Becky who blushed.

"Thank you, your Honor," Tim said as he stood.

Q. Good morning, Dr. Fields.
A. Good morning.
Q. Sir, would the heroin that you found in her system by itself without the alcohol or the citalopram likely have caused her death?
A. Yes, I believe so.
Q. So in your view the heroin amount was sufficient to cause death without the interaction of any other drug?
A. I believe given the same, the same scenario, the same situation, the same findings, I believe that I would have signed the -- I would have signed the cause of death as acute opiate intoxication.
Q. And by the way, when was this body refrigerated, you know, was it allowed to lay around for days before you did the autopsy?
A. No. As soon as it arrives at the office, it's put in a refrigerator.
Q. Do you know when it arrived at the office?
A. I don't. I can find that out for you.
Q. Was it the same day she was found dead?
A. I assume so. Again, I don't know.
Q. Okay. Now, I think I understood your testimony to be that in your opinion based on the metabolites of heroin that you found or that the Mass. State Crime Lab found in the chest cavity blood that you provided -- well, strike that.

It's your view based on what the crime lab found in terms of free morphine and 6-acetylmorphine or whatever it was, the morphine that she took, the heroin, that it was ingested minutes before her death?
A. It was a matter of minutes, yes. I don't know exactly how many minutes.
Q. And how many minutes would you estimate it to be?

A. I can't estimate that.
Q. Well, could it have been an hour before her death --
A. Yes.
Q. -- or are you thinking more in terms of an actual minute or two?
A. I can't -- without knowing the actual amount that was taken initially, it's hard to backtrack and guess as to the time that it was injected.
Q. Okay. I guess what I'm asking is: when you say "minutes" do you mean -- I mean, a year is minutes --
A. Right.
Q. -- in a manner of speaking?
A. Right.
Q. Are we talking an hour or two hours or less than an hour? What do you mean when you choose the term "minutes"?
A. What I usually mean is it's probably within an hour. I say that as an approximate interval because I can't tell you for certain that it wasn't an hour or five minutes. I can't. I have no way to know for sure the exact time interval. It's an unfortunate part of the death certificate.
Q. All right. Well, how about this citalopram?
A. Yes.
Q. That also had metabolites in your view, correct?
A. Yes.
Q. At least that's what the crime lab reported?
A. Yes.
Q. How long before death did she take the citalopram?
A. I don't know.
Q. Well, would you have an estimate that it was minutes or -- well, let me put this way: do you have any view at all based on what you've seen as to the sequence of events?
A. No. You mean which came first?
Q. Yeah.
A. No.
Q. Is it consistent with what you saw that she would have been drinking, then taken heroin, and then taken citalopram?
A. That's possible, yes.

Becky yawned. Amanda watched Becky and yawned as the Judge yawned.

Q. Now, in that police report that I just put in front of you, sir, and you based your opinion at least in part on, does it reflect that at the scene of the death there was some heroin paraphernalia in the room?
A. Yes.
Q. And does it reflect that there were prescription drugs, bottles of prescription drugs, in the room?
A. Yes.
Q. And what prescription drugs were in the room?
A. It was citalopram and Levaquin.
Q. What's Levaquin?
A. I'm sorry, I don't remember.
Q. Okay. Do you know if Levaquin has as a side effect of suicidal ideation?
A. I don't know.
Q.You don't know, okay. Do you know if on a prescription pill bottle what's reflected on the pill bottle is the dosage you're supposed to take, when the prescription was filled, the number of capsules in the bottle, things of that nature?
A. That's usually the case, yes.
Q. Did you ask anyone when the citalopram prescription bottle was filled in this case?
A. I did not.
Q. Do you know how many citalopram pills were missing from that bottle?
A. No, I do not.
Q. You don't know if the prescriptions for citalopram or Levaquin were filled two days before her death and there are 20 pills missing or if they were filled a month before her death and there's only one pill missing from each bottle or you don't know?
A. I don't know. That's something that if those – I would have to recheck the file. If those medications came to our office, they would have been counted, but I don't recall.
Q. All right. Is there anything that you have with you today that indicates whether or not those medications came to your office?
A. I'd have to look in this (gesturing). I don't know that I do.
Q. And in determining whether the cause of death was accidental or suicide, wouldn't you want to know how many citalopram or Levaquin pills were missing from each bottle?

A. I mean, that can be helpful, yeah.

“Thank you, sir. I have no further questions, your Honor.”

Woodbury scratched his chin: Any redirect, Mr. Woods?”

Zach smiled at Becky: “Yes, your Honor. Thank you.”

Q. Dr. Fields, Mr. O’Brien asked a number of questions about suicidal ideation; do you recall that --
A. Yes.
Q. -- relating to the citalopram?
A. Yes.
Q. Now, even if there wasn't -- even if Chelsea Jones had taken one pill or hundreds of pills, does this change your opinion in terms of the role that the heroin played in her death?
A. No.
Q. And given the level of citalopram in her system, the level of opiates in her system, the level of ethanol in her system, even if there were an attempt to commit suicide with the citalopram and perhaps even the alcohol, does that change your opinion about the role of the heroin in her death?
A. No.
Q. And, in fact, do you have an opinion as to whether death by an overdose of an antidepressant such as citalopram is likely?
A. I mean, it can, it can happen ... in the cases that I've seen there have been higher levels than this but --
Q. All right. Now, let me just return to that. Do you recall that Mr. O’Brien asked you a number of questions about what one might call ‘theoretical possibilities’?
A. Vaguely. I'm sorry.
Q. Let me just back up. You just testified that it's possible that someone could die simply from the citalopram?
A. Yes.
Q. Or a citalopram combination with alcohol?
A. Yes.
Q. That is possible, right?
A. Yes.

Q. Okay. Now, based on your work in this case which includes the whole variety of things that we talked about, the background information, what was found at Chelsea's bedside table, the examination, internal and external, the bodily fluids that were tested and the results are reported in the toxicology report, based on all of that totality of information, is it your opinion that that's what happened in this case; that is, that she died or that she would have died even if there were no opiates present in her system?
A. Again, I think that's highly unlikely.
Q. Okay. Let me just ask you, and I don't mean to restate what's been stated, but in your opinion, your expert opinion, what was the role that heroin played in the death of Chelsea Jones?
A. You mean physiologically, as a respiratory depressant.
Q. And what role did it play in connection with her death?
A. It played a significant role in the cause of her death.

Zach scratched his chin: Thank you, Doctor. That's all."

Becky whispered to Amanda: "Thank God," as Amanda nodded and yawned.

Woodbury took a sip of water: Any recross, Mr. O'Brien?"

"Yes, just briefly, your Honor."

Q. Sir, was this a suicide or an accidental overdose?
A. I signed the manner of death in this case as an accident.

The luscious vibrant aroma of lilacs filled the courtroom, and the Judge smiled as Josh whispered to him: "Here we go again," and Woodbury smiled and shook his head perplexed.

Q. Yeah. But you don't really know, do you?
A. It's almost hard to be 100% certain in all cases.
Q. Well, what percent certain are you?
A. I couldn't say; I can't put a number on it now.
Q. You don't know what the side effects of citalopram are including suicidal ideation? I was the one to suggest that to you; you don't know that independently, do you?

A. Again, at the time I don't recall the suicidal ideation.
Q. The Levaquin, you don't know whether that has suicidal ideation associated with it, and you don't know whether or not from her prior hospital course she had serious side effects from the Levaquin; you don't know that, do you, sir?
A. I don't know that.
Q. You don't know that. You don't know whether the Levaquin was prescribed, do you?
A. No.
Q. You don't know if she went to the hospital that day complaining of side effects that are associated with Levaquin?
A. I had information that she had gone to the hospital, and I would have to look as to why she went to the hospital.
Q. You don't know how many pills were missing or when her prescription was filled, correct?
A. I don't recall that now, no.

Timmy smiled at Becky as he said: I have no further questions."

"Mr. Woods?" Woodbury asked inquisitively.

Zach rummaged through papers on his desk before looking up at the Judge: "Nothing further, your Honor." Amanda whispered into Becky's ear: "Thank God!" as Becky and Amanda smiled as the Judge shook his head.

Woodbury looked at Zach and stared into Becky's eyes: "You may step down, Doctor. Thank you. All right, we will take a ten-minute recess for our court reporter and then I assume, counsel, you'd like to present brief oral arguments regarding this sentencing enhancement?"

Zach adjusted his tie: "Yes, your Honor, unless you'd prefer written briefs?"

"No, I don't think that's necessary, Mr. Woods … all right, the court is in recess."

"All rise," Josh said as he smiled at Becky who stood.

Amanda whispered to Becky as Zach ran out of the courtroom to the men's room: "He's pretty good" she said staring at O'Brien's back.

"Hmmm," Becky moaned as she shook her head affirmatively, "he's really good."

Twenty minutes later Josh announced: "All rise. This court is back in session."

The Judge poured a glass of water: "Mr. O'Brien?"

"Oh, I'm up first, Judge" Tim said as he smiled at Becky. "So I see two distinct issues here, your Honor. One is cause of death, and on that I see two sorts of subsets, if you will, and I don't know what the legal ramifications of one of them is.

In other words, if you were to conclude that you're not certain by whatever standard you might use, "preponderance of the evidence," whether the cause of death was accidental or suicide" ... if it's suicide, I don't know the legal ramifications -- I'm not positive. I know what position I would take, but I don't know what the legal ramifications of that are. I mean, does he have but for cause if, in fact, it was suicide? I'm not sure that I would argue that it's not.

The other issue I see with Dr. Fields is the reliability of his opinion based on his own admissions in the grand jury and in this courtroom this morning that citalopram and alcohol could have caused the death even without the heroin, never mind the Levaquin.

Your Honor, I would respectfully ask your permission for leave to brief these issues?"

Woodbury shook his head: "Granted, Mr. O'Brien."

"Amanda whispered to Becky: "Get me out of here," as Zach whispered: "Shhh."

"Mr. Woods, any final thoughts," Woodbury said as he sipped, "or would you like to brief this issue as well?"

Zach scratched his chin: "Well, certainly, I'd like the opportunity to brief these issues as well, your Honor. The government would submit first on the scientific issue that we had Dr. Fields, the Chief Medical Examiner, who explained the analysis he conducted and testified that the heroin that he found in her bloodstream was a significant cause of her death.

As the First Circuit has described it, that's more than what is required for this enhancement. This Court has had a poly substance case before. The issue is: did the death result? The issue quite frankly of suicide versus accident … this heroin, this illegal drug, sold by this defendant, resulted in Chelsea Jones' death. Dr. Fields testified to that. The death certificate shows it. The science shows it.

The issue that was raised was as a scientific theoretical matter: if it had just been alcohol and citalopram and/or Levaquin, what Dr. Fields said is that's not what this case was; there was heroin as well. Not only was there heroin, but the evidence shows that Chelsea Jones who had been out, came home, talked with her mother, made dinner, ate dinner, and then proceeded to inject herself with the heroin; and within minutes, your Honor, as Dr. Fields said he couldn't characterize exactly how many minutes those minutes were, she was dead.

The defendant, Mr. Roland Martinez, plead guilty to distribution of heroin in this case. He admitted that he sold the heroin in question to Ms. Chelsea Jones. The government believes that we have proven beyond a reasonable doubt that, in fact, this heroin, that illegal drug, sold by this defendant, resulted in Chelsea Jones' death. Once again, to reiterate, Dr. Fields testified to that. The death certificate shows it. The science shows it.

As a result, we would respectfully implore the Court to impose the sentencing enhancement of 252 months incarceration. Thank you, your Honor."

As the suffocating reek of sulphur filled the courtroom, the Judge squinched and sipped his water slowly, placing the glass down gently next to his wooden statue depicting three tiny monkeys; one monkey had his hands over his eyes, one monkey had his hands over his ears, the final monkey had his hands over his mouth: "All right. Thank you, counsel. I will take the matter under advisement."

"All rise," Josh said as Zach whispered, "I'm beat" and Becky smiled mouthing: "ditto."

Amanda listening interjected: "Difficult meeting this morning with defense, counsel?" as she smiled.

"Mmm," Zach moaned as Becky nodded and Amanda said: "Uh-huh." Zach leaned into Becky and whispered: "Have lunch with me, counsel?"

Becky smiled: "here you mean?"

"Sure. I'll buy and we'll eat out at the harbor, okay?" Zach said as he smiled and winked with his left eye.

"Okay," Becky replied as Zach whispered: "We gotta get Hill." Becky's face contorted into a grimace, and Zach said: "What?"

Becky shook her head from side to side mumbling: "Should have known you had an ulterior motive, huh?"

"What?" Zach said as he pushed the chair into the table and stood in the center aisle: "Can't I have lunch with a colleague?" Becky smiled as she watched Zach's tiny perfectly-formed ass walk down the aisle toward the double doors exiting the courtroom as she thought: "Yeah, "colleagues," huh, Mr. Woods?"

Zach abruptly stopped four feet from the double doors and turned his head and smiled at Becky, making sure she was, in fact, watching him from behind. He held the door open for her; and as she passed him by, he inhaled her savor and moaned: "Hmmm" as he adjusted himself before stepping out into the hallway.

As they stood patiently waiting for the elevator, Zach leaned into her whispering: All right, going to my office, got to return a few calls … meet me in the cafeteria in, say, half hour?" Becky nodded as a voice emanating from deep within the burrows of her mind chanted: "End this, end this, end this."

As they stepped into the crowded elevator, the voiced repeated: "End this" and Becky mumbled out loud: "Oh, shut up." Conversations ceased and silence ensued within the elevator as everyone stared blankly at each other and began to smirk, one smile at a time.

Zach leaned against Becky's left arm and whispered: "Problem?" Becky stared at her feet embarrassed and blushing as the conversations quelled the silence.

Twenty-five minutes later Becky approached the cafeteria on the second floor and smiled as she spotted Zach leaning against a column seemingly absorbed by the harbor's picturesque seascape. Becky approached him smiling: "Hi" she whispered.

"Hey, how's my girl?" Zach said with a grin as Becky's body twitched and her skin filled with goosebumps as they walked toward the salad bar. He whispered: "You wore me out," as she smiled and handed him a tray.

"I wore you out," she thought as she whispered: "I can hardly walk, Mr. Woods" as he smiled.

Becky made a heaping salad topped with bits of yesterday's buffalo chicken strips cuts into diced cubes. Zach got a small piece of halibut with mashed potatoes and opened the refrigerator and grabbed two cold Poland Springs' bottles as Becky approached. "I'm paying for my own, Mr. Woods," she said as she grinned.

Zach leaned into her and whispered: "I'm buying lunch today, Ms. Lawrence" as he smirked. "You can buy next time, okay?"

Ten minutes later as Becky stabbed her cucumber smeared in Raspberry vinaigrette Zach whispered: "We've got to move on Hill right away. Time's a ticking … knowing Timmy, he's already filed a motion to dismiss."

Becky swallowed and averted his eyes and repeatedly stabbed her romaine. Zach whispered: "What's eating you?"

"Zach, we have no case without the CW" Becky said as she stabbed a small piece of chicken with her fork and rubbed it into the dressing at the bottom of the plastic container.

"I know, right now," Zach said as he finished his fish. "Listen, I don't care about Hill. It's Veloz I want. You have any idea how many murders he's responsible for in this city alone?"

"Zach," Becky said as she slid a cucumber into her mouth and swallowed, "Hill's a baby. He's scared."

"I know," Zach said as he swirled his mashed potatoes with his spork, "Listen, if he's scared, he'll talk."

"I don't know, Zach" Becky said as she finished her salad. "I don't have a good feeling about this."

"Becky," Zach said as he placed his left hand on her knee under the table and nervously looked around observing his immediate periphery, "Give it a shot?" Zach slowly massaged her right knee and began slowly moving his hand up her inner thigh.

"Zach, stop!" Becky whispered as she pushed his hand away and slammed the dorsal aspect of her hand against the bottom of the table. "Ow" she moaned as he grinned.

"Listen," Zach said as he scooted closer to her, "Becky, we've got to move fast before, you know" --

Becky smiled and whispered into his ear: "Before Woodbury dismisses this case, right?"

"Exactly," Zach yelled and nervously looked around.

"I'll tell you what … I'll review this case this afternoon, okay?" Becky said as Zach smiled and put his head down on Becky's right shoulder. Becky looked around nervously not recognizing anyone as she gently stroked the back of his neck with her right hand. "Tired, Mr. Woods?" Becky said as her fingers stroked his hairline.

Zach placed his left hand on her knee and began riding up her thigh. "Hmmm" he moaned as Becky's ass humped the bench as her head twisted to the left and to the right fearing eyes upon her. Zach slowly pulled his head up and whispered into her right ear: "Look what you do to me, Becky" he said as her eyes followed his to the monstrous bulge between his legs. Zach's pointer finger pressed against her as her thong slipped in as she humped his finger, and he whispered: "You wet for me, baby?"

"Will you stop?" Becky said angrily as she stood and walked over to the trash throwing her empty plastic salad bowl into the receptacle. As they walked slowly back toward the Moakley, they stopped to watch seagulls landing on the deck of a ferry out by the second buoy. "Look at that" Zach said as he pointed to the flock hovering over the boat.

As they approached the garden of saltwater roses aligning the wharf, Zach whispered: "Think about Hill, will ya?" Becky shook her head repeatedly whispering: "Okay, okay," as Zach smiled and moaned "Mmm."

As the elevator door opened on the ninth floor at the U.S. Attorney's Office, Zach whispered to Becky: "See ya, beautiful." Becky grinned with her eyes and headed toward her office yawning. She booted up ECF and began reading through the docket voraciously, searching for anything that would help a potential plea. Quite by accident or sheer luck, she came upon Docket No. 122 entitled: "Rule 11 Edward Hubbard murder plea."

She opened the pdf and her mouth fell open as her tongue nervously licked her bottom lip as she read the testimony on Line 12, Page 13:

Q. You are currently a member of the 93 Bloods operating out of Fall River and Boston, is that correct?
A. Yep -- yes, sir.
Q. And you are the same Edward Hubbard who was an active member of the Bloods when you lived in Tulsa?
A. Yep.
Q. And when you lived in Miami?
A. (No audible response.)
Q. I'm sorry, Mr. Hubbard. You have to answer audibly for the record.
A. Oh, sorry … yep.
Q. I'm showing you Government Exhibit No. 8 entitled Plea Agreement. Pursuant to this plea agreement, is it fair to say that you agreed to plead guilty to federal charges?
A. Yes.
Q. As well as state charges in Tulsa?
A. Correct.
Q. And state charges in Florida?
A. Correct.
Q. Those federal charges included ten murders, did they not?
A. Correct.
Q. And you agreed to plead guilty to racketeering charges?
A. Yes.
Q. And the murder of a man named Michael Romero?
A. Yes.
Q. The murder of a man named Allen Wilkinson?
A. Yes.
Q. The murder of a man named William Mendez?
A. Yes.
Q. The murder of a man named Julio Antonio Alcazar?
A. Yes.
Q. The murder of a man named Joey Batista?
A. Correct.
Q. And the murder of a man named Miguel Ceron?
A. Correct.
Q. The murder of a man named James Dominguez?
A. Correct.
Q. The murder of a man named Tommy Rosario?
A. Correct.

Q. The murder of a man named Timothy P. Connors?
A. Correct.
Q. And the murder of a man named Richard Fuentes?
A. Correct.
Q. Is that fair to say?
A. Correct.
Q. And you agreed to plead guilty in Tulsa, Oklahoma, to the murder of a man named Roger Watkins, did you not?
A. Yes.
Q. And you also agreed to plead guilty in Miami, Florida, to the murder of a man named Peter Callahan?
A. Yes.
Q. And the brutal rape and murder of a 15-year-old girl who happened to be the daughter of rival gang member; is that correct, sir?
A. Correct.
Q. Now, this plea agreement requires you to tell the truth; is that fair to say?
A. Correct.
Q. And what do you understand the penalties to be if you don't tell the truth?
A. I do the rest of my life in jail.

Becky nervously bit the end of her ballpoint pen: "Why is Zach pushing Hill to cooperate?" She closed the pdf and twirled the pen between her thumb and pointer finger as ink jetted across her desk: "Crap," she mumbled as she reached for a Kleenex. As she grabbed the tissue, the entire contents of the Kleenex box unraveled in her right hand: "Crap" she mumbled aggravated as she cleaned the blue ink from her desktop. She stared at her hands which were now stained blue, yawned, and made a B-line to the bathroom.

She scrubbed her hands raw; and as the ink began to dissipate, she noticed blue ink traversing her right wrist and spreading halfway up her inner forearm: "Crap," she mumbled as she scoured.

Her mind drifted to Zach's enigmatic smile as goosebumps covered her arms and legs and she nervously twitched. "Good enough" she whispered out loud as she dried her hands and closed her eyes watching Zach's tongue tease her, and she smiled and jumped in the air as Amanda said: "Becky?"

"Oh, my God," Becky said as she giggled, her damp right hand plunged over her heart.

"Sorry," Amanda said smiling, "didn't mean to scare ya." Becky and Amanda giggled momentarily and walked back into the office as Becky whispered: "What's up with Hubbard? Just read his Rule 11, why isn't Zach" --

Just before they were about to open the door into the U.S. Attorney's Office, Amanda grabbed Becky's left arm and pulled her into the hallway: "Hubbard was stabbed three days after he plead in Plymouth, almost died."

"Hmmm," Becky moaned as she scratched her head.

"A week later he had open heart surgery as the blade penetrated a valve. Three days later he was in "acute undue duress" and wanted to renege on his agreement … been in solitary ever since."

"So he's still in Plymouth?" Becky whispered as Amanda's face grimaced: "Nope, he's being held in detention at Wyatt in Central Falls."

"Oh, so he's in Rhode Island?" Becky asked as Amanda whispered: "Yep, but I don't advise you bringing this up to" --

"Why the hell not?" Becky shouted as Amanda raised her pointer finger on her right hand to her lips whispering: "Shhh … 'cause Zach will take a nutty."

"Look," Becky whispered, "Hill's never gonna talk but Hubbard" --

"Maybe," Amanda said as she played with the tiny hard hairs on her chin, "so you want to give Hubbard a shot?"

"Hmmm," Becky whispered, "he'll talk or spend the rest of his life in prison … only shot we have of nailing Veloz."

"I don't recommend telling Zach about this. I can set this up for you."

"He'll blow a gasket if I sneak behind his back on this case," Becky whispered as two older women walked past them smiling as they opened the door to the office.

"Listen, if you get Hubbard to cooperate, Zach will kiss the ground you walk on -- oh, wait, forgot: he already does, huh?"

"Funny, funny Amanda," Becky mumbled as she threw her a dark glare.

"Sorry, I bad … listen," Amanda whispered as she grabbed Becky's left sleeve noticing it was wet and immediately rubbed her damp hand on her slacks, "I can set this up with the Special Agents … Zach's off next week anyway."

"Oh?" Becky whispered.

"He didn't tell you, huh? Yeah, he's taking the "fam" to Disney." Amanda watched as Becky swelled with tears … "I'm sorry," she whispered, "I'm sure he was gonna tell you himself … you know, his wife's a surgeon at the Brigham; did you know that?"

Becky shook her head and stared at her feet: "What about the Ramon trial; it's starting Monday: no?

Amanda grinned: "Oh, Zach didn't tell you: it's off. Zach dropped it down to simple distribution, and Ramon agreed to plea."

"Oh," Becky sighed, "you were saying Zach's wife's a surgeon?"

"Yeah, a cardiothoracic surgeon … brilliant. If she finds out about you two, and she probably will, she'll divorce his ass faster than you can count to three." Becky swelled with tears, and Amanda whispered: "Come on, come with me … let's take a walk."

As the elevator door opened and Becky and Amanda stepped in, Becky whispered: “I never meant for this to happen, you know,” as tears cascaded down her cheeks. Amanda hugged her whispering: “I know.”

Amanda grabbed Becky’s left hand and walked her out the back entrance of the Moakley. Peter and John smiled at Amanda and threw looks between themselves as they observed Becky crying as she passed them by.

They walked down to the wooden bench across from the harbor and sat down as Becky continued to cry: “I love him,” she said as Amanda stared into the water.

“End this,” Amanda said as she gently touched Becky’s right hand.

“He says he loves me, you know,” Becky said as tears dripped onto her skirt as she looked deeply into Amanda’s sky blue eyes.

Amanda shook her head and whispered: “Did he say that after he came or just before?”

Becky sobbed as Amanda hugged her whispering: “You’ll be all right, Becky. No matter what you decide, I will always be your friend.” Becky wiped her cheeks and momentarily grinned: “You won’t tell anyone?”

“Not a sole, Becky,” Amanda whispered, “not a sole.”

“Promise?” Becky said as she began to compose.

Amanda shook her head affirmatively as she whispered: “End this.”

“I don’t know if I can,” Becky replied as she twirled her hair into a knot by her right ear. “Tried a couple of times already but” --

“Well, then you didn’t try hard enough,” Amanda said as Becky’s hair blew over her eyes. Becky brushed her bangs back: “Best sex of my life," she whispered as Amanda smiled.

"Okay. He says he loves you … tell him if he *loves* you, he needs to leave his wife. Tell him you can't live like this. If he *loves* you, he'll let you go or leave his *unhappy sexless* marriage, right?"

A single tear fell from Becky's left eye, and Amanda wiped it away gently. Becky mouthed: "He says he hasn't had sex with her since Emily was born."

"What?" Amanda said unable to discern her words.

Becky repeated unknowingly shouting: "Says he hasn't had sex with her since Emily was born."

Amanda's eyebrows raised to the center of her forehead as she leaned in: "Shhh … and you believe that, Ms. Harvard Law?"

Becky shook her head affirmatively as Amanda grimaced and nodded her head back and forth.

"Listen," I like Zach, I always have, but I think he's full of crap … he's playing you, Becky."

Becky began to wail and Amanda whispered: "I'm sorry," stood and said: "Come on, let's walk."

Becky and Amanda walked along the Harborwalk and continued to walk long after the concrete boardwalk ended as Becky cried harder than she ever had before. Amanda whispered: "I'm sorry, Becky," occasionally bending down to pick up small shells and handing them to her one at a time.

Becky's iPhone vibrated in her blazer's left pocket. As Becky stared into the touchscreen flashing: "one missed call," Amanda whispered: "Zach, right?"

"Hmmm," Becky moaned as she slid her phone back into her pocket.

"We'd better head back before I'm out of a job," Amanda said as Becky smiled: "Thank you, Amanda" she whispered as Amanda hugged her. As they stepped onto the concrete walk Amanda stopped and Becky turned around and walked up to her cocking her head inquisitively.

"Becky," she whispered, how much you want to bet Zach left you a message telling you he's going out of town and he wants to see you?" Becky lifted her iPhone and played Zach's message: "Hi beautiful," he said as Amanda shook her head in disdain. "Listen, I'm going out of town next week. Taking Amy on vacation. I need to see you." Amanda grinned as a single tear dripped down Becky's right cheek. "I want to take you to dinner somewhere nice tonight, okay … call me babe."

As they walked toward the courthouse, Amanda whispered: "Go out with him tonight. Have a nice dinner somewhere expensive, real expensive." Becky smiled and stared at her feet noticing sand covering the tops of her black leather shoes. She bent down and wiped her shoes with her right palm.

As she stood Amanda whispered: "He'll take you to a nice hotel. Have the greatest sex of your lives … then tell him this is over; you're on the verge of a nervous breakdown. If he *loves* you, Becky, he'll end this."

"Or he'll leave his wife?" Becky interjected as Amanda shook her head: "Do they ever?" Becky nodded as she whispered: "I'm a fool" as she stared at her feet.

"Are you kidding me?" Amanda said as she hugged her: "You're one of the smartest women I've ever known … graduated valedictorian at Harvard Law, right? This isn't about intellect, baby." Amanda slowly pulled away from Becky's hug and stood a foot away whispering: "It's up to you. I can't tell you how to live your life or what to do."

As they knelt down and inhaled the saltwater roses, Amanda whispered: "You ever have an affair with a married man before?"

Becky shook her head and stared intently into her eyes: "Nope."

"Listen," Amanda whispered as she cut a white rose with the edge of her thumbnail and placed it delicately into Becky's open left palm: "It's none of my business, but how many men you been with?" Becky raised the rose to her nose and inhaled as she shook her head back and forth …

"You were a virgin before Zach? Oh, my God," Amanda said arching her brows as Becky stared at her shoes. "Pick your head up and hold it high," Amanda said as left right hand picked up Becky's chin forcing her face upwards, "end this tonight," she whispered. "Here," Amanda handed her a business card which had Amanda's handwritten scribble on the back, "508-535-7739."

"That's my cell. You call me any time, okay? I mean, any time." Becky whispered: "Thanks" – as Amanda rolled her eyes and shook her head -- "No, I mean it, Amanda, thanks" as they walked up the concrete walk and approached the rear entrance to the Moakley as Becky's iPhone vibrated in her pocket.

"Guess who?" Amanda quipped as she held the door for her friend. As they stepped into the elevator, Becky pressed voicemail and held the phone between Amanda and her left ear: "Hi, beautiful. Listen, where are you? Just went down to your office … call me, okay?"

As the elevator doors opened, Amanda said: "Look at that, 4:00 already. I'm out of here," she said with a beaming smile and reached and touched Becky's left forearm: "Have a great weekend … call me," she mouthed as she walked into the ladies room. Becky walked into the office and whispered "hi" to the receptionist and walked with her head down towards Zach's office.

Zach was standing in the doorjamb as Becky approached his office, and he pulled her abruptly into his realm and closed and locked the door behind her. He momentarily studied her face and raised his eyebrows whispering: "You okay?" as he pressed into her while his hands reached around her and grabbed her buttocks tightly.

“Mmm,” Becky moaned as Zach pushed into her and her body swayed. His right hand slid between her inner thighs, and he began slowly massaging her through her hose as they dampened and clung to her vulva.

“Ever been to Clio’s?” Zach asked as he massaged her ass with his left hand. Becky nodded her head from side to side as Zach slid both hands to her hips and peeled her hose to her knees; he pressed his face against her as his right pointer finger crept inward, and he fingered her tantalizing her slowly. Her body involuntarily humped his meandering finger as she inhaled his unique scent.

“Oh, God,” she mumbled as he lapped and pushed his tongue in deeper. He pulled his face away and looked up at her while he licked his lips, and his right hand began playing with her as she humped his hand. Zach stood and pulled her against him as he kissed her neck and moaned.

“Listen, I’m gonna go down first. Got a cab waiting out front by the meters. I’ll get in. Wait five minutes and meet me in the cab, okay, babe?” Zach unbuttoned the first three buttons of her shirt as she pressed against his erection causing his zipper to bulge and rub into her stomach irritating her skin.

She placed her left hand on his zipper and pulled the zipper down cupping him as he gently pulled her left breast from her bra as he licked around the circumference of her large light brown areola as liquid began dribbling down her inner thighs, slowly catching at her scrunched-up pantyhose wrapped around her knees.

With his right hand he teased her clit as he sucked her nipple hard as she broke out into a full body sweat. Slowly he released her nipple and buttoned her shirt as his tongue licked her lips. She turned her head as she could smell herself on his lips. He stuck his now sopping right hand into his cotton brief and adjusted himself as she watched licking her bottom lip.

“Mmm,” he moaned as he whiffed his fingers … “five minutes, beautiful,” he whispered as he walked away from her and unlocked the door.

Becky stood in his office and faced the harbor trying to peel her pantyhose up. As she pulled the hose over her right thigh, a slow dribble cascaded to her knee and she mumbled: “Ah, Gross.” She managed to pull the hose under her skirt and headed to her office, booted down her PC, shoved the Hill file folder into her briefcase, locked the door, and headed down the hallway past reception toward the ladies room.

As she pushed the door open, her mind suddenly freeze-framed to when she was 13 and sitting with her mother’s brother, her Uncle Chuck, on the living room sofa. He had his beat-up Gibson in his lap and an old Boombox covered with Zeppelin stickers on the coffee table in front of them. She closed her eyes and he said with a huge smile: “Greatest guitarist since Jimmy Hendrix, blues guy from Texas, listen to this,” and Becky started to sing softly: “Well, I'm a lovestruck baby I must confess, life without you darlin' is a solid mess, thinkin' ‘bout you baby gives me such a thrill, I gotta have you baby, can't get my fill … I love you baby and I know just what to do.”

Becky walked into the ladies room quickly observing that it was empty and she was alone. She walked into the handicapped stall and peeled her pantyhose down to her ankles. She stepped out of the stall and threw them into the trash underneath the paper towel dispenser. She leaned over the first sink and filled her hands with soap creating a sudsy foam. She walked back into the stall, closing the door with her back. She stood, her back holding the door closed, as she cleaned herself and sang out loud:

“Every time I see you make me feel so fine, heart beatin' crazy, my blood run wild.” Becky closed her eyes, her mind flashing to cramming the last night before the bar. It was 3:30 a.m. and she couldn’t focus her eyes any longer. She closed her book and diligently began searching for LoveStruck Baby on Google, and YouTube brought her right to it. Her head bounced as she began to jump around her apartment suddenly revitalized, adrenaline rushing, coursing through her veins as she watched Stevie Ray Vaughan play his guitar riff behind his head.

Becky broke out into a smile and began singing loudly as she closed her eyes and saw Zach eat her slowly as she sat on the edge of the bed: "I'm a lovestruck baby. Yeah, I'm a lovestruck baby. You got me lovestruck baby, and I know just what to do." Becky smiled as she thought: "Now what?" as suds seeped down her inner thighs. She grabbed the toilet paper roll which fell out as she touched it which she caught in midair just before it hit the floor.

As she wiped the soap away with the toilet paper, she sang: "Sparks start flyin' every time we meet, let me tell you baby you knock me off my feet; your kisses trip me up they're so dog gone sweet, you know baby you can't be beat. I'm a lovestruck baby. Yeah, I'm a lovestruck baby … (da-na-na-na) you got me lovestruck baby (da-na-na-na) , and I know just what to do" she sang as she air-guitared Stevie Ray's solo at the end.

She washed her hands and dried them on a paper towel. As she stood waiting for the elevator, she hummed: "I'm a lovestruck baby. Yeah, I'm a lovestruck baby. You got me lovestruck baby." She walked out of the Moakley holding her briefcase in her left hand, clutching her cell in her right reading it as she walked through the glass doors: "one new text: "where are you? … Z"

She slid the iPhone into her blazer pocket, smiled, and sang softly: "I'm a lovestruck baby" as Zach opened the rear right door of the cab for her, and she slid in next to him as he smiled and whispered: "Every time I see you make me feel so fine, heart beatin' crazy, my blood run wild."

Zach grabbed Becky's left hand in his right palm and whispered: "I'm a lovestruck baby; yeah, I'm a lovestruck baby; you got me lovestruck baby, and I know just what to do" as he kissed her cheek and she blushed and the cabbie yelled: "Get a room, will ya … Jesus!"

The cab pulled in front of the restaurant at 4:40, and Zach held the door for Becky. Her ankle twisted as she exited, and Zach caught her before she fell onto the curb. Becky's mouth dropped open as Zach handed the cabbie a 50 and said: "Thanks, buddy … keep the change."

Becky stared at the menu perplexed: "Everything's in French," she muttered. Zach ordered the lobster bisque, and Becky finally settled on just about the only thing she understood on the menu: "crispy fried chicken."

Zach smiled at Becky as she picked at her plate. "Not good?" he whispered.

"No, it's fine. Kind of spicy is all," Becky said as she peeled off the batter and slit it into her mouth making a face. Zach yelled out "waiter" as he motioned him over with his left hand in the air.

"No. Really, it's fine, Zach," Becky whispered as the waiter approached.

"Yes, sir?" the young boy with enormous eyebrows that met in the center of his nose said as he inquisitively noticed Becky's plate full of batter.

"Yeah, this is just too spicy for her. Can you" --

"Sure," the waiter said as he picked up her plate and smiled. What would you like, Miss, instead? It's on the house."

Becky stared at Zach as he winked at her with his right eye: "Um, how 'bout just a Caesar salad?"

"No problem," he replied as he carried her plate in his left hand and ran his right hand through his greased-back black hair.

Zach pulled his chair closer to Becky and kissed her as the waiter disappeared. "I got something for you," he whispered as he pulled out a small rectangular metal bulb.

"What's that?" Becky said as her eyebrows raised as Zach placed his left hand on her bare knee.

“A toy for you,” he whispered as he moaned, “Mmm.” He flicked a button on the underside of the bulb, and it began to vibrate and hum. “You’re gonna like this,” Zach said as he placed it in his left hand and it vibrated softly up her inner right thigh.

Becky nervously looked around the restaurant as she pushed his hand out from under her skirt. “Zach!” she whispered, “stop!” Zach smiled and put his hand back on her knee as her salad arrived. Becky ate her salad voraciously as Zach played with his mashed potatoes creating a sort of volcano in the center of his plate as Becky smiled.

Zach whispered: “Listen, I’m sorry I didn’t tell you about Disney next week.” Becky stared at the bottom of her bowl stabbing croutons as he spoke: “Let’s get out of here” he whispered with a smile as Becky’s eyes looked up at him and glared.

“What?” Zach said as he raised his brows.

“Nothing,” Becky mouthed as he waved the waiter over: “Check please?” he said with a grin. Zach grabbed Becky’s right hand in his left, and they walked into the lobby of the Eliot Hotel chatting and giggling.

Zach whispered: “And it was hysterical, picture this: her first dance recital, five years old. The music stops and all the other little girls looked dumbfounded and petrified as Emily starts dancing in the center of the stage and singing at the top of her lungs: “We’re off to see the wizard, the wonderful Wizard of Oz.”

Becky giggled as Zach stopped in front of the main desk. He looked at the young man behind the counter: “Zach Woods” he said as he winked at Becky who nervously began twirling her hair.

“Hi, Mr. Woods,” the clerk said with a smile: “Room 218” as he placed the hotel card on the countertop: “You’re all set. Have a good stay” he whispered as he smiled at Becky who continued to twirl her hair with her right hand.

Zach grabbed Becky's right hand in his left palm and led her to the elevator. As they stepped in, Becky broke free of his tight grasp and leaned her back into the back wall feeling the railing against the small of her back. As the doors closed, Zach approached her and pinned her against the wall: "Feel this," he whispered as she groaned.

Zach led her down the hallway, and they stopped in front of 218. Becky whispered as Zach opened the door: "We have to talk."

"Okay," Zach said as he placed the "Do not disturb" sign on the front of the doorknob and closed the door behind her. "Later" he whispered as he began to kiss her as his hands unhooked her skirt from behind. He fumbled with the zipper and continued to kiss her as her skirt fell to the floor.

"Get naked, baby," he said as he walked into the bathroom smiling, and she heard the door lock. Becky undressed hanging her suit on the hanger rack next to the bathroom and adjacent to the door hovering from the ceiling. She stood naked at the foot of the bed and threw the rose faux-embroidered comforter on the floor in front of the TV. She climbed into the king-sized bed and pulled the sheet up to her neck as Zach walked toward her slowly fully erect. As he stood next to the bed, Becky sat up and opened her mouth widely as he slid in.

As she scraped her teeth against his rim, he shrieked: "Ow," and she stopped and opened her eyes and looked up at him searching for a cue: "No, it's good, keep going; put your teeth on me," he whispered as she bit down. As he felt his ejaculation imminent, he pulled out and said: "Lay down, baby."

Becky lied back uncomfortably on the double pillows under her head. Zach kissed her and threw one pillow onto the floor as he kissed her neck and slowly made his way down to her breasts. As he went from one nipple to the other, sucking insanely hard, Becky heard an odd buzz and twitched and opened her eyes. He stopped suckling for a minute and looked up at her pulling on her left nipple with his teeth as he held the metal vibrator between his thumb and forefinger, and it vibrated insanely in his left hand.

"Sit up," he whispered as Becky complied smiling. "Move back," he said as he licked his lips and squeezed her right nipple as she shimmied against the headboard. Gently Zach spread her legs apart and placed his tongue inside of her. Liquid impregnated the mattress as Zach rubbed his tongue back and forth, up and down, gently against her clit. As he suckled, he placed the small metal bulb into her ass and her magma gushed onto his face.

"What does it taste like?" Becky whispered as Zach giggled. Zach smiled and looked up into her eyes: "Poland Springs, baby, Poland Springs."

"Oh, God," Becky screamed as her juice continued to dribble down both inner thighs. Zach pulled his lips away softly and whispered: "On your knees."

Becky turned around and placed her knees on the waterlogged mattress as Zach licked her anus and placed the cold metal deep inside of her. She humped and screamed as her cascading waterfall erupted.

"Oooh, you like this, baby?" he whispered as she screamed and humped his left forearm. After 20 minutes the mattress was drenched, and Zach stood up and said: "Get up for a minute?" He grabbed the comforter from the floor and placed it neatly across the bed. As he leaned over the mattress tucking in the comforter between the mattress and the box spring, Becky hopped on top of the bed and bent down on her knees and began licking his anus as her right hand reached around him and began jerking him off forcefully.

Zach closed his eyes and was transported in his mind to the Cape Cod National Seashore inside of Nickerson State Park. He was standing on the beach looking up at the magnificent cliffs; as she swallowed and released, the waves crashed onto the beach. And with his eyes still tightly shut, he felt the ejaculate rise as he whispered: "Ah-ah, stop."

He sat on edge of the bed and motioned for her to lie down with his left hand: “On your stomach, baby” he whispered. Becky lied down on the comforter as he pulled her wet thighs apart with both hands. He stuck his tongue inside of her playing with her lips delicately maneuvering his tongue as he placed the vibrator deep inside her ass as she screamed: “Oh, God,” and humped him wildly.

“Come up on your knees, baby,” he said as he grinned and rubbed the bulb against her labia as fluid splurted through the air. He placed the metal deep inside her as he whacked his erection against her ass. “What do you want, baby?” he said as he bent down and licked her engorged lips softly from behind as fluid doused his chest.

“Oh, God,” Becky screamed as she humped his tongue and with her right hand cupped his sack from underneath.

“Say it,” he whispered as Becky bit her tongue as Zach’s middle finger entered her anus as his tongue continued to play with her outer lips. He mumbled: “You are so beautiful,” as he jammed his finger deep inside her ass, and she climaxed yet again saturating the comforter.

“Oh, God,” she screamed: “Fuck me.” Zach entered her from behind; and as he rode her wildly, he placed the vibrating bulb against her lips as she screamed: “Oh, God … harder.” He plunged as hard as he could inside of her as she screamed “harder,” and Zach smiled as her clear lava dribbled down his thighs. He slowly pulled out and began teasing her with his tip, placing it against her inner lips, and then whacking himself against her inner thighs.

“Say it,” he said as he plunged the vibrator deep inside her and turned it on “high.”

“Fuck me,” she screamed as she humped; “Oh, my God” she whispered as her body convulsed.

“Turn over,” he said as he grinned and slowly backed away staring at her inner lips as he began to masturbate with his left hand on his immense erection. Becky slowly turned over and spread her legs as far apart as physically possible and closed her eyes as he plunged inside of her.

As he rode her, he placed the vibrator inside her anus as she screamed “Oh, God” and her pelvic floor contracted.” He slid out of her and stood by the bed. “Come here, baby,” he whispered as her ass clung to the comforter. She stood in front of him, and they kissed as his fingers played with her labia. He grinned as he teased her with his fingers and kissed her neck as she screamed: “Oh, God.” Zach fixed the disheveled comforter and tucked in the corners and said: “Turn over.”

Becky spread her arms across the bed as her ass hung over the side of the frame. Zach spread her legs apart and placed the bulb deep inside her as he entered her anus. “Ow, what the f-” she screamed as he whispered: “Sorry, babe … say it” and simultaneously pulled out, rubbing his tip against her inner lips as he gently rubbed the metal bulb across her anus.

“Put it in,” she pleaded as she humped, “Zach, please put it in.” He continued to tease her and smiled as her juice dripped onto the floor. “Say it” he whispered as she began to explode.

“Fuck me,” she cried as he entered her. She squeezed him firmly inside her using her pelvic floor muscles contracting tightly as she cried: “Oh, my God” and he smiled and whispered: “Oooh, you really do like this,” as he inserted his middle finger deep within her ass as he mounted her and her volcano exploded.

“I can’t move,” he whispered with a grin as he humped her and she contracted her muscles around him as he ejaculated. He slid his finger out as he came and rode it over her inner lips as cum rushed down his legs submerging the comforter.

“I love you,” he whispered as her pelvic muscles squeezed him tightly; he laughed and pressed his face against her back as her translucent broth dripped from his balls, and he giggled. She continued to hump him as fluid cascaded down his legs.

"I gotta lie down," he whispered still giggling as she released him. She crawled across the comforter and lied down on her stomach feeling the dampness saturating her skin. Zach climbed on the bed and collapsed on his back and closed his eyes. He fell fast asleep with his right hand cupping himself firmly. Becky's multi-faceted orgasm continued as he slept. She turned her head toward him and whispered: "And he sleeps" as she gently kissed his lips, and he turned his head away from her.

Becky tiptoed to the bathroom and filled the tub with steaming hot water. She bathed as she hummed: "I'm a lovestruck baby … you got me lovestruck baby."

Twenty minutes later Becky exited the bathroom surprised to see Zach wide awake sitting up leaning his back against the headboard. "Hi beautiful" he whispered as she approached him wrapped in a white towel. As she approached the bed, she dropped the towel as he smiled: "Hmmm, come here."

She walked around the bed and hopped on yelling: "Gross!" Zach smiled as he grew hard in his left hand whispering: "It's not gross; it's beautiful." Zach stood up still cupping himself with his left hand and walked over to the small table with two wide wooden chairs situated by the window. He raised the blind halfway allowing a beaming streetlight to shine in as Becky stood naked by the bed.

"Come here," he said with a grin, slapping his right hand against the seat.

"Don't you ever get enough?" she said with a smile as she sat down on the chair and he sat Indian style on the floor at her feet. "Shimmy to the edge," he said as he grinned. "Never," he whispered as he began to lick her clit. As his tongue teased her, Becky spread her legs and put both feet on the edge of the chair and shimmied her ass to the very edge of the seat.

Zach licked her lightly and slowly as he inserted his middle finger inside her and fluid dripped onto the seat, meandering its way toward the edge, and slowly dripping onto his bare knees. “Oh, my God,” she screamed as her muscles contracted.

“Stand up, baby” he said as he pressed himself between her inner thighs. She reached down with her right hand and grabbed his tip firmly as he moaned: “Bend over.” She bent over and he sat down on the wet vinyl seat and began licking her ass as fluid continuously erupted and streamed down her inner thighs toward her ankles. Unconsciously she stuck the pointer finger of her right hand deep inside her as he whispered: “Oooh, turn around.”

She turned around and released her finger as he shook his head: “I want to watch you,” he said as his left hand began masturbating. Zach whispered: “Sit down,” and pulled the other chair closer across from him. Becky sat down facing him. “Put your feet up,” he whispered as he pulled on himself and grinned.

Becky put her feet on the sides of the seat and began touching herself as Zach watched intensely as he grabbed his sack. He slid off his wet chair and pushed the chair toward the window. He sat down in front of Becky’s chair as she whimpered: “Watch me” and she inserted three fingers deep inside her. Zach reached up and began licking her anus as Becky screamed: “Oh, God,” and Zach whispered: “Come here.”

Becky slid off the chair and placed her knees on the carpet in front of him and cocked her head back smiling. Zach pushed her chair away and began slapping her ass with his cock as he wiggled her clit between his thumb and pointer finger of his left hand as she moaned.

“Say it,” he whispered as she leaned forward and screamed as she inundated the floor: “Come inside me.”

That’s not it, baby. Say it,” he whispered as he fiddled.

“Fuck me,” she screamed. He inserted himself as deep as her body would allow as Becky yelled: “Ow.” Zach pulled out and began tantalizing her by rubbing his tip against her lips as he slowly stuck his middle finger in and out of her. She angled her body onto him, and he kept teasing her as she whispered: “Put it in; please, put it in.” He continued to tease her and giggle as she pleaded: “Oh, my God, Zach; put it in, please put it in.”

“You getting sore, baby?” he whispered as he sat back on his knees and licked her clit from behind. “Put it in” she cried as he licked her lips, and she screamed.

“Say it, baby,” he whispered as he rubbed his cock between her wet thighs.

“Fuck me,” she cried as he thrust into her. “Harder,” she screamed as she drowned the carpet. He dug into her as hard as he could as she reached behind and under her and cupped his balls with her left hand: “Oooh,” he screamed as he came inside her.

Becky moaned “mmm” as she whispered: “Oooh, you like that, baby?” as Zach collapsed on top of her, her left hand still clenching him as he giggled and whispered: “I love you, Becky.”

Zach grabbed the pillow he had thrown on the floor earlier and delicately placed it under her head as his body collapsed onto her. He remained inside her for twenty minutes as they lied on the carpet until slowly he fell out. Zach sat up and leaned his back against the foot of the bed as Becky sat up and cuddled next to him.

Becky cupped his balls in her left hand, and he grew hard as she tightened her clench. “Mmm” he moaned as she leaned forward and cupped her mouth tightly around him. As he became erect he mumbled: “ah-ah” and she opened her eyes as she began to gag as he grew immense within her mouth.

“How many times can you go?” she said softly giggling as he said: “Come here.” Becky leaned her back against the bedframe as Zach spread his body across the floor, closed his eyes and stuck his tongue inside her. “Oh, my God,” she screamed as he moved his tongue into her anus and flicked her clit with his right pointer finger, occasionally squeezing it with his thumb. Zach gagged temporarily as his mouth filled with her heaping juice as she screamed: "Oh, my God."

Zach slowly opened his eyes as he gently licked her inner lips, spreading her labia apart gently with his left hand. "You wanted to talk?" he whispered as he licked her anus and jammed his middle finger inside of her as she raised her buttocks in the air and cum projectily splurted and splashed against the dresser across from the bed.

Zach sat up and leaned his back against the bedframe as his left middle finger continued to tantalize her: "You want to talk?" he whispered as she shook her head side to side: "No … oh, my God" she panted heavily as he shoved his entire fist inside her: "I love you," she whispered as she got on her knees.

"I love you," he whispered as he wiggled her with his pointer finger from behind as he grew immense and pushed himself between her inner thighs. As he continuously stimulated her, he whispered: "Say it, baby," as he plunged deep within her and she screamed: "Ow!"

"Oooh, you are hurting," he mumbled as he slid out slowly and rubbed his rim against her clit; as he gently pushed himself in and calculatingly slid out, fluid gushed down his thighs and he mounted her again.

"Oh, my God," she screamed as her pelvic floor contracted against him as he licked his pointer finger wet and stuck it deep inside her anus. "I want to get on top" she whispered as he slid out and shimmied against the foot of the bed. As she stood in front of him, her crotch at his face level, she spread her legs and he gently wiggled his tongue against the tip of her clit as cum splashed across his face and chest.

Becky sat in Zach's lap and arched her back swallowing him deeply inside. He closed his eyes and screamed: "Ahhh," as he ejaculated and she felt a stabbing pain deep in her back. She thought: "I gotta pee," as her body collapsed onto him as he forcefully grabbed her left breast and bit down on her nipple with his front teeth as she screamed in cataclysmic orgasm and erupted in his lap.

They lied on the floor side by side with their eyes closed moaning for several minutes before Zach opened his eyes and stared at the back of her head: “Becky?” he whispered. Becky turned her head toward him and opened her eyes.

“How many men you been with?” he asked as he leaned forward and gently kissed her lips. Becky shook her head back and forth as her eyes filled with tears as Zach’s eyes widened and his brows raised. “Seriously?” he said as he sat up wiping his still wet hands on his damp thighs.

Becky sat up and they both leaned against the bed as he put his left arm around her shoulders. “How many women you been with?” she whispered as he grinned. “You mean in my whole life?” he asked as he coyly smiled.

“Mmm,” Becky moaned.

“Five,” he mumbled -- “no, six” he whispered as he leaned forward and kissed her gently on the lips, his tongue swiping her upper lip. “It’s different with you” he said as he grinned.

“Different?” Becky asked as she mumbled: “Oh, my God, I’m soaked.”

“Mmm,” Zach moaned, “I know.”

“Different how?” Becky asked as Zach hugged her.

“Feels like the first time with you,” he whispered as he licked her earlobe and she pulled away from him giggling: “Yeah, right.”

“No, really,” Zach said with a smile as he slowly raised his left hand and gently twirled her right nipple as it grew hard in his grasp.

“Don’t think I’ve ever been with a woman who actually climaxed before,” he said as his mouth suckled her erect nipple as her right hand played with his dark hair.

"Really," she whispered, "you're so good," she said as he looked up at her and whispered with her nipple gently between his front teeth: "You think?" He continued to suckle her drawing a faint amount of milk. "Mmm," he moaned as she began to rock her waist.

Zach released her nipple and kissed her neck as he whispered: "It's the way you move to my touch," he said as he kissed her lips and stuck his tongue into her mouth. They kissed for five minutes as he laid her back down on the carpet cupping her buttocks with both hands as she pushed into him, and he grew erect once again.

"Seriously," she whispered into his left ear: "how many times can you go?" as her right hand tightly grasped his erection. As she jerked him, he giggled: "I don't know," he said with a grin as he stood, and she closed her teeth on him. She bit down on him and pushed him into the back of her throat as her pointer finger entered him from behind. She began pulling back and slowly and gently licking him. He turned around and she stuck her tongue deep within his anus as her right hand jerked him off.

"A-h-h-h!" he screamed as her tongue went deep inside. She slowly pulled her tongue out and whispered: "Oooh, you do like that baby?" as he turned around and said: "Put it in." She bit down on him and gently scraped her teeth against his rim as his left hand pushed the back of her head into him. As he slid down her esophagus, he screamed: "A-h-h-h!" as he ejaculated and she temporarily gagged and slowly pulled off.

"You okay?" he moaned as he swayed and pushed her head into him. "Hmmm" she groaned as she lifted her head up and put both balls inside her mouth and sucked slowly and gently. "I gotta sit down," he whispered as he giggled and sat on the edge of the bed, and she continued to suckle him. He lied back on the wet comforter and grew small as she looked up smiling. Slowly she released him and whispered: "You done finally, huh?"

"Hmmm," he groaned as he shimmied his body toward the

headboard ignoring the dampness under him. Becky walked into the bathroom holding herself barely able to walk thinking: “Oh, my God; I gotta pee, I gotta pee” as urine dripped down her inner thighs as she stood just outside the bathroom as Zach fell into a deep sleep. Becky unrolled some toilet paper and didn’t even attempt to wipe herself as she stood and turned the faucet on the tub to hot.

As the bathroom filled with steam she sat in the hot water. “Ow,” she mumbled out loud as she thought, “Geez, can’t even touch myself,” as she slowly got on her knees and dangled her clit into the hot water and felt some relief. She cleaned herself with the Dial on the rim. She sudded her right hand and gently attempted to clean her crotch as she yelled: “Ow” as the soap burned her engorged raw tissues.

Zach cleared his throat as he watched her face squinch in pain and whispered: “hurting?” as she sat into the water and smirked. He knelt down by the bathtub rim with his knees on the wet towel and whispered: “Come up on your knees.”

With his left hand he splashed hot water up inside her and she moaned “hmmm,” the hot water comforting her and stifling the pain. Exhausted she sat back down in the tub and he stood erect before her. She said with a grin: “Can I?”

Becky got back on her knees and rubbed the Dial between her hands. She placed the soap on the rim which fell into the water and she cleaned his cock and his sack before whispering with a devilish grin: “Turn over, baby.” Zach turned over smiling and Becky cleaned his buttocks before gently inserting her soapy pointer finger into his anus. “Ow” he screamed as the soap burned.

“Sorry, babe,” she said as he hopped into the tub splashing water onto her face and hair. He leaned his back against the opposite wall of the faucet and motioned for her to sit between his legs. As she leaned her back against his chest, his right hand slowly touched her clit under the water and she screamed: “Ow!”

“Oooh, you really are sore,” he whispered as he placed his hand on her thigh.

“Yeah, and all of a sudden,” she said concerned as she twisted her head to face him, “I feel like I gotta pee constantly.”

“Great,” Zach mumbled: “Listen, your bladder’s just like irritated. They sell crap in the pharmacy. We’ll stop on the way out and get you something” he whispered as he kissed the back of her neck, and her body pushed deeply into his chest. His right hand found the bar of soap floating next to him. He picked it up and began lightly rubbing it across her breasts, cleaning as he stroked. He placed the bar on the rim and began splashing water onto her chest as her nipples became hard and erect.

She stood up in the tub and he cupped her buttocks with both hands as he leaned forward and placed his tongue inside of her and gently reached upwards. She turned around; and as his tongue licked her clit, her juice bubbled down her legs and dripped into the now lukewarm tub. “Sit” he whispered, “I think you’re done tonight” he said as she sat back down in the water.

As she pressed her back into his chest, she whispered: “I love you, Zach.” He cupped his hands under each breast and firmly tightened his grip: “I love you too, Becky,” he said as she felt his erection against the small of her back.

Becky stepped out of the tub and wiped herself off as Zach watched smiling. She walked out of the bathroom and dressed. She buttoned the final button of her shirt as Zach walked out soaking wet: “Got a towel?” he whispered as their eyes locked on her damp white towel at her feet. She picked it up, and he turned with his back toward her as she began patting him dry. As she reached down with the towel by his ankles, goosebumps shot up his spine and he turned around fully erect.

“Seriously?” she said as she smiled and began wiping the towel across his chest. “Look what you do to me” he said as he threw her one of his amazing enigmatic smiles, and she opened her mouth and laid her teeth against his rim. Their eyes locked as she whispered: "Seriously?"

"Mmm," he moaned as he grew immense within her jaw. She attempted to kneel down but her skirt was too tight and she couldn't maneuver. She looked at him dumbfoundedly as he whispered: "No problem" and he unlatched her skirt and as he pulled the zipper, her skirt fell to the floor over the wet towel.

She picked her skirt up and hung it on a hanger as he grinned. As she leaned upward to hang it, he dropped to his knees and pushed his face against her buttocks. "What are you doin', baby?" she whispered as she grinned and moaned.

Slowly he took his head away and she turned around as he stood in front of her. She knelt down on the carpet, her knees aching, as she swallowed him. After a few minutes Zach started to wobble and lose his equilibrium as he whispered: "Stop. I gotta sit down … I don't feel so good."

He stumbled over to the bed and whipped the comforter and the fitted bedsheet onto the floor and sat on the bare mattress at the edge of the bed. Becky ran into the bathroom and grabbed the wet washcloth he had used to meticulously clean her. She ran the cold water and held the washcloth under the faucet.

Zach had his head between his legs. Becky sat down on the floor in front of him and gently began to pat his forehead and temples with the freezing cold cloth. "Thank you" he whispered as she smiled. She placed the washcloth on his neck as his erection returned. "You want?" she said as he smiled and nodded. He grabbed the cloth and stuck it on his forehead as she swallowed him and bit down hard on his queue. He lied back on the bed sticking the washcloth under his left armpit as Becky leaned her body forward digging her knees into the carpet.

She pulled on him as hard as she could, utilizing her jaw muscles as she scraped her teeth gently across his rim. Zach closed his eyes and watched as the waves crashed onto the beach and screamed: "A-h-h-h!" as he pushed himself down her throat. As Becky swallowed, she sopped the carpet under her feet.

Zach lied back, his left hand playing with her hair as he groaned. "Gotta take a shower" he said as he slowly sat up, and she delicately released him. She swirled her tongue against his tip as he grinned and lovingly leaned forward and kissed her forehead. As she leaned back so he could stand, he looked down at her whispering: "I love you, Becky," as she grabbed his balls and opened her mouth and cocked her head back.

"Oh, my God," he said as he chuckled and remained small. Becky grinned as she said: "You're done," and he smiled as she released him.

"Get dressed, beautiful," he said as she watched his ass walk away from her. She walked over toward the bathroom door and picked up the damp towel and dried her inner thighs and crotch as she heard the shower run. She walked over toward the table near the window and cleaned both seats with the towel in her right hand. She threw it overhead and it landed on the mattress as she sat down and stared out into the night in a zombie-like trance, her mind repeating: "I gotta pee; oh, God, I gotta pee, I gotta pee."

Zach walked out of the bathroom as Becky stood by the doorjamb, her legs squeezed tightly together and her body crunched awkwardly forward. "Hmmm" Zach said as he slid his brief on watching her make a mad dash toward the toilet. He smiled at her as she closed the door. As she tried to wipe herself, she began to cry: "Something's wrong," she mumbled out loud. "Ow!" she cried as she attempted once again. Becky opened the door, her face pale, and her expression sullen and somber.

Zach, now fully dressed, walked toward her: "You okay?"

"Something's wrong," she said as she put her head down. Tears streamed down her cheeks as Zach lifted her chin with his left hand. "I can't even wipe myself," she muttered.

"You'll be okay, baby. You're just sore. Come on, let's get out of here," he whispered as he hugged her and she pressed into him. Zach and Becky walked hand in hand into the elevator. Becky smiled as Zach continuously yawned. They walked out of the Eliot Hotel, and Becky sneezed as they broke hands.

Zach pointed across the street: "Look at that," he said with a grin as he pointed to the CVS directly across the way. He grabbed Becky's hand as they crossed, and he smiled while whispering: "You're walking funny, baby."

"Very funny, Mr. Woods," Becky quipped as they stepped onto the sidewalk. As they walked through the automatic double glass doors, Zach spotted a bench just inside the pharmacy and pointed: "Sit. I'll be right back."

Becky sat down on the bench and winced in pain; one thought permeating the meandering burrows and landscaped crevices of her inner mind: "Oh, my God; I gotta pee."

Five minutes later Zach approached the bench holding a small white bag with the CVS emblem and a Classic Coke in his left hand. He sat down next to her and handed her the Coke bottle. He opened the bag and tore open the top of the cardboard box which had "UTI Relief" sprawled across the front, "Maximum Strength Tablets, Fast Relief for Bladder and Urinary Tract Infections, Pain & Burning." He opened the plastic wrap with his teeth and slid two tiny maroon pills into her open left palm. She put them on her tongue and guzzled the Coke.

Zach handed her the bag with an assortment of products. "What's this?" she whispered as he cuddled close. "Listen, take these pills for a few days. If you're still having pain and having to pee a lot," Zach said as he smiled, "you know you might need to see your doctor, okay?"

Becky cuddled close, her left shoulder tightly fitting under his right armpit. She turned her head toward him and inhaled his pheromonal cocktail and felt her juice dripping from her thong as he groaned:

“Hmmm.”

“Listen, when you get home tonight, put some petroleum jelly, you know, all around.” Becky scrunched up her nose and whispered: “Seriously? That’s gross.”

“Mmm, smear it inside like” … Zach licked his bottom lip as Becky swayed to his hormonal release.

“Gross,” Becky whispered as Zach gently placed his right hand on her right cheek and tilted her face toward him: “It’s not gross, baby,” he whispered as she smiled; “there’s nothing gross about you,” and he kissed her gently on the lips.

“You might walk funny next couple of days,” he said with a grin as he mouthed “I love you,” as she nestled her head across his chest and watched as his bulge grew. Becky handed Zach the Coke, and he downed it in one heaping gulp.

“Let’s go, baby,” he said as he stood and threw the empty coke bottle into the trash. They walked across the street spotting a taxi parked outside the hotel. Zach grabbed Becky’s right hand, and they rode back to the courthouse silently, occasionally catching each other’s glance and smiling. As they pulled past Courthouse Way, Zach said: “Hey, park right here, okay?” Becky’s face went pale as she tried to stand as Zach giggled as he held the door open and pouted his lips.

“Shut up,” Becky said as Zach threw a 10 and a 20 onto the front seat. “Thanks buddy,” Zach said as he giggled watching Becky hobble onto the sidewalk. Zach whispered into her left ear as he leaned down: “Follow me, I’m gonna take you home, baby.”

They walked toward the Moakley, and Becky grabbed his right sleeve: “Zach” she said scared and squeezing her legs together. Zach started giggling as she pinched his forearm: “Shut up.”

“Sorry,” he giggled, “come on, baby,” and Becky followed him into the courthouse. Zach stood outside the ladies room door for five minutes waiting impatiently staring at his cell. "Shit, it's really late," he mumbled as he stared at the touchscreen: "11:25 … damn, hope she's sleeping," he said in his mind as Becky opened the door.

"You okay?" Zach asked as he grinned. Becky shook her head up and down and mouthed: "thank you." She followed him to the elevators leading to the garage. As the elevator door closed, and Zach cornered her into the far right wall she whispered: "Never been down here before," as he grinned and humped her. Zach smiled as Becky walked, her legs hardly spreading. He pouted as she struggled to sit in the passenger's seat. "Ow," she screamed as her face scrunched as she sat. "You poor thing," Zach said as he smiled and she hit his right arm: "Shut up, Zach."

Zach sat down in the driver's seat of his brand new black Mercedes and stared at Becky: "I'm sorry, baby," he whispered as he leaned toward her and kissed her, his tongue licking her bottom lip as she moaned. "Give me that bag," he said with a smile, "and lift up your skirt."

"Zach, I can't, please … I can't move right now," Becky said with tears in her eyes as she lifted her skirt to her stomach. "I know, baby," he said as he gently put his head between her legs and licked her vulva over her thong. "Ow, don't," Becky screamed as his tongue meandered inward and her juice sopped onto his leather seat as his tongue licked her gently as her body flinched.

"Shhh," Zach said as he lifted the Vaseline from the CVS bag. He stuck the pointer finger of his right hand into the jelly and said: "Spread 'em." She held her breath as she picked her ass off the leather and slid her thong to her ankles. "I'm gonna destroy your car," she whispered as he took his blazer off while shimmying it under her as he smiled.

Slowly Zach rubbed his petroleum-laden finger into her swollen vulva, and she humped his hand as she screamed: "Ow … oh, my God, Zach." Zach dipped his finger back into the Vaseline and stuck it deep inside her as she yelled: "Oh, my God."

He stuck his finger back into the container and slowly inserted his finger deep inside her ass as she began to hump his hand: “Better?” he whispered as he grinned coyly.

“Mmm,” Becky moaned as he attempted to release his finger: “Don’t move,” she whispered as she began to masturbate and contract her pelvic floor. Zach licked his lips as he watched her manipulate and soak the car mat.

“You’re turning me on, baby,” he whispered as he slid his finger in and out as she squeezed. Zach stuck his pointer finger into the jelly and played with her engorged clit as Becky mumbled: “Oh, my God, Zach,” as he unzippered his pants with his left hand while his right fingers played incessantly with her as she moaned and humped his finger still imbedded inside her anus.

Becky slowly slid toward him; and as she sat in his lap, she screamed: “Ow” as he inserted his jellied finger deep inside her ass: “We don’t have to do this, baby,” he whispered as he pushed the automatic lever for the seat to slide back to the rear.

“I can’t move,” Becky whispered as she leaned back against the steering wheel. Zach removed his finger and stuck it back into the goop and began playing with her clit wiggling it gently as Becky bounced in his lap. Zach smiled as he felt her lava jettison under his ass, soaking the driver’s seat, and slowly dripping down the backs of both legs. She lunged on him as he ejaculated and wiggled his goopy finger across her clit. Simultaneously as they moaned they screamed: “A-h-h-h” as Becky whispered into his right ear: “Don’t move, don’t move, don’t move,” as she exploded.

Zach giggled as he shriveled inside of her as she continued to whisper: “Don’t move,” as liquid pooled onto the car mat at his feet. Zach opened his eyes and reached for the Vaseline. He inserted both forefingers into the container; and as she lifted herself off of him, he smeared it all over her swollen protruding tissues. “Ow” she screamed as she sat down on his blazer as he giggled.

“Oooh, you’re really swollen, baby,” Zach said as he pouted and

Becky spread her legs as far apart as she could squinching in pain as he gooped a mound of Vaseline around her vulva and looped it deep inside her anus and began pinching her clit lightly between his fingers as she moaned and closed her eyes.

She opened her eyes and whispered: "Zach, stop," and placed her right hand on top of his forearm as his tongue licked his top lip as he stared at her vulva and Becky climaxed again, her magma flying projectily and splashing across the glove. Zach giggled as he removed his fingers and leaned toward her left ear: "You're right, you are gonna destroy my car."

"Mmm," Becky whispered as she smiled, "and your blazer and the seat and the floor." Zach smiled, wiggling his pants up, and turned on the ignition as he grinned and pulled the saturated blazer toward him: "Come here." Becky moved toward him and he kissed her gently as she stroked her right nipple through her blouse.

"You're killing me," he said as she smiled as they stopped at the exit to the garage under the Moakley, and Zach stared at her: "So?" he said with his foot on the brake.

"So?" Becky said as she inhaled his imbibing chemical savor and moaned: "Hmmm."

"Where we going?" Zach said as she smiled: "Um, Granite Street, Braintree."

"Seriously?," Zach said with a smile, "Geez, I could have just walked you to the T, huh?"

"Yeah," Becky said as she smiled widely, "but then we wouldn't have had so much fun," as he grinned and she placed her left hand across his zipper as he enlarged and moaned "mmm" as he yawned, and Becky leaned in and kissed his right cheek: "Geez, how many times can you go, Mr. Woods?" Becky whispered with a wide-eyed grin …

Half an hour later Zach smiled: "You're killing me, baby," he said as he smiled as Becky stroked him over his zipper. As he pulled onto Granite Street, Becky's face scrunched. He pulled over to the right as Becky whispered: "here," and as Zach threw the Mercedes into park, she stared at him intently.

"Hurting, huh?" he whispered as she shook her head. "You live alone?" he asked as he kissed her lips.

"No, have a roommate but she's out of town … in Denver visiting the 'fam,' you know."

"Good," Zach said as he turned the ignition off, "I'm carrying you to bed." Becky smiled as he opened the car door and whispered: "Shimmy that ass over here, beautiful."

Zach lifted her gently from the seat and slammed the door with his right foot as he carried her up the concrete stairs and into the foyer of her complex. She dropped the CVS bag and gently Zach put her down. As she began walking through the glass door into the complex, Zach whispered: "Nope" and picked her up cradling her in his arms as he placed the CVS bad on top of her groin and she giggled. He walked toward the elevator and whispered: "Where we going, baby?"

"Third floor," she said as she nestled her head into his shoulder. As they stepped inside the elevator, Zach whispered: "Oooh, you're really wet," as Becky smiled: "yeah, and goopy," as the doors opened.

"322," she whispered as he put her down in front of her apartment. She opened the door and he swooped her into his arms and whispered: "Bedroom?"

Becky pointed with her right hand to a hallway just off of the living room, and Zach ran down the hallway with her giggling in his arms. Gently he placed her on top of her Laura Ashley comforter and sat down on the edge of her bed unbuttoning her shirt. "Zach," she whispered.

“Yeah?” he said as he peeled her shirt off and she whipped her bra toward the door. “I love you,” she said as he leaned forward and gently licked her right nipple. As he suckled her, he reached both hands around her back and unlatched her skirt and fumbled with the zipper until he finally freed it. He gently pulled her skirt down and slid it off at her ankles and threw it into the hamper by the door.

He locked the door and slowly walked toward her licking his bottom lip as she whispered: “Zach, I can’t right now.”

He pouted as he peeled her thong from her and threw it overhead into the hamper. She lied naked on her bed with tears in her eyes. He knelt down and picked up the CVS bag that she’d dropped at the side of her bed. As he licked his bottom lip, he opened the Vaseline and whispered: “Spread ‘em, baby.”

He stuck his pointer finger, middle finger, and ring finger simultaneously into the goop and smeared it all over her vulva as she winced. Slowly he inserted his middle finger deep inside her anus as his pointer finger wiggled her now immensely swollen clit. “Oh, God,” she screamed as he smiled. He spread her legs apart as far as they would go and slid his body down to the edge of the bed, his legs dangling over, so he could watch as he smeared the goop inside.

He looked at her with a menacing stare as he wiggled her clit and her body tensed and she screamed: “Ow!”

“I’m sorry, baby,” he said as he stood by the head of her bed: “I gotta go” he whispered as he adjusted himself and smiled as she watched and licked her lips. Slowly Becky sat up on the bed, and he knelt down and kissed her softly and gently on the lips. “Take a couple more of these magic little pills in a couple hours” he said as he smiled and walked toward the door staring at her bare breasts. “I’ll call you at some point next week from Disney,” he said as he grinned and mouthed: “I love you.”

Becky laid back down listening to the front door slam as she stood naked and attempted a mad dash to the bathroom, squeezing her legs together as she stood in the doorjamb as urine dribbled down her legs. Ten minutes later as the bathroom filled with steam and the mirror clouded, she sat in a burning hot tub smiling. She leaned her back against the rim temporarily whacking the back of her head into the protruding faucet. "Ow" she mumbled as she smiled and closed her eyes and watched as Zach's tongue tortured her as he whispered: "I love you, Becky."

Becky opened her eyes and said: "What are you doing to me, Zach … he's playing you, he's playing you." She dunked her head under the hot water as her mind shuffled to a song that resonated, a song she hadn't heard in many years. She sat up and applied a gob of Pantene on the top of her head as she began to sing:

"You live in a church where you sleep with voodoo dolls and you won't give up the search for the ghosts in the halls; you wear sandals in the snow and a smile that won't wash away, can you look out the window," Becky, "without your shadow getting in the way?

Oh, you're so beautiful, Zach, with an edge and a charm but so careful when I'm in your arms … 'cause you're working building a mystery, holding on and holding it in; yeah, you're working building a mystery and choosing so carefully."

Becky sudded her scalp and as shampoo dripped from her temples, she started to scream:

"You woke up screaming aloud, a prayer from your secret god, you feed off our fears and hold back your tears, you give us a tantrum," Zach, "and a know-it-all grin just when we need one, when the evening's thin … oh, you're a beautiful, a beautiful fucked up man, you're setting up your razor wire shrine … 'cause you're working building a mystery, holding on and holding it in. "Yeah, you're working building a mystery and choosing so carefully."

Becky dunked under the water and scrubbed the suds from her scalp as she watched as Zach went down on her and she waterlogged the bed. She lifted herself out of the tub still humming as she wrapped a penguin beach towel around her breasts and walked slowly, conscious of keeping her legs as close together as possible as she walked into her bedroom.

She slipped into a black-and-white teddy and hopped into bed; and as she closed her eyes, she began to smile as she hummed just before passing out:

"Yeah, you're working, building a mystery, holding on and holding it in; yeah, you're working building a mystery and choosing so carefully"….

The sun blinded Becky's eyes at 6:25 a.m. She turned over and put her head under the pillow. She tried to turn over but the pain between her buttocks could not be ignored. "Oh, my God" she mumbled as she held herself thinking: "I gotta pee." She stood up and walked with her legs clenched together toward the back of her bedroom door. She swiped her bathrobe off the hanger and slid it on as she ran down the hall.

Becky walked into the kitchen and set her Keurig to brew a Green Mountain Columbian as she peered down noticing that her bare crotch was clearly visible, and she blushed as she tied her bathrobe tightly around her waist. She took her coffee back to her bedroom and sat on the edge of her bed. She placed the mug on her nightstand as she bit open the UTI magic relief pills and swallowed two while downing half her mug. She struggled to dress herself, still unable to wear a thong as it rubbed irritatingly across her swollen vulva. She smiled as she thought: "Time to buy some old lady undies," as she made her way into the living room and turned on her PC.

There were ten new emails, nine from Zach sent from his iPhone, and Becky nodded her head back and forth as she smiled and opened the first timed at 12:35 p.m. from the evening before: "Hi, just got home. Can't stop thinking 'bout you."

Becky smiled and nodded her head raising her eyebrows as she opened the second email timed at 12:55: "Hi, miss you already … Z." She clicked on the third as her eyes widened and her jaw dropped: "Don't want to wash, still smell you on my fingers … Z."

“Seriously?” Becky said out loud as she read the last email timed at 5:45 a.m.: “Hi beautiful … listen, here is my calendar for the week. I trust you, implicitly and explicitly. Please find time to work on the ‘Hill’ plea. Maureen O’Malley is available to consult, told her you were brilliant, didn’t need any help, but she’ll be there if you need her (p.s. How’s my girl?)”

Becky’s face grew pale and her eyes stared at the floor: “How’s my girl, how’s my girl?” repeated in her mind as her body twitched and she opened the pdf attached to the email and briefly glanced at the docket.

“Bench trial with Woodbury Tuesday 9 a.m.” she read out loud … “hmmm, nice of you tell me, Zach” she mumbled as she smiled and began to hum: “Yeah, you’re working building a mystery and choosing so carefully.”

She queued his calendar to print on her Laserjet as she walked into the kitchen and brewed another cup of coffee. She grabbed the two freshly printed pages and read over his busy docket as she downed her mug. She walked slowly trying not to move her legs too far apart as she walked into her bedroom and grabbed a scrunchie off the bureau. She threw her hair up into a loose ponytail and screamed “Ow” as she bent down to pull her jeans up.

“Oy,” she whispered as she sat on the edge of her bed running her right hand over her engorged vulva and squinched her nose as she closed her eyes and whispered “Zach.”

Becky walked back to her PC and went onto ECF, went to Query, and typed in “12-30225.” As the case queued listing all of the named defendants, she clicked on “Edward Hubbard” and scrolled through the docket until she came to an intriguing motion entitled: “Motion to Rescind Rule 11 Plea.” She opened the pdf and began chewing on the cap of her pen:

“Now comes the Defendant, Edward Hubbard, seeking to rescind his former Rule 11 guilty plea” … Becky’s eyes skipped through the next several paragraphs of dense legalese until she came to the fifth bullet point:

"The Defendant, Edward Hubbard, was promised protection in exchange for his cooperation and truthful testimony against several of the named defendants herein … AUSA Zachary Woods assured the Defendant that he would be placed into the Federal United States Witness Protection Program (WITSEC) as he awaited trial. However, Mr. Hubbard remained in the general population at Wyatt Detention Center and was viciously attacked approximately three days later on September 12, 2009, while sleeping in his cell. Defendant Hubbard received more than 20 lacerations and was airlifted to Massachusetts General Hospital where he underwent emergency cardiac surgery" …

Becky skipped to the last sentence of the last page: "Defendant Hubbard remains in solitary confinement at Wyatt and wishes to recant and rescind his former Rule 11 plea … Timothy O'Brien, Federal Public Defender's Office, State of Massachusetts, 51 Sleeper Street, Boston, MA."

"Hmmm," Becky mumbled as she mutilated her pen cap, "interesting." Becky printed several pdfs from Hubbard's docket. She stood over the HP as it hummed thinking: "He's the one. He's the one."

Becky heard the unique zing of a new email and smiled, knowing intuitively it was Zach. She hunched over her PC as she opened it: "Hi, babe … leaving in an hour. I'll call ya … how you walking today, beautiful?"

Becky nodded her head back and forth as her face took on a solemn pout: "Now, I'm his whore," she said in her mind: "Now, I'm his whore." Becky turned around and shuffled the newly printed pages into a neat bundle as another zing echoed. She opened the email and smiled as she read: "(p.s. I love you, baby … Z.)"

Sunday it poured all day as Becky sat at her PC researching and ingesting every nuance and seemingly unimportant enigma of the Veloz case. At 2:30 her cell rang: "Hi," Amanda whispered, "you know who this is, Becky?"

Becky smiled as she said: "Hi, Mandy."

"Wondering how you are?" Amanda said as Becky smiled: "Sore, real sore, but okay."

Amanda giggled: "Sore, huh? … Had a good night, I take it?"

"Unbelievable," Becky whispered blushing as silence crept in. "Um, um, um" --

"You end this?" Amanda said as she raised her brows.

"Um, um, um," Becky stammered as she searched for her words.

"You didn't … I knew it, Becky" --

"I can't, Amanda," Becky said as she stared at the floor and pouted.

"You can't or you won't?" Amanda asked as Becky swallowed her gum and momentarily gagged.

"I can't … I, I, I --"

"You love him, that's what you're gonna say, right? Jesus, Becky."

"I do, Amanda. I do," Becky said as she unwrapped another piece of Juicyfruit.

"Uh-huh," Amanda said as she paced and nodded as Becky chomped her gum, "he's gonna hurt you, you know." Becky bit her tongue and yelled "Ow" as Amanda whispered: "You know he's never gonna leave her." Becky stared at her feet as Amanda nodded her head back and forth nervously biting her bottom lip. "It's not my place to judge you, Becky."

"Aren't you?" Becky said as a single tear fell from the corner of her left eye. "I tried to end it; I just can't right now," Becky said as she blew a tiny bubble from her gum. The Juicyfruit stuck to her lips, and Becky tried to wipe it off with her fingers as the gum stuck to her hand: “Can I call you right back?” she whispered as she stared at her gummy hand.

“Sure,” Amanda said as Becky placed her iPhone on the desk. Becky washed her hands in the kitchen sink: “She’s right,” she said out loud as she scrubbed the gum off her fingers, “he’s never gonna leave his family ... he’s playing you,” as she wiped her hands on the kitchen towel hanging off the stove. She shook her head and watched as Zach licked her from the floor, and she grinned and whispered: “Zach.”

Becky dialed Amanda’s number and just as Amanda said “Hi,” Becky began nervously spouting: “Listen, been doing a lot of thinking about the Veloz case. I want to meet with Hubbard.”

“Eddie Hubbard, seriously?” Amanda said excitedly as she began to bite her thumbnail.

“Seriously, he’s the only one who can nail Veloz.”

“Hmmm, maybe,” Amanda said as she dropped her Android, “sorry ‘bout that,” she said as Becky chuckled … “you know he’s recanted, trying to rescind his plea.”

“Yeah, I know but I think I can reach him. I want permission to go to Wyatt tomorrow. I want you to come, ‘k’?”

“Okay,” Amanda said as she examined her intact Android, “listen: put a call in to Angela … only way Hubbard will cooperate is if you get him the hell out of there.”

“Already did,” Becky whispered, “spoke to her at noon.”

“Oh?,” Amanda said as she smiled and thought, “you go girlfriend.”

“Yeah, explained the whole Veloz scenario, the whole Hill saga. She agreed to place him into federal protection and release him immediately, you know, that is, if he'll cooperate."

"Wow," Amanda whispered, "unbelievable … you're great, you know that?"

"Yeah? Thanks," Becky whispered: "Listen, meet me in front of the Moakley at 8 a.m. tomorrow morn, okay?"

Amanda paced as she whispered: "Um, Becky, we need some marshals with us, don't you think?"

"Amanda, I'm not stupid," Becky said as Amanda's mind reeled: "Oh, really … you're fucking Zach, aren't ya?"

"Okay … maybe I am," Becky said as she grinned, "Marshals, Pete and John, they're taking us to Wyatt in a white van. Be there at 8?"

"You're not stupid," Amanda said, "just a little, say, confused I think ... see ya tomorrow, Becky."

"Amanda?" Becky whispered.

"Yeah, girlfriend?" Amanda said as Becky grinned.

"Thanks, Mandy" Becky whispered as she squeezed her thighs together and winced and mouthed: "Ow."

"See ya tomorrow, girlfriend," Amanda said as urine dripped down the inside of Becky's left thigh."

The second Becky hit disconnect, her iPhone buzzed in her palm. Becky glanced at the screen: "Zach" it displayed.

"Hi beautiful," he whispered, "miss me?"

"Hmmm," Becky moaned as she smiled.

"Listen, can't talk long … wife's in the shower and Emily's passed out cold. How's my girl?"

Becky's body began to convulse; she closed her eyes and heard her father's raspy voice: "How's my girl?, how's my girl?" She opened her eyes and twitched as she ran her right hand across her vulva which remained highly engorged: "sore."

"I bet," Zach whispered: "taking them little magic pills?"

"Mmm," Becky said as Zach giggled.

"Listen, I got a call from Angela … be careful with Hubbard, will ya?"

"What do you mean?" Becky whispered as she yelled: "Why am I whispering?" as Zach giggled.

"Um, he's a dangerous dude; you'll be fine. If you can get him to cooperate, I told Angela to, um, you know, give you free reign but" --

"Zach?" Becky said as she clenched her thighs together.

"Yeah?" Zach said as he grinned and unhooked his zipper and stuck his left hand into his shorts cupping his erection: "Hmmm?"

"Miss me?" Becky asked as she grabbed her right breast and squeezed it through her shirt and bra causing milk to ooze from her sore nipple.

"Mmm," Zach moaned as he began to masturbate, "you have no idea -- shit, Becky, gotta go," he whispered as he hit disconnect as Becky stared at her touchscreen as the rain pelted against the window and a dark shroud descended upon her. She walked slowly into her bedroom and climbed into bed and stripped naked. She closed her eyes and whispered "Zach" as she watched as he looked up into her eyes and whispered softly: "I love you, Becky."

"Ow" she screamed as she attempted to turn, grabbed the Vaseline from her nightstand, and inserted her pointer finger in. She played with herself as she smeared the goop inside of her, closed her eyes, and watched as Zach licked her from the floor as she fiddled and smiled as she felt her juice run down her thighs. She closed her eyes and whispered "Zach" and fell fast asleep….

Becky watched hovering above a twin bed; there was a little girl who seemed oddly familiar and a middle-aged man who lied next to her naked under The Little Mermaid comforter. The little girl sobbed as her father whispered: "harder." A woman appeared in the doorway. She screamed: "Bobby, what are you doing!" as the little girl wept and the old man came as he whispered: "Shhh." Becky awoke at 3:12 and sat up in her bed. "How's my girl?, how's my girl?" repeating in her mind as tears streaked her cheeks.

Becky stepped into the metal detector in the lobby at 7:15 and her mind moaned: "Coffee, I need coffee" as she walked into the coffee shop on the ground floor. "Hi, Alan," she said with a grin.

"Hi, Becky, how you doing?," Alan said as he smiled and poured the Dunkin' blend into a large styrofoam cup: "cream and sugar, right?"

"Yeah, please, Alan … thanks," Becky said as he placed it on the countertop and she slid a 5 into his open right palm as her stomach growled and Alan giggled: "Hungry?"

"Mmm," she moaned, "um, give me a coffee roll too, will ya -- oh, and keep the change."

Becky tried to sit down at the rear table facing the magazine rack. Her face scrunched as her ass made contact and her hose rubbed ferociously against her swollen anus. "Oh, my God," she thought as she felt liquid ooze from both nipples: "What the hell is wrong with me?" she thought as she inhaled her large coffee roll and downed half her coffee as she grinned as her mind's eye flashed backwards to her straddling the edge of the bed and Zach on his knees licking her insanely to orgasm. Again, milk infiltrated her bra. "Jesus, what's wrong with me?" she thought as she felt liquid ooze down her right thigh.

Becky walked out of the main entrance of the Moakley and walked over to the white van parked behind a yellow cab. The door opened as Peter smiled: "Hi, Becky."

"Hi, Pete," Becky said with a smile as she hopped in and stared at her cell: "7:45." Peter smiled at Becky: "So have a nice weekend, Becky?"

"Yeah, great … you?" Becky said as she sat down and winced.

"Great, yeah -- well, had my grandson's graduation Saturday … five hours!" he exclaimed exasperated.

"That's great … I know, so boring, right?"

"Um, yeah … that's putting it nicely," Peter said as Becky chuckled: "Where'd he go to school, Pete?"

"MIT, he's a brilliant kid."

"Good school, Pete; that's awesome" Becky said smiling as Amanda approached the van and Peter opened the door for her. The van pulled in front of the Donald W. Wyatt Detention Center in Central Falls at 9:20. Peter looked at Becky and smiled: "Listen, girls, you're not allowed to bring anything in. I mean like anything: no jewelry, no phones, nothing."

Amanda took out her hoop earrings and began to unhook her 18-inch gold chain from around her neck. Becky took off her Harvard ring and her bracelet as Peter smiled: "Yeah, and your purses too." Amanda placed her jewelry inside the inner zipped pocket of her brown leather bag as Becky said: "What about this?" holding up her briefcase.

"Na. You're an attorney; they'll let that in." Becky carefully placed her jewelry inside her purse as Peter smiled: "John will be in the van waiting for us ... ready?"

As a guard buzzed them into the facility with Peter out front and

Becky and Amanda nervously giggling behind him, a female officer smiled: “Ladies, come with me please.” Becky and Amanda were lead into a small room as Peter smiled as the guard waved a wand over his body and Peter began emptying his pockets and handed him his firearm.

The female officer waved a wand over Amanda as Becky watched smiling. “Please turn around” she whispered as she patted Amanda down. Amanda giggled as Becky was frisked and Becky whispered: “Yeah … what’s so funny, Amanda?”

Peter joked with the hefty male guard as Becky and Amanda followed them down a long white hallway with columns painted in beige. They approached two massive double glass doors and a buzz annoyingly sounded as the doors opened. They were led into a small conference room where Eddie Hubbard sat smoking a cigarette as his left hand twirled a Marlboro pack.

“Mr. Hubbard?” Becky said as she approached and shook his right hand as he stood, “Becky Lawrence.” Hubbard smiled at her as he blew smoke away from her face: “How you doin’?” he mumbled as he coughed.

“This is Amanda Jenkins.” Amanda smiled nervously and sat down at the table mouthing “hi.”

“Hi,” Hubbard said as he put out his cigarette into a tiny glass ashtray and winked at Amanda causing her body to twitch.

“Peter Walsh,” Pete said as Hubbard grabbed his left hand and seized him with a vice grip mumbling: “Hey, how you doin.”

Two armed guards entered the conference room and closed, then locked the door. Amanda tapped Becky’s left arm as she sat down at the table looking inquisitively.

“Protocol, sorry,” the 300-pound-plus armed guard said, as he smiled and sat down next to the door.

“Um, Mr. Hubbard,” Becky said, “I was told Tim O’Brien would be here?”

“Yeah, he’s, um, running late,” Hubbard said as a buzz echoed loudly.

Tim O’Brien was standing just outside the conference room door as the hefty guard’s Motorola began to squeak: “Defense attorney, let him in.” The guard stood and unlocked the door as Timmy rushed in panting: “Sorry” he said out of breath as Becky stood, and they shook hands.

“Nice to see you, Becky” Tim said as he winked at her and sat down next to Hubbard. “How you doin?” Hubbard mumbled in his raspy tone as Tim smiled: “Sorry, everyone … traffic.”

Becky shook her head as Timmy smiled at her: “Mr. Hubbard, I think you know why we’re here.”

Hubbard shook his head and nervously lit another smoke: “Call me Eddie?”

Becky smiled: “Okay, Eddie.” Becky opened her briefcase and pulled out Hubbard’s Rule 11 plea. She placed it in front of Tim as Eddie glanced through the first page recognizing it and stared at her as he blew a smoke ring into the ceiling.

“Eddie, if the Judge approves your pending motion and rescinds the plea, you will go to trial; you understand that?”

“Hmmm” Eddie moaned as he blew another smoke ring and Becky coughed.

“If this case goes to trial, you will be found guilty and you will spend the rest of your life in prison; you know that?”

“So?” Eddie said as his eyebrows arched and he coughed on his smoke.

“Not only will you face murder, corruption, and RICO violations here in Boston, but the States of Oklahoma and Florida will seek the death penalty; you understand?”

Eddie nervously looked at Timmy who affirmatively nodded as he placed his hand on Hubbard’s right forearm for reassurance.

Becky stared straight on into Hubbard’s eyes: “There is no excuse for the delay that occurred that caused you to be brutally attacked.”

“Yeah, I almost fuckin’ died ‘cause of you people” Hubbard muttered as Tim grabbed his right forearm nodding his head back and forth whispering: “Shhh, let her speak.”

“I know,” Becky said as she stared straight on into his bulging eyes: “I can’t make excuses or justify what happened.”

Hubbard put out his cigarette and lit another coughing as he stared at Becky.

“I can only tell you that if you will reconsider and cooperate with the government now” … Becky reached into her open briefcase and pulled out a ten-page stapled document entitled: “Cooperation Agreement” and placed it in front of Hubbard. Tim was straining to read it over his shoulder as Becky smiled and handed him a duplicate copy: “For you” she whispered as he grabbed it and mouthed: “Thank you.”

Tim read through the copious agreement as Hubbard whispered to him intermittently, and Timmy held up his right hand whispering “Shhh.” Becky smiled at Amanda who winked at her as Tim said: “Could I have a minute with my client, please?”

Becky and Amanda rose from their respective chairs and walked toward the door. Peter whispered to the guard playing Angry Birds on his iPhone: “They need a minute.”

“Oh, sure” he said as he stood and slipped his cell into his bulging right pocket. Becky smiled at Amanda as they stared at his butt crack as he pulled up his pants and they giggled noticing his American Dad brief. Amanda deliberately knocked into her, and they both broke out into an enormous, radiating mutual smile.

Five minutes later the conference room door opened and a tall lanky guard smiled: "All set, counsel."

Becky, Amanda, and Peter walked into the room as Hubbard lit a smoke and Tim whispered into his left ear causing Hubbard to giggle.

"How you doin?" Hubbard said with a grin as he blew smoke upwards into the ceiling causing the light to reflect its hazy waves. "Just got one question: this says in exchange for my cooperation and substantial assistance" --

"You'll be released immediately," Becky interjected, "today, right now" … Becky stared at Hubbard who whispered to Timmy as he smiled and said: "He needs protection."

Becky stared momentarily and grinned at Tim: "Eddie, you will be placed into the Federal United States Witness Protection Program today, this afternoon, as soon as possible. You will be released from Wyatt today, given a new identity. We will arrange for you and your family to be flown to an undisclosed location."

Hubbard blew a smoke ring and smiled: "You got a deal, counsel" he said as he grinned.

Timmy smiled at Becky who blushed: "One little caveat, Ms. Lawrence: Mr. Hubbard has been contacted by an influential local author who is writing a book called "The Assassin." Hubbard has already been given $250,000 for his assistance."

"His assistance?," Becky repeated as she grinned as her mind flashed back to Second Year Criminal Law 300. She watched as her Professor, Professor White, paced nervously in front of the podium:

"Let's talk, people, a little bit about the Federal Son of Sam Law.

We're at "Title 18," people, "Crimes and Criminal Procedure, Part II, Chapter 232A, 18 USCS § 3681 (2000) § 3681: Order of Special Forfeiture."

"Ms. Lawrence," Philip White said as he winked at her, "could you read this to the class please?"

Becky stood as her hands shook as she read:

"Upon the motion of the United States Attorney made at any time after conviction of a defendant for an offense under section 794 of this title or for an offense against the United States resulting in physical harm to an individual, and after notice to any interested party, the court shall, if the court determines that the interest of justice or an order of restitution under this title so requires, order such defendant to forfeit all or any part of proceeds received or to be received by that defendant, or a transferee of that defendant, from a contract relating to a depiction of such crime in a movie, book, newspaper, magazine, radio, or television production, or live entertainment of any kind, or an expression of that defendant's thoughts, opinions, or emotions regarding such crime."

"Ms. Lawrence, thoughts?"

Becky remained standing as she spoke: "I don't think it's right that the government has to make an order like this. It should be automatic; defendants who are found or plead guilty should not be able to profit from their crimes, sir."

"Becky?" Amanda whispered as she kicked her shin under the table. Becky's eyes widened as the pain radiated straight to her brain jarring her into the present tense.

"I see," Becky said as Tim continued: "Mr. Hubbard will be given another $250,000 after the book is published."

"I see," Becky said as she thought, "unbelievable!"

"And he's already been contacted by "Dreamtime" to possibly

produce his life story. They gave him $250,000 up front; and if the movie is actually produced, they're searching for funds, he'll receive another quarter of a million at release."

Becky stared at Amanda as she thought: "Son of a bitch … guy admits to killing 20 people and makes a million bucks and now he walks free … what the hell am I doing?"

Becky stared at Tim as he tried to decipher her inner thoughts through her contorted facial cues. "All right. That's no problem, but here's my caveat, Mr. Hubbard: "Aside from this one book and this one movie deal, you will not profit in the future: deal?"

Hubbard whispered to O'Brien and stood, laying his smoldering butt into the ashtray. He outstretched his right hand, and Becky stood and grinned as they shook hands firmly. The buzz of the door blasted and the short stalky guard opened it as five FBI special agents approached.

"These agents will process you into WITSEC and arrange for your immediate release. I will need you to appear in Courtroom No. 1 at the John J. Moakley United States Courthouse on Thursday at 9:00 a.m. to briefly rescind your motion to withdraw your Rule 11."

Hubbard stared at Becky and mumbled: "Rule 11?"

"Your plea, Mr. Hubbard, and advise the judge of your intention to testify against" --

"Veloz?" Hubbard interjected as he stared at her.

"Jose Veloz," Becky said as Tim whispered into Hubbard's ear.

"Immediately after Thursday's hearing you and your family will be transported to another state. The agents will advise you further."

Hubbard approached Becky as she gasped for air and hugged her as guns were drawn. "It's okay" Becky whispered as the agents simultaneously disarmed, and Hubbard whispered: "Thank you, Ms.

Lawrence … you won't regret this."

Becky followed Peter and Amanda into the hallway thinking: "I already do, Mr. Hubbard; I already do."

As they walked down the long white hallway with an uneven floor, Becky whispered into Amanda's left ear as she tripped: "Now I'm making deals with the devil" and Amanda shrugged her shoulders as she whispered: "This is our only chance to nail Veloz, and he's been murdering people for 20 years."

Becky shook her head and stared at her feet as Amanda read her mind and pinned her into the wall momentarily: "Listen to me: everything Hubbard did was ordered by Veloz. You're doing the right thing here."

Becky grinned as she mouthed: "You think?"

"No, I know." They continued to walk following Peter who waited for them before the double glass doors raising his eyebrows whispering: "Problem, counsel?"

Becky grinned: "No, no problem, Pete," and mouthed to Amanda who was smiling at her, "thank you."

As they walked through the foyer, Amanda whispered as she deliberately bumped into Becky's left side: "You know that old expression, Becky" -- Becky stopped short as Peter held the main door to the Wyatt open for them as Becky shrugged her shoulders.

-- "you know," Amanda said as she smiled, "you got to walk a mile in someone else's shoes, right?" Becky smiled as she saw Zach smiling at her on his knees lapping her as she whispered to Amanda: "I miss him already." Amanda rolled her eyes back and shook her head as Becky whispered: "Pathetic, huh?"

Peter walked a hundred feet in front of them as Amanda leaned into her: "Good job today, counselor" as Becky grinned and they hopped into the van. Becky closed her eyes as Amanda joked with Peter. Her mind fixated on Hill's brief colloquy in Zach's office, which had seemingly unraveled before her eyes:

Q. Are you aware that Christopher Russo, ten years old, was caught in the crossfire, shot in the back, and is now a quadriplegic?
A. Nope.
Q. And if I told you that Chris Russo will spend the rest of his life in a wheelchair and will need 24-hour medical assistance, how would you feel?
A. Um, like shit.
Q. Uh-huh. Do you feel personally responsible being a member of the Bloods?
A. Fuck you.
Q. Excuse me, Mr. Hill?
A. You heard me, you cretin.

As the van pulled in front of the Moakley, Becky's iPhone vibrated in her black slacks. She walked following Amanda and Peter into the courthouse holding her phone away from the sun and angulating it, attempting to read the screen: "Zach …how'd it go, babe?"

Becky texted: "Made deal" as she walked inside the courthouse and lost reception. Amanda was waiting for her in between the two sets of double heavy glass doors: "Let me guess?" she whispered as Becky smirked. As they walked through the metal detector, Becky grabbed Amanda's left sleeve: "So what's this bench trial with Woodbury tomorrow?"

Amanda started giggling as they walked into the coffee shop: "Interesting actually."

"Oh, do tell," Becky said as her phone read, "message sent."

"Okay," Amanda said as she leaned against the brick façade as Alan yelled: "Hi Becky."

"Hi, Alan," Becky replied as Amanda leaned forward: "This shouldn't be too long … guy murdered his wife with a coat hanger. He's been in prison now for, I don't know, long time, and sued the

State of Massachusetts for violating his Eighth Amendment rights by refusing to follow the advice of several experts to provide him essential medical care, i.e., Sex Reassignment Surgery."

"Oh, I know this case," Becky said as her eyes widened and her brows raised.

"Yeah, you know, says 'he's a man trapped in a woman's body.'" Becky nodded her head as Amanda whispered: "he's at MCI Framingham … anyway, Woodbury already found and issued an order that the Department of Corrections, the defendant, had been deliberately indifferent to the plaintiff's serious medical need for sex reassignment surgery and ordered the Department of Corrections forthwith to take all actions reasonably necessary to provide sex reassignment surgery as promptly as possible."

"Yeah, I read about this," Becky said as she bobbed her head and Alan yelled: "The usual, Becky?"

"Yes, please. Thanks, Alan … you want something?"

Amanda yelled: "Hi, Alan, I'll have the same."

"Hi, Amanda," Alan said with a grin as he turned around and began pouring coffee into the styrofoam containers.

"I don't get it, Amanda. Why would an Assistant United States Attorney be involved here?"

"No, the federal government isn't involved in this case; Woodbury wants you to sit in and advise him."

"Oh," Becky said as they walked toward the counter, and Alan placed their large regulars in front of them, "this is the case the Judge wanted me to consult and advise."

"Thanks, Alan," Amanda said as she threw a 10 on the counter and Becky picked it up and placed it gently into his right open palm. "Thanks, Becky," Alan said as he smiled.

“It’s for both,” Amanda said smiling: “on me today, girlfriend.”

“Thanks, girlfriend,” Becky said as Alan reached out with his right hand extended holding the change.

“You keep it today, my friend,” Amanda said as the girls walked toward the elevator.

“Still don’t understand why the Judge wants my input on this” Becky whispered as they stepped into the elevator, and Amanda pressed “9.”

“He likes you a little,” Amanda said with a smile. “Also, you’ve got a 2:00 status, Zach’s case, of course; um, you might want to briefly look at the pending motion on this one.”

“Sure,” Becky said smiling as the elevator stopped on the ninth as Becky’s iPhone began to buzz. Becky stared at Amanda who shook her head back and forth as Becky whispered: “I’ve got to take this.”

“Hi, Zach,” Amanda yelled as she walked toward reception with her coffee.

Becky answered as she walked toward the glass wall overlooking the harbor: “Hey” she whispered as the sky darkened.

“Hey,” Zach whispered, “good job today, counselor.”

“Mmm, thanks,” Becky said as she grinned.

“Listen,” Zach whispered as Becky strained to hear, “my wife knows.”

“What?” Becky shrieked as she stared at her touchscreen dumbfoundedly, “how?”

White noise infiltrated reception and Zach began to scream: “Becky?” which was muted through the surrounding chaos,

"Becky?" The call dropped and Becky opened the rim of her coffee and began to sip. She glanced at the screen as it said "11:22," and it vibrated in her palm.

"Hey," Zach whispered.

"Hey," Becky said smiling as coffee dribbled down her chin. "Hold on a sec," she whispered as she placed her coffee on the marble tile and swiped her chin with the back of her left hand. She held the cell nestled between her right ear and shoulder as she picked up the coffee with her left.

"Sorry," she said, "how, Zach: you tell her?"

"Um, no -- well, not in words I guess."

"Huh?" Becky said as she took another heaping gulp.

"Emily fell asleep real early last night, like 8:30. We'd spent the day at the water park and, you know, wore her out."

"Hmmm," Becky said as she took another sip.

"My wife tried to kiss me; I turned my head. She tried to hug me, but, um, I just pulled away."

"Thought you said you haven't had sex with her since Emily was born?" Becky whispered and then guzzled.

"Yeah, and she had no interest … 'til last night."

"So?" Becky asked as she downed the rest of her coffee.

"So I couldn't touch her. She kept trying to, you know, and I couldn't touch her."

"Zach" --

"Becky," Zach interrupted, "she cupped me, you know, trying to get me" --

"Hard?" Becky asked angrily.

"Yeah, and I pulled away. She starts freaking on me: "Who are you fucking, Zach?, who are you fucking?"

"And you said, Mr. Woods?" Becky said as she grimaced and thunder erupted in the sky just outside the panes.

"I just looked away … she started freaking out."

"Zach," Becky whispered, "I don't know what to say."

"Where are you right now?" Zach asked as he groaned and stuck his left hand down his shorts.

"On the ninth, on the balcony, watching the sky opening up" Becky whispered as Zach moaned.

"Do a favor for me?" Zach said as he groaned and began to pull on himself. "Go to your office, lock the door, and call me back?"

"Okay," Becky said, "give me five."

"Becky?" Zach said as he began to breathe heavily.

"Yeah?" Becky asked as she thought: "He'll full of shit … he's playing you, he's 'building a mystery and choosing so carefully.'"

"I love you," Zach whispered as he pulled his brief down to his knees.

"I love you too, Mr. Woods," Becky whispered as she hit disconnect and ran to the ladies room mumbling out loud: "Oh, my God … I'm not gonna make it."

Five minutes later Becky locked her office door and sat at her desk and booted up her PC. She walked over to the window and watched as the rain pelted against the glass as she dialed “Zach.”

“Hi beautiful,” Zach whispered, “you alone?”

“Mmm,” Becky answered as she lowered the blind.

“What are you wearing, babe?” Zach asked as he stood in the hotel bathroom naked sitting on the toilet cupping his balls in his left hand. “Do something for me, Ms. Lawrence?” Zach said as he began to masturbate and moan.

“Anything, Zach,” Becky said as she closed her eyes.

“Get naked, will ya?” Zach said as he moaned.

“Zach, I can’t; I’m” --

“Hurting, huh? Okay, beautiful,” Zach whispered as he panted, “close your eyes. I’m eating you, baby, can you feel it?” Becky’s body began to sway as she pulled her pantyhose to her knees.

“Mmm,” Becky moaned as Zach whispered: “Take your pointer finger of your right hand and very slowly put it in your mouth and make it wet for me.”

“Zach,” Becky whispered, “what are you doing?”

“Take that wet finger and put it inside you … I’m licking your ass, baby.”

“Oh, God,” Becky whispered as her juice dribbled down her right inner thigh.

“You wet for me?” Zach said as he stood continuing to cup himself with his left hand as his right hand masturbated as he licked his bottom lip.

“Mmm,” Becky said as she began to delicately touch her clit as she winced. “You’re pushing my head in deeper and deeper” … Becky began to moan as cum dripped down both inner thighs meandering to her knees.

"Very slowly wiggle that wet finger in and out for me … now, close your eyes."

"Oh, God, Zach," Becky stammered as she dropped the cell to the floor … "sorry," she whispered as she smiled.

"Now take that wet finger and slowly rub it across your anus for me?"

"Zach," Becky whispered as she moaned.

"You wet?" Zach said as he felt his ejaculate approach.

"Ahhh" she moaned as he giggled: "Now put that wet finger back inside your ass, close your eyes; can you see me licking you, baby?"

Liquid began pouring down Becky's legs. "Hold on a sec," she whispered as she slid her pantyhose off her ankles and sat at her desk. She put both legs onto the desktop and grabbed an empty water bottle and began gently putting it inside of her with her left hand as she held the iPhone with her right.

"Oh, God," she whispered as cum dripped onto the chair underneath her.

"What you doing, baby?" Zach said as he panted and masturbated.

"Zach," Becky moaned as her torrent drenched the floor, and Zach sat back on the toilet and came onto his stomach."

Becky closed her eyes as she listened to him climax and stuck the bottle as deep as it would penetrate as she whispered: "What are you doing to me, Zach?"

Zach giggled as he wiped his hand onto a wet towel he picked up from the floor. "Becky," Zach whispered as he sat back down on the toilet and cupped himself with his left hand, "you still wet?"

Slowly Becky lifted the bottle out; and as she did, she screamed: "Ahhh" as she stood and her juice deluge flooded her thighs.

Zach grew hard within his left palm as Becky moaned. "Sit down, baby, and spread your legs for me?" he whispered.

Becky sat back down in her sopping chair and threw her legs up, each foot delicately balancing on the desk's rim. "Now, close your eyes. You're sitting on the edge of the bed in the Eliot Hotel and slowly, very slowly, I'm inserting my tongue inside you." Becky began to hump the chair as liquid dripped from the seat onto the floor under her desk. She stuck the pointer finger of her left hand inside her as he spoke:

"Now I'm teasing you, baby … licking you softly, gently, the tip of my tongue wiggling your clit."

"Zach," Becky screamed as she climaxed and saturated the floor. She looked down and noticed a heaping, good-sized puddle of liquid under her desk and shook her head back and forth.

"I miss you," she whispered as she grabbed a handful of Kleenex and patted herself dry as her face contorted in pain.

"Shit! Gotta go, babe," Zach whispered as Becky stared at her touchscreen. Slowly she dressed herself and began cleaning her seat with a wad of scrunched-up Kleenex as liquid ran down her right inner thigh and her nipples stood erect. She lightly touched her right nipple through her blouse and said: "Ow, what the f- ... my nipples hurt; Jesus, what the hell is this?"

After Becky cleaned her chair and rolled her pantyhose up each leg, her iPhone vibrated on the desk. She picked it up noticing her touchscreen was blurry. It said: "Wife walked in with Em … how's my girl? … Z."

Becky's body convulsed and she swelled with tears as she sat down in front of her PC. She closed her eyes and heard her father's voice: "How's my girl?, how's my girl?," as she twitched. She opened her eyes and whispered "Zach," and opened her email occasionally feeling herself drip intermittently, saturating her pantyhose: "Crap, I'm in court at 3 today?" she mumbled as she perused Zach's weekly calendar.

Becky looked at the motion hearing pending at 3:00: Docket No. 07-cr-10924. Chan v United States of America, et al. She went onto ECF and queried the docket and pulled up the pending motion. It read: "Motion for Judgment as a Matter of Law or in the Alternative a New Trial." She quickly scanned the document.

"Defendant requests that the court order a new trial pursuant to Federal Rule of Civil Procedure 59. As grounds, Defendant Washington states that the evidence presented at trial showed that every sexual encounter between the Plaintiff, Kristen Chan, and the Defendant, Moses Washington, was consensual in nature."

"What's this?" Becky said as she continued to scan: "This Court previously ruled that, because of the inherent imbalance of power between an inmate and a correction officer, it could not agree with the majority of courts that have ruled that voluntary sexual encounters do not, as a matter of law, rise to the level of a constitutional violation.

The Court stated that, given this inherent imbalance, true consent cannot be determined as a matter of law. Rather, the facts must be presented and the issue determined at trial" … "Hmmm," Becky moaned as she momentarily closed her eyes and whispered "Zach."

"Consensual sexual relations between an inmate and correction officer do not amount to Eighth Amendment violations. In *Freitas v. Ault*, 109 F.3d 1335 (8th Cir. 1997), the Eight Circuit held that as a matter of law sexual conduct between two consenting adults, even in the inmate-correction officer context, does not amount to cruel and unusual punishment because "welcome and voluntary sexual interactions," no matter how inappropriate, cannot as matter of law constitute 'pain' as contemplated by the Eighth Amendment" …

“Seriously, Zach?,” Becky mumbled, “this is a loser.”

“Based on the evidence presented and the jury’s finding regarding the consensual nature of each and every sexual encounter, there can be no finding as a matter of law that Washington violated Chan’s right to be free from cruel and unusual punishment. Judgment should enter, therefore, in the defendant’s favor as to claims alleging violations of the Federal and Massachusetts Civil Rights Acts; or, in the alternative, the Court should order a new trial because the jury’s finding that there was no assault or battery is inconsistent with the finding that Washington violated Chan’s Eighth Amendment rights.”

Becky sighed and queued the pending motion to print. She then opened the Opposition to the Motion and began biting the cap of her pen as she read:

“Regarding their initial encounters,” the plaintiff testified: “I just thought it was a friendship. I thought he was being nice, and it was refreshing after being in a facility where, you know, you're looked at -- you're looked down upon. You know, you're an inmate; they think they're better than you. You're kind of like a caged animal. You don't feel worth too much, and he was nice to me. He talked to me. He made me feel human” ….

“On July 5th, 2003, Defendant Washington asked the plaintiff to meet him in the gym (Trial, Day II, Page 58):

“I was sitting on a bench when he approached me and put one of his legs in between my legs. He asked what I wanted to do, and I shrugged. He told me to come with him and took me to a supply room. Then he unzipped his pants and pulled out his penis. He sat on a chair and called me over to him. He said: “You do me a favor, I do you a favor” as he held his penis in his right hand.
I sucked him; he pulled out a rubber glove and ejaculated into it” …
“Jesus” Becky mumbled as she mutilated her cap between her teeth:

“This was the first of fifty to one hundred sexual encounters between Chan and Washington over the next year occurring in at least twenty-three different places in the prison. The Defendant admitted to often using rubber gloves for "protection," and on one occasion he used a plastic bag"… "Gross" Becky mumbled as she continued to peruse the motion in opposition:

"On cross-examination, Chan was asked:

Q. You could have told him no, correct?
A. You think I could have told him no? I don't think I could have told him no.
Q. I'm just asking for a yes or no, Ms. Chan.
A. No, I couldn't have told him no.
Q. Well, but you never told him no?
A. I just said I couldn't tell him no. This was an environment where you do what you are told: I'm an inmate; I'm supposed to do what I'm told to do. If I'm told to mop the floors, I mop the floors; if I'm told to remake my bed because it's not made well enough, I remake the bed; and if I don't do what I'm told to do, there's consequences to not doing what you're told to do."

"There came a time when Ms. Chan testified she knew that she was being 'used' (Trial Day II, Page 61):

A. I wanted it to end. I didn't know how to stop it . . . I wanted it to end because it was very clear to me I was being used. Like I said, it was maybe five times that we had intercourse out of 100 times that I gave him oral sex. That's nothing, that's not a relationship, that's being used. It's being degraded. It's dirty. It's not what I wanted … I was very ashamed."

"What a loser this one is" Becky said as she queued it to print as her eyes focused on the next excerpt ("Trial Day II, Page 71):

"Q. Did you feel like you had to go along with his sexual demands to keep your rights?
A. Yes, I did."

Becky continued to skim as she stared at her pen cap and placed it on the desktop:

“During the same time period Washington had sexual encounters with at least four other inmates. Although the individual sexual encounters may have been ‘consensual’ -- meaning that the inmates did not outright refuse -- the jury could have come to the conclusion that these ‘relationships’ were coercive. Even Washington recognized that he knew he was abusing his power and ‘taking advantage.’

To be sure, the pain caused by sexual misconduct is not necessarily the same type of physical harm as from beating or excessive force, but it is no less serious, and indeed, in some ways may be even more harmful ... sexual misconduct of guards may cause: significant depression, nausea, frequent headaches, insomnia, fatigue, anxiety, irritability, nervousness, and a profound loss of self-esteem, and these effects are ‘more than enough evidence to satisfy the objective component of the Eighth Amendment.’ Women Prisoners, 877 F. Supp. at 665, rev'd on other grounds.”

“Oy,” Becky said as she skimmed: “The case against Washington could not have been more straightforward. Over the course of almost a year he had Chan perform fellatio fifty to one hundred times, sometimes three times in one night. He confessed to her that he was abusing his authority and taking advantage of her. He knew of her personal background of being molested and raped beginning at age 9, and yet he engaged in this reckless conduct.

In addition to being reckless with her mental health, he was also reckless with her physical health. He used plastic gloves or bags as ‘protection’ when they had intercourse. Indeed, it appeared that it became a game for him, with multiple inmates and sexual encounters in at least twenty-three different places in this small facility. Washington wrote ‘reports’ about rumors as a decoy so as to avoid detection.

The evidence at trial was overwhelming; Washington knew of the risk of harm and was intentionally and deliberately indifferent to it ... the defendant’s motion is premised upon the assertion that Ms. Chan consented to all of the multiple instances of sexual abuse by

Defendant Washington … however, as this Court already has noted, in denying summary judgment on this same issue, that 'a relationship between an inmate and a guard is presumptively coercive.'

Recognizing that, Massachusetts law states that 'an inmate shall be deemed incapable of consent to sexual relations with a person who is employed by or contracts with any penal or correctional institution in the Commonwealth (M.G.L., c. 268 §21A)."

Becky began nervously twirling her pen in her right hand as she read:

"Noting that while consensual sex does not constitute cruel and unusual punishment merely because it occurs in a prison," this Court wrote: "Sex within a prison is simply not the same as sex outside, particularly between a female inmate and her male captor; the relationship between them is inherently unbalanced. A female inmate must rely on her male captor(s) for basic necessities, phone privileges, visits with her children, protection from harm from them or other inmates, health needs.

The men in these circumstances have absolute power over women. Should she wish to end the relationship -- and the termination of coercive relationships is often fraught even in the outside world -- she cannot simply 'leave.' [Docket No. 138, p. 18-19] Thus, the defendant's argument that the plaintiff 'consented' is absurd, even if legally possible.

"It is absurd, Zach!" Becky said as she began biting her fingernails.

"As set forth above, the defendant's motion fails to show that there was no legally sufficient evidentiary basis for a reasonable jury to find for the Plaintiff as this jury did. Accordingly, the defendant's motion for a new trial should be denied."

"Oh, this should be fun" Becky said under her breath as she smiled and walked over to the HP to retrieve the documents in queue. She shuffled the papers together into a neat pile as she mumbled:

“Coffee, coffee, I need coffee.” She placed the stack onto her desk and picked up her cell which read: “2:14” … “coffee,” she mumbled as she stepped off the elevator on the ground floor and walked into the coffee shop.

“Hi, Becky,” Alan said, “the usual?”

“Hi, Alan, please,” Becky sighed as Alan smiled: “Long day, huh?”

“For sure,” Becky said as Alan turned around to pour.

“Pelting out there,” Alan said as he placed the cover onto the styrofoam.

“Thanks, Alan,” Becky said as she placed a 5 into his open right palm. Alan refused to take it, and it fell onto the countertop: “Nope, on me this time,” Alan said as he turned around and put the cream back into the small fridge.

“You’re so great,” Becky said as she opened the rim and began to sip: “Mmm, coffee,” as she yelled: “Thanks, Alan,” and strutted toward the elevator sipping slowly.

Amanda was standing outside Becky’s office, her back leaning against the wall as Becky approached sipping her coffee. “Hey,” Becky whispered as she walked into her office.

“Hi,” Amanda said following her inside, “you ready for this motion?”

Becky picked up her coffee and guzzled it and then sat down at her desk stammering: “Um, um, yeah, I guess, but” --

“I know. Another no-win, you know” Amanda said as she stood and fixed her skirt. “Jury gave Chan like 75k.”

“That’s all?,” Becky said as she finished her coffee and threw the empty cup into her trash can, “could have done a lot better, I suspect, with, you know, better counsel, huh?” Amanda smiled and nodded her head as she walked toward the door: “Ready?”

“I guess,” Becky said with a conniving grin.

Becky and Amanda sat down at the plaintiff’s table as Josh whispered: “Hi, Becky,” and Becky smiled and mouthed: “Hi, Josh.” She looked over at the defense table and smiled at Kristen Chan who smiled back as her attorney stood with his right hand extended and walked toward her: “Hi, Andrew Fishman.”

“Hi, nice to meet you,” Becky said as Josh whispered: “You guys ready?” as counsel took their seats.

Josh announced: “All rise” as Woodbury smiled at Becky and sat at the bench as he whispered in a raspy tone: “Good afternoon, everybody. You can be seated but introduce yourselves before you sit down. You are?”

“Good morning or good afternoon, your Honor. Andrew Fishman for the Plaintiff Kristen Chan.”

Becky stood as Woodbury poured water into his glass: “Good afternoon, your Honor. Rebecca Lawrence for the Government.”

Woodbury took a small sip before he spoke: “There is a motion pending. Counsel, I have read the motion for a new trial and the opposition. Please do not regurgitate your briefs … do you want to start, Ms. Lawrence?

“Well, I think there's sort of a ‘disconnect’ between the facts of this case. It's our contention, and it has been, you know, all along, your Honor, that this was a consensual sexual relationship. (Becky thought: “Oy,” what am I saying?)

Whether there is a legal argument as to whether an inmate can ‘consent,’ factually speaking, this was a consensual sexual relationship, your Honor.” Becky heard a voice whisper from the witness box: “Charlie, Charlie, Charlie.”

Woodbury took a small sip of water: “Then how did your client get convicted of rape?”

Becky thought: “Oh, here we go” … “He didn't get convicted of rape, your Honor.”

Woodbury placed his glass on the bench and with his eyebrows raised: “Then, what was he convicted of precisely, Ms. Lawrence?”

“It's a statute under the Public Justice Chapter, not the crimes against the Person Chapter, of Mass. General Law 268, Section 21A, and that's an important distinction here because under the Public Justice Chapter” --

“Uh-huh, and what does it provide?”

Becky scratched her head: “It actually uses the phrase ‘sexual relations.’ Any employee of an institution cannot have ‘sexual relations’ with an inmate, and ‘consent’ is not a defense in a prosecution, in a criminal prosecution … so that's what he was charged with, that's what he was convicted of, your Honor. He was never charged with rape.”

“I see, Ms. Lawrence. Did he go through a trial? Was he charged?

“No, your Honor; he plead.”

“Okay,” Woodbury said as he raised his glasses off his nose, “Ms. Chan, I mean, the story that she tells, however this may have begun, she tells a story of many of the -- what is it -- 50 to 100 sexual incidents that, however it started, that it became nonconsensual at some point. All you have to do is read that 12-page letter, her handwritten letter, which is something that she did on her own without the aid of the lawyers who were contemplating litigation, and she wrote it on her own.

And if you read that 12-page statement, Ms. Lawrence, it's very difficult to see how any reasonable jury could have concluded that this was a consensual sexual relationship. It starts off with, Ms.

Lawrence:

'Up to three times a night he would come into my room, wake me up for me to give him oral sex. I just have never known how to stop it, and I feared that if I stopped the sexual relationship I would be punished, severely punished, and sent back to the main prison facility.'"

Becky said to herself: "What am I arguing here?" as she spoke: "Your Honor, she may have a hundred explanations as to why she did what she did, but the bottom line is: what she did was consensual by all outward indicia of how she conducted herself.

It's the fact that she proposed to Moses Washington where to go to have sex; it's the fact that she voluntarily went to a designated spot when she didn't need to."

Woodbury said: "Excuse me, Ms. Lawrence, but let me just say here at the outset: I will address the arguments briefed in detail below. I pause to note, however, that the jury's verdict was entirely consistent with the trial record in this case.

The defendants have argued that Chan, even though a prisoner, had consented to the sex and that the consent negated any finding of serious harm. As such, they argued, a jury could not possibly find that there was no 'assault and battery' and yet find a violation of the Eighth Amendment.

The plaintiff countered in their opposition that inmates cannot consent as a matter of law and that *all* sex is a per se violation of the Eighth Amendment.

The jury's verdict belies both contentions. As I noted in refusing to hold on summary judgment that a prisoner's arguable consent *as a matter of law* vitiated the possibility of serious harm under the Eight Amendment:

'Sex in prison is a complex and risky phenomenon; 'consent' is not easy to determine amidst the power dynamics between male captors and female inmates. The analysis is contextual and for the fact finder. An inmate may acquiesce to sexual encounters with a guard, such that they would not meet the formal requirements for assault and battery, and yet those sexual encounters may nevertheless be coercive and intimidating under the circumstances.

Three former inmates and two guards testified at trial that the prison had a highly charged sexual environment. There were a few guards, and at least two of them, Terrence Jackson and Moses Washington, who admitted to having sexual contact with many female inmates. Elsa Jones, an inmate, testified:

'You have men, you have a bunch of women, and 9 times out of 10 the women are overtly flirtatious and sexual because, and I'm not saying it's anyone's fault, but they don't see men very often and it's kind of how it goes, you know. That's just how it is.'

Indeed, around the same time as Washington's misconduct, a scandal broke out at the police barracks when authorities discovered that civilian staff, while employed at the police department, were engaging in sexual contact with female inmates on work crews from SMCC. Interviews as part of the investigations into sexual misconduct at SMCC revealed that inmates 'kept the peek,' meaning they stood watch, while guards had sexual encounters with inmates. (Trial Ex. 12, Investigation Report, July 28, 2004.)

Further, inmates referred to "the Horticultural Room" within the prison as the "Hotel." Sexual contact also took place in the kitchen and in closets. One inmate said that 'all the inmates knew' about Chan and Washington. Trial Ex.13, Investigation Report.

It was apparently also well-known that Washington had sexual contact with multiple inmates. An inmate told investigators that girls had 'story time' when they gossiped about Washington's penis and the fact that it was discolored. Indeed, Washington conceded that he had sexual relationships with five inmates, some of them at the same time.

There was substantial evidence to suggest that the relationship between the Plaintiff, Ms. Chan, and the Defendant, Mr. Washington, was, in fact, coercive. The case against Washington could not have been more straightforward in my opinion, Ms. Lawrence."

Becky thought: "This is over" as she stared at the floor and the fragrant vibrant essence of lilacs permeated the courtroom.

Woodbury took a small sip of water as he cleared his throat: "The jury found that the sexual contact was nonconsensual and consisted of approximately 50 to 100 encounters of oral, vaginal, and anal sex."

Amanda whispered: "Becky," as Becky leaned forward, "this is over."

"I know" Becky mouthed as Woodbury nodded his head in disapproval as he stared at Becky: "Is there a problem, Ms. Lawrence?"

Becky stood: "No, your Honor. I'm sorry."

Woodbury grinned: "Counsel, please know that I have read your respective briefs on these issues in their entirety and unless either of you have a persuasive oral argument to proffer that has not already been briefed, I will forthwith execute an order delineating my findings that I have briefly articulated here … Mr. Fishman?"

"No, your Honor, I will rest on my opposition."

Woodbury sipped from his water: "Ms. Lawrence?"

Becky stood as she addressed the Court: "No, your Honor, the government will rest on our papers."

"In that case this hearing is adjourned. Good day then, counsel" Woodbury said as Josh stood: "All rise" he said as the evanescence of lilac began to wane, and Josh looked at Becky mouthing: "Smell that?"

Becky and Amanda walked in silence toward the elevator occasionally catching each other's glance. Becky pushed the arrow up as her cell vibrated in her blazer pocket. Amada stared at Becky reading her emotions on her sleeve: "Can't win 'em all, you know" she said as Becky smirked as her iPhone continued to vibrate.

As the elevator opened on the ninth, Amanda whispered: "You're beat, huh? It's been a long day; why don't you get out of here?"

Becky nodded as she reached for her cell as Amanda quipped: "Yeah, wonder who that is" …

Becky rushed to the ladies room and stood next to the toilet with her thighs tightly clenched: "Crap, I'm not gonna make it" she mumbled out loud as urine dripped down her right thigh. She closed her eyes: "What's wrong with me?" she said in her mind as her cell rang in her pocket.

Becky walked into the U.S. Attorney's Office exhausted with her head pinned to her chest. She opened her office door and stood aghast. On the center of her desk was a large glass vase holding 24 long-stemmed red roses. "Zach" Becky thought as she approached the flowers searching for a card. Her face turned white and her body filled with goosebumps as she trembled as she read the small beige card: "How's my girl?" it read … "your secret admirer."

Becky walked over toward the window and stood peering into the harbor, watching intently as the rain pelted against the glass as her iPhone rang: "Hi, beautiful" Zach whispered as Becky smiled.

"Hi" Becky said as she turned her head and smiled at the bouquet. "Thank you, Zach" Becky said as she blushed, "the flowers, they're beautiful."

"Like you," Zach whispered, "You okay; you sound funny?"

"Yeah, I'm okay," Becky said as she heard a voice deep within:

“How’s my girl?, how’s my girl?,” it echoed as she twitched as she watched the raindrops melt against the glass.

“What’s that noise?” Becky whispered as she touched her nipple through her bra and winced as searing pain engulfed her brain.

“Sorry, parade, babe.”

Becky yawned as she heard: “How’s my girl, how’s my girl?” as her body trembled and her hands shook.

“You sound tired?” Zach said as he stepped into the bathroom, locked the door, and unzippered his shorts.

“Yeah, I’m beat … long day, Mr. Woods” Becky said as she smiled.

“You alone right now?” Zach whispered as he stuck his left hand into his brief and cupped his balls in his palm as he grew monstrous.

“Mmm,” Becky whispered as she walked over to her door and closed it, locking it as she walked toward the harbor.

Zach began to moan and Becky closed her eyes watching Zach’s tongue scintillate her labia as his head lapped her from the floor. Becky whispered: “Close your eyes, Zach. You’re in my mouth, Zach; my teeth are grinding on your rim”….

“Ahhh,” Zach moaned as he ejaculated as Becky heard: “How’s my girl?, how’s my girl?” as she began to nervously twirl her hair.

“Becky?,” Zach whispered as he wiped his right hand on his left thigh, “scared to ask but, um, how’d the motion hearing go?” “What do you think, Mr. Woods?” Becky said as Zach grinned.

“Hmmm, that good, huh -- shit, gotta go, babe” he whispered as he hit disconnect.

Becky walked over to her desk and stared at her cell which read: “4:35.” She yawned and thought: “I’m outta here,” as she walked out of her office, her eyes tearing, her mind now a blank grey slate.

Becky ate a Lean Cuisine beef stroganoff in bed thinking: "Crap, I didn't even look at tomorrow's bench trial" as she finished her dinner and laid her head down against the pillow. She closed her eyes and fell asleep as she whispered "Zach" and she heard as her eyes darted behind closed lids: "Charlie, Charlie, Charlie."

Her alarm blasted at six a.m. along with her iPhone's simultaneous buzz, and Becky awoke exhausted. She sat up and yawned as she shut off her alarms. "Oh, my God," she said as her eyes opened, "I gotta pee." As the hot water hit Becky's chest, her body twitched as her nipples, hard and erect, tingled.

"What the hell is this?" she said out loud as she turned her back and stared at her protrusions irradiating pain neuronic pathways to her brain.

As Becky dressed, she hummed: "Yeah, you're working building a mystery and choosing so carefully" … she sat on the edge of her bed to pull her knee highs on and closed her eyes as Zach forcefully entered her from behind; Becky smiled as she began to sing out loud:

"Oh, you're so beautiful with an edge and a charm, but so careful when I'm in your arms," and walked into the kitchen moaning: "coffee." She set the Keurig to brew and began to gag wildly as the spice of coffee percolated through the air.

She ran into the bathroom and dry heaved over the toilet thinking: "Oh, my God … what's wrong with me?"

Becky walked back into the kitchen and grabbed a small pint of half-and-half from the fridge. She poured it into her mug; and as she brought the coffee to her mouth, she gagged and it spilled onto the floor. She leaned over the kitchen sink dry heaving as she thought: "Great … now I'm sick," as she spilled the coffee into the sink.

Becky sat down at her PC and turned her computer on. She read through Zach's calendar for the day: "9:00 bench trial, Courtroom

No. 1, 02-00235, Michelle Rosen v. Department of Corrections, et al."

Becky highlighted the docket number and cut and paste it into ECF. Her eyes widened looking at the voluminous docket. She went through it until her eyes focused on Docket No. 600 entitled: "Supplemental Memorandum in Opposition to Attorneys' Fees and Costs, filed by Zachary Woods (12/2/2012)."

Becky walked into the Moakley at 7:45 tired and yawning. "I gotta pee" she said in her mind, "I gotta pee" as she smiled at Peter and mouthed: "hi" as she walked through the metal detector and then ran toward the ladies room on the first floor. As she exited she momentarily contemplated "hmmm, coffee" but dismissed the notion as her nipples tingled: "What's wrong with me?" she said out loud as she waited for the elevator.

Becky walked into the U.S. Attorney's Office smiling and saying "hi" to everyone she passed. She walked into her office and put her heavy briefcase on the desktop. She opened it and began visually scanning the motions pending.

Her eyes focused on Page 8 of the Motion filed by the Plaintiff: "The importance of obtaining electrolysis throughout the litigation was made clear through plaintiff's testimony at trial:

Q. Why are you bringing this action?
A. Because I'm a transgendered woman and I've been denied access to the appropriate medical care for treating my condition.
Q. What medical care do you want?
A. At this point I'm seeking sex reassignment surgery and the completion of the hair removal.
Q. What do you see when you look at your body in the mirror?
A. I see something ugly and something repulsive.
Q. What areas of your body do you focus on?
A. My face and my genitals mostly bother me.
Q. Why do they bother you?
A. My face because it's still got hair on it. Despite the several laser hair removal treatments I've had I still have almost a full beard

because in the process -- everybody involved in this process, we all had black beards when this process started many years ago and now we've all got white beards, and the laser doesn't remove gray or white hair. So I mostly still got a full beard and I have to shave every morning."

"Give me a break," Becky mumbled as Amanda stood in the doorjamb smiling. "Hi" she whispered as Becky looked up.

"Hi … come in," Becky said with a grin as Amanda sat down facing her across her desk.

"Reading through Rosen's motion, huh?"

"Mmm," Becky moaned as she smiled: "Can't really figure out why Woodbury wants me there" Becky said as Amanda smiled.

"I know; you know he's gonna award attorneys' fees and full costs" … Becky nodded in agreement as Amanda whispered: "probably just wants an opposing point of view, you know."

Becky smiled as she put the motion on her desk: "And why would I be the one to offer and engage in this enlightened quid pro quo?"

"I don't know, Ms. Lawrence … you tell me?" Amanda giggled as Becky smiled. "Listen, you don't really need me there, do you?"

"No, not unless you're dying to attend?" Becky said as she grinned and watched as Amanda opened the rim of her coffee. As the coffee beans perforated her mucous membranes, Becky began to gag.

"You okay?" Amanda whispered as Becky swiveled her chair and placed her head down between her knees. Amanda put the coffee down on Becky's desk and walked over toward Becky staring at her intently.

Becky looked up as the nausea passed and Amanda whispered: "You sick?"

"Mmm," Becky moaned as she shrugged, "I don't know what's wrong with me," Becky said as her eyes teared and Amanda returned to her seat and guzzled her coffee down.

"Nauseous, gotta pee constantly, and my nipples hurt" Becky said as she gagged.

"Oh, shit," Amanda exclaimed as she put the coffee down on her desk, "you pregnant?"

Becky's jaw dropped and her eyes widened: "No … no way."

Amanda looked at her inquisitively: "Your nipples hurt, tingle?"

Becky shook her head back and forth as she whispered: "No way, can't be; I'm not pregnant, Mandy."

Amanda rolled her eyes as she guzzled her coffee and finished it. She stood and threw it into the trash as Becky's eyes filled with fright as her face grew pale.

"I'm just sick," Becky said as she thought: "Oh, my God … that's ridiculous, I'm not pregnant."

"Um, none of my business, but, um, what you using for, um, you know, protection?" Amanda asked as she searched for her lip gloss.

Becky looked down at the floor as Amanda stood: "Seriously … what is he pulling out?"

Becky continued to stare at the floor as Amanda shook her head. Becky slowly lifted her head and whispered: "I wouldn't know this soon, Mandy"….

"Oh, yeah; are you sure about that?" Amanda said as she walked toward the door and Becky stood and walked toward the glass overlooking the water and shook her head from side to side: "That's ridiculous; I'm not pregnant" she said as a single tear rolled down her left cheek, and she stared out into the harbor.

Becky walked into Courtroom No. 1 at 8:35. She was alone in the courtroom or so she thought. Charlie stared at her from the witness box as Becky sat at counsel table perusing the pending motion.

"What the hell am I doing here?" she said in her mind as Charlie blew a fine mist toward her enveloping her in lilac balm.

"Hmmm," Becky moaned as several attorneys walked up the main aisle and the door behind the bench buzzed as Josh walked in.

"Hi, Becky," Josh said as he grinned and walked toward her. Becky stood and met him halfway between the clerk's bench and the government's table.

Becky whispered: "Josh, I'm not sure why I'm here."

"I know," Josh said with a giggle in his voice, "this case has gotten a lot, like a lot, of media coverage, and I think the Judge just wants your opinion. Everybody's mad at him."

"Oooh … why me?" Becky whispered.

"I don't know; he likes you a little" Josh whispered as he smiled and returned to the clerk's bench.

Becky turned around and as she approached counsel table two attorneys outstretched their hands: "Hi, Richard Kennedy, Department of Corrections … "Hi, Linda Cohen, Department of Corrections." As Becky shook their hands in turn, she shuffled her motion papers together and slid them into her briefcase. She moved down to the very end of counsel table to allow them room.

The door buzzed and two armed marshals led in the defendant in an orange jumpsuit, aiding him to walk as his feet were shackled, his hands cuffed behind his back. The defendant had long greasy hair and threw a menacing look at Becky as she stared. Charlie filled the courtroom with the musk of sulphur as Kennedy looked at co-counsel and said: "Smell that?"

Charlie smiled from the witness box watching as counsel gagged; and as Becky began to gag, he blew a fine mist of lilac dust toward her as Kennedy whispered: "Smell that?" and Becky smiled as she stared into the witness box and heard: "Charlie, Charlie, Charlie."

"Oh, my God," Becky said to herself, "I'm losing it" … "who the hell is Charlie?" she said out loud.

Kennedy smiled at Cohen and they both stared at her. Kennedy scratched his chin and said: "Excuse me, Ms. Lawrence?"

Charlie smiled and rose above the witness box as Becky whispered: "Sorry, thought I heard you say something."

Kennedy grinned at Cohen and they all giggled as flowers scented the air. "That's all right," Kennedy whispered, "thought I heard something too … and what's that smell?" he said: "Smell that?" as Becky giggled: "Lilacs?"

Josh stood and bent down to buzz in the Judge. "All rise" he said as Woodbury took the bench.

Woodbury sat behind the bench and smiled at Becky: "You may be seated."

Josh announced: "This is the matter of Michelle Rosen vs. The Department of Corrections, et al, Docket No. 00-02355. The Court is in session. You may be seated. Would counsel please identify themselves for the record?"

"Good afternoon, your Honor. For the Plaintiff Mark Wolfe and Christina Wang from Bingham, and Michelle Rosen is seated at counsel table as well."

Kennedy stood: "Good afternoon, your Honor. For the Defendants Richard Kennedy, and with me is General Counsel for the DOC, Linda Cohen."

Woodbury winked his left eye at Becky as she stood: "Good morning, your Honor; Rebecca Lawrence for the Government."

"Thank you, Ms. Lawrence," Woodbury said as he smiled: "Okay. As always, I'd like to try to assure that we have a clear and common sense understanding of where we are and what's on the agenda today, which requires placing this hearing in some context.

In my September 3rd, 2012, memorandum and order concerning the alleged Eighth Amendment violation I found that the Plaintiff, Michelle Rosen, had proven that the defendant, the Department of Corrections, had violated his Eighth Amendment right to adequate medical care for a serious medical need.

Because it was proven that sex reassignment surgery was the only adequate care for the severe gender identity disorder from which the plaintiff is suffering mental anguish, severe mental anguish and the risk of suicide, I ordered the sex reassignment surgery."

Simultaneous conversations began erupting all through the courtroom, and Becky turned her head befuddled by the sheer number of spectators assembled behind her.

"Excuse me" the Judge said as the courtroom quieted. "As a result, the plaintiff is the prevailing party in the one-count complaint alleging a violation of his Eighth Amendment rights. As the defendant recognizes, under 42 United States Code, Section 1988(b), the plaintiff is therefore entitled to an award of reasonable attorneys' fees and costs. The rate at which the attorneys' fees can be awarded, essentially, an hourly rate, is limited by the Prison Litigation Reform Act, 42 United States Code, 18 Section 1997e.

Originally, the plaintiff requested $644,573 in fees and an additional $161,873 in costs for a total of $806,446.

Now, this hard fought struggle has involved a uniquely unpopular cause: the rights of an inmate, a convicted murderer sentenced to life in prison, with an unpopular diagnosis, Gender Identity Disorder or "GID," seeking a little known medical treatment: sexual reassignment surgery. That reviled trifecta -- inmate, GID, and sexual reassignment surgery, and its inevitable companion, a fusillade of publicity -- has hardened the Department of Corrections' ("DOC's") resolve to fight to the last redoubt necessary medical treatment for the Plaintiff, Michelle Rosen.

On September 16th, 2012, I ordered the parties to meet regarding attorneys' fees and related outstanding miscellaneous cost issues. The Plaintiff offered to waive attorneys' fees if the Department of Corrections would agree to simply comply with this Court's judgment and to provide Rosen with sexual reassignment surgery. Even before the parties' meeting, the Defendants announced their appeal. The parties have conferred but have not reached any agreement regarding fees or costs which bring us here today.

As an aside, this case has been heavily briefed and litigated. I implore the parties to limit their oral arguments to matters heretofore unbriefed.

Mr. Wolfe, you may proceed."

"Thank you, your Honor. Let me start by addressing a fundamental problem in this case: the DOC has denied Rosen her prescribed treatment not because of a lack of belief in the diagnosis, or a failure to understand Rosen's anguish or the risks of inaction, but motivated, as this Court found, by a desire "to avoid public and political criticism."

That desire alone has motivated the DOC's conduct in this litigation, where it left no avenue unexplored in its efforts to avoid taking unpopular action. Rosen now seeks an award for the fees and costs directly and reasonably incurred in proving an actual violation of the Plaintiff's rights.

What your Honor is asking, I think, is about the two issues under the Criminal Justice Act, um, with regard to the fees. The first is the rate, the appropriate rate, the rate that is authorized by the, um, judicial conference or is it the rate that is actually funded by Congress; and the second issue is, um, depending on which rate it is, is it the rate payable at the time of the award or at the time the work was done? So with respect to whether it's the, um, rate authorized by the judicial panel or the rate actually funded by Congress, courts have split on this issue."

Becky began staring at the floor as her mind repeated: "And bla, bla, bla … boring!" as Wolfe rambled on page after page after page citing a myriad of cases on point. Becky continued to fixate on the floor as Woodbury interjected:

"Well, let me put it this way, counsel: the rate established by the judicial conference is the proper rate to use; I have the discretion to use a different hourly rate for each year or to use the rate as of today, and my present inclination is to use the rate as of today essentially for the reasons stated by the Supreme Court in ***Missouri vs. Russo."***

As Woodbury went on citing the case, Charlie stared at Becky who was engaged in a colloquy in her mind: "he doesn't love you, Becky … you know he's playing you; you're just a good lay" she said as her eyes filled with tears and the balmy odor of lilac infiltrated the courtroom as Charlie giggled. The spectators all began a simultaneous chit-chat which turned into a blazing roar muffling the Judge's oratory.

"Excuse me," Woodbury said as Becky smiled and looked up at him, "As I was saying, counselor, I don't think it's a question of not compensating for reasonable hours incurred; it's a question of whether if the maximum rate is appropriate, as I think it is at the moment, for core work, is it also appropriate for noncore work?"

A spectator stood and yelled out: "unbelievable!" and his voice echoed throughout the large domed courtroom. Woodbury whispered to Josh: "Get him out of here." Becky turned her head and watched as two CSOs led the spectator out of the courtroom as he yelled: "This is such bullshit … bad enough the people are paying for sex reassignment for a cold blooded murderer, now the taxpayers are gonna pay this freak's legal expenses … gee, maybe I should just commit a federal crime and have my sex change paid for free, huh, Woodbury?"

“He’s not wrong” Becky thought as Woodbury grinned at her. “Get me out of here” she thought as Woodbury stared at Wolfe: “You want to say something, Mr. Wolfe?

Wolfe stood: “Yes, your Honor, please. As I cited in my brief: “Awarding fees in favor of prevailing civil rights plaintiffs is “virtually obligatory.” *Parker v. Town of Swansea*, 310 F. Supp. 2d 376, 387 (D. Mass. 2004); *Nazario v. Rodriguez*, 554 F.3d 196, 200 (1st Cir. 2009)

As this district court has recognized, ‘Prisoner cases are particularly unpopular” and “in the vast majority of cases, the Court cannot find counsel willing to represent pro se civil rights litigants.”

Civil rights cases are more efficient and more cost-effective when there are competent counsel on both sides than when one party litigates without counsel. Thus, where there are lawyers or organizations that will take a plaintiff’s case without compensation, that fact does not bar the award of a reasonable fee.”

Woodbury interjected: “Why are you citing me your brief in its entirety, Mr. Wolfe? I read it; I assure you, I read it.”

“I’m sorry, your Honor. I will just end by saying: for the foregoing reasons, this Court should allow this Motion for Award of Attorneys’ Fees and Costs and award Rosen’s counsel the total amount of $806,446.25 in attorneys’ fees and costs. Thank you, your Honor.”

Woodbury shook his head as he continued: “I will issue a written order, I expect, rather quickly. The appeal, as described to me, did not raise or rely on unsettled issues of law; instead, it relied, as explained to me, on factual findings I made based on a detailed description of the evidence I heard and my assessment of credibility.

The defendants are absolutely free to continue to pursue their appeal, but as I know lawyers sometimes like to say, “The meter is running.” If, as I expect, the order I issued requiring sex reassignment surgery is affirmed by the First Circuit, then the plaintiff will be entitled to additional attorneys' fees.

As I said, I will issue a written decision; and since I've studied these issues in some detail, I don't expect to change my mind in any material respect, but until I write that decision I can't calculate the precise amount of award."

"Your Honor," Kennedy said as he stood, "may I briefly address one issue?"

"Sure, Mr. Kennedy, proceed."

"Your Honor, I believe that the courts are split regarding the implemented versus funded rates for attorneys' fees. We, of course, would prefer the lower rate to be applied to this case. Again, with regard to the historic versus the current rates, we agree that the statute is somewhat silent on that issue, but we would argue that the purpose of the Prison Litigation Reform Act on attorneys' fees is to assure that reasonable rates apply, that fees are kept reasonable, and the states are not forced to pay huge amounts with regard to the attorneys' fees in those cases."

"Mr. Kennedy," Woodbury interjected: "That's why they're capped, but in all honesty, it appears to me that you're simply regurgitating your brief."

"I'm sorry, your Honor," Kennedy said as Becky smiled and squirmed in her chair.

"Mr. Kennedy, do you have anything to add that's not contained in your voluminous opposition to your brother's motion?"

"No, your Honor."

"Okay, then this hearing is adjourned. I will take the matter under advisement and issue a written order. Thank you, counsel."

"Boring," Becky said to herself as she promptly stood as her ass ached from the hard wooden seat. Josh smiled at her and whispered: "Judge would like to see you, Becky. As Becky stood and walked toward him, she leaned in and whispered: "Wow, this was boring, huh?"

Josh smiled: "Tell me about it," as he buzzed her into the back of the house. As Becky stepped through the door into the Judge's robing room, she jumped as the Judge stood smiling behind her: "Scared ya, huh?" he said as Becky smiled.

"Hi, Judge," she said as she sat down.

Hi, Becky," Woodbury said as he hung his robe and whispered, "Come on, come take a walk with me?"

As they stepped out into the back of the house, Woodbury whispered: "Look at that" as the sun formed a rainbow prism in the sky. "Come on, let's go outside."

"Yeah, so I couldn't figure out the DVD player, right; we got this new Amazon Smart TV and I'm like utterly dumbfounded and bewildered, can't figure it out, right? My three-year-old granddaughter Annie … she walks over to the TV, plays with a few buttons, and the movie plays." Becky giggled as the Judge laughed: "Kid's smarter than I am."

"I don't know about that, your Honor" Becky said as he held the door open for her as they exited the Moakley and walked toward the harbor.

"I have to say: you are positively glowing, Ms. Lawrence."

Becky thought: "Oh, my God," as the Judge continued: "Seriously, it looks like the U.S. Attorney's Office agrees with you, Ms. Lawrence, huh?"

Becky blushed as she thought: "Yeah, and I'm probably pregnant … oh, my God!"

"I don't have to tell you the public's in a bit of an uproar over this case" Woodbury said as he knelt down and picked a white saltwater rose and handed it to Becky who blushed and inhaled its sweet earthy fragrance.

"It's funny … I was real skeptical when this trial began, thought it'd be 'a cold day in hell' before I allowed sex-change operations paid for by the taxpayers."

"Hmmm," Becky moaned as she nodded as she sniffed the rose.

"But Mr. Rosen or um, Ms. Rosen, I guess I should say, has been victimized and deprived of constitutionally protected rights."

"Judge," Becky said as she shook her head, "I don't know how to say this" --

"You don't agree; do you, Ms. Lawrence?"

"No, sir, I don't," Becky whispered as she inhaled the flower's essential essence.

"That's precisely why I had you sit in today, Becky, wanted to pick your brain a little here."

"Oh, okay, Judge. Pick away"….

Woodbury smiled as Becky giggled and whispered: "Here's something you don't know: Rosen repeatedly tried to perform a sex change himself."

"Aw," Becky said, "gross."

"Yeah, actually had the tip sewn back on last time he attempted."

"Oh, God," Becky said as rose oil saturated her palm.

"Anyway, here's the golden question: I have to award costs and fees here, but to what extent?"

Becky and Woodbury walked along the harbor, and Becky tasted the salt on her lips as she spoke: "Judge, I'm really not sure I'm the one to ask this" --

"Yes, you are, Ms. Lawrence. Continue."

"Okay. You're right, the First Circuit will affirm your decision in this case; the Defendants can appeal it all the way to the Supreme Court if they like, but you have to award attorneys' fees and costs, but I think only on the issue you decided."

"Hmmm," Woodbury moaned as he smiled.

"You denied the electrolysis claims so I think you should deny the costs associated."

"Interesting, Ms. Lawrence, and a valid point," the Judge knelt down and picked up a clamshell and passed it to Becky as she smiled: "You really are glowing, you know that?"

"Thanks, Judge," Becky whispered as Woodbury hugged her and whispered, "Zach treating you all right upstairs?"

Becky's face contorted into an awkward expression as the Judge's eyebrows raised.

"Sure, of course," Becky said as the Judge studied her confounded expression: "You sure?"

"Sure, he's great," Becky whispered as the Judge smiled … "You know you could probably be making three times your salary if you switched to defense?"

"I know, Judge," Becky whispered as they walked back toward the Moakley smiling.

"Do me a favor?" Woodbury said as he gently grabbed Becky's left sleeve as they stood on the concrete walk a hundred yards from the courthouse.

“Anything,” Becky said as she stared into his intense blue eyes.

Woodbury smirked and whispered: “Research this issue about costs for me. I’ll have my law clerk Timmy, you know Timmy, send you the cases on point, but it’s your input I want here, okay?”

Becky smiled and the Judge grinned as they walked into the Moakley laughing and giggling as the Judge beamed talking about his eight-day-old grandson Elijah: “Kid’s smart too … eight days old, he watches as I leave the room and cries; I walk back in and he smiles and coos.”

As they walked toward the front of the courthouse, the Judge whispered: “I’m outta here” and as Becky began to walk away, the Judge whispered: “Becky.” Becky turned around and met the Judge halfway in the hallway. The Judge leaned in toward her and whispered: “Having a family is really important … keep it in the back of your mind, okay?”

“Okay, Judge,” Becky said as she grinned with her eyes.

“Seriously,” Woodbury whispered, “your whole life can’t be the law, Becky; there’s so much more.” The Judge kissed Becky’s left cheek as she smiled and whispered: “I know … thanks, Judge.”

“Write that up for me in the next few days, Ms. Lawrence?” he said as the elevator to the garage opened, and he winked at her and stepped inside.

“I will, Judge,” Becky said as the elevator door closed, and she thought: “Oh, my God; I gotta pee. Oh, my God!” and ran to the ladies room on the ground floor.

She stood up and leaned into the back of the stall door and her nipples burned against the inner rim of her bra: “Ow” she moaned as adjusted her breasts within their metal prison.

“Becky walked slowly into the coffee shop, her mind fixated on her current dilemma; she repeated over and over again in her head: Am I pregnant? Am I? No … oh, my God!”

“Hi Becky,” Alan said with a grin, “thought you weren’t in today.”

“Hi, Alan,” Becky said as she smiled, “No, I’m here … have a bit of a stomachache so skipped the morning coffee ritual, you know.”

“You want now?” Alan asked as she smiled: “No, but how ‘bout tea? You got tea, Alan?”

As Becky stood leaning over the countertop, the distinctive fragrance of freshly ground coffee beans percolating infiltrated her membranes and she began to gag.

“You okay, Becky?” Alan asked as he poured hot water into a medium styrofoam cup on top of a teabag.

“Yeah, I’m okay,” Becky mumbled gagging as she turned away and blocked her nose which temporarily quelled her gag.

“Thanks, Alan,” Becky mumbled as she placed a 5 in his open right palm.

Alan refused it: “No, it’s on me.”

“Thanks, Alan,” Becky said as she turned around abruptly and gagged, dry heaving halfway to the elevator. She pressed the button and placed her tea on the trash receptacle as she lifted her iPhone out of her blazer pocket. It read “3:45,” and she said out loud under her breath: “psyched!”

Becky sat in her office slowly sipping her tea when the intercom buzzed: “Ms. Lawrence?”

“Yes,” Becky said as she stared at her phone on her desk.

“Line 2 please. It’s rather important, I think.”

"Thanks, Jenny" Becky said as she picked up the phone and hit Line 2: "Becky Lawrence. Can I help you?" Becky said as she took another sip of her boiling tea.

"Yes, I hope so. My name is Charlene Richards. I've never dealt with you before, Ms. Lawrence; you new?"

"Excuse me," Becky said as she took another sip, "I don't mean to be rude, but who are you?"

"My name is Charlene Richards. My son killed himself in prison five years ago. Your boss knew he was innocent and let him rot in Bridgewater State for 12 years."

Becky closed her eyes as she heard: "Charlie, Charlie, Charlie" whispered from the radiator. She turned her head toward the radiator, and Charlie blew a fine mist of lilac-infused dust toward her. Becky's eyes widened as she said: "I'm sorry, Ms. Richards. I don't understand."

"Okay. In a nutshell my son was accused of repeatedly molesting and raping my granddaughter; this was 1997. I knew he was innocent. He was found guilty in Suffolk, was sent to Bridgewater; your boss, Zachary Woods, he was the prosecutor when it came up federally; it was actually one of the first cases tried in Massachusetts under the Adam Walsh Act."

"Oh, my God," Becky said to herself as she moaned "uh-huh," listening intently and took another sip of tea.

"Evidence first came to light ten years after he was tried, convicted, and incarcerated at the Bridgewater State Hospital for Sexual Predators."

"What evidence exactly, Ms. Richards?"

"My granddaughter signed an affidavit unequivocally recanting her prior testimony. She was 24 years old when she came to me crying

Christmas Eve 2008. With tears streaming down her face she said: 'Grammy, Daddy never touched me. Mommy made me do this … I ruined his life and mine.'"

Tears cascaded down Becky's cheeks, and she closed her eyes. She was nine and her father lied next to her naked in bed rubbing her inner thigh: "You know, Becky, girls like you" he said as Becky wailed shaking, staring at the receiver: "Girls like you, Becky, have to nurture their intellect."

"Ms. Lawrence?" Charlene whispered, "Ms. Lawrence?"

"Yes?" Becky said as she wiped her tears with the back of her left hand and snorted as she held back.

"I knew all along it was a lie," Charlene said as her voice cracked, and she began to bawl.

"How?" Becky asked as tears streamed.

"They were in the middle of a real contentious divorce. Charlie's wife, Lorraine, she'd been having an affair for a real long time. She was a raging alcoholic; she'd lost her license several times, you know, multiple DUIs; she knew Charlie was a good man and he'd get custody so she" -- Charlene Richards began sobbing and couldn't catch her breath long enough to speak.

Becky was crying inconsolably and for more than three minutes both women conversed without speaking.

"Charlene?" Becky whispered in a crackled voice as Charlene spoke: "So I took my granddaughter to Charlie's lawyer's office the very next day. She told him: "My daddy never touched me."

Becky was sobbing as Charlene spoke, her hands trembling as she heard: "Charlie, Charlie, Charlie"…. Becky grabbed a pen from the top drawer and said: "His lawyer's name, please?"

Charlene whispered: “Timmy, Timmy O’Brien.”

“Tim O’Brien, you mean, from the Federal Public Defender’s Office?”

“Yep, he’s the one.”

“I’m sorry, Charlene,” Becky said, “please continue” as both women stopped crying and momentarily recomposed.

“So Timmy had her disposition taken.”

“Her disposition -- oh, you mean her deposition?” Becky interjected.

“Yeah, yeah, her deposition, that’s it. She testified that her mother made her say these awful things, that her Daddy, my Charlie, never touched her.”

Tears swelled behind Becky’s lids; and as Charlene Richards sobbed, her voice trembled and shook as she spoke: “Then he said he needed an affidavit?” Charlene said with a question imbedded in her tone.

“Yep, an affidavit,” Becky said as she heard: “Charlie, Charlie, Charlie” and tears dripped onto her chin and into her open mouth.

“So,” Charlene said as she cried, “after that Timmy said we had to have a hearing with the Judge.”

“Do you remember what Judge, Charlene?” Becky asked.

“Wood something.”

“Oh, God,” Becky said in her mind, “Oh, God.”

Charlene wiped her face dry with the backs of her hands nestling her cell between her right ear and her shoulder: “So he set up something called, um, a revelation hearing?” Charlene said with trepidation.

“Yep, a revocation hearing, that’s right,” Becky mumbled.

“Your boss couldn’t make it that day,” Charlene said as tears flowed, “so he sends in this woman lawyer who knows nothing about this case; she was hostile ... Timmy did a real good job, though. He put my granddaughter Lacy on the stand. She cried for over an hour as she recanted. She just kept crying and saying: “My daddy never touched me; my mother made me do this.

I remember seeing Charlie next to Timmy; he cried as much as Lacy and kept yelling: “It’s okay, baby. I love you.”

Becky became hysterical as Charlene whimpered into the phone. “The bitch,” excuse me, I’m sorry” --

“It’s okay” Becky mumbled as she cried. Becky closed her eyes as her father molested her with his fingers, her daddy softly repeating: “It’s okay, baby; Daddy loves you.” She forced her eyes open as Charlene continued:

“So the woman starts screaming that we need more time for additional discovery. Timmy pleads with the Judge saying, you know: “Your Honor, there are no other victims. The only person Charlie Richards has ever been accused of molesting or raping is his daughter Lacy. He’s been in custody now continuously since 1997 for a crime it appears he didn’t commit.”

Tears dribbled down Becky’s cheeks as she heard: “Charlie, Charlie, Charlie.”

“So,” Charlene began to cry so hard her speech became unintelligible, “so” --

“Take your time,” Becky whispered as she grabbed a Kleenex and began dotting her cheeks.

“So the Judge agreed and scheduled another hearing three months away. Timmy pleaded with the Judge to reconsider. He wouldn’t. Lacy cried so hard she had to be escorted from the courtroom by armed guards. She cried: "Please, your Honor, please let him out. It's me who should be in jail."

Becky's eyes swelled again with tears as both women sobbed. "Charlie, Charlie, Charlie" overwhelmed Becky's auditory input. She stared at the radiator from whence it came as lilacs flooded the air.

"The Judge wouldn't listen. Charlie put his head down on the table and cried as the Judge denied release. That night my son hung himself with the shoelaces from his Nikes, and his blood is on Mr. Woods' hands. Worst of all, I think he knew all long he was innocent."
Becky was blubbering, couldn't stop crying, couldn't catch her breath as she closed her eyes and heard: "Charlie, Charlie, Charlie"…

"Why do you say that, Charlene?" Becky asked as she began nervously twirling her hair.

"Because Zach deposed Lacy several times and her story kept changing. He even told me that he wasn't sure he could put her on the stand 'cause she's so, um, 'unreliable' I think is the word he used. Yep, she was 'unreliable,' that's what he said.

Ms. Lawrence, I have filed suit against your boss and the United States Attorneys' Office and the United States of America. I don't want money. Money can't bring Charlie back to me," she sobbed, "I want my son's name cleared. I want the charges dismissed, and his name exonerated. Do you understand?"

Becky stopped crying as soon as she heard the words "filed suit." She wiped her face with a Kleenex and blew her nose before she spoke: "Ms. Richards, what's the case number or the docket number for Charlie's case, please?"

"Um, I don't know … I can get it if you'd like," Charlene said as she blew her nose, "hold on."

Becky closed her eyes and said to herself: "Your father's been dead for years … you gotta let it go; just gotta let it go" as she heard: "Charlie, Charlie, Charlie" as lilac mist blew across the room, and Becky sat back smiling as she inhaled the perfumed fragrance.

"Got it … it's Docket No. 97-10019-CPW ... Ms. Lawrence?"

"Call me, Becky."

"Becky, that's pretty … um, I'm sorry to lay this on you, but your boss won't take my calls; he won't return my letters."

Becky closed her eyes and said: "Zach!" as Charlene continued: "You want the docket number to my case?"

"Please," Becky replied as she inhaled the ambient lilac.

"It's 13-10029-PBS; also, Charlie's case is on appeal; the First Circuit is reviewing … Charlene began to cry and her voice tremble: "Worst of all, worst of all, Becky, my granddaughter, she's, she's suicidal. She can't live with what she's done. She turned to heroin after Charlie died. OD'd twice, twice they resuscitated and brought her back … then last week she slits open her throat with a razor blade."

Tears streamed down Becky's face as Charlene cried: "She's okay. Well, alive anyway … still in the Brigham."

"I will look into this, I promise you" Becky sobbed as Charlene whimpered: "Thank you. God bless you" and hung up the phone. Becky walked over toward the glass overlooking the harbor, grief engulfing and encapsulating her very spirit of humanity as an avalanche of tears cascaded down her cheeks.

"Zach" … she whispered repeatedly as she cried and closed her eyes and heard: "Charlie, Charlie, Charlie."

After five minutes of sobbing Becky recomposed and sat down in front of the PC. She went onto ECF and queued Docket No. 97-

10019, U.S. vs. Charles Richards. She went to "docket report" and selected "all." She scrolled down all the way to the bottom of the docket to the indictment. She skimmed the document quickly and exited the pdf and continued to scroll upwards searching for the trial testimony.

"12/2/2002, Trial Day 1, Suffolk clerk's notes: Commonwealth vs. Richards." Becky momentarily paused as she looked at her right hand noticing mascara smeared all over her fingertips. "Crap" she said out loud as she licked her fingers with her mouth and rubbed under her eyes, further reddening her skin.

"Direct/Cross/Redirect Examination of Lacy Richards; Direct/Cross, Redirect/Recross of Leonard Grassion, M.D., Ph.D., forensic expert."

Becky searched upwards in the docket until she came upon Docket No. 189, "Transcript of Trial Day 2, Suffolk clerk's notes, Commonwealth vs. Charles ("Charlie") Richards."

Becky opened "189" and went to the Index on Page 3. She jotted down quickly where the direct and cross of Charles Richards began and the Direct and Cross page numbers for the expert.

She went to the top of the pdf and hit "go to Page 32" and she cried as she read:

CONTINUED DIRECT EXAMINATION BY MR. WOODS:

Q. Mr. Richards, your daughter testified crying on the stand for almost two hours yesterday about the repeated raping and molestation she endured throughout the course of almost five years. Are you really going to ask this Judge and jury to discount her testimony?
A. I never touched her. I don't know why she's saying these things. (Witness cries.)"

Becky's eyes swelled with tears again as she focused:

Q. Mr. Richards, why on earth would your daughter make these things up?
A. I don't know, Mr. Woods, but she is (Witness cries.)
Q. Mr. Richards, why don't you just save your breath. We all know what you did.
A. (Witness cries.)

Tears once again began tumbling down Becky's cheeks as she scanned and absorbed the next three pages of heartbreaking testimony, almost every answer containing: "(Witness cries.)" Becky went to "go to Page 196:

"RECROSS-EXAMINATION OF LEONARD GRASHION, M.D.

Q. Doctor, is there any doubt in your mind that Lacy Richards may be fabricating?
A. No.
Q. Maybe you're not understanding, Doctor ... I'm asking you is it theoretically possible that Lacy is not being candid?
A. Well, anything is possible, I suppose, if that's what you're asking.

MR. WOODS: Objection, your Honor, speculation. How can --
THE COURT: Overruled. He's an expert. He can speculate.
MR. O'BRIEN: Thank you, your Honor. May I proceed?
THE COURT: Please.

Q. Doctor, it is possible that Lacy is not being entirely candid; isn't it possible, sir?
A. Of course, anything is possible, Mr. O'Brien.
Q. Thank you. Are you aware, Dr. Grassion, that there may, in fact, be extenuating circumstances in this case; namely, Charlie and Lorraine Richards were in the middle of a contentious divorce, Lorraine Richards is admittedly a raging alcoholic --

MR. WOODS: Objection, your Honor.
THE COURT: Sustained.

Q. Okay, I'll rephrase. Doctor, you are aware, are you not, that there are extenuating circumstances in this case?

A. I suppose.
Q. You suppose. Lacy's parents are in the midst of a contentious divorce, her mother is a raging alcoholic and has a long history of drug abuse; would you think, Doctor, that it's possible that Lorraine Richards may, in fact, have manipulated Lacy in this case?
A. No, I don't.
Q. Doctor --
A. Children must be believed. You're asking me, sir, 'is it possible?' Anything's possible. Maybe Lorraine Richards made this whole thing up, told it to Lacy when she was very young … we know from renowned memory experts that memories can be influenced in young children, but, sir, children must be believed when they come forward.

Becky stopped reading and glanced at her iPhone; it was 5:15 and she was tired. She tore off the single sheet she wrote upon from the yellow legal pad on her desk and rolled it up and tucked it into her blazer pocket. She booted her PC down while yawning and walked out of her office, her mind fixated on one thought: "Oh, my God … I gotta pee."

Two hours later Becky finished her scrambled eggs and while sipping a cup of tea went onto ECF. She queried 97-10019, selected "most recent date first" and perused the docket. Her eyes quickly focused on Docket No. 310, Revocation Hearing U.S. V RICHARDS 9/9/2009. She opened the pdf and scrolled down each page quickly until she came upon:

"REDIRECT EXAMINATION BY MR. O'BRIEN:

Q. Lacy, I know how hard this is.
A. (Witness cries.)
Q. I only have a few more questions for you.
A. (Witness cries.) I told you, I told all of you: I lied. It was all a lie.
Q. I know, Lacy, but please just a few more questions.

THE DEFENDANT: "Stop it, will you?"
THE COURT: Mr. Richards, please sit down. Mr. O'Brien, I will not tolerate such outbursts in my courtroom.

MR. O'BRIEN: Yes, your Honor.

(Whereupon, an off the record discussion commenced between defense counsel and the defendant.)

Q. Lacy, one more question. Please tell the Court one more time why did you lie?
A. My mother said he did all these things. She said he fingered you every night, he made you touch him … (witness cries.) I was a just little kid. After awhile I really believed these things happened.
Q. And why do you know now that your father never touched you?
A. (Witness cries.) By the time I turned 15, after she nailed my dad and sent him to prison, like every night, like all the time, she'd just start making more shit up, you know.
Q. No, I don't know. Please explain.
A. Like we'd be sitting on the couch and she'd say, like, you know, remember when you told me your dad licked your pussy? How'd it feel? Did you like it? That's when I knew (witness cries) what she did, what she made me do. She was just making shit up, and I swear she got off on it.
Q. So you're telling us that by 15 you realized that your mother was making up stories and --
A. Yeah, (witness cries) and feeding 'em to me.

MR. WOODS: Objection, your Honor.
THE COURT: Sustained, form. Rephrase.

Q. Lacy, how old are you today?
A. I'm 24.
Q. Do you believe that your father, Charlie Richards, ever molested you?
A. No, I don't.
Q. Do you believe that your father, Charlie Richards, ever raped you?
A. No, he didn't. He never touched me; my mother made me do this, I told you (witness cries.)

Becky's eyes filled with tears as she went to "Go to end."

"THE COURT: This is perhaps the most troubling revocation hearing I have ever entertained in this court. If what Lacy Richards is now saying is true, then this case is perhaps one of the greatest travesties to unravel in the history of American Jurisprudence. Mr. Richards --
MR. RICHARDS: Yes, your Honor?"
THE COURT: -- I am going to launch a full investigation into this, you understand?
MR. RICHARDS: Your Honor, I can't do another three months. I've done 13 years for a crime I didn't commit; I can't do any more time.
THE COURT: Mr. Richards, please understand I can't just release you today. I am ordering a full psychiatric examination to be conducted on Lacy Richards.
MR. RICHARDS: "Your Honor, don't do that; please don't do that. She's really vulnerable right now. You saw her. She's falling apart. She's suicidal. She says she doesn't deserve to live.
THE COURT: If, in fact, your daughter was manipulated by your now ex-wife, I promise you Lorraine Richards will be facing federal indictment. In the meantime, Mr. Richards, I will order a full and comprehensive investigation into your background.
I understand, Mr. O'Brien, that there are no priors?
MR. O'BRIEN: "That's correct, your Honor.
THE COURT: Then this hearing is suspended until 12/21 @ 10 a.m.
MR. O'BRIEN: Your Honor, please, my client informs me he can't do any more time.
THE COURT: This hearing is adjourned, Mr. O'Brien.

(Whereupon, the proceedings concluded at 3:55 p.m.)"

"Wow," Becky mumbled as she rose from the chair and ran down the hallway toward the bathroom holding her crotch with her right hand. She stood in the doorjamb as her roommate Sara Wilkins watched her while exiting her bedroom: "Having a problem, Becky?" she said giggling as Becky stood with her thighs clenched praying: "Please God, let me make it, let me make it."

As her head hit the pillow, Becky passed out in seconds and promptly dreamt the nightmare she'd always dreaded that emanated from deep within the recesses of her mind ... there was a little girl;

she was nine. A middle-aged man was lying next to the child naked and forcing her tiny hand to stroke him. “Harder” he whispered as the child cried. “Becky,” her daddy whispered, “harder, he said, as tears streamed down her tiny face; and as she violently gagged, the monster forced her head down deeper upon him.

Becky forced herself into consciousness, her eyes fixated on a black-and-white maze of squares, a bright white light at the end of the tunnel in her mind. “Open your eyes” she said as her eyes opened and she stared into the dark ceiling, her entire body doused in sweat, perspiration dripping from the back of her neck and sliding from her temples, dripping onto her pillow.

Becky sat up and looked at her alarm clock: “2:34 … crap” she mumbled as she raced to the bathroom. She splashed cold water onto her face and stared into the mirror. Cast in the reflection she was herself at nine. She splashed cold water again onto her face and began her ritual chant: “It was just a dream, Becky,” she said out loud, “It was just a dream,” as her body twitched.

Becky hopped back into bed and tossed and turned unable to escape the internal horrors of her mind. Every time she closed her eyes and was just about to nod off she watched the old man fiddle with the child in the dark.

By 4:25 Becky decided it was time to get up as she thought: “That’s it, I’m done,” and stepped into a steaming shower. “Ow” Becky screamed as the hot water caused her nipples to burn, sending tingling sensations from her hypothalamus through her sympathetic nervous system. Goosebumps filled her skin as she trembled, and she abruptly turned around involuntarily cupping her breasts as they ached and screamed in pain.

As the hot water streamed down her back, she closed her eyes and whispered: “Zach” as she touched herself and a small trickle began to dribble down her right inner thigh. “I miss you” she whispered as she cleaned and stimulated herself, stopping just before she climaxed. As she dried herself, she closed her eyes and smiled as Zach teased her incessantly with his tongue. “Say it” he whispered as he teased.

Becky turned on her PC as she sipped her tea unable to shake the monster's naked image from the inner cobwebs of her mind. She opened her email and smiled as she opened the first sent at 8:38 p.m. from the evening prior: "Hi Beautiful, can't stop thinking 'bout you ... Love Z."

Becky closed her eyes as she sipped: "Love Z" she said out loud as she grinned. She opened each new email from Zach chronologically, each containing a small blurb of an imminent pretrial motion hearing or status conference. The last email simply read: "Friday, 10 a.m. U.S. vs. Roetengwa, 07-cr-10358, Sentencing. Real interesting case, my love" … "my love" Becky repeated as she smiled and sipped her tea; "read the 'unsealed' indictment, you'll see … Love Z."

Becky went onto ECF and went to query. She plugged in "07-10358" and scrolled down the docket as she smiled as her mind repeated: "Love Z" … she sipped her tea as she opened the indictment.

"The Grand Jury Charges that:

1. Rwanda is one of the smallest countries in Africa, with approximately 7 million people , and is peopled" -- "peopled" Becky questioned, is that a word -- "by two main ethnic groups, the Hutu and the Tutsi."

Becky's eyes scanned the document as she began to read:

"4. The killings spread throughout the countryside as Hutus, armed with machetes, clubs, guns, and grenades, began killing Tutsi civilians … women who were Tutsis and identified as such at roadblocks were at times not killed, but were taken into custody, imprisoned by the Hutu under deplorable inhumane conditions, and repeatedly raped and sotomized."

"Jesus" Becky said out loud as she queued the indictment to print and continued to scan the indictment until her eyes fixated on

“Excerpted Testimony of Dr. Jeffrey Clark, Page 102:

“Over a hundred days 800,000 people were killed, most of them Tutsis, some moderate Hutus as well. Most of them were killed with hand tools, machetes; some from shooting, some with grenades. It was a violent orgy of neighbor, Hutu neighbor largely, killing Tutsi neighbor, people they knew or might have grown up with, the type of catastrophe that could not have occurred without the government having a large role in protecting those people who had been conspiring and planning what we call a ‘genocide.’ That's the background from which this defendant was coming to the United States.”

Becky scanned each page quickly and settled her focus on Page 13, (“Trial Day 4, Testimony of Elizabeth Ashley Payne, Page 46:)

“Q. Aside from obvious policy reasons, were there reasons to keep people who may be involved in the genocide out of the United States?

A. Yes, we had learned from history that people who commit these types of war crimes after, you know, there's a period of unrest they tend to flee. They tend to go places where they can hide. They tend to go places where it can be difficult for them to then be extradited, if required; and it's important that the United States be a leader in the world of showing that we are not going to be a safe haven for people who commit acts of genocide. We will not be a safe haven for people who participate in war crimes. And we wanted to send a signal that we will watch closely, we will do our best in order to screen out any of these individuals that may be looking to come to the United States as a safe haven, so it had very important policy implications as well.

Q. And was the issuance of a visa, the restriction of travel essentially, was that important to the strategy on how to deal -- by the U.S. Government on how to deal with that, with the genocide?

A. Absolutely. We wanted to also send a signal. Unfortunately, it's usually the elite in countries because they're in power that engage in these acts, and we know that it's important to powerful elite families to travel. They want to have an education in the United States for their children. They want to be able to see medical doctors in the United States. We've got the best medical care in the world. There are reasons why it's important to them that they can freely travel around the world; and, again, it's from a policy perspective, we wanted to send the message that no matter how powerful you are, no matter how elite you are, if you engage in acts of genocide, if you engage in war crimes, you're not going to come to the United States for medical care; you're not coming to come to the United States for an education."

"Damn right," Becky said as she exited the indictment as she scrolled. Her eyes fixated on the

"EXCERPTED CLOSING ARGUMENT BY MR. WOODS (Trial Day 8, Page 197):

As I just told you, ladies and gentlemen of the jury, this defendant was actually very active politically. She said in her application for a visa seeking asylum that she was not a member of any political party. That was a lie. She said that her husband was not a member of any political party. That was a lie.

Then you're going to hear that she said in her application that her husband was not a member of the secret police ... another bold-faced lie. "A member of the secret police" … ladies and gentlemen, he was the director of the secret police during the whole genocide.

That's why these questions matter. That's why lying about those things matter. Because why would somebody say answers like these to those questions? Why would somebody lie about their political affiliations? And if this person is lying about these things, then I ask you: what else are they lying about?

I would like to end by echoing something that I said during my opening statement to you about eight days ago. The U.S. is the envy of the world. Our borders are open to visitors. They are open to immigrants. They are open to people who want to come here to seek asylum. You learned that during the course of this trial information was gathered in connection with this defendant seeking to find out about her background, seeking to find out whether she was eligible for a visa, seeking to find out whether she was eligible for asylum, seeking to find out whether she was perhaps in the category of people who are barred from getting asylum because of information she may have been a 'persecutor' in her home country.

That's what this case is about. This case is about this defendant lying, lying to get a visa to get into this country, and then once she was in the country, lying to get asylum -- to seek asylum and providing evasive information to prevent U.S. officials from figuring out how she had spent the genocide, what her party affiliation was, what her husband's party affiliation was, what her husband did for a living before and during the genocide, and what she did or what she saw -- I should say, what she saw in Butare during those, by her own admission, at least six weeks that she spent at this hotel (indicating) in the vicinity of this roadblock (indicating) where hundreds of thousands of people were hacked to death while alive with machetes."

"Jesus, Zach," Becky mumbled, "he's so good."

"It's a crime to enter this country by lying, and it's a crime to seek asylum by lying. It's a crime to game the system by concealing facts that matter, material facts, facts that matter to officials in trying to determine whether you are eligible for the benefit you're seeking, and that is precisely what this defendant did. This case is not about whether the defendant committed acts of genocide. It's not about whether her husband committed acts of genocide, and it's not about what may or may not have happened to Tutsi who went through this roadblock during the genocide. That's not what this case is about.

The question in this case, the question for you, is a far simpler one. The question is: did she lie? That's the question. Did she lie? And did she, in so lying, did she obstruct the integrity of the process, the integrity of the visa process, the integrity of the asylum process?

Ladies and gentlemen, we know she lied, the evidence proves to you beyond all reasonable doubt she lied, and I would respectfully ask you to come back with a verdict for the Government."

Becky printed Zach's Sentencing Memorandum as she closed her eyes and listened to Charlene Richards cry as she yelled into the phone: "Your boss knew he was innocent."

"Zach," Becky mumbled as she set the Keurig to brew more hot water as she placed two Lipton tea bags into a large mug. "Zach, I miss you" she mumbled as she rubbed her abdomen with her right open palm. "Na, I'm not pregnant," she said as she continued to rub her belly, "ridiculous," she moaned as her nipples ignited in electrified sensation, "ridiculous."

Becky arrived at South Station at 6:58 and walked across the street to the Walgreen's. She stood in Aisle 7 astounded at the sheer array of home pregnancy kits on display. "I'm not even really late yet," she said to herself as she read the indications for use, "can detect pregnancy HCG hormone in as little as one day late." Nervously, she placed it on the counter as the young clerk smiled at her.

Becky arrived at the Moakley at 7:30 nervous and agitated from not having slept well the night before. She walked into the coffee shop and immediately began gagging as the coffee vapors suffocated her auditory and olfactory sensors. She ran toward the elevator, her right hand blocking her mouth as she dry heaved, and stepped inside.

"I'm starving," Becky thought as she reached into her purse and pulled out a fresh wad of Juicyfruit as her cell vibrated in her right front pocket. She unraveled the stick of gum and shoved it in her mouth and placed her briefcase on the elevator floor as she held the iPhone toward the ceiling. She twirled it to read: "one missed call … Zach." She smiled as the elevator opened on the ninth and walked toward the balcony toward the conoid glass wall overlooking the harbor. She placed her briefcase on the tile and dialed "Zach."

"Hey," Zach whispered.

"Hey," Becky replied as she smiled.

"Miss me?" Zach whispered as he coughed.

"Mmm," Becky moaned … "Zach?"

"Yes, beautiful?"

"Got a real distressing call yesterday about you" Becky said as her grin turned into a grimace, and she turned her back from the blinding rays of the sun.

"Oh?" Zach whispered as he closed the bathroom door and locked it grinning. He unzippered his jeans and sat on the toilet as he undressed.

"You gonna tell me?" Zach said as he brought his brief down to his ankles, and his left hand held himself tightly.

"Yeah, um, Charlene Richards called me" Becky whispered as she heard Zach groan. "What you doing there, Mr. Woods?" Becky asked as she began to smile.

"What do you think I'm doing?" Zach asked as he began to pant and masturbate as he whispered: "Where are you?"

"Outside the office on the ninth," Becky whispered as Zach said, "Okay. Get into your office. Call me back when you're alone, 'k,' babe?" Becky stared at her iPhone as the call disconnected. She strolled past reception thinking: "he didn't even acknowledge what I just said."

Becky walked into her office and closed and locked the door. She lowered the blind and dialed "Zach."

"Hi, babe," Zach whispered, "alone?"

"Mmm," Becky replied as she felt a lone trickle drip into her thong.

Zach whispered: "What you wearing, doll?"

"Zach, really, we need to talk" --

"Later, I know you want to talk about "Charlie Richards."

"Yeah, I do," Becky said as Zach whispered, "close your eyes for me."

"Zach, I" --

"Shhh," Zach whispered, "close your eyes. Get naked."

Becky unzippered her black pants and slid them to her knees.

"In-person, we need to talk about that case in-person, okay? Damn case haunts me, babe, will haunt me to my grave."

"Okay," Becky said as she took her pants off and slid her thong down to her ankles as Zach grabbed his balls with his left hand and grew immense as he whispered: "You naked for me?"

"Mmm," Becky moaned as she sat in her chair.

"Miss me?" Zach whispered as he began to masturbate with his left hand stretching his rim.

"Mmm," Becky whispered as she threw both legs up onto the desk, slowly balancing the arches of her feet against the desk's rim as her chair pulled out slightly from the desk.

"Close your eyes, baby," Zach whispered: "You're sitting on the edge of the bed. I'm kneeling on the floor as I lick you." Tiny droplets oozed onto her seat as she began to wiggle her finger delicately against her engorged vulva as she moaned: "Zach."

"Zach?" Becky whispered.

"My tongue is tickling you, teasing you; slowly I'm rubbing it back and forth tantalizing as my fingers slide deep inside you. Take a finger and wet it for me, baby, 'k'?"

"Oh, God," Becky moaned as Zach whispered, "I'm close" as he stood and voraciously wacked off staring at the toilet as he closed his eyes.

Becky closed her eyes as liquid deluged her seat, and she whispered: “My mouth is wrapped around you.” She grinned as she listened to Zach pant: “my teeth are scraping against you as you yell: “I like that … ahhh, harder.” Becky stuck her wet finger deep into her anus as her juice dripped onto the floor.

“Ahhh,” Zach groaned as he felt the ejaculate rise within, “I turn you over and I insert my tongue into your ass as you erupt all over me.”

“Oh, God,” Becky said as she began to hump the chair and orgasm.

“Say it,” Zach whispered as he ejaculated.

“No, Zach,” Becky yelled as a puddle formed under her desk.

“Ahhh,” Zach groaned as his semen released over his stomach, and it began to drip down each bilateral hip. “Listen,” Zach said as he began wiping his abdomen onto a washcloth, “I’ll be home early Friday. Meet me in town early, okay?”

“Why?” Becky asked with a coy smile as she continued to flood the floor.

“You know why” Zach said as he gripped his sack firmly cupped in his left hand.

“Why?” Becky said as she continued to tease herself.

“You wet for me?” he whispered as she groaned and whispered: “Yeah, the minute I hear your voice.

“Mmm, I like that … got a new toy for you, baby.”

“Zach?” Becky whispered as she stood and stared in disbelief at the fluid accumulated in her seat. She moved her chair a couple inches back and stood perplexed staring at the puddle under her desk.

“Yeah?” Zach whispered as he retrieved his brief from the floor and sat on the toilet, slowly pulling his brief up to his knees.

“Nothing,” Becky said as she thought, “tell him. Tell him what … you think you might be pregnant? No, stupid. Shut up.”

“Everything okay, Becky?,” Zach said as he raised his brief and cupped himself through his brief and felt his bulge grow within his left palm as he moaned, “I’m hard again … God, what you do to me, Becky.”

“I’m okay,” Becky whispered as she grinned and grabbed the Kleenex box and began wiping herself dry as tiny pieces of tissue eroded and stuck to her vulva and her inner thighs. “Great” she said as she felt the Kleenex sticking inside of her.

“Listen, after that sentencing Friday there’s like nothing else on the docket. Check out at like 3. Walk down to the Marriott on Long Wharf. I’ll meet you in the lobby, ‘k’? We’ll have a nice lunch/dinner and then” --

“And then?” Becky said as she peeled shredded pieces of Kleenex from her thighs and rolled them into tiny balls within her fingertips.

Zach grinned as he whispered: “You’re gonna sit on my face for a few hours.”

As Becky closed her eyes watching Zach’s tongue play with her; her waterfall erupted and creamy liquid began pooling down her thighs as tiny pieces of shredded tissue stuck to her skin.

“You wet?” Zach whispered as he grew hard and stuck his left hand into his brief.

“The minute I hear your voice,” Becky whispered and immediately thought, “don’t say stupid shit like that … Jesus, Becky.”

“Yeah?,” Zach said as his voice raised an octave, “So you hear my voice and you’re wet, huh?”

“Mmm,” Becky moaned as Zach whispered: “Shit, they’re back ... gotta go.”

Becky sat down in her wet chair and placed the empty plastic bottle deep inside her as her fingers played with her engorged inner lips. Her nipples tingled as her orgasm consumed her. Her left hand shoved the empty bottle deep within. As the plastic molded and crinkled inside her, she stood and laid her arms over the desk. She squeezed the bottle inside her with her pelvic floor as she closed her eyes and watched as Zach entered her from behind. As she humped, she stuck her wet pointer finger deep inside her ass and the ensuing deluge engulfed her.

Her cell vibrated on the desk, and she stood slowly peeling the water bottle out gently as liquid splashed against the side of the desk and dribbled down the interior walls. “One new text,” it read, “sorry babe … Friday! Love Z.”

Becky used the last of her Kleenex sopping up the fluid from her seat and throwing it haphazardly on top of the puddle under her desk. She waited for five minutes for her legs to air dry before she even attempted pulling her slacks on. Once dressed, she sat at her desk staring at the tiny Walgreen’s bag teetering at the desk’s edge. She nodded her head and grabbed the bag and walked down the hall, past reception, and into the ladies room.

She sat on the toilet fully dressed as she read the instructions. She opened the plastic envelope with her teeth and peeled her slacks down to her knees and peed on the indicator. “Oh, God, I need a shower,” she mumbled in her mind as the inside of her slacks stuck to her sticky thighs.

She placed the indicator on the toilet paper dispenser and got dressed as she whispered with her eyes tightly shut: “Please God, let it be negative, please God” … as Becky buckled her belt, she turned around, her mouth agape as her tongue protruded. The indicator panel had turned from pink to a deep blue in the interim.

“Oh, my God,” Becky said out loud as she opened the stall door and tossed the indicator into the trash under the paper towel dispenser. She walked over to the sink and washed her hands as she whispered in her mind: “I’m pregnant ... oh, my God.”

Becky sudded her hands and walked back into the stall. She managed to get soap suds all over the door handle before leaning it closed with her shoulders. She pulled down her slacks and cleaned her inner thighs and her vulva as bubbles slowly cascaded down the inside of each leg, stopping at the knee high barrier. “Ow” she mumbled as the soap momentarily burned her. She pulled ten individual pieces of paper towel down from its skew and walked back into the U.S. Attorney’s Office with her head down on her chest, one thought radiating in her mind: “I’m pregnant, oh, my God … he’s gonna kill me.”

Becky walked into her office and lifted the blind. She threw her pile of paper towels onto the puddle under her desk and walked back toward the harbor watching as the sky turned an ominous grey and thunder boomed as lightening sparkled before her over the water. She rubbed her abdomen with her left hand as her nipples tingled and stood erect. As she rubbed her stomach, she whispered: “I love you already” as she closed her eyes and fantasized Zach’s enthusiastic reaction.

As the rain pelted against the glass, Becky stood in a fixed trance rubbing her stomach and smiling. “Becky!” Amanda said sternly as Becky jumped and her body twitched in fear. Becky stared at Amanda and they began giggling as Becky whispered: “God, you scared the shit out of me, girlfriend.”

Becky walked over to her office door and closed it as Amanda ripped open the rim of her large regular coffee and began to sip slowly. “What’s up?” Amanda asked trying to decipher Becky’s contorted bewildered facial expression.

“I’m pregnant” Becky whispered as Amanda took a heaping gulp and placed her styrofoam on the desk as she coughed.

"Told ya," Amanda said as the corners of her eyes wrinkled in smile, "what you gonna do?"

Becky began to pace behind her desk as she nodded her head back and forth whispering: "I don't know, I don't know … guess I'm gonna have a baby."

"Zach know?" Amanda said as she held her head back and downed half the coffee.

Becky nodded as Amanda shook her head: "None of my business, but maybe, maybe" --

"What?" Becky said as she stopped pacing as stared at Amanda sternly.

"Maybe you should do something about this."

A single tear dropped from the corner of Becky's right eye as she shook her head as Amanda spoke: "You know he's married. He has a family. You really want to raise a baby by yourself? Think about your career here ... Jesus, you just started and" --

Tears streamed down Becky's face as she walked over toward the radiator and watched as the raindrops hit the glass as her cheeks soaked, and she swallowed the salty taste of her tears. Amanda came up behind her and Becky turned around as Amanda hugged her tightly: "Whatever you decide, I'm your friend; I'll stand by you," she whispered, as Becky sobbed.

"I love him" Becky said as she wiped her cheeks.

"Yeah?," Amanda said with her brows raised returning to her chair as Becky sat down at her desk, "well, you think you love him" she said as she finished her coffee and coffee dribbled down her chin. "Listen, I'm gonna go do some crap. I'll email you everything you're going to need for the Veloz hearing tomorrow. Take it easy today, huh?"

As Amanda stood in the archway, she turned around as Becky looked up at her: “Call me any time, okay?” as Becky mouthed: “thank you.” As Amanda stepped out into the hallway, Becky yelled: “Amanda!”

Amanda turned around and walked back through the doorjamb as Becky whispered: “Don’t tell anyone.”

Amanda said: “Who am I gonna tell?”

Becky mouthed: “No one.”

“Okay” Amanda mouthed as she grinned.

“Promise?” Becky asked as she booted her PC on.

“Promise,” Amanda quipped as she stepped out of her office and walked slowly toward reception.

Becky spent the morning researching the Veloz case on ECF. As she diligently searched through the docket, she came upon Docket No. 408 entitled: “Psychiatric Evaluation of Rose Perez Veloz by Dr. Leonard Grassion.”

Becky opened the pdf as she yawned. She tried to focus on the document in view, but her mind wandered to the tiny embryo growing inside her womb. She leaned back in her chair as it creaked and closed her eyes watching Zach play with her with his tongue as she started to sing:

“Show me love, show me life; baby, show me what it's all about … you're the only one that I’ve ever needed, show me love and what it's all about”….

Becky began reading the psych eval. as she watched Zach smile at her and hummed:

“I love you, I miss you, I’ll make sure everything will be all right; I’ll give you my heart if you just give me love every day and every night … show me love, (yeah), show me life (all right); baby, show me what it's all about. You're the only one that I've ever needed (show me love), show me love, and what it's all about … yeah!"

Becky leaned forward in her chair as she read: "(Recorded Interview with Rose Veloz:)

Q. Please state your full name.
A. Rose Perez Veloz. People call me "Rosie."
Q. Rosie, how old are you?
A. Fifteen."

Becky continued to scroll and skip most of the next three pages as she hummed: "Show me love, show me life; baby, show me what it's all about …you're the only one that I've ever needed, show me love and what it's all about, yeah!"

Becky's eyes focused on Page 7, starting at Line 22:

A. (Affiant cries.)
Q. I know this is hard, Rosie. When is the last time you saw your father, Jose Veloz?
A. Um, I don't know … like four years ago maybe.
Q. Have you had any contact with him whatsoever in the past four years?
A. Yeah, um, he sends me birthday cards, Christmas gifts, you know, and, um – oh, yeah, last Christmas a huge box was delivered to my front door. Thank God my mother wasn't home; she was at work. It was addressed to me. I opened the box. Inside the box was a smaller box. I opened the smaller box. Inside was an even smaller box. There was like ten boxes inside this mega box, you know. When I got down to the last box, there was an envelope inside. Written on the outside was: "For my Rosie. I love you, Daddy." Inside was 5,000 dollars just for me.
Q. Wow, what a Christmas present, huh?
A. Yeah.
Q. What happened to that $5,000, Rosie?
A. Oh, it's gone now.
Q. Did you give it to your mother?

A. No. Yeah, right. I ain't stupid.
Q. Did you buy something for yourself?
A. (Affiant nods head.)"

Becky hummed: "Oh, show me love, show me life" as she read:

Q. What did you do with the money, Rosie?
A. Bought drugs, had a good time.
Q. What kinds of drugs, Rosie?
A. Weed, coke, shrooms, you know.
Q. How long have you been using drugs, Rosie?
A. Um, on and off, you know, since I was 11."

"Oy" Becky mumbled as she hummed: "Oh, show me love; yeah, show me life. Baby, show me what it's all about" as she smiled as Zach stood naked and erect in front of her. She shook her head several times back and forth as she focused on the pdf in view:

Q. Rosie, can you tell me why your Daddy was sent away four years ago?
A. Yeah, he beat my mother up pretty bad one night. She was being a real bitch I guess. I don't know; I wasn't even home. He fractured her skull and sliced her face and raped her supposedly.
Q. You have doubts about what happened?
A. Yeah, I do.
Q. You know your mother was in a coma for three weeks?
A. I know.
Q. You know she received multiple stab wounds and 117 stitches?
A. Yeah.
Q. Yet, you have doubts?
A. Yeah, my father never hit her before. At least, I never seen it.
Q. Rosie, your mother was violently raped; do you know she received 24 stitches in her anus as a result of this attack?"

"Oh, gross … was that really necessary? Jesus, no wonder this kid does drugs" Becky said out loud as she spinned her chair around to face the harbor, stood and slowly walked over toward the radiator patting her belly and humming:

"Show me love, show me life; baby, show me what it's all about. You're the only one I've ever needed … show me love and what it's all about."

Amanda walked into Becky's office watching her rub her stomach affectionately, and Amanda nodded her head: "Becky." Becky turned around and smiled as her left hand unconsciously patted her stomach.

"Amanda, what's with Veloz's kid, Rosie?"

"Um, yeah, you don't want to go there."

Amanda sat down in the chair across from Becky's desk as Becky walked around the desk and pulled up a chair next to her whispering: "Well?"

"Veloz's wife Magdalena filed for divorce. Veloz gets the papers served to him by some constable; he shows up dead floating in the Charles a few days later ... the night he's served with the divorce papers, Veloz freaks, beats the literal shit out of her, raped her with a broom handle, perforated her bladder, punctured her spleen."

"Jesus," Becky whispered as she stared at the floor.

"She's in a coma for like a month after all the surgeries ... four months later, night before the domestic abuse trial in the New Chardon, asshole sends some Bloods to her house. Kid was there. They threw Rosie in the bathroom, barricaded the door with some bureau. She listened as for hours as they gangbanged her mother. Raped and beat her for hours, Becky. Kid didn't talk for months; she was in a psych ward at Mass. General for like five months."

Becky whispered: "Oh, my God."

Amanda stared at her: "Next morning Maggie calls the DA, drops the charges. She'll never talk to you."

Becky placed her right hand over her face as Amanda moved it with her left hand: “Becky, don’t even go there; Maggie will never talk to you and the kid, Rosie, she’s” --

“Fucked up, huh?” Becky whispered as she stood and walked toward the window, watching the rain pelt against the glass as the sky turned black and roared.

Amanda stood and ironed out her skirt with the palms of her hands as she walked toward Becky and whispered: “He’s such a piece of shit” … Becky nodded her head up and down as she said: “I’m gonna nail this son-of-a-bitch.”

“Hope so,” Amanda said as she stood next to Becky, and they watched as lightening illuminated the sky over the harbor as the turbulent Atlantic crashed onto the shore.

“Zach’s been trying to nail Veloz for years,” Amanda whispered as Becky continued to watch the breaking waves. “We finally got him, slam dunk, and this case is falling apart at the seams.” Becky stared at Amanda as Amanda nodded her head back and forth: “I’m gonna nail him” Becky whispered as Amanda grinned.

“Come on; come have some breakfast with me?” Becky said as Amanda grinned and followed her toward reception. Becky and Amanda walked into the caf engaged in a legal debate over the death penalty. Becky was a die-hard proponent of capital punishment, and Amanda tried unconvincingly to sway her.

Becky ordered an “everything bagel” with cream cheese as Amanda ordered a breakfast sandwich on a croissant. Becky started gagging involuntarily as the aroma of coffee perforated her nostrils. “Go sit down,” Amanda whispered as she smiled watching Becky gag, “I got this. Jesus, you’re making me nauseous. Go sit down, will ya?”

As Becky turned around and began to walk away, her right hand covering her mouth, Amanda whispered: “Want some coffee?”

Becky turned around smirking: “Very funny, Amanda. How ‘bout some OJ instead, please.”

The cafeteria was empty as Becky stared at her touchscreen: "Wow," Becky thought, "it's only nine o'clock" as she sat down in the table closest to the glass wall overlooking the Boston Harbor. Rain continuously dripped down the conoid wall as Becky watched the buoy intermittently swallowed by the rippling waves.

"You okay?" Amanda said as she placed the tray on the table. Becky nodded as she inhaled her bagel.

"Hungry, huh?" Amanda said smiling as Becky woofed it down. "Hmmm" Becky moaned as Amanda smiled. Amanda was on her third bite of her breakfast croissant when Becky finished her bagel. She looked at her inquisitively: "You have kids?" Amanda smiled. "You do … I knew it."

Amanda reached into her purse and pulled out her wallet. She flipped it open and passed it to Becky as Becky smiled. "This is Alaya. She's five. And this tiger, Dylan; he's three now. So weird, seems like he was just born."

"They're so cute, Amanda" Becky gushed as she stared intently at the photographs. Husband's a marine, he's in Afghanistan, been there for like three years now. He's seen Dylan on leave twice; once for five days when he was first born and then last year for ten days."

"Wow, so you're" --

"Yeah, I'm a single mother, working 50 hours a week to boot. It's hard, Becky, raising kids alone." Becky smiled at her with a new understanding of her plight and a keen insight that threw Becky's brain into a bizarre one-sided colloquy in her mind: "Geez, she knows what she's talking about. How can I even think about raising this baby alone? What's the other choice? There is no choice; what the hell am I gonna do?"

"You'll be okay," Amanda said as she grabbed her right hand and Becky's mind began to clear, "it's hard but"….

Lightening flashed in front of them as Becky jumped and Amanda spilled her coffee onto the table. As the vapors infiltrated Becky began to retch and couldn't stop. "Go" Amanda said as she cleaned the table with her napkin and began to gag herself watching Becky dry heave. Becky ran to the bathroom just outside the Court of Appeals and made it into the stall before she regurgitated her bagel.

As Becky splashed cold water against her face, soaking her hair and her neck, the incense of lilac infused the air, and Becky smiled as she closed her eyes and inhaled the savory fragrance deep into the intrinsic fibers of her soul. She closed her eyes and heard: "Charlie, Charlie, Charlie," smiled and mumbled: "I'm starving" as she walked out of the bathroom humming:

"Show me love, Zach; show me life, baby, show me what it's all about … you're the only one I've ever needed, show me love and what it's all about, yeah!"

Amanda smiled at Becky as Becky sang and screamed: "Oh, my God, Robyn Carlsson; I love that song!" as Becky mumbled: "I'm starving, Mandy" and Amanda smiled and whispered: "Stay put." She walked back into the cafeteria and bought Becky another "everything bagel" with cream cheese. "To go" she said smiling as it was bagged.

As Amanda waited in line to purchase Becky's breakfast, she hummed: "Show me love, show me life; baby, show me what it's all about" Amanda handed Becky the small white bag. Becky opened it as she inhaled the onion spewing: "You're a doll," she whispered as she hummed: "bump bump bump … bump, bump bump," as Amanda smiled and hit the up arrow quietly singing: "Baby, show me what it's all about, yeah!"

Becky spent the day on ECF preparing for the Veloz hearing the next morning. She walked back into the cafeteria as the sun blinded her eyes. She got a small salad topped with tuna and a piece of pita and sat at her desk. As she finished her salad, she noticed her roses were wilted as the water had evaporated. She stood up and leaned over her desk; and as she touched a single pedal, it broke off and floated through the air landing on her yellow legal pad.

She walked over toward the radiator and stared up into the beautiful blue sky dotted with innocuous white puffy clouds as her eyes followed a rainbow prism just above the water's periphery, and her mind reeled: "Your boss knew he was innocent," she heard as she closed her eyes, "and he let him rot." Becky shook her head and rubbed her abdomen as her eyes filled with tears, and her cell vibrated off the desk onto the floor.

Becky picked up her iPhone as the touchscreen displayed: "one next text: "missing you … Z." Becky held her phone as a mic and sang loudly, unashamed and uninhibited as she walked back toward the harbor: "Show me love, show me life; baby, show me what it's all about."

Becky walked past reception 15 times between one and four o'clock and into the ladies room. At 4:10 as she walked past reception, Jenny smiled at her from her desk whispering: "Problem?"

Becky blushed and shook her head back and forth as she smiled and gently rubbed her stomach: "No, too much coffee, you know."

Becky awoke at 4:46 as the monster moaned in her dream, and she sat straight up in bed and rubbed her eyes ... she walked into Courtroom No. 1 at 9:45 spotting Amanda at counsel table. She smiled as Amanda nodded and watched her walk down the aisle. "Hey" Becky whispered as Amanda grinned. "You know you're like glowing today" Amanda said as Becky blushed.

"Hi, Becky," Josh said from the clerk's bench.

"Hi, Josh," Becky whispered as she smiled and approached him, "listen, is there any way I could talk to Hubbard for a minute?"

Um, yeah, I guess so … he's walking in right now."

"Oh, right … sorry, was thinkin' he was in lock-up, I bad" … Becky walked back toward counsel table and whispered to Amanda: "I got this, I got this."

"Yeah?" Amanda whispered, "I don't know, Becky."

Josh stood as he hung up the phone on the bench: "Becky, make it quick, though; Judge wants this called at 10 sharp, 'k'?" Josh pushed "1, 2, 3, 4" and a buzz echoed throughout the courtroom as Josh disappeared into the back of the house. Hubbard walked behind Timmy O'Brien who smiled at Becky as they approached.

"Hi, Becky" Timmy said as he shook her right hand and inhaled her scent. Becky smiled as Josh reappeared whispering: "five minutes, counsel" and smiled as he poured fresh water into the Judge's decanter. Becky sat down next to Hubbard and whispered: "I'm gonna put you on the stand. You need just to affirm that you will be cooperating for the government and testifying against Veloz."

"That's it? That's all?" Hubbard said as Timmy whispered: "Yeah, this should be quick." Becky nodded and smiled at Timmy as Hubbard said: "Maybe I should move, huh?" and hit Timmy with his left shoulder. Becky walked into the aisle as Timmy yelled: "Becky."

Timmy smiled as he leaned in and whispered: "I was wondering, um" --

Becky stared at him intently watching his nervous mannerisms unfold. Timmy adjusted his tie and cleared his throat: "I was wondering if maybe you'd like to, um, have dinner sometime?" he whispered as Amanda smiled and stared at the floor.

Becky smiled with her eyes as she rubbed her stomach, and Timmy smiled as Becky's stomach rumbled: "Hungry?" he said as Becky giggled.

"Hmmm," Becky smiled as she thought, "always now."

"Don't answer me just now … just think about it. I really like you" he whispered as she grinned and walked toward counsel table. She turned her head back just as she sat down next to Amanda and grinned knowing Timmy was watching her gait. She thought: "He's kind of cute," as Amanda whispered: "Oooh, he likes you."

"All rise" Josh announced standing as the courtroom filled with spectators stood. Woodbury sat at the bench and mumbled: "You may be seated.

Josh announced: "This is the matter of the U.S. vs. Veloz, et al, Criminal Docket No. 12-30225. Would counsel please identify themselves for the record?

Becky stood as the Judge smiled and poured a glass of water. "Rebecca Lawrence for the Government, your Honor."

"Good morning, Ms. Lawrence" Woodbury said as he sipped his water.

"Good morning, your Honor" Becky said as Amanda smiled.

"Timothy O'Brien, Federal Defender's Office, for Mr. Hubbard, your Honor, who is present."

"Good morning, Mr. O'Brien, Mr. Hubbard," the Judge muttered.

"Michael J. O'Connor for Defendants: Jose Veloz, Julio Ramirez, Chico Hernandez, and Eric Jones, your Honor."

"Good morning, Mr. O'Connor. We're here this morning for a status conference that you requested, Ms. Lawrence. Let me just say, counsel, at the outset, this case, as I've already delineated in prior sessions, is ripe with appellate issues.

You may proceed, Ms. Lawrence."

"Thank you, your Honor. The government calls Edward Hubbard to the stand."

Josh stood as Hubbard walked toward the witness box, and Charlie floated above it watching from the ceiling: "Please raise your right hand, sir. Do you solemnly swear that the testimony you will give will be the truth, the whole truth, and nothing but the truth, so help you God?

"I do," Hubbard said as Woodbury mumbled: "You may sit, sir."

"Here?" Hubbard asked pointing to the witness box.

"Yes, thank you," the Judge said as he winked at Becky who blushed and stood from her chair.

"Thank you, sir," Hubbard said as he sat in the witness box, and Charlie floated to the ground and stood next to him. Hubbard felt a cold mist and shivered as Becky began her examination.

Q. Please state your full name for the record, sir?
A. Edward Charles Hubbard.
Q. How old are you, sir?
A. 42."

Woodbury cleared his throat: "Counsel, we all know Mr. Hubbard's background."

Becky smiled: "I'm sorry, your Honor."

"Proceed please, Ms. Lawrence" Woodbury said as he winked at her and Timmy smiled.

Q. Mr. Hubbard, you have signed a plea and/or a cooperation agreement with the government in this case; is that correct?
A. Yep.
Q. Your Honor, I'd ask that the cooperation agreement be entered into evidence as Government Exhibit No. 1 for this hearing?

"Granted. I assume there's no objection, Mr. O'Connor?"

"No objection, your Honor.
"Q. Mr. Hubbard, please take a look at Exhibit No. 1 which I've

placed on the overhead. Can you see it?"

Amanda fumbled with the document aligning it perfectly and zooming into the text.

A. I see it.
Q. Is this the cooperation agreement you executed in this case?
A. Yep.
Q. I want to ask you about the signed written agreement. In that agreement what did you promise to your understanding?
A. I promised to help law enforcement with their investigations and to be truthful when I get called up for questioning.
Q. And what's your understanding of what the government promised you in this signed agreement, if anything?
A. Immunity.
Q. Pursuant to this agreement, is it fair to say that you agreed to plead guilty to federal charges?
A. Yes.
Q. As well as state charges in Tulsa?
A. Correct.
Q. And state charges in Florida?
A. Correct.
Q. Those federal charges included ten murders, did they not?
A. Correct.
Q. And you've agreed to plead guilty to racketeering charges?
A. Yes.
Q. And the murder of a man named Michael Romero?
A. Yes.
Q. And the murder of a man named Allen Wilkinson?
A. Yes.
Q. The murder of a man named William Mendez?
A. Yes.
Q. The murder of a man named Julio Antonio Alcazar?
A. Yes.
Q. The murder of a man named Joey Batista?
A. Correct.
Q. And the murder of a man named Miguel Ceron?
A. Correct.
Q. And the murder of a man named James Dominguez?

A. Correct.
Q. The murder of a man named Tommy Rosario?
A. Correct.
Q. The murder of a man named Timothy P. Connors?
A. Correct.
Q. And the murder of a man named Richard Fuentes?
A. Correct.
Q. Is that fair to say?
A. Correct.
Q. And you agreed to plead guilty in Tulsa, Oklahoma, to the murder of a man named Roger Watkins, did you not?
A. Yes.
Q. And you also agreed to plead guilty in Miami, Florida, to the murder of a man named Peter Callahan?
A. Yes.
Q. Now, this plea agreement requires you to tell the truth; is that fair to say?
A. Correct.
Q. And what do you understand the penalties to be if you don't tell the truth?
A. I do the rest of my life in jail."

The pungent funk of sulphur blew from Charlie's lips toward the Judge's bench as he squinched his face, and Becky began to gag. Charlie nodded his head back and forth, and Becky closed her eyes trying to compose as she heard: "Charlie, Charlie, Charlie."

"Jesus," Hubbard yelled as he blocked his flaring nostrils with his right hand.

"Josh," Woodbury whispered as Josh shrugged his shoulders, "here we go again, right?"

Proceed, please, Ms. Lawrence."

Q. Mr. Hubbard, I'm now showing you Exhibit No. 8 from a prior proceeding dated almost 15 years ago to the day. Do you see that?
A. Yep.
Q. This is a plea agreement, is it not, executed by you?

A. Yep.
Q. And this plea agreement, Exhibit No. 8, provided that you receive a sentence from 12-and-a-half to 15 years in prison?
A. Correct.
Q. And what sentence did you actually receive?
A. Fourteen years.
Q. Did you also receive a sentence of supervised release?
A. Five years supervised, yeah.
Q. Have you served that sentence as you sit here today?
A. Yes -- well, not the release yet.
Q. And regarding the period of incarceration, did you serve that in a federal maximum security facility?
A. Yes, Butner, and then I was transferred back to the Wyatt.
Q. I see. Did this prior plea agreement require you to cooperate against the
Defendant in this case, Jose Veloz--
A. Yes.
Q. -- as well as other individuals, is that fair to say?
A. Yep.
Q. Now, this plea agreement requires you to tell the truth; is that fair to say?
A. Correct.
Q. What do you understand the penalties to be if you don't tell the truth?
A. I'll do the rest of my life in jail."

Woodbury cleared his throat: "Ms. Lawrence, please proceed."
Becky smiled as her eyes met the Judge's: "Yes, your Honor."

Q. Now, I'd like to direct your attention to Page 4 of the plea agreement marked as Exhibit No. 8. Your Honor, I'd ask that that be introduced in this case as Government Exhibit No. 2.

Woodbury sipped from his water: "Admitted. Continue please, Ms. Lawrence."

Q. And before we get to this -- withdrawn. Directing your attention to Paragraph 6A it says: 'The defendant agrees to cooperate fully with law enforcement agents and government attorneys. He must

provide complete and truthful information to all government law enforcement personnel. He must answer all questions put to him by any government law enforcement agents or government attorneys and must not withhold any information' … and did you do that, Mr. Hubbard?
A. Yes, I did.
Q. Did you provide information about all the individuals that you were asked about?
A. Correct.
Q. And did those individuals include many members of the 93 Bloods out of Fall River and Boston, is that correct?
A. Correct.
Q. And, ultimately, pursuant to the plea agreement that's been marked as Exhibit No. 2 that we've been discussing, you pled guilty to those charges as well as the ten murder charges in federal court?
A. Correct.
Q. And that essentially increased your sentence, is that fair to say?
A. Correct.
Q. When were you released from prison?
A. The other day after we talked.
Q. And you have been incarcerated from 2000 until through 2014?
A. Correct."

Woodbury cleared his throat: "Ms. Lawrence, please proceed. I'm quite familiar with the background of this case.

Becky said: "I'm sorry, your Honor."

"Please, Ms. Lawrence, proceed."

"Yes, your Honor," Becky said as Woodbury grinned.

Q. Mr. Hubbard, one last question: trial is now slated in the case of U.S. vs. Veloz, et al, to begin in three months; it is your intention to testify against Jose Veloz in this matter pending in this court?
A. Yes, it is. I will.
Q. Thank you, Mr. Hubbard. No further questions."

"Mr. O'Connor?" the Judge whispered as he cleared his throat and sipped his water.

O'Connor stood and whispered: "No questions, your Honor." Timmy stood smiling at Becky: "No questions."

"Mr. Hubbard, you may step down. Thank you. Counsel, if there are no other issues for the Court to take up, then I will adjourn this proceeding. Ms. Lawrence?"

"Nothing further, your Honor."

Michael O'Connor smirked as Woodbury smiled at Becky: "Nothing further, your Honor" he whispered as he stood and mouthed "hi" recognizing Becky for the first time.

"Hi" Becky mouthed back.

"Good day, counsel. The Final Pretrial Conference will be July 28th, 2014; I look forward to seeing all of you then."

"All rise," Josh said as the Judge left the bench and the courtroom.

Amanda pulled on Becky's sleeve and whispered: "Good job."

"You think?" Becky said as Tim smiled at her from across the aisle.

"Yeah, you did g-o-o-o-o-d," Amanda said smiling as Timmy followed Hubbard toward the back of the courtroom. As he approached the heavy wooden double doors, he turned around and Becky and Timmy's eyes locked as he grinned and walked out of the courtroom.

Becky whispered to Amanda as she stood: "I don't feel too good."

"Great," Amanda sighed, "and it begins. Come on." As Amanda and Becky walked down the main aisle, Charlie blew a fine lilac mist, and Becky smiled as her nausea dissipated as the lilac consumed her. She smiled as Amanda held the door for her whispering: "Smell that? Feeling better, huh?"

As Becky walked out of Courtroom No. 1 a middle-aged woman grabbed her left sleeve as spectators surrounded Becky effectively caging her: "Ms. Lawrence. My name is Maria Batista." Becky stared into the woman's wrinkled eyes and a lump developed in her trachea as she coughed.

"Mr. Hubbard admitted to murdering my son Joey in broad daylight; he shot him in the back of the head." Tears streamed down Maria Batista's jaundiced skin as an obese man began to scream: "My name is Jimmy Rosario. Hubbard sliced my brother's throat; he was 19. He left him to bleed out; did you know that?"

Becky's eyes swelled with tears as the crowd ignited into a blazing fury. Amanda ran back into Courtroom No. 1 and exited within seconds with two armed CSOs who fumbled to try to reach Becky in the center of this angry, hostile mob.

"How could do you this?" Maria Batista wailed as Peter reached the center and stood in front of Becky guarding her as individual voices screamed simultaneously in a futile attempt to be heard over the roar of the crowd. Peter looked into Becky's eyes and yelled: "That's enough, folks" as a young teenage girl looked deeply into Becky's eyes. With tears cascading down her cheeks, she whispered: "I'm Angelina Ceron. Eddie Hubbard killed my father."

Becky began to cry as Amanda reached her and hugged her as CSOs with guns drawn descended upon the mob. One by one spectators were led down the hallway screaming at Becky as they turned their heads to chastise her just one last time. The last spectator left of her own accord as she pushed Peter's hand away who attempted to continually grab her left arm to escort her.

Becky watched as Maria Batista walked with CSOs surrounding her. She stopped as she hit Courtroom No. 4 by the elevators, turned around, as tears dripped onto the marble tile. Becky sobbed in Amanda's arms as Amanda led her back into the courtroom.

Becky and Amanda sat on the bench in the last row in silence.

“Come on,” Amanda whispered: “I’m still hungry” as Becky’s stomach grumbled. They grabbed an early lunch and took their salads outside to enjoy the warm spring day. The sky had cleared and the sun blazed high in the sky. They sat under a white umbrella overlooking the Boston Harbor as they ate in silence.

“Zach’s back tomorrow” Amanda said as Becky chewed her pita and Becky stared out over the water. “Look, whatever you decide, I’ll be here for you.” Becky’s eyes swelled with tears as she placed her right hand on Amanda’s left forearm: “Thanks” she mumbled as she began to cry staring into her salad.

“You need to tell him as soon as possible, I think” Amanda said as Becky wiped her cheeks, embarrassed as several people stared at her with pity as she looked left and right feeling their judgmental eyes upon her.”

“Amanda, I can’t get Maria Batista’s face out of my mind … I love Zach, you know” Becky whispered as Amanda pouted. Becky looked at Amanda and said sternly: “What?”

“Nothing” Amanda said as her cheeks pinkened.

“What?” Becky said as she slammed her right arm on the table, and it wobbled.

“That’s what all women say, Becky. Oh, my husband beats me sometimes, but, oh, I love him. My boyfriend cheats on me all the time with my friends, but, oh, I love him.” Becky nodded her head up and down as tears swelled within her lids.

“Look, maybe I’m wrong … maybe Zach will do the right thing here, whatever the hell that is, but just stop saying: ‘I love him,’ okay?”

“Okay,” Becky said as she closed her eyes and licked the salt off her bottom lip as she heard: “Charlie, Charlie, Charlie.” Becky walked back into the Moakley half-listening to Amanda’s story about Dylan chasing butterflies in the backyard.

“You’re not even listening to me, are you?” Amanda asked as they stepped into the elevator.

“No, I am,” Becky said as Amanda grinned: “Yeah, what’d I just say?”

Becky stared at her feet as Amanda giggled: “It’s okay. You’ve got a lot on your mind these days, huh?”

“Yeah,” Becky said as she gently rubbed her stomach with her left hand. The elevator opened on the fifth to allow people to exit as Amanda whispered to Becky: “You gotta stop doing that or everyone’s gonna know.”

“Doing what?” Becky asked as she unconsciously stroked her belly.

“That,” Amanda said as she pointed to Becky’s hand. Amanda began rubbing her abdomen stroking it gently: “You see?”

Becky’s face turned pale as her eyes widened: “Oy,” she mumbled under her breath.

“Yeah, ‘oy,’” Amanda repeated smiling as Becky chuckled.

Friday morning Becky arrived at the Moakley at 8:25. She couldn’t get Charlene Richards’ sobbing voice out of her head. As she walked through the metal detectors, her stomach rumbled as her bladder cried out for attention. Becky stood in front of the ladies room on the ground floor humped over as she squeezed her thighs together thinking: “Please God, let me make it” as urine dripped slowly down her right leg, and she dashed into the bathroom.

Her nipples were screaming on fire as she washed her hands in the sink and momentarily closed her eyes hearing Charlene Richards whimpering: “Grammy, Daddy never touched me. Mommy made me do this,” it repeated, replaying on the scratched CD in the funnels of her mind.

Becky walked into the coffee shop and stood as far from the counter as she could as she yelled: “Hi, Alan ... large tea with two sugars, please, no cream.”

“Hi, Becky” Alan said as Becky began to gag as she slowly approached the counter. She stood with her right hand over her nose as she heard: “Charlie, Charlie, Charlie,” and the essence of lilac inseminated the air as the coffee vapor dissipated.

“It’s Friday,” Alan said with a smile as he placed her large tea on the glass countertop. Becky placed a 5 into Alan’s open right palm and whispered: “Have a good weekend, Alan.” She picked up her briefcase with her left hand and grabbed the tea in the right and walked away as Alan yelled: “Becky, your change.”

“Keep it, Alan; it’s on me today,” she said as Alan smiled and yelled: “Have a good one, Becky.”

Becky’s cell vibrated on her desk, and she answered as she smiled: “Hi, Mandy.”

“Hi, girlfriend. Listen: sentencing’s been postponed … I’m off today; Alaya’s sick, you know, coughing, sneezing, whining”… “Mommy!” Alaya screamed as Becky giggled.

“So a real vacation day, huh?” Becky said as Amanda chuckled.

“Call me later -- oh, wait, you’re going out with Mr. Wonderful today, forgot; I bad … I’ll talk to you tomorrow, girlfriend.”

Becky hit disconnect and sipped her tea slowly, occasionally booking it down the hall to the ladies room. “What’s with me today?” she whispered to herself as she walked back into her office for the tenth time in less than two hours. She sat at her PC, opened ECF and queued in Docket No. 97-10019. “U.S. vs. Charles Richards,” appeared at the top of the screen as Becky heard: “Charlie, Charlie, Charlie.”

She went into “docket report” and scrolled down until she came upon Docket No. 188, “Trial Day 1, Suffolk clerk’s notes: Direct/Redirect/Cross of Lacy Richards.” Becky cried as she read the trial testimony starting on Page 61:

Q. Lacy, I know this is hard. How many times did your father penetrate you?
A. (Witness cries.) What do you mean ‘penetrate’?
Q. I’m sorry. You testified that your father, Charlie Richards, began molesting you at age 7; is that correct?
A. Yes.
Q. You testified that initially he “diddled,” that was your word; isn’t that correct?
A. (Witness cries.) Yes.
Q. You explained “diddled,” did you not?
A. Yes. (Witness cries.)
Q. You further testified that your father began forcing you to perform fellatio on him soon thereafter, is that correct?
A. “Fellatio”?

Tears streamed down Becky’s cheeks as she began nervously tapping her right foot against the bottom of the desk as she heard: “How’s my girl?”

Q. I’m sorry. Fellatio, oral sex, your father made you perform oral sex on him you testified?
A. Yes. I didn’t like it (witness cries.)
Q. How many times would you estimate that you were made to do this?
A. I don’t know (witness cries.)
Q. More than 10 times?
A. Uh-huh.
Q. More than 20 times?
A. Uh-huh (witness cries.)
Q. More than 50 times?
A. (Witness cries.)
Q. Let’s move on. At some point when you were approximately nine your father began having intercourse with you, is that correct?
A. Yes. (Witness cries.)

Q. Do you remember the first time this happened?
A. Yes.
Q. Can you tell us what you remember, Lacy?"

Becky began whimpering and wiping her tears with her left hand as she read:

A. The first time was when my mother went to stay with my grandparents in Ohio. My papa had a heart attack so my mom went out there to -- (witness cries.)
Q. To help take care of him?
A. Yes.
Q. Can you tell us what happened, Lacy, that first night?

MS. LORRAINE RICHARDS: "I'm gonna fuckin' kill you."
THE COURT: "Please escort Ms. Richards out of this courtroom."

Becky stood up and walked toward the harbor as tears soaked her chin and dripped onto her chest. "She made all this up?" she thought as she closed her eyes as her father whispered: "Girls like you, Becky, girls like you" … Becky stood crying peering out over the water searching her mind for clarity as her cell vibrated in her right front pocket. She stared at the touchscreen as she wiped her cheeks:

“No way, it’s 2:10?” she said out loud as she hit connect:

“Hey,” Zach whispered, “how’s my girl?” Becky heard her father’s voice emanating from the deep wells: “How’s my girl, how’s my girl, how’s my girl?” Becky twitched, feeling goosebumps covering her skin, as tears streamed down both cheeks as she searched for her words. “How’s my girl” repeating ad infinitum in her mind: “How’s my girl?”

“You okay?” Zach said as Becky whimpered.

“Yeah,” Becky mumbled as she wiped her cheeks.

“Plane was actually on time; I’m at the Marriott Longwharf, beautiful.”

“Okay,” Becky said “Give me five,” as she hit disconnect, booted the PC down, and lowered the blind. She left her briefcase on the floor, grabbed her purse, and scooted down the hall in a mad rush to the ladies room. She slowly dipped a paper towel under the faucet to clear the black from underneath her eyes which had stained her cheeks. She rubbed gently as she thought: “He never touched her … I don’t know,” as she reapplied her mascara as she heard: “How’s my girl?”

Her stomach rumbled as she put on her strawberry lip gloss and rubbed her lips together. “Well, she said as she stared at her reflection, “it looks like you’ve been crying, Miss” she said out loud as she stared at her raccoon eyes.

She walked out of the Moakley with her head hung low, unable to clear her mind from the terrors she’d absorbed as the horrors of her mind replayed and the monster spoke, and she talked to herself as she always had: “Let it go, Becky,” she said, “just let it go.”

She walked into the foyer of the hotel and spotted Zach sitting on the brown leather sofa. He smiled as he stood, and she thought: “What a babe” as he approached her and hugged her tightly whispering: “Let’s go.” They walked into a restaurant just off the main foyer, and

Zach listened to Becky's stomach growl. "Hungry?" he said with a coy smile.

They waited for the hostess to show them to a table as Becky moaned "Hmmm" as she stared at her feet. Zach placed his left hand under her chin and slowly raised it. "You okay?" he asked as he studied her red swollen eyes: "You been crying?"

"Mmm," Becky moaned as her body began to sway to his pheromonal savor, and Zach groaned as he felt her body tingle and twitch as she stared into his eyes. As they walked to the table, Zach whispered: "Miss me?" as he pulled the chair out for her to sit. "Mmm," she said as she smiled and whiffed his unique aroma.

"Crappy vacation," Zach mumbled as the waiter approached: "Ready?" he asked as Zach passed a menu to Becky. "Take your time, folks; I'll be back," he said with a wide-eyed smile in a creepy sort of way.

"Why crappy, Zach?" Becky whispered as he grabbed her right hand and gently rubbed her forearm where it met the wrist.

"Well, Emily had a blast, but I'm wiped … need a vacation from this vacation, you know what I mean? And, um, my wife is convinced I'm having an affair."

Zach lifted Becky's right hand to his mouth and gently kissed her open palm as Becky became saturated and squirmed in her chair.

"I love you," he mouthed as the waiter reappeared, "miss me?"

"Mmm," Becky moaned as she smiled at the short bald waiter and grinned: "I'll have the Buffalo Chicken Salad with the Raspberry vinaigrette on the side please."

"Sir?" the waiter asked as he winked at Becky sending mysterious chills down her spine: "creepy" she thought as she grinned back.

"I'll have the 10-inch rib eye with mashed potatoes and green beans," Zach said as his eyes focused on Becky's breasts.

"So Emily really had the time of her life … Disney's so incredible for kids, you know." Zach and Becky giggled as Zach nervously rambled, detailing "Emily anecdotes" of mystery and enchantment as she meandered through Disney's imaginary worlds of wonder.

As Zach finished his meal and began playing with the mashed potatoes on his plate, creating an erupting volcano, Becky whispered: "Zach, tell me about Charlie Richards."

Tears filled Zach's eyes as he spoke softly: "Charles Richards, I was convinced he was the devil incarnate at the time. It was my first case as an AUSA trying under the Adam Walsh Act." Becky, sensing Zach's trepidation and sorrow, grabbed his left hand and gently placed it into her right palm.

"It was 2006 when the case was first transferred from the state to us … you read the trial testimony?" Zach asked as Becky nodded: "I read it."

"Compelling, riveting, horrendous, you think?" Zach asked as Becky nodded her head and finished her salad and began stroking the top of Zach's left hand cradled within her right palm.

Zach pulled his hand from Becky's grip and began playing with his potatoes: "Lacy recants and then DNA evidence proves his innocence."

"DNA evidence, what do you mean?" Becky asked as Zach stared at his potato volcano, arranging green beans as pooling lava.

"Yeah. When the kid was like 13, her mother, a real whack job, Lorraine, takes her up to the Brigham, tells the doctors she was raped by her father the night before." Zach dropped his fork and raised his right hand to his forehead as Becky grabbed his left hand and stroked.

"Did a rape kit, got semen."

“I don’t understand, Zach ... when did you know that it wasn’t Charlie?”

“After Lacy recanted I ordered DNA from Charlie … sent it off to, you know, the Mass. State Crime Lab; results came back ten days later. The semen from the rape kit didn’t match. I should have done it before his trial” … tears spilled from the corners of Zach’s eyes as Becky stared at his erupting mashed potato volcano oozing green been lava concoction.

“Jesus,” Becky said as a single tear fell from her left eye, and Zach wiped it with his thumb.

“The day of the revocation hearing my wife is in labor. Emily was born while Lacy cried on the stand.” Tears began to stream down Zach’s face as Becky began to cry.

“I should have been there. I should have done something … instead, I was so wrapped up and ‘lovestruck’ with my newborn, had like tunnel vision, you know, couldn’t see anything but my baby.”

Zach pushed Becky’s chair closer, and they hugged as they cried. He kissed her neck and she felt his tears drip down the inside of her blouse. He pulled away momentarily; and as tears streaked his cheeks, he whispered: “Charlie Richards hung himself that night in his cell.”

Becky mouthed: “I love you,” and Zach held her, both of them crying as Zach whispered into Becky’s left ear: “I dream about him all the time. I see his black eyes as he hangs from the rafters, his neck twisted as his tongue dangles. There’s pictures of it … haunts me, baby.”

Becky wiped her tears with the backs of her hands and took a sip from her lemon-infused water as Zach whispered: “Let’s get out of here,” and Becky nodded as he leaned in and gently kissed her lips. She swallowed tasting his salty tears.

As they walked out of the restaurant, Zach held the hotel card in his right palm. She smiled as they grabbed hands and walked toward the elevator. As the elevator closed, Zach whispered: “Say something.”

“I love you,” she said as she leaned her body against him and felt his erection protruding through his Levis. He grabbed and cupped her buttocks with both hands as he pressed into her small, petite frame and whispered: “You wet for me?”

Becky smiled and nodded as the elevator landed on the third floor. As she stepped out, Zach picked her up and carried her down the hallway as he whispered: “I love you, Becky.”

Zach put Becky down in front of Room 328. She watched as he opened the door and giggled as he picked her up again and carried her through the threshold. As he walked toward the bed, the door closed of its own accord as he gently placed her on top of the comforter. “Don’t move, baby” he whispered as he grinned and ran into the bathroom.

Becky began stroking her stomach thinking of the embryo metamorphosing into a fetus within her womb: “It’s a boy” she whispered as she smiled and sat up and unbuttoned her blouse, throwing it onto the floor. By the time Zach exited the bathroom Becky was naked and had a white sheet pulled up to her neck as she leaned against the headboard which creaked as she moved.

Zach walked toward her naked and fully erect as he smiled and held a purple plastic-molded dildo in his right palm. “Watch this” he whispered as he sat on the edge of the bed as his left hand pulled the sheet down exposing Becky’s large breasts and her hard protruding nipples. She studied what he held in his open palm. It looked like a monkey sticking his tongue out while holding his thumb up in the air. He flicked a metal switch on, and the monkey’s tongue vibrated as the top of his hand twitched in opposition.

Zach ripped a tissue from the dispenser on the nightstand and placed the “monkey” on it as his left hand reached under the sheet and began teasing her as he leaned forward and kissed her. She swallowed his tongue as she groaned and placed the balls of her feet on the mattress as she leaned her back against the headboard. Zach placed his head between her thighs and began licking her left inner thigh slowly as she watched him staring at her. “You are so beautiful,” he whispered as he grinned and began licking her clit.

Becky’s nipples were on fire and the tingling sensation flooded her brain as liquid drowned the mattress. She closed her eyes as Zach grabbed the monkey from the nightstand. She heard the vibrator buzz as he laid it across her clit as his tongue reached deep inside of her.

“You like it?” he whispered watching as she humped and her torrent deluged in orgasmic waves. “Ahhh,” she screamed as projectile liquid splurted through the air and Zach giggled, staring at her perfectly formed internal “rose.” Becky’s body slid down as she humped him until her head hit the pillow as liquid dribbled down her thighs. He placed the monkey’s head deep inside of her; and as the monkey’s hand teased her clit, he stuck his tongue deep inside her anus as she screamed: “Oh, God, Zach … oh, God.”

Slowly Zach pulled his tongue back as he smiled and whispered: “Say it, baby?”

“Ahhh,” she moaned as she humped the vibrator, and he began licking her clit, softly whispering “Say it?”

“Fuck me,” she screamed as Zach pulled the dildo out and whispered: “Turn over.” He rubbed his cock against her vulva teasing her as her juice inundated the mattress.

“Put it in,” she pleaded as he continued to tease her and giggle. She reached her right hand down under and forced him into her. As her body squeezed him, he pulled out.

He knelt down and licked her clit slowly and gently as she screamed: “Put it in, Zach.” He licked her for over an hour until she screamed: “Put it in, Zach, please.”

As he tortured her and placed the tip of his tongue on the tip of her clit, he whispered: "What do you want, baby … say it."

"Fuck me," Becky screamed as he plunged forcefully inside her whispering as he giggled: "I can't move … ahhh, don't move." As her pelvic floor contracted, he ejaculated and collapsed on top of her back. He reached his left hand between her thighs and played with the very top of her clitoris as he remained within and liquid pooled onto the mattress as her burning nipples pressed against the sheet.

"I love you," she whispered as his pointer finger incessantly teased her … "Zach?" Becky asked.

"Yeah?" Zach whispered.

"I gotta pee," she said as he giggled and fell over next to her landing in a sopping mess and groaning as she grabbed her crotch with her left hand and ran toward the bathroom.

She walked out of the bathroom and walked toward the bed slowly as liquid cascaded down her legs. Zach was lying on his back with his eyes closed as she placed her mouth on him. He grew immense immediately as she bit down on him, her teeth scraping gently against his rim as he moaned: "Ahhh."

With his eyes closed, he was transported to the National Seashore; and as the waves crashed against the cliffs, he ejaculated; and as she swallowed, he whispered: "Oh, God … I love you, Becky."

Becky laid her dampened naked body next to him, and he spooned her as they both fell into a deep sleep. After an hour Zach awoke and began squeezing her nipples as she screamed: "Ow."

"Ow?" Zach mumbled, "ow?" He sat up and leaned his back against the headboard as he mumbled: "Ow?" She sat next to him and cupped his balls in her right sweaty palm as he grew and inquisitively stared into her eyes. "What are you gonna get your friend soon?" he whispered, his brows raised.

Becky shook her head from side to side, and with her left hand gently rubbed her abdomen as she stared into his eyes. “No way” Zach said as he watched her hand navigate her flat muscular stomach. Becky shook her head affirmatively, scared, holding her breath, petrified of his impending explosion.

“You’re pregnant?” he asked as he scratched the stubble forming under his chin.

Becky’s eyes filled with tears as Zach screamed: “That’s awesome. Really?” as his left hand rubbed her stomach gently, and he leaned in and began kissing her left nipple as she winced in pain. He shimmied his body toward the lower part of the deluged mattress and groaned: “Oooh” as he lied on the puddle underneath. He licked her slowly and gently as he whispered: “You’re gonna have my baby.”

As he drank her sweet clear stew, milk began flowing from her nipples as oxytocin secreted from her posterior pituitary sending millions of neurotransmitters into climatic hyperdrive. Zach picked his head up and watched the milk drip slowly onto her abdomen.

“Close your eyes,” he whispered as he lapped up the milk with his tongue, slowly licking her stomach, then gently rubbing his tongue against the outer parameters of her areola. He began suckling her right nipple as he inserted the monkey deep inside her. She placed her left hand on the back of his head and pushed it hard against her inflamed nipple as she humped him ferociously. As he drank her milk, she climaxed and he whispered: “Turn over, baby”….

Two hours later as darkness engulfed Room 328, Becky opened her eyes and smiled as Zach spooned her. She listened as he lightly snored and fell back into a deep sleep as she heard: “Charlie, Charlie, Charlie.”

On July 28th Becky arrived at the Moakley at 7:15 singing as she walked through the metal detector. She quieted temporarily as she said “hi” to Peter and John, rubbed her stomach lightly with her left hand and hummed: “Show me love, show me life (all right); Baby, show me what it's all about; you're the only one that I’ve ever needed, show me love and what it's all about, yeah!"

Becky ran to the ladies room as she sang an octave higher: "Show me love, show me life; Baby, show me what it's all about" as her iPhone ignited in the right back pocket of her navy slacks. She whispered: "Zach" as she retrieved the phone and stood next to the ladies room clenching her thighs tightly.

As the signal faded the call went to voicemail and Becky hummed "show me love" as she walked into the restroom smiling and enthusiastic as she said: "ten o'clock, Veloz, ten o'clock." She walked into the coffee shop as Alan smiled: "Hi, Becky, tea?"

"Please, Alan. Thanks," her cell vibrated madly in her back pocket as Becky picked up her briefcase in her left hand and grabbed the large tea in her right. She walked out the back entrance and sat on the bench across from the harbor. She opened the rim of her tea and sipped it with her left hand as her right hit "connect."

"Hey, beautiful," Zach whispered as Becky blushed.

"Hey," Becky said as she took another swig.

"Potential hiccup," Zach whispered.

"Hiccup?" Becky asked as she sipped.

"Mmm, O'Connor filed a motion to stay, says the "government's withholding evidence crucial to defense."

"Are we, Mr. Woods?" Becky asked as she downed her tea.

"Well, define 'withholding,' Ms. Lawrence? You here, Becky?" Zach asked as he heard the distinctive sound of a steamship horn blow wildly.

"Mmm," Becky said as she placed her tea on the ground at her feet. "Guess what?"

“What?” Zach asked as he grinned.

“Had an ultrasound yesterday … baby’s 18 weeks.”

There was a long uncomfortable pause before Zach whispered: “Yeah … we need to talk, Becky.”

Becky closed her eyes fantasizing Zach kneeling before her begging her to marry him as she smiled and rubbed her abdomen and internally hummed: “Show me love and what’s it all about, yeah!”

“Becky?” Zach whispered: “Woodbury’s gonna approve this, you know.”

“I know,” Becky said as she picked up her tea and guzzled it, “maybe you should just turn over everything, Mr. Woods.”

“Funny … Becky?” Zach asked as he paced in his office spotting Becky sitting out on the bench across from the harbor.

“Yeah,” Becky asked as she smiled.

“I see you.”

Becky stood and faced the Moakley and attempted to look for Zach’s office, but the sun was blinding and Becky couldn’t focus.

“Becky,” Zach whispered, “come see me?”

“Okay,” Becky quipped as she finished her tea and walked up the concrete as Zach watched until she was out of sight. Becky was still talking when the call dropped as she entered the Moakley. She walked into Zach’s office at 7:30 and placed a small sonogram into his open left palm. He held it up to the light and shook his head as he mumbled: “I can’t see anything.”

Becky retrieved the small ultrasound and held it toward the sun shining through the conoid wall and pointed as she smiled: “See, that’s his head.”

"His?" Zach asked as he walked over toward the door and closed it. Zach placed both hands on her stomach as he whispered: "Oooh, you got a baby bump … 'his'?"

"It's a boy," Becky said as she smiled, and Zach hugged her whispering: "I really do love you, you know."

"I love you too, Mr. Woods," Becky said as she broke free of his arms and sat down in the chair opposite his desk. Zach sat and smiled: "Let's get to work. Here, read this."

Becky read Michael J. O'Connor's motion to stay in its entirety. She looked up as Zach whispered: "What?"

"Zach, don't play games with me, will you?"

Zach threw her a calculated enigmatic smile as Becky nodded her head back and forth: "You can play all you want with opposing counsel but"...

"Yeah. Well, he's got everything now, no rabbit left in my hat." Becky giggled as he perused the Veloz docket, and Amanda walked into Zach's office.

"Hey you," Becky said as Amanda smiled: "Hey."

"Hi, Mandy," Zach mumbled as he temporarily moved his eyes off the docket.

"Hi, Zach … look, I just read O'Connor's brief."

"Here we go," Zach said as he smiled at Becky who blushed.

"You know Woodbury; he's gonna move the trial date now," Amanda said with her hands on her hips as she nodded her head.

"Yeah, I know … get off my back, will ya?" Zach quipped as Becky smiled.

"You know you love me, Zach," Amanda said as Becky shook her head back and forth. Amanda's mouth dropped open as she stared at Becky: "No way. Stand up … look at this, a baby bump," she exclaimed as her right hand felt Becky's hard, small protruding abdomen.

"Um, can we get to work here?" Zach said as he grinned, and Becky blushed as Amanda continued to rub her stomach.

"Stop it, will ya?" Becky said as she walked toward the curved glass wall.

"Oh, my God," Amanda sighed as she stared at the small sonogram in Becky's seat. Amanda held it up to the light and shrieked: "it's a boy, isn't it?"

Zach threw daggers at Amanda as Amanda sat in Becky's empty chair and stared at her feet avoiding Zach's scowl.

"Can we get to work, Mandy, you think?"

"Yes, sir," Amanda said as she walked toward the glass and whispered to Becky: "Oh, my God!"

Becky and Amanda walked into Courtroom No. 1 at 9:30 surprised to see a room full of spectators already seated. O'Connor was talking with Josh leaning over the clerk's bench and didn't see Becky as she strolled into the courtroom. Charlie watched Becky as she walked down the main aisle and blew a kiss in her direction, filling the courtroom with the smell-o-vision of lilac.

Becky smiled as she inhaled her favorite fragrance and sat down next to Amanda whispering: "Smell that?" as Amanda smiled and nodded whiffing the air: "Hmmm, it's lilac" as Charlie smiled.

"How you feeling?" Amanda whispered; and as they engaged in idle chit-chat, the minutes flew. Every bench in the courtroom was packed full of bodies, and Becky didn't notice the defendants led into the courtroom by the armed CSOs. She didn't notice Timmy O'Brien trying desperately to get her attention.

Josh whispered: "Becky," and Becky jumped out of her skin and twitched as Josh laughed, "sorry, didn't mean to scare ya … where's Zach?"

Becky shrugged her shoulders and looked at Amanda who made a silly face as Zach ran up the aisle adjusting his tie: "Sorry, Josh" he whispered as Amanda vacated her seat, and Zach sat down next to Becky. "Sorry, baby" he whispered, was talking to defense counsel on a sentencing this coming Monday … lost track of time, you know."

Josh announced: "All rise," as Woodbury entered the courtroom and sat at the bench.
Woodbury mumbled: "You may be seated," and the sound of a thousand buttocks smacking the hard unforgiving benches echoed throughout the courtroom as Charlie smiled from the witness box.

"This is the matter of the U.S. vs. Jose Veloz, et al, Docket No. 12-30225. Would counsel please identify themselves for the record?

Zach stood as he winked at Becky who stumbled to stand: "Zach Woods and Becky Lawrence, your Honor, for the United States.

"Good morning, counsel," Woodbury said as he shook his head glaring at Zach.

"Michael J. O'Connor, your Honor, Federal Public Defender's Office for the Defendants: Jose Veloz, Julio Ramirez, Chico Hernandez, and Eric Jones."

"Good morning, Mr. O'Connor," the Judge said as he winked at Becky.

"Timothy O'Brien, your Honor, Federal Public Defender's Office for the Defendant Edward Hubbard, sir.

"Good morning, all. As an aside, Mr. Woods, according to my watch, it is now 10:15."

Zach stood: "Yes, your Honor."

"What time were we scheduled to begin this hearing, Mr. Woods?"

"Ten a.m. sharp, your Honor," Zach said as his voice trembled, and he looked at Becky as she grinned.

"Uh-huh. Mr. Woods, my patience is wearing thin. Do you understand?"

"I'm sorry, your Honor. It won't happen again."

"You're quite right, Mr. Woods. It won't happen again. Do you know why it won't happen again, Mr. Woods?" Woodbury said as Zach's face grew pale.

"The next time you are late to my courtroom, Mr. Woods, I will find you in contempt of court. Do we understand each other, Mr. Woods?"

"Yes, your Honor. I'm very sorry … something came up."

Woodbury raised his right hand into the air and made a slicing motion directly underneath his chin across his neck silencing Zach as the courtroom filled with the heavenly scent of lilac, and Charlie and several spectators began an overenthusiastic giggle.

"Now, until 9:00 this morning I understood we were going to have our final pretrial conference on this case."

Zach stood holding his tie against his chest: "Yes, your Honor."

"Then my law clerk hands me a motion to stay, quite a compelling motion, Mr. Woods. You've read it and dissected it, I assume?"

Zach stood: "Yes, your Honor," he mumbled as once again the

courtroom filled with giggles. As the Judge's eyes widened, the room silenced except for Charlie who was insanely giggling silently from the witness box.

O'Connor stood and as he smiled at Zach, he said: "Your Honor, if I may address my pending motion before the Court?"

"No, Mr. O'Connor. Have a seat please."

"Yes, your Honor" O'Connor said as he sat down, and Becky whispered to Zach: "He's pissed. Here it comes; hold on, babe."

"Mr. Woods" the Judge said as the courtroom grew so eerily quiet you could hear a pin drop.

"Yes, your Honor?" Zach said as he stood and looked at Becky who stared at Josh and began to smile before concentrating his eyes on the clerk's bench.

The Judge poured a glass of water and said as he stared at Zach: "Do you enjoy wasting my time, Mr. Woods?"

"No, your Honor. If I could explain" --

"No, Mr. Woods, you may not explain. Please sit down. The pending motion for discovery filed by Mr. O'Connor is granted. Mr. Woods, how long have you been trying cases before me?"

The courtroom erupted in giggles as the Judge's eyebrows raised. Zach stood: "Um, 17 years, I think, your Honor."

"Uh-huh," Woodbury said as he sipped from his glass, "Mr. Woods, how many cases have you tried before me, a guesstimate, sir?"

The courtroom erupted in giggles as Charlie blew a fine lilac power into the air and the dust meandered toward Becky and she smiled as she stared through the ghost and heard: "Charlie, Charlie, Charlie."

"Thousands, your Honor," Zach said as he stared at the floor.

"Mr. Woods, how did you think I would rule when I discovered that the government is withholding crucial evidence from defense?"

"Yes, your Honor," Zach whispered as multiple individual conversations ensued.

Woodbury took another sip of water and waited for the audience to stifle … "Mr. Woods, as I've told you numerous times, this case is ripe with appellate issues and now on the eve of trial I discover that you are withholding evidence that may possibly exonerate these defendants."

"That's not true, your Honor … 'exonerate'?"

"Mr. Woods, sit down. Do not interrupt me."

Zach stood: "I'm sorry, your Honor."

"Sit down, Mr. Woods. This is my final warning to you: Turn over all exculpatory and inculpatory evidence you possess immediately to the defense. If you withhold, Mr. Woods, I will find you in contempt. Do we understand each other, Mr. Woods?"

Zach stood and mumbled as his eyes avoided the Judge's scowl: "Yes, your Honor."

"The final pretrial conference in this case will be October 31st at 4:00 p.m. unless anyone has a scheduling dilemma?"

Zach stood: "Your Honor, most respectfully, that's Halloween and" --

Woodbury smiled: "I understand that, Mr. Woods; you have trick-or-treating plans, do you?"

The courtroom ignited into a blazing roar of laughter as Woodbury stared out glaring at the crowd as silence ensued.

“Okay … Josh.” Josh leaned over the bench and spoke with the Judge. Woodbury smiled at Becky as Josh whispered calendar dates into his left ear. Becky mouthed: ‘hi” and he smiled affectionately.

“Okay, the final pretrial conference will be November 5th at 11 a.m. … Mr. Woods?”

Zach stood: “That’s fine for the government, your Honor. Thank you.”

Woodbury took a sip of water as O’Connor fumbled through his Blackberry: “That’s fine for defense as well, your Honor.”

Timmy stood and smiled at Becky as she blushed and the Judge grinned: “That’s fine for me too, your Honor.”

“Very well. Thank you, counsel. We are adjourned.”

Zach whispered to Becky: “That went well, huh?”

“Yeah, great,” Becky said as Charlie smiled.

“We’ve got to talk,” Zach whispered as his face contorted into a grimace.

“You mean now?” Becky asked as she twirled her pen in her right hand. Zach grabbed the pen with his left hand and nodded his head. They waited for the courtroom to clear; and as Amanda said: “See ya,” Zach whispered into Becky’s ear, “Come on; let’s get some breakfast. We’ll eat outside.”

Zach and Becky ate their bagels sitting on a bench overlooking the harbor, watching as seagulls landed ten feet in front of them on the pebbly sand. Once they were finished, Zach said: “Come on, come take a walk with me.”

Becky walked at Zach’s left side as he occasionally stopped and picked up a rock and skidded it into the water. They giggled as seagulls argued amongst themselves over a floppy French fry at the water's edge.

"Becky, I want you to think about this real seriously, okay?"

"Think about what, Zach?" Becky whispered.

"Do you know how hard your life will be raising a baby all by yourself?" Zach asked as he stopped and stood in front of her.

"What are you saying, Zach?" Becky asked as her eyes swelled with tears.

"I love you. I think you should have an abortion." Becky felt her blood pressure escalate, and she slapped him as hard as she could across the left side of his face, leaving a handprint impression in his skin.

"Seriously! You're serious? You wait until I'm five months along to tell me to get an abortion." She pushed his chest and he backed up several feet as his shoes hit the water as the tide began to creep in.

Becky started to walk away from him, her face turned red as she began to talk to herself as she mumbled under her breath: "You love me … you love me!"

"Becky," Zach whispered from behind, "Jesus, stop!" Becky stopped walking and stood her ground staring at her feet as Zach walked in front of her: "What do you want to happen here? Just tell me, Becky, what do you want from me? If my wife finds out about this 'baby,' she'll take everything, I mean 'everything,' and I'll never see Emily again. Is that what you want?"

Tears poured down Becky's cheeks as she turned away from him as he screamed: "You're so selfish. You're fucking up my life."

Becky turned around and smacked him as hard as she physically could as she screamed: "I'm selfish? I'm fucking up 'your life'!" Zach grabbed his face with his left hand as he mouthed: "Ouch … Becky!"

“Becky,” Zach whispered as he placed his left hand on her right arm, and she pulled away and screamed: “Don’t touch me. Just don’t touch me.” She walked with her back toward him crying, unable to catch her breath. Zach screamed: “I love you … where are you going?” as an elderly couple stared at him in contempt.

“What the hell are you looking at?” Zach shouted. He turned around and faced the ocean, watching the waves crash onto the beach, occasionally running toward seagulls, and smiling as they flew away. “Becky!” he screamed as she walked with a singular purpose, to put as much distance as she could between them.

“I’ve never hit anyone before” -- she thought to herself -- “well, except Zach,” as she walked toward the Moakley at a fast clip while mumbling: “you love me … you love me?” as tears streamed down her cheeks. Becky walked across the bridge at the Fort Point Channel and walked around the Financial District bawling, talking to herself almost continuously searching for some scintilla of mental clarity: “You love me … oh, my God. I’m such a moron,” she whispered as she cried and walked darting the sun. It was 97 degrees out; and as Becky walked, her clothes became saturated as she swallowed and tasted the salt of her tears as her suit clung to her skin.

She leaned against One Financial Center and sent a text to Amanda: “Hi, going home early; I’ll put a leave slip in on Monday … call me later, ‘k’?” Sixty seconds later Becky’s cell vibrated: “one next text: You okay? … Amanda.” Becky’s hands were shaking and she hit two letters as she sobbed: “n-o.” Her iPhone rang and she answered as her head pounded.

“Becky?,” Amanda whispered, “what’s wrong?” Becky began blubbering and hysterically mumbling: “I, I, I can’t” -- she whimpered into her iPhone soaking the touchscreen with her tears.

“Where are you?” Amanda asked.

“I don’t know,” Becky sighed as she looked around, and strangers stared at her pouting as she sobbed.

“All right, I’ll let everyone know you’re sick today, had to leave early. Meet me down by” --

“Meet me on the bridge, ‘k’?” Becky stammered as she attempted to compose and wiped the tears from her cheeks. As Becky walked back over the bridge, people stared and contorted their faces as Becky thought: “Geez, I must look like a freak … look how they stare.”

The mascara stained her fingertips as she rubbed the skin under her eyes. She spotted Amanda pacing nervously a hundred yards ahead. Amanda ran toward Becky and tears streamed down her cheeks as Amanda hugged her tightly.

“Come on,” Amanda whispered and Becky followed her down toward the pier. Occasionally, Amanda looked into Becky’s eyes and shook her head back and forth spasmodically. They walked in silence as the wind blew Becky’s hair back and twisted it into salty knots. As they stepped off the boardwalk and hopped down to the beachfront, Becky stopped walking and stared out into the ocean as tears slid down her cheeks: “Zach wants me to get an abortion,” she whispered as she stared blanketly into the waves.

“Isn’t it a little late?”Amanda screamed as she mumbled: “prick” and Becky whispered: “Shhh.”

Amanda walked toward the water and Becky followed as she said: “Look at you, you’re soaked” … Becky walked into the water leaving her heels on the sand and took her pantyhose off and immersed her hose in the sea. She wiped her wet hose across her forehead and the back of her neck; and as her body temperature plummeted and began to regulate, she finally caught her breath. Amanda watched as Becky submerged her arms and splashed saltwater onto her face and smiled.

They sat down on the sand and Becky whispered: “I’m a moron, Amanda.”

"No, you're not. Listen: Don't make any decisions right now, okay? Just go home, take a shower, you know, put your feet up, have an ice cream, and think about things. Zach's scared shitless … it's real now, you know; you're starting to show, and he's running scared."

Becky stared into the sand and whispered: "The only decision I have to make is figuring out how I'm going to ask for an internal transfer. I don't think I can work with him … Amanda, I hit him."

Amanda nodded her head back and forth, "Yeah? I probably would have beat the shit out of him" she said as Becky grinned, and they giggled watching a naked two-year-old chasing a gull as he, in aggravated exasperation, threw his pale at the bird in archaic frustration.

"Listen, you call me any time, day or night. Don't make any decisions right now, and, um, maybe"…

"Maybe?" Becky asked as the sun illuminated her pretty face.

"Maybe you should just put a little distance between you and Zach right now, you know?" Becky nodded as Amanda helped her to stand. Amanda walked Becky back toward the Moakley, and they walked around the courthouse and across the street to the Silver Line. They hugged and stuck to each other in sweat as the sun beat across their backs. Becky walked down four concrete stairs leading underground into the station and turned around, and Amanda smiled and waved as Becky said: "I love you, you know."

Amanda smiled: "I love you too, girl … go." Amanda walked into the Moakley stomping her feet and biting at the bit. She ran into the elevator and stormed into Zach's empty office. She looked around noticing his blazer was absent from its usual spot hanging on the back of his door and his monitor was black. She walked up to reception and stared at Jenny seething: "Where's Zach?"

"Oh, he left for the day, Mandy" Jenny whispered as Amanda shook her head and internally fumed as her cheeks reddened. "Of course, he did" she mumbled to herself as she walked out of the office and into the hallway and began to pace in front of the conoid wall: "Of course he left early … couldn't face her, selfish prick."

Becky sat on her black leather recliner in front of the living room air conditioner and sipped lemonade as she flicked channels incessantly on her Amazon Smart TV when she came upon one of her favorite movies from 1988. She watched as C.C. Bloom asked her best friend Hillary if she'd slept with her director, the director of her new off-Broadway play, the man she longed to touch … "Zach" Becky mumbled as she began to cry as Bette Midler's face contorted in anger and resentment.

Becky bawled as she sipped her lemonade and became hysterical as Beaches ended and Hillary died; and as Midler sang: "You are the wind beneath my wings" Becky sang along out of pitch, closed her eyes, and watched as Zach slowly leaned in and whispered: "I love you, Becky."

She heard her iPhone ringing from the hamper in the bathroom. "Please God, let it be" -- she ran to the bathroom and kicked the metal hinge protruding from the doorjamb. She hopped in pain toward the hamper and scattered to retrieve her cell. "One missed call," it said across the touchscreen, "Amanda."

Becky hopped back into her recliner, closed her eyes, and saw Zach standing erect before her, watched his head cock back as she swallowed him; and as she slept, she heard: "Charlie, Charlie, Charlie."

Two hours later Becky awoke with her neck aching as she was wrenched in an awkward position. She sat up and twisted her neck from side to side as her iPhone buried under her began to vibrate: "Please God" she whispered as she dug into the cushion.

"One next text," it displayed: "You okay girl? … Amanda." Tears streamed down Becky's face as she hit reply: "Yeah, sad … TTYT."

Becky looked up and noticed that Beaches was playing again. She flicked on the menu to discover that AMC was playing it back to back for the next 48 hours. She fell back asleep as her iPhone buzzed: "One next text."

Becky awoke and stared at her touchscreen: "I'm sorry, I love you … Z." Becky cried as she placed the iPhone on the ottoman and walked over toward the window and watched as the sun set and the pink sky ignited with exuberant florescence. Her cell vibrated as tears streamed down her chin … "Zach," she whispered as she cried and hummed: "Show me love, show me life, Baby, show me what it's all about … you're the only one I've ever needed; show me love and what it's all about" as tears fell into her open mouth and she tasted the salt of her grief.

Becky walked with a marked limp toward the ottoman: "Please call" it read as Becky's tears clouded the screen. She put it on the coffee table and walked into her bedroom as her stomach rumbled. She stripped naked and got into bed. She fell asleep as she rubbed her belly and whispered: "I love you already."

Becky awoke as the sun rose at 5:25 a.m. and her stomach roared for attention. She ran to the bathroom and vomited as her day began. She splashed cold water on her face and headed into the kitchen starved. As she woofed down three sunny-side eggs with two pieces of toasted rye bread, dunking them intermittently into her dribbling yoke, her cell phone buzzed from the living room.

Becky ran to the living room and sighed as her touchscreen displayed: "one next text." She smiled as she read: "Hi, it's Saturday. Kids sleeping at Grandma's tonight, dropping 'em off soon, let's go shopping, girlfriend … Amanda."

She dialed Amanda who answered as her kids fought in the background: "Hey," she whispered as Dylan shrieked: "That's mine" and pulled the watergun out of his sister's hands.

"Hi … got your hands full, huh?" Becky said smiling as her right hand patted her belly.

“Hmmm,” Amanda moaned and shouted simultaneously: “Alaya, stop it! Listen, Becky, can I call you back?”

“Sure” Becky said with a giggle as she hit disconnect. She read Zach’s text over and over again: “I’m sorry, I love you … Z.” She plugged her iPhone into the USB attached to her PC and booted it on as she walked into the bathroom. She stepped into the shower; and as the hot water pelted against her shoulders and upper back, she rubbed her stomach with soap and whispered: “Zach.” She closed her eyes and heard: “How’s my girl?” as her body twitched, and she opened her eyes as the shampoo blinded her.

At noon Amanda beeped just outside Becky’s complex as Becky leaped to her feet from the front stoop. “Single, huh?” she said as she smiled and hopped into the front seat … “Where we going, girlfriend?” Becky said as Amanda smiled.

“How ‘bout my new fav store?” Amanda said as she giggled and Becky yelled: “TJ Maxx! I love it, and besides look” ... Becky picked up her overhanging Imagine Dragons t-shirt and showed Amanda that her pants were unbuttoned and ballooning at the waist.

“Hey, I got maternity clothes for you real cheap too. Come on, we’ll stop at my place first.”

Amanda put on a face as Becky said: “What?”

“Um, nothing, just don’t mind the mess, ‘k’?”

Twenty-five minutes later Amanda pulled in front of her small white house with black shutters on Spring Street in Holbrook and parked her white new Maxima in the driveway. Becky gasped as she smiled staring at the tall wild flowers in bloom darting through the tiny front yard. There were red and white roses meandering along the white picket fence, and Becky leaned down for a fragrant whiff.

“Come on,” Amanda said as she walked into the house as Becky sneezed. Becky stepped over Tonka trucks and Legos scattered on the living room floor. “Told ya,” Amanda said as Becky smiled:

"Ah, it's not so bad, girlfriend."

Amanda led Becky upstairs to her master bedroom and pulled out two large white plastic bins from under her box spring. She opened them and said: "Bargain basement price on all this," as Becky smiled and began rummaging through the bins.

Becky tried on three pairs of pants, shocked at how well they fit. "Wait," Amanda shrieked, "lookie what I got" … Becky followed Amanda to her closet as Amanda pulled out several dress suits with elastic waists. "Can I" --

"Sure, try 'em on," Amanda said smiling as she sat on the edge of the bed as her legs dangled off the floor. "This is gorgeous, Mandy," Becky said as she looked in the mirror at the black pantsuit that molded to her frame. An hour later Amanda and Becky carried the two large white plastic bins and loaded them into Amanda's trunk. Amanda laid half a dozen suits and two maternity dresses across the double car seats, and they sped off laughing toward the Westgate Mall.

As Amanda pulled into the garage and turned off the ignition, she whispered: "Hear from, um, Mr. Wonderful yet?" Becky displayed Zach's text, and Amanda grabbed the iPhone: "I'm sorry, I love you … Z." Amanda nodded her head up and down and whispered: "You call him?"

Becky nodded her head back and forth as Amanda smiled: "Good girl. Don't. Let him wallow a little." Becky smiled and the girls spent the day rummaging through the discount racks at T.J. Maxx and Marshalls. By 3:30 Becky couldn't ignore her rumbling belly as Amanda smiled: "Hungry?" and giggled: "Come on."

Becky and Amanda sat in a dark booth in Bertucci's and devoured a large pepperoni pizza as they talked and giggled as Becky's iPhone vibrated in her pocket.

"Wonder who that is?" Amanda said with conniving grin.

Becky looked at the touchscreen: "One next text." It read: "Where are you? … Zach." Becky flashed her screen toward Amanda as she grinned. "Don't answer, Becky. Let him wallow."

"Maybe I could just hit like "missing you" or "at the mall?" Becky asked as Amanda shook her head back and forth as she nervously bit her bottom lip.

"Don't respond. You want him?" Amanda asked as Becky nodded. "Then don't respond. He thinks he lost you. He's out of his mind right now. Let him wallow. Let him suffer a little."
Becky nodded her head as Amanda grinned, and Becky smiled: "So this is the game we play, huh?"

"Yeah, my friend … the game of love, the game of life" Amanda said with a smile as Becky giggled. "Haven't you ever heard the expression: if you love something, set it free; if it comes back to you" --

"It's yours?" Becky interjected as Amanda smiled, "always thought that was crap.

"I don't know, Becky; guys like the chase, especially a cocky prick like Zachary Woods."

"Amanda, he's not a" --

"Seriously, Becky, he is. If you want him, you need to learn to play the game." Becky nodded her head as Amanda whispered: "Is he that good?"

Becky smiled and whispered: "Oh, my God, Amanda." Amanda bumped her left shoulder into Becky, and they giggled like teenagers as Amanda whispered: "does he eat you?"

"Amanda," Becky shrieked as she shook her head up and down and whispered, "for hours and hours and hours, girlfriend."

"Hmmm," Amanda sighed, "Make him wallow." Becky's cell began to play her new ringtone, her favorite tune from The Kooks:

"So now you pour your heart out, you're telling me you're far out, but you're not about to lie down for your cause, but you don't pull my strings 'cause I'm a better man moving onto better things … well, uh oh, I love her 'cause she moves in her own way. Well, uh oh, she came to my show just to hear about my day."

Amanda yelled: "Oh, my God, The Kooks! I friggin' love them." Becky went to answer and Amanda grabbed her wrist and shook her head back and forth whispering: "no" as the song continued to play: "So won't you go far; tell me you're a keeper, not about to lie down for your cause and you don't pull my strings 'cause I'm a better man, moving onto better things … "well, uh oh, I love her because she moves in her own way."

Amanda and Becky started to sing out of tune: "Well, uh oh, she came to my show just to hear about my day, but, uh oh, I love her because she moves in her own way, but, uh oh, she came to my show just to hear about my day."

Amanda and Becky giggled as the waiter smiled and said: "You know they're coming to Boston this summer," and Amanda smiling at Becky said: "So we got a date, girlfriend?" as Becky shook her head, and they sing in unison and in perfect pitch: "Well, uh oh, I love her because she moves in her own way. Well, uh oh, she came to my show just to hear about my day."

"I'll get the tickets," Becky said as she smiled and her cell vibrated in her palm: "Please call … Love Z." Amanda whispered: "how much you want to bet he's drinking his sorrows away?"

Amanda and Becky walked out of Bertucci's still singing: "Well, uh oh, I love her because she moves in her own way," as Amanda's Galaxy began to sing:

"There is no pain you are receding, a distant ship smoke on the horizon … you are only coming through in waves, your lips move but I can't hear what you're saying. When I was a child" -- "Ma?,"

Amanda answered as she stopped walking, “seriously?”

“Okay. No, it’s fine. I’m at the mall with a good friend.” Becky smiled as Amanda whispered: “Give me an hour.”

“What’s up?” Becky said concerned deciphering Amanda’s serious expression. “Nothing, Alaya doesn’t feel good … she’s crying so, you know, I’ll go over there and tell her a bedtime story; and when she passes out, I’m going home and getting loaded.”

“Getting loaded?” Becky asked with a smile.

“Yeah, haven’t had a drink in almost a year and I’m long overdue” Amanda said as she pressed the remote and the doors unlocked. Half an hour later as they sat in the Maxima just outside Becky’s complex, her iPhone buzzed: “one next text: “Where are you, babe?” Becky flashed the screen toward Amanda who whispered as she hugged her: “Had fun today.”

“Me too” Becky replied as she smiled.

“Remember, let him wallow,” she whispered, “make him come to you,” as Becky whispered: “Thanks, Mandy.” Amanda shut off the ignition and helped Becky carry in the bins of clothes into her apartment. Amanda spread the suits out onto the couch as Zach appeared in the doorway wasted.

“Mr. Wonderful’s here,” Amanda whispered as Becky turned her head toward Zach who stammered: “Hi, Mandy.”

“Hi, Zach -- woe, you’ve seen better days, huh? Excuse me,” she said with glaring sarcasm as she squeezed by him in the doorjamb. “See ya, Becky,” she said with a smile as she threw Zach a menacing look.

“Bye, Mandy,” Zach said as Becky carried her suits into her bedroom and put them into her closet. Her stomach hurt as her tight jeans dug into her midriff, and she stripped and slipped on her bathrobe. She walked back into the living room and stared at Zach who looked wasted staring at the floor as the jamb supported his weight.

She walked over to the couch and sat down as he began swaying, his head leaning against the doorjamb as he spinned. He walked in as their eyes locked and the door swung closed behind him. She stared at the floor at her feet as he sat down in front of her on the floor.

"Look at me," Zach said looking disheveled, his eyes tiny red slits as he'd spent the day with a good old friend, Jim Beam. As the whiskey infused her mucous membranes, she whispered: "You drunk?"

"Mmm … define 'drunk,'" Zach moaned as he stared at her bare legs. "I'm sorry," he whispered as tears filled her eyes, and he buried his head against her baby bump. Her bathrobe tie came loose as his head shimmied, and Zach smiled as she inhaled his distinctive pheromonal tang mixed with whiskey, and her knees spread apart as his left hand peeled her thong down to her knees and his warm tongue entered her and she screamed and stood: "Zach, don't;" and as she stood naked above his head, he reached up and suckled her clit in his mouth.

"Oh, God," she screamed as her juices began to flow, and he lapped as her translucent liquid drowned his chin. "I am such an asshole," he whispered as she sat back down on the couch and spread her legs as she pushed the back of his head against her and wept as her internal volcano exploded and liquid splurted through the air.

Zach stood swaying staring at her wet cheeks: "Come on," he whispered as he helped her to stand. He led her into her bedroom knocking his shoulders intermittently into the walls as he staggered, and he locked the door as her bathrobe fell to the floor. She stood naked beside her bed staring at her round belly: "Look at me," she said as she cried hearing her father's voice: "Girls like you, Becky"….

Zach stood in front of her as his right hand gently felt her baby bump: "I'm looking at you," he whispered as he sat on the edge of the bed and pushed his face gently against her abdomen, "you are the most beautiful thing I have ever seen."

"Sit," Zach said as his left hand pounded the bed's edge. Becky sat down next to him as he whispered: "I'm sorry." His left hand touched the right side of Becky's face cupping it gently in his massive hand as he kissed her, and she tasted whiskey and cigarettes and slowly lied back on the bed.

He kissed her neck as her body humped the air. He began licking her neck as she giggled. He squeezed her right nipple between his forefingers as he suckled her left nipple and drank her milk as she sopped the mattress. "Ow" Becky screamed as her nipple ignited sending neurons into disarray.

He licked her abdomen as she twitched, and goosebumps filled her arms and legs. "My baby" he whispered as he licked her belly, and she shimmied her body toward the headboard and opened her legs as he buried his head into her engorged vulva. "Oh, my God," she screamed as he ate her delicately and lapped as his middle finger inserted deeply inside her ass. An hour later as Zach watched smiling as her volcano erupted, he giggled insanely as Becky pleaded: "Put it in, Zach; please, put it in."

"Turn over, baby," he whispered as he stared at her inner lips. Becky turned over and got on her knees. He licked her anus as she pleaded: "Put it in, Zach," as her juice dribbled down her inner thighs. "I'm wasted," he whispered, "I'm sorry, but, um," as he giggled, "this might be quick."
He mounted her as his right middle finger rubbed her clit back and forth, and she squeezed him inside of her as hard as she could, and he ejaculated and giggled. "Sorry," he whispered as he collapsed on top of her, his weight throwing her into her waterlogged mattress. Her pelvic floor contracted repeatedly as he giggled and drooled on her back. Slowly he pulled out and whispered as he diddled: "Turn over, baby."

Becky turned over as Zach on his knees watched her as she laid her head against the pillow and he whispered: "Put your feet up, baby." He licked her clit softly and gently, his tongue meandering toward her ass slowly with calculated orgasmic intent. As he licked her, she whispered: “Ahhh” and he fell asleep ten minutes later with his tongue deep inside her.

“Zach?” Becky whispered as she raised her head and smiled, watching him sleep as she climaxed again, and he began involuntarily drinking her as she released. He opened his eyes and watched her orgasm, and he licked his lips as his erection grew immense, and he giggled: “I gotta pee, baby.”

Zach stood up swaying and walked toward her bedroom door as she whispered: “Zach.”

Zach turned around and with an enigmatic grin: “Yeah?”

“I’ve got a roommate, remember?”

Zach stumbled toward the foot of the bed, grabbed his jeans off the floor and sat down struggling to pull them up to his waist. He attempted as he giggled to zipper them over his immense bulge finally leaving the zipper down as he giggled and she smiled. Three minutes later Zach walked into her bedroom smiling as Becky was on her knees, fingering herself as she moaned.

Oh, my God,” he said as he grinned and slid his Levis to the floor and began licking her from behind, watching her vulva swell and contract and cupping his sack as she masturbated. “Put it in” she pleaded as his tongue began suckling her clit hard, pulling on it as she humped her fingers.

“What do you want, baby?” he whispered as he smiled and drank from her fountain. He slid into her as her fingers continued to play with her inner lips, and he lost his erection and whispered: “I’m sorry, baby … I’m wasted.”

Becky giggled and said: “Zach, stand up.” He stood next to the edge of the bed as she dangled her legs over the side and swallowed him, her teeth scraping against him. He closed his eyes and swayed and screamed: “Ahhh.” And as the ejaculate rose from deep within, just as he was on the cusp of release, he pulled out of her mouth and said with a coy smile: “Turn over, baby.”

Becky hopped off the mattress and kneeled on the floor in front of him, spreading her arms over the bed as Zach whispered: “Say it.” Becky shook her head and buried her face into the bed’s edge as her body humped the air.

“Say it,” he whispered as he knelt down and smacked his cock back and forth against her inner thighs as his fingers played an orchestral symphony with her labia. As he whacked against her ass, he wet the tip of his pointer finger of his left hand and wiggled her clit madly as she screamed: “Oh, my God, Zach … put it in.”

“Say it, baby,” Zach whispered as her juice flowed up his forearm.

“Fuck me!” she screamed as he plunged inside of her as she erupted, and he immediately ejaculated deep within her. As he climaxed and moaned, she whispered: “I love you, Zach,” as his left hand caressed her stomach, and he whispered as he felt her intense uterine contractions groping him from within as he giggled and whispered: “I love you too, Ms. Lawrence.”

They climbed on top of the bed and Zach spooned her as he fell fast asleep, both hands on her baby bump. As she lied naked in his arms exhausted, listening to him sleep, she closed her eyes and heard: “Charlie, Charlie, Charlie.” She momentarily opened her eyes and rubbed his forearms, pressing them against her midriff tightly, and she whispered in her mind: “Zach,” and fell fast asleep.

At 10:05 Becky opened her eyes as Zach’s ringtone blared from his jean pocket on the bedroom floor, and she smiled as she listened to his new ringtone: “If I could talk, I’d tell you; if I could smile, I’d let you know; you are far and away, my most imaginary friend.”

“Zach,” Becky whispered as she nudged his left arm. Zach didn’t move. “Zach, wake up!” Zach sat straight up listening to: “Khmer Rhouge and genocide qua, your place or Mein Kempf, now I’m giving the dog a bone, slight hunch without the vaguest clue to keep the blood balanced, now we're coming around again."

"Jesus," Zach mumbled as he raced to his jeans and retrieved his cell. "Hey," he whispered as he rubbed his eyes, and Becky leaned her back against the headboard.

"Where the fuck are you, Zach?" his wife screamed. "I've about fucking had it. Answer me!"

Zach grinned at Becky as she closed her eyes and listened: "I'm at a bar, drinking … what the fuck do you want?" he screamed as Becky winced: "Oh, my God," she thought, "this is how they talk to each other?"

"Get your ass home now; you hear me?" his wife screamed as her voice echoed loudly.

"Laura, fuck off," Zach screamed, "I'll be home on my time … why don't you take a little purple pill; that always makes you feel better."

"Fuck you!" his wife screamed as Zach sat on the edge of Becky's bed trying to wake up. Becky stood up and ran to the bathroom as urine dribbled down her thighs, and Zach giggled watching naked from the edge of the bed.

Becky returned to her bedroom surprised to see Zach hadn't moved. As she approached him, he untied her white terry bathrobe and she knelt down on the carpet on her knees. "I gotta go" he mumbled as she swallowed him, and his erection caused her to temporarily gag. He lied back on her bed as Becky pulled on him sucking her mouth like a vacuum, scraping her teeth against him as he screamed and ejaculated down her throat. He sat up and stroked the back of her head as he grew small inside her mouth.

"Fuck it," he said as Becky stood and Zach whispered, "Come here" as he patted the center of the soaked mattress. Becky dropped the bathrobe on the floor and straddled the bed. "Put your knees up, baby" he whispered as he shimmied on his back underneath her. Becky sat on his face as he teased her with his tongue as his hands clenched her buttocks and she screamed as she sat straight up. As her orgasm consumed her, he inserted his entire fist inside her and watched her as she humped and swallowed his hand.

Slowly he slid his fist out and shimmied his head out from under her torrent. She turned around and sat on her knees as he bent down and tortured her clit with his tongue as he whispered: “Say it.” Becky leaned forward and threw her breasts on top of her arms and whispered: “Put it in” as her juice saturated the mattress.

He continued to slowly lick her clit as she pleaded: “Oh, God, Zach, put it in.” He licked as he giggled: “Say it, Becky.”

“Fuck me,” she screamed as he plunged inside her while his left hand played with her vulva incessantly as she screamed: “Oh, my God, Zach … oh, my God, harder.”

“Harder?,” he whispered, as he slid out from her and liquid engulfed the mattress. “Come here” Zach whispered as he stood next to the bed holding his cock in his left hand. Slowly Becky peeled her skin from the deluged mattress and stood in front of him. “Turn over and bend down, baby.”

Becky turned around and bent over as Zach thrust into her from behind so deeply it hurt. “Ow” she shrieked as he whispered: “It’s okay,” and he reached down with his left hand in front of her and began playing with her clit, wiggling it as she humped him. He waited until he felt her orgasmic release before he banged her with increasing force from behind.

“Harder,” she screamed as liquid inundated his thighs. He plunged as hard and as deep as he could thrust as she yelled: “Ow.”

He pulled out and smiled: “You said ‘harder,’ remember … you okay?” as he slid out.

Becky nodded as Zach sat on the edge of the bed and said: “Turn over and come here.” Becky stuck her ass in his face, and he bit her ass as he spread her cheeks far apart and licked her anus. As his tongue dug in deep, his right hand reached around and under, and he fucked her with his fingers as her warm juice sopped the floor. Zach shimmied off the bed and onto the wet carpet as Becky stood watching him panting.

“Come here,” he whispered, “on your knees.” Becky sat down on the floor and dug her knees into the carpet and screamed: “Zach” as Zach thrust into her from behind as Becky’s orgasm exploded in seismic waves. As he banged her, he reached down with his left hand and played with her clit as fluid drowned the carpet, and Zach giggled as he released and whispered as he wiggled her: “You like that, baby?” and collapsed on top of her on the carpet as she giggled.

The tang of whiskey flooded her nostrils as Zach kissed the back of her neck whispering: “I love you … I gotta go” and slowly pulled out of her. “I can’t move,” Becky whispered as Zach stood and giggled: “Yeah, you stuck to the floor, huh?”

Becky sat up slowly and Zach pulled her up by her right hand as he stared at her immense nipples protruding, hard and erect. He sat down on the bed and pulled her toward him as he suckled her right breast and milk filled his mouth as her liquid dripped onto the floor.

Zach released her nipple slowly and smiled as he watched her juice running down her legs. He licked her inner thigh and moaned: “Hmmm” as he raised his head and pressed his face between her breasts. He stared into her eyes as he cupped her right breast and began suckling her nipple. “I gotta go, baby,” he whispered as he held her right nipple in his teeth.

She sat down on the edge of her bed and watched as Zach dressed. “You okay to drive?” she asked as he smiled. “I’m fine, baby,” he said as he tucked his t-shirt into his pants. Fully dressed, he sat down on the edge of her bed and tied his Nikes as she leaned against the headboard and yawned.

“I’m gonna leave her,” Zach said as he smiled watching Becky yawn and her eyes water as his cell phone began to scream: “If I could talk, I’d tell you; if I could smile, I’d let you know, you are far and away, my most imaginary friend."

"Shit," Zach said as he hit the button to ignore the call and slipped his iPhone into his right front pocket. He leaned in toward Becky and kissed her gently on the lips. She rubbed her tongue against his bottom lip tickling him. As he giggled, he whispered: "Get some sleep, baby" and Becky watched as Zach left her bedroom and began to cry as she heard the front door close.

She stripped her bed and threw her soiled bedsheets and mattress pad into the hamper by the door and walked into the hallway and opened the linen closet as she began to hum: "If I could talk, I'd tell you; if I could smile, I'd let you know … you are far and away, my most imaginary friend."

As she shut off the light on her nightstand and shimmied her body under her crisp clean sheets, she closed her eyes as her room filled with the luscious scent of white lilac, and she said out loud under her breath: "Zach" as she fell fast asleep.

Zach dashed into Courtroom No. 1 at 10:08 a.m. as Josh grinned: "Judge is pissed."

"Damn" he whispered under his breath as he sat next to Becky and leaned in toward her right ear: "he's gonna castrate me" as Becky smiled and whispered: "Yeah?"

Josh buzzed in the Judge and announced: "All rise" as Woodbury took the bench with an angry, hostile demeanor.

"This is the sentencing hearing in the matter of the U.S. vs. Charles Grady, Esquire. Would counsel please identify themselves for the record?

Woodbury poured a glass of water as he stared at Zach with a menacing scowl.

"Zach Woods and Becky Lawrence for the Government, your Honor."

“Good morning, your Honor. Mark Gould, your Honor, from Gould & Storrs, for the Defendant.”

Zach remained standing as the Judge sipped his water: “Your Honor, I want to start out by apologizing to the Court for being late.”

“Mr. Woods, you are in contempt of court. Every time you show up late to proceedings held in this chamber you will be fined $100. Please make the check payable to the Clerk of Court.”

Amanda began smiling and Becky stared at the Judge as he grinned at her and the incense of freshly-cut lilac diffused throughout the courtroom.

“Your Honor, I’m deeply sorry.”

Woodbury chuckled: “You’re going to be very sorry in the near future, Mr. Woods. Let’s proceed, shall we, counsel?”

“Yes, your Honor,” Zach said as he smiled at Becky who was on the verge of cracking up.

Zach cleared his throat: “Your Honor, as you're aware the defendant stands before you having admitted to very, very serious crimes; specifically, the defendant who was a highly-educated, long-time member of the criminal defense bar in Massachusetts has admitted to using his attorney IOLTA account to launder over $2,000,000 in drug proceeds.

That money was then used, among other things, to basically buy freedom, your Honor, for incarcerated state court defendants facing drug charges; many of whom, once their freedom was purchased with the money laundered through Mr. Grady's IOLTA account, fled and became fugitives in the system.

These are incredibly serious crimes. The government believes that there is no excuse, in light of the information in the presentence report regarding Mr. Grady's background, his education, what appears to have by all accounts been a loving and stable family in which he was raised, there's no excuse for this conduct."

Woodbury put his glasses on: "Because this defendant is being held responsible for laundering funds in the amount of $2,329,015, and that figure falls between 1 and 2-and-a-half million, a 16-level increase is warranted pursuant to Guideline 2B1.1(b)(1)(i), rendering a base offense level of 24. Do counsel agree with those calculations?"

Mark Gould stood and smiled at Zach as he spoke: "Yes, your Honor."

Zach stood and held his tie to his chest: "Yes, your Honor."

Woodbury took his glasses off and laid them gently next to his water glass: "Does the defendant wish to address the Court before sentence is imposed?"

Mark Gould smiled as he stared at Zach who focused on the floor in front of the clerk's bench: "No, your Honor."

"Then would the defendant please stand. This is a sad day, not only for you, but for the entire legal profession, and, particularly, the criminal defense bar of Massachusetts, which is composed of a uniquely talented group of professional attorneys.

You have disgraced not only yourself but all of the rest of us who hold our profession in high esteem, and for what ... something like $30,000 over a five-year period. And beside that paltry amount, what did you accomplish? You bought the freedom of accused drug traffickers, a great many of whom absconded, and for all we know are trafficking in drugs to this day.

It is incomprehensible to me that someone of your intelligence, background, and education could have committed such a heinous and stupid crime. You are an attorney, a criminal defense attorney at that. You know what crime is and what it does to society in general and to its innocent victims in particular.

How could you have done such a thing? I know that in one way you are very fortunate because if your attorney had not worked out an agreed plea with the government, I would have reasonably sentenced you to a guideline sentence of 87 months. I would have done that not only to punish you, but also to send an even louder and clearer message than the one I am now going to send to any other attorney, or professional for that matter, that such conduct will not be tolerated. Our profession deserves better."

Amanda whispered: "Oooh" to Becky who smiled as she inhaled the savory lilac permeating the air.

Woodbury took a sip of water: "Pursuant to the Sentencing Reform Act of 1984, and having considered the sentencing factors enumerated in Title 18 of the United States Code, Section 3553(a), it is the judgment of this Court that you, Charles M. Grady, are hereby committed to the custody of the Bureau of Prisons to be imprisoned for a term of 66 months. This term consists of terms of 66 months on each count to be served concurrently.

Upon release from imprisonment, you shall be placed on supervised release for a term of two years. This term consists of terms of two years on each count, all such terms to run concurrently.

Within 72 hours of release from custody of the Bureau of Prisons, you shall report in person to the district to which you are released. No fine is imposed as it is found you do not have the financial ability to pay a fine.

While on supervised release you shall comply with the following terms and conditions: first, you shall comply with the standard conditions that have been adopted by this Court, and described in Sentencing Guideline Section 5D1.3(c), and which will be set forth in detail in the judgment and committal.

You shall not commit another federal, state, or local crime, and shall not illegally possess a controlled substance. You shall refrain from any unlawful use of a controlled substance, and you shall submit to

one drug test within 15 days of release from imprisonment and at least two periodic drug tests thereafter, not to exceed 50 tests per year as directed by the probation office.
You shall submit to the collection of a DNA sample as directed by the probation office, and the following special conditions also apply: within six months of sentencing or release from custody, whichever is later, you shall cooperate with the examination and collection divisions of the Internal Revenue Service.

You are to provide to the examination division all financial information necessary to determine your prior tax liabilities, and you are to provide the collection division all financial information necessary to determine your ability to pay.

You shall file accurate and complete tax returns for those years for which returns were not filed or for which inaccurate returns were filed, and you shall make a good faith effort to pay all delinquent and additional taxes, interest, and penalties.

Finally, the following special conditions apply: you are prohibited from possessing a firearm, destructive device, or other dangerous weapon. You are to participate in a program for substance abuse treatment as directed by the United States Probation Office, which program may include testing not to exceed 50 tests per year to determine whether you have reverted to the use of alcohol or drugs.

You shall be required to contribute to the costs of services for that treatment based upon your ability to pay or the availability of third-party payment. You are not to consume any alcoholic beverages, and you are to participate in a mental health treatment program as directed by the probation office. You are required to contribute to the costs of services for that treatment based upon your ability to pay or the availability of third-party payment.

It is further ordered that you shall pay to the United States a special assessment of $500, which shall be due and payable immediately. It is further ordered that you shall self-surrender at an institution designated by the Bureau of Prisons four weeks from today, and that facility will be designated by the United States Marshal between this date and then.

Mr. Grady, to the extent that you have a right to appeal, you must appeal within 14 days. If you cannot afford an attorney, an attorney will be appointed on your behalf. Do you understand that?"

The defendant stood and said in a crackled voice: "Yes, your Honor."

Woodbury smiled at Becky: "Then is there any further business then to come before the Court in these proceedings?"

Zach stood: "Not from the United States, your Honor."

"No, your Honor," Mark Gould said as he smiled at Becky. "Thank you."

Woodbury sipped his water slowly and placed it on the bench: "In that case then, we are adjourned ... Mr. Woods, approach."

Zach whispered to Becky: "Here it comes" as she smiled and said: "You deserve it, Mr. Woods," and he sneered at her and smiled at Woodbury as he approached the bench.

Josh stood: "All rise. Court is in recess." Zach walked around the clerk's bench and Woodbury stood and walked toward the opening in the bench: "I'm sorry," the Judge whispered, "that I had to do that in open court."

Zach said: "No, I'm sorry, your Honor. There's no excuse for me being late and keeping you waiting every day."

Woodbury smiled: "Make the check payable to the clerk … be seated; we're gonna call the next case now as Josh tells me all parties are present, and, of course, this sentencing ran a little late," he said with a grin as he winked at Zach, and Zach whispered: "I'm sorry, your Honor" and returned to counsel table.

Becky whispered to Zach: "Everything okay?"

He whispered back: “I love you” as Josh announced loudly: “everyone here for the next sentencing in U.S. vs. Rainy?”

Timmy O’Brien yelled: “Here and present” as he walked toward the front of the courtroom and smiled at Becky mouthing: “Hi” as Zach threw him an angry, inquisitive look.

Josh leaned over the Judge’s bench and whispered: “All set, your Honor.”

“Thanks,” Woodbury whispered as he smiled at him and Josh smiled as he turned and faced the open courtroom: “All rise. This is the sentencing in the matter of the U.S. vs. Greg Thomas Rainy. Would counsel please identify themselves for the record?”

“Good morning, your Honor,” Zach said as he smiled: Zach Woods and Rebecca Lawrence for the Government.”

Timmy stood and smiled at Becky as Zach fumed: “Good morning, your Honor. Timothy O’Brien, Federal Public Defender’s Office, for the defendant who is present.”

Woodbury smiled at Becky as his eyes darted between Zach and Timmy: “You may be seated. You may proceed, Mr. Woods.”

Zach stood: “Your Honor, my esteemed colleague will address the Court.”
Woodbury grinned as Becky stood: “Good morning, your Honor.”

“Good morning, Ms. Lawrence” the Judge said as he grinned and sipped his water.

“Your Honor, in this case Mr. Rainy's crime is appalling. It involved an unmitigated abuse of trust and had a profoundly devastating impact on so many innocent victims. For over 48 months Greg Rainy made the cold, conscious, and calculated decision to steal, and he didn't just steal on a whim; he decided exactly who he would steal from, and he chose his victims carefully to ensure he would not get caught.

Quite frankly, your Honor, Mr. Rainy is a financial predator. He stole from the most vulnerable members of our society. He stole from at least two retired widows who had worked their entire lives in public service to save for their retirement. He stole from an 80-year-old man who worked his whole life to save for his retirement, and he even stole from a church congregation that had been saving money to build a new church.

Your Honor, Greg Rainy's victims are not just nameless, faceless banks; they are real people, and many of those victims are standing here today. These victims are people Greg Rainy met face-to-face, people whose life stories he knew, people whose dreams he was hired to achieve their financial goals. And knowing all of this, he met them and lied to their faces, and he showed them fake documents to advance his conniving scheme.

Your Honor, the impact of Mr. Rainy's crime is very tangible, and it goes far beyond pure numbers of financial loss. Mr. Rainy has shattered the lives of so many victims in this case, leaving them to ask how such a close person could have deceived them. He's also left them to wonder if they'll ever see their hard-earned life savings they had earned. As the Court is well aware, many of these victims have submitted victim impact statements, and some of the victims here today do wish to be heard."

"Please proceed, Ms. Lawrence," Woodbury said as Charlie rose from the witness box and blew a fine mist of lilac dew toward Becky who sneezed.

Woodbury leaned forward: "Josh?" Josh shrugged his shoulders and smiled as Becky said: "Your Honor, the Government calls Mr. Walter Thabian, who's sitting in the front row of the court."

The old man walked slowly over toward the witness box, and Becky nodded as he took the stand:

“I am a 90-year-old retired man who lived in West Quincy for 54 years. As a child I spent eight years in foster care as a ward of the state. When I graduated from high school during the depression, I signed onto Mass. Highway to work on a project in western Massachusetts for three years.

When World War II ended, I was offered a position in a factory at the Gillette Company. I spent my entire career at Gillette, retiring from a middle management position in 1979 ... while at Gillette I was forwarded many opportunities and was able to provide for my family while saving for the future.

My wife and I had hoped to travel and enjoy a long restful retirement. However, in May of 1969 our plans changed forever. My son was severely injured in Vietnam, 100% disabled, and my wife and I cared for him at home for the next 25 years. In fact, I took an early retirement from Gillette in order to take care of him and my wife.

My focus for investing changed after my son was injured. I decided instead to look at ways to save to ensure that my son and wife would always be provided for; that my daughter would have access to funds for unforeseen expenses, and that my grandchildren would be able to further their education.

I had known Mr. Rainy since he was a child living in the neighborhood and from the church. In January of 2006 Greg Rainy suggested I withdraw monies from an annuity I had to invest in a tax-free shelter. He convinced me that it was a good investment. I paid penalties to withdraw the money to invest with Mr. Rainy.

In September of 2008 I was rushed to the hospital and ended up having emergency surgery. During my hospital stay Greg phoned me to inquire about my health and even visited trying to talk to me about withdrawing my funds from AIG while I was being wheeled into surgery.

What I believed at the time was an example of Greg's concern for my health and welfare, apparently, was a desperate attempt by Greg to steal additional monies from me. I cannot help but wonder if Greg was perhaps praying for a different outcome: if I had died, no one would have known the amount of money that he stole from me.

While I understand that Greg Rainy is being sentenced for the theft of monies, money is not the most important thing he stole from me. I believed in Greg. I believed he was a true friend who cared about my well-being. I no longer feel that I can trust anyone outside my immediate family.

For 89 years I felt like an intelligent, astute man who was able to make positive independent financial and life decisions; and in a few short months, Greg Rainy took that away from me. (Victim cries.)"

Woodbury whispered: "Thank you, sir. You may step down. Are there any further victims who wish to be heard?

Becky smiled as she said: "Yes, your Honor. The Government calls Robert Simmons to the stand."

"Your Honor, my name is Robert Simmons; I'm the 'RC' that was mentioned in the pleadings. Recently, I have been hearing some articles or seeing some articles that kind of indicated to me if one wants to get into crime, white-collar crime is the place to go. No. 1, you have a better chance of getting away with it; No. 2, very often the penalties are very light.

It's really not so much the money that was taken in this, this venture, as has been mentioned many times: the abuse of trust, that I think hurt even more than the loss of the cash. It was interesting what was mentioned this morning in talking about how the victims were chosen that it was not a universal thing, but they were chosen which kind of makes me feel like maybe I am kind of a weak individual because as was indicated as 'one who could be easily duped,' and like the previous gentleman, we were duped twice.

We were duped once in April of '07, and, again, in November of '07 for the sale of our home. Many of our family were hurt. We were on a mission in Albania for 18 months. It wasn't until we were there for about 14 of those 18 months that we were alerted to the fact that this was happening; and it was our daughter, who I don't think knew what she was signing up for when she agreed to be our Power of Attorney for that 18-month period of time, and who did a marvelous duty in following through and helping as much as she could along with the help of our son who lives in Ashland, and so many lives were, were very much interrupted as a result of this experience.

I guess I should have been a little suspicious when every time a document needed to be presented Greg was willing to come by the office and drop it off and talk about it. Nothing was ever sent through the mail. Now, I know exactly why that is the case.

I'm here both as a victim myself but also as a part of a group of victims who took a person's relationship, trusted that relationship, and signed checks over to that person, expecting a return.

These aren't wealthy people. These are church-going people; these aren't people that understand tremendously the financial system. These are people that only felt one thing, and that was a trust for someone that reached out on a regular basis and shook their hands, came to their houses on a regular basis, and promised to them that they were going to get a return on an investment because Greg said it was so.

When you have that kind of confidence in that kind of relationship, at times your judgment is clouded by that trust, and that trust was betrayed. It was betrayed to me on two occasions where I was approached with these investments and the fact that they were guaranteed returns; and, in fact, I was given a very formal looking bound document which stated as such.

I'm not a stupid man. I run organizations as large as 160 million dollars in revenue, but I trusted in a person, and I trusted in a document, and that person took that trust and betrayed me. Not only did he betray that trust, but he also impacted a relationship that I have with my closest friend.

I was introduced to Greg by a person that worked with me for 22 years who knew Greg for many, many years and said: This is a person that you can trust. In November of 2008 I lost my job unexpectedly. One month later I got a call from this trusted friend who said to me: Check the Quincy paper, and Greg had been indicted or arrested.

In November of 2008 as a senior executive there was not a lot of jobs out there. The time between that call and the next six months I spent many nights wide awake, with my wife, spent many times not being able to really trust anyone as was reflected in an earlier statement, and a strained relationship because of Greg's behavior with one of my best friends."

"Thank you, sir. Please step down. Are there any other victims who would like address the Court?" No, then I will hear from counsel for the defendant, Mr. O'Brien?"

Timmy O'Brien stood and adjusted his tie as he spoke: "Thank you, your Honor. Your Honor, the defendant wishes to address the court."

"Proceed," Woodbury said as he smiled at Becky who grinned.

The defendant rose: "First of all" --

Woodbury put his glasses on: "Would the defendant please rise."

"I'm sorry" he whispered as he stood: -- "I want to say to everyone in the courtroom today that I accept and have accepted full responsibility for all of the bad decisions and judgments I've made and the unhappiness I've caused on all these good people.

I had many chances to go to the authorities, and I didn't; and for that reason and many others, I'm incredibly sorry. I've shamed my family beyond repair along with everyone else.

You know, for the longest time, especially when it was clear to me that these investments were doomed that I made, I would get up in the morning before everybody was up, and look in the mirror, and say: What in God's name have you done to hurt all these good people?

The pain of knowing this and the unhappiness I had caused became overwhelming to me, and I did not want to live anymore. I came dangerously close to ending my life many times and could not go on feeling the way I did. I sought professional help, and started to look at things a little differently.

I hurt people that not only liked me, but as you can see, people that loved me. For my family and my kids, I know I have to face this wrong and basically try within my power and skills to make this not go away; that will never happen as this will be with me for the rest of my life (Defendants cries.)"

"Thank you, Mr. Rainy," Woodbury said as the defendant sat down next to Timmy and wailed.

Timmy stood: "May I address the Court, please?"

Woodbury nodded as Timmy smiled at Becky.

Timmy smiled at Becky as he spoke: "In this particular case, your Honor, it is sad for everybody. There is no question in my mind. As I look back and I look in the eyes of these people, I can do nothing but feel sorry.

Let me begin by saying a couple of things just to clear up a couple of misunderstandings. First, Mr. Rainy, in essence, self-reported this crime. He wasn't caught. He indicated to his partner that he had done something wrong, that he knew he was gonna have to deal with it, but that he could not continue to go on, and he voluntarily extricated himself from that situation.

There was no investigation going on by either the SEC or the U.S. Attorney's Office. He self-reported to his partner. In this particular case, your Honor, it's extremely sad because unlike most situations, this was not a question of greed.

This was not a question where Mr. Rainy was taking these people's money and putting it in his pocket. It wasn't that he was taking the money and buying fancy vacations for himself or cars. He had fallen prey like untold numbers of people that there was an investment out there that was, in essence, riskless; that any time you nailed up a nail into a piece of wood, you were gonna sell that for some exaggerated profit, and you were going to make money for everybody.

Everybody was doing it. It worked out. Nobody understood the frailties of the fundamental that the real estate market could not continue to go on. It is sad for everybody.

This was an effort that he earnestly believed in. He didn't buy one car. He didn't gamble ten cents. He didn't put drugs in his system. He didn't drink to excess at that time. He did what he thought was going to give everybody a return.

When it started going bad, he made the quintessential error, an error that unfortunately too many people make: he began to chase. He began to say: it's going bad; if I can just get another few dollars, we'll put this back on track. We're gonna make a little less profit, but we're going to sell these units. Everybody's selling them. Everybody's doing this. He was going to get the money back, not only for these people who he told what the investment was, but for those he deceived.

And there's no question, your Honor, as he stands before you, there's no question he deceived these people. Eventually, when he realized that there was no return, that there was gonna be no return, he stood up and he told his partner: I've done something very bad here, okay, and he walked away."

Woodbury shook his head back and forth as the courtroom filled with the putrid stench of rotten eggs, and Charlie giggled from the witness box.

"I understand what you're saying, Mr. O'Brien; I'd like you to specify just, you know, why this Court should deviate or depart from something that the guidelines in a sense discretionarily impose?"

Tim smiled at Becky as she raised her eyebrows and sat down next to Zach: "What I'd say, your Honor, is because this does not fit the classic fraud case as most fraud cases, and I will show you by example, Bernie Madoff."

Woodbury sipped from his water: "By what?"

Timmy stared at Becky as he spoke, and the Judge's brows raised curiously: "Your Honor, by giving an example of another case; let's take, for example, the Madoff case, and we don't even come close to anything like that here, because that was money he was using personally, your Honor. That was money that he was actually taking. Madoff was living 'the high life' on other people's money; there never could have been a repayment.

In this particular situation, it's not the classic case: this money didn't go to him personally. It wasn't used by him personally. This isn't the classic stealing we see here in federal court. It's stealing from them, no question, because they should have had the right to make that decision; they should have had the right to say: Hey, listen I have this real estate deal. I think it's a good deal. You want in?

That's where we are, but this isn't that classic Madoff case where he was taking the money for himself and using it personally and squandering it on yachts and a lavish lifestyle; he was using it to further what would have been an investment that had it worked everybody would have gotten their money back with a high return. It wasn't a Ponzi scheme, your Honor."

Woodbury smiled at Becky as she stood: "Your Honor, the government recommends a 96-month period of incarceration, a $15,000 fine, a three-year period of supervised release, a $1,400 special assessment, and restitution in the amount of $3,736,734.42."

Woodbury looked around the courtroom before his eyes settled upon the defendant:

“Would the defendant please rise. The Court is imposing the following sentence: a term of imprisonment of 84 months on Counts 1 through 14 to be served concurrently with credit for time served.

The reason that I reduced the recommendation of the United States, which was well-founded, was that the money that the defendant obtained from the victims was not primarily used for his own personal selfish consumption.

Three years supervised release, restitution in the amount of: $3,736,734.42. The individuals and corporations and the amounts due will be specified in the written judgment, but the ultimate restitution will be $3,736,734.42.

A special assessment is imposed in the amount of $1,400. In addition, the Court makes the judicial recommendation that the defendant participate in substance abuse treatment. In addition, the Court makes the judicial recommendation that the defendant be designated to a facility commiserate with security where the Bureau of Prisons can afford appropriate psychiatric and/or psychological care of the defendant's documented mental health needs.

Lastly, the Court makes the judicial recommendation that the defendant be designated to a facility which is closest to the defendant's family in Massachusetts.

With respect to the restitution, any payment made that is not payment in full shall be divided proportionally among the individual victims named until such time as those victims are fully compensated.”

After Woodbury recited the specific conditions and paused, Becky stood: “Your Honor, we would ask for a quick report date here.”

Timmy stood and smiled: “Your Honor, is this necessary?”

Becky smiled back at Tim: “Your Honor, since Mr. Rainy has been out on release it appears that he has abided by all of the conditions of release; although, he is now facing a very serious period of incarceration and the risk of flight here is" --

Woodbury shook his head: "Here's what I'm going to do: I'm going to allow him to self-report to the United States Marshalls' Office one month from today to give him an opportunity to tidy up his personal affairs."

Timmy interjected: "Thank you, your Honor" as Becky nodded her head back and forth biting her bottom lip, and Timmy grinned.

Woodbury looked at the defendant who was crying: "Mr. Rainy, you have a right to appeal this sentence. You must file an appeal within 14 days of today's date. If you cannot afford an attorney, one will be provided for you.

On a personal note, Mr. Rainy, you will spend a long time incarcerated, but you are a relatively young man and will still be relatively young upon release. Please use your intellect and financial acumen to help society rather than victimize it further. I don't anticipate ever seeing you before me again. Good day, counsel. This proceeding is adjourned."

"All rise," Josh said as he smiled at Becky who whispered to Zach: "What's your problem?"

"I don't like how he looks at you, Becky," Zach whispered as Timmy walked out of the courtroom behind the defendant.

Becky bit her bottom lip: "You jealous, Mr. Woods?"

He leaned in and whispered "Mmm" into her left ear, and she smiled as she inhaled his pheromones dancing before her, and he said softly: "You're mine" and she felt a tiny trickle drip down her inner left thigh.

As the courtroom cleared, Becky and Zach flirted with each other and giggled amongst themselves before Becky leaned toward him whispering: "Show me love, show me life … Baby, show me what it's all about," and Zach kissed her cheek and said: "You're driving me crazy," as Josh walked into the courtroom from the back of the house and looked at Becky with an inquisitive grin.

"Everything okay in here, counsel?" he said as he smiled and Zach stood as Becky leaned back and blushed: "Sure, everything's hunky dory, Josh."

"Hunky dory?," Josh repeated as he winced, "hunky dory, Becky?"

"Bye, Josh," Becky said with a smile as she followed Zach down the main aisle and Josh yelled:

"Everything's hunky dory? Get outta here. See ya, Becky." Becky turned around giggling as Zach held the door open for her and smiled: "See ya, Josh" as Zach whispered: "I can't walk" and Becky's eyes followed his downward, and she giggled as his zipper protruded into the air.

Zach pulled her into the conference room on the right directly across from the court reporter's office. He closed the door and moved a 52-inch television over to block its exit. She smiled as she backed away from him toward the rear wall stacked five-feet high of black exhibit binders.

"What do you want, Mr. Woods?" She said as he pressed into her and grabbed her buttocks in both hands. She reached between them and unhooked his button and with both hands shimmied his zipper down as he pressed into her. Zach walked toward the large conference table in the center of the room and mouthed: "Come here."

"What do you want, Mr. Woods?" Becky teased him as she walked over toward the table; and as she stood in front of him, he reached under her skirt with both hands and pulled her pantyhose down to her ankles. "Take it off," he commanded as he took his shoes off and his slacks fell to the floor. She sat on the edge of the conference table and just as she removed her hose from her ankles, Zach stood directly in front of her naked and immense.

He pulled a chair in front of her and sat down so that his face was eye level with her vulva. He reached in between her legs with both hands and slowly spread her legs apart as he smiled and backed the chair up a foot and began eating her. Becky exploded and her juice dripped off the table's edge as she moaned: "Oh, God," and Zach looked up at her as his tongue licked her clit and whispered: "Shhh … unbutton your blouse; I want to see you" as he continued to wiggle her wildly.

Slowly she unbuttoned her blouse as he looked up into her eyes. He stood and inserted his middle finger of his left hand deep within her as his right hand fumbled to remove her right breast from her bra. She humped his finger as her juice continued to drip from the table's edge. He stared at her erect nipple; and as he coddled it in his mouth and tasted her sugar-infused milk, he looked up into her eyes and whispered: "What do you want, baby?" as she moaned and sweat saturated her forehead.

He smiled and inserted his soaked middle finger into her anus as he bit down on her nipple and she whispered: "Put it in, Zach. Oh, God, put it in."

He licked around her areola as milk jettisoned from each nipple and he smiled as he said: "Turn over, baby." Becky stood on her feet and turned around and leaned her weight into the table's edge feeling liquid soak her abdomen. Zach knelt down with his knees pressing into the hardwood floor as he spread her legs and wiggled her clit madly as his chin sopped.

"Oh, God," she moaned as he continued to gently wiggle as he whispered: "Say it, Becky."

"Oh, God," Becky sighed, "Put it in, Zach; put it in." Zach shook his head back and forth and stuck his middle finger deep inside her ass as he bit down on her clit and her waterfall deluged onto his bare thighs. He teased her until she was humping wildly as sweat beaded from her temples and dripped down the sides of her face as she screamed: "Fuck me!"

"Shhh," he whispered as he smiled: "Turn around, put your ass up here." Becky turned around and hopped up onto the edge of the table. As he wiggled her clit between his forefingers, he whispered: "Na, you're not ready yet."

He pulled the chair toward the table and sat down and sucked on her until she orgasmed, and he watched as her lava erupted and inundated the floor forming a puddle under the table. Tears cascaded down her cheeks as he continued to tease her as she violently humped his tongue: "Put it in, Zach, please" she begged.

He looked up at her as he held her clit between his teeth gingerly. He slowly pulled his mouth from her and her molten lava erupted as he whispered: "Stand against the wall." Becky's skin squeaked as she slid off the table and stepped into her juice on the floor.

"Oh, my God," she whispered as she looked at the puddle under her bare feet. Zach smiled as Becky dropped to her knees and swallowed him. She rode him as hard as she could, using her mouth as a human vacuum and biting down on his rim as she pulled. He fucked her mouth for a few minutes; and just as he felt the semen rise, he pulled out and walked toward the rear wall cupping his sack in his left hand.

"Come here," he mouthed as Becky stood and wobbled over toward him, "turn around." Becky leaned into the wall as Zach dropped to his knees and whispered: "Open" as he spread her legs apart. He rode his tongue between her anus and her vulva until liquid jettisoned and dripped down her legs as he giggled. He stood and jammed into her as her pelvic muscles contracted around him repeatedly forcing his ejaculate to inseminate.

As he came, she reached underneath and grabbed his balls with her right hand and whispered: "I love you, Mr. Woods." He giggled as the last of the semen exploded within her as he whispered: "I love you too, Becky. Turn over."

As he came loose, fluid inundated the floor and Becky turned around as Zach kissed her and she turned her head squinching her face.

“What?” Zach asked as he forced her head to face him.

“I can taste it,” she said as she made a face.

“Best thing I’ve ever tasted,” he whispered as he walked toward the table and pulled out a chair: “Sit and take that off.” Becky took her shirt off and walked toward the chair as her juice drenched her legs: “Zach, I’m soaked,” she whispered.

“I know, baby,” he said as he smiled, “take that off,” as she unhinged her bra and it fell into the puddle at her feet. Zach picked it up: “Oooh,” he said with a smile, “shimmy that gorgeous ass to the edge here for me; you’re not done yet.”

Zach sat Indian style on the hardwood floor as his tongue sent Becky into an orgasmic frenzy. Her juice jettisoned and splattered against the wall opposite the table as she continuously moaned: “Zach, Zach, Zach,” and fluid drenched Zach’s lap as he grinned. She began to hump him wildly as he gently bit her clit and whispered: “Say it.”

“Fuck me!” she screamed as he smiled: “Shhh … bend over.” Becky leaned against the saturated edge, her nipples screaming as they touched the cold, wet formica. He plunged deep into her from behind; and as he rode her, his left pointer finger played with her clitoris wiggling it lightly as he intermittently stuck his finger deep within her ass.

As her cataclysmic orgasm reached its zenith and her pelvic muscles squeezed him toward ejaculation, her juice flooded his legs as he whispered: “I love you, Becky.”

Becky’s pelvic floor rhythmically repeatedly contracted; and as Zach screamed “Ahhh” as he ejaculated, she whispered: “Shhh.”

As Zach dressed he giggled as he stared at the puddle under the table. He watched as goosebumps caused Becky to twitch uncontrollably. He placed his blazer over her shoulders and kissed her. As he stuck his tongue into her mouth, she winced and turned her head away from him. He giggled as she whispered: “yuck.”

"Get dressed," he said as he moved the television stand away from the door, and it scraped against the floor. "She covered her ears as the sound vibrated and reverberated within her mind. "I'll be right back." Becky smiled as she watched him leave and closed the door.

As she dressed she looked at the walls seeping onto the floor and mumbled: "Oh, my God" out loud as her eyes stared at the puddle under the table. Zach walked in humming with a gigantic wad of paper towels in his left hand. He closed the door and smiled as he laid paper towels on top of the puddle and began swiping the wall as he giggled.

Becky cleaned the table and the chair as Zach hummed: "If I could talk, I'd tell you; if I could smile, I'd let you know … damn, Becky, can't get that song out of my head" he whispered as he turned his head toward Becky who continued to clean and giggle as she sang: "You are far and away, my most imaginary friend."

Zach and Becky ate lunch under a white umbrella overlooking the harbor. They giggled and laughed all through lunch; Zach rambled, telling endless anecdotes recanting his most precious childhood memories, occasionally nervously glancing his periphery to make sure no one was watching. No one was.

As he finished his salad, he whispered: "O'Brien likes you, you know." Becky smiled and nodded her head as she whispered: "Jealous?"

"What?" Zach said exasperated.

Becky whispered into his left ear: "You are jealous, Mr. Woods?"

"Just stay away from him, will ya?" Zach said as they threw their salads away and headed back into the Moakley.

Becky returned to her office at 1:05 exhausted. She sat at her desk and stared blanketly into the double monitors as Amanda walked in.

“Hey you,” she said as she sat down, “woe, you looked wiped.”

“Yeah,” Becky said as she yawned as Amanda nodded her head: “Um, Becky, you check your messages lately?”

“I have messages?” Becky said with a grin as her eyes watered.

“Um, yeah, like a lot; actually, your voicemail’s full … you’d better check. Listen, I’m going for a cup of coffee; you want?”

“Na” Becky said as Amanda walked away, and she picked up the phone and pressed “Intraoffice voicemail.”

Tears streamed down her cheeks as she listened, every message started the same and ended with their voice cut off: “Ms. Lawrence, my name is Amy Romero. I want to know how you live with yourself? How do you look in the mirror? My daughter Eva was raped and murdered by Eddie Hubbard; she was 15. This piece of shit admitted to it, and you gave him immunity?”

“Ms. Lawrence, my name is Steven Ceron … Eddie Hubbard murdered my father 12 years ago. He destroyed my entire family. My mother killed herself. How do you live with yourself, Ms. Lawrence? You’re a prosecutor? How do you look in the mirror?”

After listening to seven messages, Becky hit “delete all” and walked over toward the harbor searching her soul for answers she didn’t possess. She closed her eyes and watched as Maria Batista’s tears stained her jaundiced skin: “Mr. Hubbard admitted to murdering my son Joey in broad daylight; he shot him in the back of the head.”

Zach walked into Becky’s office humming and stood gaunt as he watched Becky cry. She looked at him as tears dripped onto her blouse. Zach closed and locked the door and walked up behind her and hugged her placing both open palms around her baby bump: “What’s the matter?” he whispered as she sobbed.

She turned around and faced him as he held her. After five minutes of blubbering and soaking Zach’s collar with tears and mascara, she said: “Maybe it’s not the right thing, Zach.”

Zach kissed Becky on the lips and tasted her salty tears as he whispered: “What are you talking about, baby?”

“Letting Hubbard walk free. He’s a murderer. Did you know he killed and raped a 15-year-old, Zach, and I set him free”… Becky began wailing as Zach held her whispering: “Think about Veloz, baby … Hubbard’s nothing; he’s just a pawn, a gorilla carrying out orders; you know that.”

Becky backed away a few inches and wiped the tears from her cheeks as Zach peered out over the water. “He was ordered to rape and murder a 15-year-old little girl, Zach?” Becky whispered as her eyes swelled with tears again.

Zach turned around to face her and grabbed her into a bear hug. He held her in his arms as he whispered: “I love you, Becky” and squeezed her and felt the baby kick his abdomen.

“Oh, my God,” Becky said, “did you feel it?” Zach dropped to his knees and pressed his face gently against her stomach as the baby squirmed and kicked him and Zach giggled: “I feel it; he’s talking to me.” As the captivating essence of lilac permeated her office, Becky stopped crying and whiffed the air, and Charlie giggled as he sat on the radiator watching the baby kick Zach’s cheek.

“Wow, he’s already mad at me,” Zach whispered as he kissed her stomach and the baby violently kicked his lips as Becky giggled and Zach looked up into Becky’s eyes as he mouthed: “I love you.”

Two weeks later Becky smiled as she opened the front door to the Moakley staring at the white handwritten sign taped to the door: “Bring your kids to work day, Friday, July 26, 2014.” Zach arrived at 8 a.m. with Emily pulling on his sleeve. Becky walked into Zach’s office as Emily stared at her and approached cautiously. Becky stared into Zach’s eyes as Emily grabbed Becky’s left hand and led her to the center of his office where she said: “Sit.”

Becky tried to sit but was having difficulty navigating her 24-week-old fetus to the floor. Zach giggled as he helped her to sit down. Emily gave her purple crayon to Becky, and Becky watched astounded as Emily sketched a dragon in near-perfect artistic precision. Emily smiled at Becky who stared at her sketch as her eyes bulged: "Color him purple, Becky" Emily said as Becky leaned over feeling the baby kick her inner left calf.

Here?" Becky asked as Emily smiled. Zach leaned his back against the desk and watched as Emily dropped her pencil and placed her small right hand against Becky's abdomen. The baby kicked Emily's palm, and her eyes sparkled as she screamed: "Daddy, there's a baby in there."

Emily hopped into Becky's lap as Zach smiled: "Gentle, Em … remember, there's a baby in there," and Emily smiled and looked into Becky's eyes: "What's his name?"

"I don't know yet," Becky said as she hugged her, and Emily smiled at Zach who blew her a kiss that she caught in midair. "You're really very talented," Becky said as Emily began to draw a tongue rising from the dragon's mouth and slid out of Becky's lap and laid across the floor, her tongue licking her bottom lip as she concentrated intently. Zach pulled Becky to stand as she whispered: "She's really good," as Zach smiled and nodded.

At 10:30 Zach and Emily walked into Becky's office; as Emily ran toward her desk and plopped in Becky's lap, Zach whispered: "Can you cover the motion at 11?"

Becky nodded as Emily slid out and stood next to her with a curious expression: "Can I?" she asked as Becky nodded, and Emily placed both hands on her stomach gently. The baby squirmed and kicked her left hand as Emily giggled in delight and Zach smiled: "Courtroom 1. Meet us for lunch at noon?"

"Please," Emily said as she motioned with her right hand to whisper to Becky, and Becky leaned forward to hear the secret. Emily threw her arms around Becky's neck and kissed her cheek and whispered as Zach strained to hear: “Your baby’s special, you know” as the room filled with the aroma of lilacs in bloom, and Emily skipped around Becky’s desk before skipping toward the door screaming: “Come on, Daddy.”

Zach followed Emily and turned around and smiled at Becky in the doorjamb as he inhaled the infused lilac and puckered his lips into a kiss. Emily watched smiling as Becky caught it in midair as she pulled on his sleeve: “Come on, Daddy,” and skipped into the hallway.

Becky yelled as Zach turned around: “Case Number?”

“I forget … it’s Williams -- no, Hunter, U.S. v. Hunter … sorry” he said as Emily dragged him away.

Becky went onto ECF and went to query. She plugged in “Hunter” and 200 names popped up in view. She perused the list looking for CPW attached to a number as Amanda walked in. “Here” she said as she handed Becky a document entitled: “Evidentiary Review Hearing to determine whether the Respondent still meets the Criteria for Commitment under USC 4248.”

Becky smiled as she shook her head: “You know how good you are” she said as Amanda grinned: “Yeah, I know.”

Becky’s eyes centered on the bold-faced title: “Findings of Fact and Conclusions of Law and Order, Introduction: “The United States seeks to civilly commit Respondent Rod Hunter as a “sexually dangerous person” under Section 302(4) of the Adam Walsh Child Protection and Safety Act of 2006 (“Adam Walsh Act”), Pub. L. No. 109-248, Title 111, § 302(4), 120 Stat. 587, 620-22 (2006), codified at 18 U.S.C. §§ 4247-4248.

In order to commit Mr. Hunter, the government must prove by clear and convincing evidence that he is “sexually dangerous.” Under the Adam Walsh Act, a person is sexually dangerous if he “has engaged or attempted to engage in sexually violent conduct or child molestation and … is sexually dangerous to others.” 18 U.S.C. §

4247(a)(5).

In order to determine that someone is sexually dangerous to others, a court must find that he "suffers from a serious mental illness, abnormality, or disorder as a result of which he would have serious difficulty in refraining from sexually violent conduct or child molestation if released." Id. § 4247(a)(6).

Mr. Hunter concedes that he has engaged in sexually violent conduct or child molestation spanning three decades"… "Oy" Becky moaned as Amanda sat down in the chair across from her desk: "Keep reading … it gets better."

Becky's eyes scanned until she reached: "Sexual and Relationship History." Amanda opened her coffee and gulped it as Becky read:

"Mr. Hunter's childhood was also plagued by his frequent victimization of sexual abuse. At the age of seven, a neighborhood boy forced Hunter to perform oral sex with a similarly-aged child. (Trial Day III, Page 12:)

Q. Now, there are incidents of abuse that you experienced of a sexual nature as a young child that have been discussed in various reports submitted to the Court. I think the first one is when you were age 7?
A. Yes.
Q. Would you describe what happened; where were you first?
A. That happened out at, I believe it was, a work site where they were building a school, and there was an older boy there, and I was with another kid that was around 7, and he forced me to perform oral sex on the boy.
Q. On the other boy?
A. Yes, on the other boy."

"When Mr. Hunter was ten or eleven, a fifteen-year-old boy forced Hunter to perform oral sex on him during a game of 'doctor.'

At approximately age thirteen Mr. Hunter performed oral sex on a boy in diapers. (Trial Day II, Page 189:)

Q. Can you describe your memory of what happened that afternoon for the Court?
A. One day in the afternoon, I believe it was, I was walking around and I saw a boy about the same age as me playing with his younger brother in the garage. And I approached them, and I think we started talking about penises, and I don't know exactly. You know, it's a long time ago, I don't remember exactly what happened, but I believe I pulled the boy's diaper down; he was like two, and I performed oral sex on him.
Q. For how long?
A. I don't know ... maybe a couple minutes, if that long. He liked it.
Q. How do you know that, Mr. Hunter?
A. The baby liked it. He got erect.
Q. And what was going through your mind when you did that?
A. It was kind of a normal thing to me. It had been done to me, so, you know, I didn't understand what I was really doing.
Q. What was the reaction of the boy's brother?
A. I don't know if he was fascinated or interested, you know. He was watching what I was doing, you know."

"At the age of sixteen Mr. Hunter shot a similarly-aged boy with a BB gun after the boy refused to engage in oral sex; the pair eventually performed oral sex on each other on multiple occasions."

Becky looked up at Amanda as she guzzled her coffee, gulped, and said: "Keep reading." Becky skimmed through a myriad of molestation allegations and kept perusing:

"Sometime in his mid 30's Mr. Hunter testified that he became addicted to child pornography, amassing approximately 50,000 images of children, some as young as three-years-old. His addiction became so severe that if he was missing a specific picture from a series, he would scour the internet for hours until he found it. (Id. at 52.)

According to Mr. Hunter, he primarily viewed images of males between the ages of thirteen and twenty, but collected images of children of a variety of ages for the purposes of trading with other collectors. Hunter's preoccupation with child pornography became very disruptive to the rest of his life. He reported spending between 12-14 hours on the internet and masturbating to child pornography between 2-3 times per day. (Ex. 25 at 9.)"

Becky continued to scan the Conclusions of Law until her eyes focused on "**B. Hunter's Testimony:**

"At trial Hunter testified extensively about his past offending. He also specifically addressed the question of whether he continues to be attracted to children. He stated: 'Yeah. I would say I still had an attraction. I mean, I don't know; I'm not around any 13-year-olds now so . . . I mean, I feel like I don't, but I can't be honest and say that.

It's not an honest statement if I say I'm not attracted to them, I don't know if that's honest or not. We've got guys in prison but, you know, there ain't no 12-year-olds in prison. I know I would never have sex with a 13-year-old, you know, no matter if they looked 20, you know, I don't care; it's just illegal, and I know the damages I can cause that person, you know, psychological damages."

When asked about his molestation of infant males, Hunter responded (Trial Day III, Redirect Examination, Page 210:)

"A. Well, I know now it was very wrong but….
Q. But, what, Mr. Hunter?
A. At the time I don't know then if I knew it was 'wrong.' I mean, after all it had been done to me, and besides, the baby liked it."

Becky's mouth fell open and she said: "Oh, my God, 'the baby liked it'" … and looked up at Amanda who finished her coffee and whispered: "Keep reading. I gotta pee." Amanda walked out of the office and watched as Becky placed her right hand over her face and continued to scan:

Q. Mr. Hunter, you testified on direct examination that you became a fan of the Grateful Dead?
A. Diehard.

Q. And you followed them around the country?
A. Yeah.
Q. So where did you go with the Grateful Dead?
A. Well, I went all over the country, almost every state in the country.
Q. During this period had you talked about any sexual experiences that you had in treatment?
A. Can you repeat that?
Q. Yes. Sorry about that. During this period of your life did you have sexual encounters?
A. Yes, I had a sexual encounter with a boy that I met at a Grateful Dead show. He was, I believe, 13.
Q. Could you describe the circumstances of that encounter?
A. I met him in the parking lot. He was high on something. I don't know what it was. I think it was nitrous, and it led to me following him and then performing oral sex on him for the concert tickets."

During the course of his treatment for sexual predators while incarcerated at FCI Butner the respondent acknowledged engaging in either oral and sexual intercourse with as many as 100 minor male children spanning the course of more than three decades (Trial Day III, Page 232:)

Q. Mr. Hunter, how many children have you been intimate with would you estimate?
A. You mean since I was a kid?
Q. No. Let me rephrase. How many children have you had sex with since you were, say, a legal adult, 18?
A. I don't know … a lot, but I didn't force 'em. They wanted it. They liked it.
Q. Mr. Hunter, how many?
A. I don't know, 89, 90, no more than a hundred … and it wasn't like I was raping 'em; they liked it."

Tears streamed down Becky's cheeks as she closed her eyes as her father whispered: "How's my girl?" She walked over toward the harbor and spotted 200 children in a circle spread out on the grass. They were playing some kind of game Becky couldn't decipher.

Amanda walked into Becky's office with another large cup of coffee in her right hand as Becky wiped her cheeks dry with a Kleenex as Line 3 lit up and began to buzz on Becky's desk as the intercom played: "Ms. Lawrence, Line 3."

Becky stared at Amanda as she opened her coffee, scared to connect. "Becky Lawrence" she said as she dotted her cheeks with her left hand: "Josh?"

"Yeah. How ya doing?" he said giggling.

"Oh, good. You?" Becky said as Amanda smiled and Becky shrugged her shoulders.

"I'm good now … listen, this motion hearing is canceled."

"You're kidding?" Becky said as she grinned at Amanda who raised her brows and cocked her head back to guzzle.

"Yeah, Hunter filed a motion last night, wasn't entered into ECF 'til this morning."

Becky sat in her chair and perused the docket: "I don't see it, Josh."

"Hmmm, exit and go back in to query … you know, it needs to refresh" Josh said as Becky exited ECF and hit "query" and focused on Docket No. 218, Motion To Cancel Hearing filed by Jennifer Anderson."

"Just wanted to catch ya before you headed down is all" Josh said as Becky opened Docket 218.

"Thanks, Josh. That's awesome ... I hate this case."

"Yeah, don't we all … sicko! See ya, Becky."

"See ya, Josh," Becky said as she looked at Amanda and whispered: "Look at this," pointing to her monitor. Amanda walked around the desk and sat in Becky's chair as they read:

"Motion To Cancel Hearing: The Respondent, Rod Hunter, by his counsel, respectfully shows the Court that:

1. The 18 U.S.C. 4248 review hearing is scheduled for August 19, 2013, in Boston.

2. The Respondent, Rod Hunter, is presently in custody at FCI Butner, North Carolina.

3. He is now in Phase 4 of the Sex Offender Treatment Program at Butner, is benefiting from it significantly, and believes he is relatively close to graduation from it.

4. Such graduation would likely result in a 'certification' pursuant to 18 U.S.C. 4248(e) ...WHEREFORE, the Respondent, Rod Hunter respectfully prays the Court that the 18 U.S.C. 4248 review hearing scheduled for August 19, 2013, be canceled."

"This sicko thinks he's gonna get out?" Amanda said as she looked up at Becky. Becky shook her head and whispered: "Over my dead body," as Amanda smiled and said: "Come on, let's get out of here."

"Where we going?" Becky asked as she followed Amanda toward the door. Becky stopped in the doorjamb and turned around and looked back toward the harbor as Charlie opened his mouth while sitting on the radiator and blew a fine lilac mist toward her. She inhaled as she sighed: "Ahhh," and smiled as Amanda yelled: "Coming, girlfriend?"

Amanda and Becky walked outside the rear entrance of the Moakley and walked following the concrete path toward the harbor. Emily ran toward them as Zach yelled: "Emily!" and smiled as Emily hugged Becky, wrapping her arms around her upper thighs.

"Becky, Becky," Emily yelled as Amanda smiled and grabbed Becky's right hand and led her toward the grassy knoll where the children were assembled in a circle. "Sit" Emily said as Zach helped her onto the grass.

“She’s adorable,” Amanda whispered to Zach as they stood watching Emily as the leader encircling the crowd while they chanted: “Ring around the Rosy” as Becky mouthed to Zach: “Oh, my God!”

“Thanks,” Zach whispered to Amanda, “and where’s your little brew today, Mandy?”

“Um, daycare … this was just, um, so much fun last year” Amanda whispered as Zach giggled: “Yeah, I remember, your son screamed all day.”

“Yeah, it was fun,” Amanda said smiling as Becky’s face contorted into a grimace. Amanda pointed to Zach who stared at Becky and walked over toward her. “Come on,” he said as he helped her to stand whispering: “You okay?”

“Yeah, just” --

“Just? Zach whispered.

“It’s stupid, think I’m having contractions … it’s stupid; it’s too early.”

“Yeah,” Zach said as he whispered to Amanda, “can you watch her?”

“Sure” Amanda whispered and she watched Zach lead Becky down toward the harbor who hunched over grasping her belly.

“Zach,” Becky whispered, “I’m scared.”

“You’ll be okay. It’s probably just false labor, you know; it happened to Laura too … come on, come take a walk with me?”

Zach and Becky walked along the harbor as her contractions passed. He helped her off the boardwalk and gently lifted her onto the sand. “Emily adores you, you know” he whispered as he kissed her left cheek.

“Zach?” Becky whispered as she took her heels off and felt the warm sand under her feet as tiny gritty particles stuck between her toes.

“Yeah, beautiful?” he said as he smiled and gently touched her belly with his left hand as the baby kicked.

“She reminds me so much of myself when I was young,” Becky said as she hunched over and her face went pale.

“Really, how?” Zach asked as he grinned as Becky stood as her contractions waned, and they walked along the shore hand in hand.

“I don’t know. Can’t put my finger on it … she’s really gifted, huh?”

“Yeah, been drawing like that since two.” Zach knelt down and picked up a tiny shell. He gently placed it into Becky’s right open palm as he whispered: “Listen, Laura’s coming here at 2 to” --

“To pick up Emily, huh?” Becky said as Zach helped her to sit in the sand.

He grabbed her right hand and placed it into his left palm as his right hand massaged her fingers: “She can’t meet you” he said as he kissed the back of her hand.

“So you want me to disappear?” she said as her eyebrows funneled into a frown as her right hand rubbed her abdomen softly.

“Yeah. I mean, there’s nothing else going on today; why don’t you take off?” … Becky stared out into the ocean; and as the waves crashed onto the shore, she whispered: “You’re not gonna leave her, are you?”

Zach stared into the ocean and then at her abdomen, watching as it moved of its own accord.

“Answer me,” Becky said as tears swelled behind her lids, and she wobbled onto her right side in the sand and tried to stand. Zach helped her to her feet as she pulled away from him.

“I can’t, Becky,” he whispered as she nodded her head back and forth and walked away from him as he yelled: “Becky … Becky … Becky!”

“That’s it,” Becky said to herself mumbling as she walked; “I’m done” she mumbled as she felt her blood pressure rise, and the baby fell asleep in her abdomen with its knee angulating into her sternum. As she walked into the rear of the courthouse, she talked to herself repeatedly in her mind: “He’s playing you, you idiot … he’s playing you.”

She smiled at Peter who said: “Hey, nice day out there, huh?” She stepped into the elevator as her anger grew. By the time the elevator reached the ninth, she was irate and mumbling under her breath: “Selfish prick. I’m done. This is over. I’m done.”

She stormed into her office and with her right hand banged her office door closed so hard and with such force that her plaques trembled on the walls. Becky started banging things as she mumbled: “You love me?”

She walked over toward the dead bouquet of roses still sitting on the edge of her desk. She lifted the heavy vase and banged it on the desk; the desk wobbled under her fury and debris floated through the air causing her to sneeze as she repeated: “You love me?”

She picked up the vase in her right hand and threw it over her head toward the trash can. She missed and glass splattered and splintered into microscopic slivers all over the floor. “I should clean that up” she mumbled out loud as she walked over toward her bookcase and began heaving Criminal Law and Civil Torts one by one, throwing them onto the floor causing caustic vibrations at her feet.

“Prick,” she mumbled as she walked over toward her desk and began dismantling file folders with her teeth and shredding documents on her desk causing pyramids of paper filament to align on the floor at her feet. She walked over and looked out into the harbor; and as she closed her eyes, she watched Zach lick her as he whispered: "I love you."

"You love me," she screamed as she walked over to her desk and with her right hand swept everything on her desktop onto the floor as Amanda walked in.

"Hey," she said as her smile turned into a curious warped glee, her eyes deciphering Becky's discombobulation as she attempted to interpret the chaos darting the periphery: "Problem?"

As Becky's cheeks reddened and her face contorted into an anger snare, Amanda stared at the broken glass at her feet. "Talk to me, girlfriend" she whispered as her eyes roamed the cyclonic disarray.

"He's a prick," Becky said as Amanda broke out into a wide-eyed smile: "And?"

Becky stared at the broken glass as she whispered: "He's not leaving her."

"And?" Amanda asked as she walked over the splinters which crackled under her feet toward Becky.

"I'm done," Becky mumbled as Amanda stared into her eyes: "Yeah?" she whispered as she grinned.

"Yeah," Becky said as her belly jumped and Amanda giggled, sliding her right hand over her baby bump and feeling the baby squirm.

Amanda lifted her Galaxy out of her purse and smiled as she spoke: "Yeah, need maintenance on the ninth please, Room 9018." Becky started grinning as she stared at her stomach perplexed, watching it rise and fall and spasmodically jumping as the baby hiccupped.

"Yeah, Rebecca Lawrence's office; we had a little accident up here." Becky smiled as Amanda giggled: "Yeah, broken glass, you know … thanks."

Amanda smiled awkwardly at Becky as Becky said: "What?"

"I'm proud of you," Amanda whispered as she hugged her and glass crunched under her heels. "It's not over" she whispered as Becky pulled away.

"I'm done, Mandy ... help me clean up this pigsty?"

As Becky and Amanda placed the law books back onto the bookcase shelves, Jeremy entered dragging a large cart behind him. He smiled as he stuttered: "Hi B-b-b-b-b-ecky" he said smiling as he stared at her shoes.

"Hi, Jeremy," Becky said as she stared through him as Amanda whispered, "He's so creepy" as Jeremy's eyes focused on Amanda's sandals: "Oooh, I like your s-h-h-h-h-o-e-s" he said as he smiled, and Amanda giggled as she said with a crazed glaze: "Thank you, Jeremy."

"Woe," Jeremy said as he stared at the glass slivers, "Don't you worry, B-b-b-b-ecky, I'll have this spic and s-p-p-p-p-a-n in no time." As Amanda heaved the last heavy book onto the top shelf, she whispered to Becky: "He gives me the willies."

Becky nodded and mouthed: "He likes shoes" as Jeremy collected the glass into a red dustpan. "You know," he said with exuberant exhilaration: "It's almost Groundhog Day, just six more months, you know."

Becky placed her right hand over her forehead and sighed as Amanda giggled: "You like groundhogs, Jeremy?" As he picked up the last remaining splinters of glass and discarded them into the trash can next to Becky's desk, he smiled: "Are you kidding me? I love g-g-g-g-g-g-roundhogs."

Becky leaned in toward Amanda: "Shhh, don't get him started" as Amanda giggled.

“Gotta get me a v-a-c-c-c-u-m,” Jeremy said as he disappeared and stomped down the hallway as Becky and Amanda began chuckling: “Oh, my God, Amanda … never bring up groundhogs.”

“Come on,” Amanda said smiling, “he’ll clean this up. Let’s get outta here” she whispered smiling snidely as Becky grinned, grabbed her purse, and followed Amanda down the hallway.

As the elevator door opened, Emily ran into Becky and threw her arms around her thighs. “Hi, Becky!” Emily screeched as she hugged her legs and Becky whispered: “Hi, Sweetie” as she stroked the top of her hair and sneered at Zach who mouthed: “Let’s talk.”

Becky shook her head back and forth as Emily ran toward the entrance to the U.S. Attorney’s Office and opened the door screaming: “Come on, Daddy.”

Zach leaned in toward Becky as Amanda said: “Let’s go” and he whispered softly into Becky’s left ear: “We have to talk” and stepped out of the elevator smiling at Emily. Becky stated softy with no facial contortion: “There’s nothing to discuss” as the elevator door closed.

Becky and Amanda sat on a bench overlooking the inner harbor. Amanda giggled as she watched Becky’s stomach rise and fall: “Alaya used to get hiccups all the time,” she said as Becky smiled.

“It feels so weird, Amanda” Becky said as Amanda nodded: “Tell me about it” as she placed her right hand on Becky’s abdomen and giggled insanely as the baby kicked the palm of her hand.

“You want some advice?” Amanda said as Becky nodded and bit her bottom lip moaning: “Hmmm, do I have a choice?”

Amanda smiled: “No, you don’t … end this.”

“I already did,” Becky said as she broke out into a wide smile as Amanda’s hand jumped off her belly, and Amanda rummaged through her purse searching for her Galaxy. “Crap,” she said as she stood: "I've got a meeting in five minutes. Come on, girlfriend; let's go."

Becky couldn't seem to lift her ass off the bench, and Amanda smiled as she extended her right hand and pulled Becky to a wobble. Becky followed Amanda up the concrete walk whispering: "What time is it?"

"Almost 2" Amanda said as she pressed the elevator up arrow. As the elevator arrived on the ninth, Amanda grabbed Becky into a hug and felt the baby kick her. "Ow" she giggled as she whispered: "I'm proud of you … call me" and flew toward reception.

Becky made a B-line to the ladies room. As she washed her hands, she closed her eyes and watched Zach as he licked her from the floor. She felt a trickle dribble down her inner left thigh as an attractive blond walked in.

"Hi," she said to Becky as she entered the stall.

"Hi," Becky said smiling: "wow, friendly" she thought as she dried her hands and reached for her makeup bag. Becky applied a little mascara and stared at her enormous stomach in the reflection as she heard her father's voice: "Girls like you, Becky"….

"Hi, Laura Woods," the stranger said as she placed her right hand on Becky's abdomen feeling the baby jerk. "Woe," she giggled as Becky's face turned pink, and she leaned toward her smiling: "Becky Lawrence" she mumbled as the woman stared into her eyes.

"Do I know you?" Laura asked with sincerity, "you look so familiar somehow?"

"I don't think so," Becky said smiling as she thought: "Holy shit."

"How far along?" Laura asked as she turned on the faucet.

"Six months," Becky answered feeling an immediate warm connection she couldn't quantify.

"Oh, you're Becky … you work with my husband Zach?"

"Yeah," Becky mumbled as she stared at Zach's pretty skeleton wife.

"It's so nice to meet you. Zach adores you, you know," Laura said as she reached for a paper towel.

"You have no idea," Becky thought as she stammered, "Nice to meet you too," and left the bathroom as tears filled her eyes. "She's nice," she mumbled as she wobbled past reception and down the hallway. "And she's pretty," she thought as she walked into her sparkling office, the smell of Lysol causing her to gag.

"Prick," she said out loud as she sat at her desk and turned on her PC and went onto ECF. As Becky queried next week's calendar and began plugging in docket numbers and searching through PACER, Laura Woods walked into Becky's office smiling. Becky looked up as Zach stood in the doorjamb.

"Hi," Laura said as she sat down in front of Becky's desk, and Zach stumbled into the room mouthing to Becky behind his wife: "I'm sorry." Becky glared at him as he mouthed: "I love you." She nodded her head and forced a fake smile as she stared at Laura who immediately turned her back and stared into Zach's eyes. She stared at Zach and then at Becky; her neck wrenching between them as the tiny hairs on the back of her neck became rigid.

Becky stood and smiled at Laura as Laura stood and Zach approached. "So you married, Becky?" Laura asked as she stared at Zach staring at the floor.

"No," Becky said as she shook her head and stared at Zach. Laura's hazel eyes darted between them as Becky thought: "She knows."

"Wow … so you're going this alone, huh? I respect that … Zach?"

Zach's eyes remained on the floor as he said: "Yeah?"

Laura's face became pink and then a muted red as she stared at Becky as Becky continued to glare at Zach, and he continued to stare at the floor averting his wife's eyes. Laura walked over toward Zach and slapped him as tears fell from Becky's eyes, and she turned around and walked over toward the harbor. "God forgive me," she internalized as Charlie blew a freezing cold vapor toward her causing her body to twitch. "She knows," she thought as Laura began pushing Zach toward the rear of her office.

"You're fucking her, aren't you?" Laura screamed as she pushed Zach backwards and his head smacked into the bookcase causing rippling vibrations through the floorboards.

"What's the matter with you?" Zach screamed as he placed his right hand on the back of his head and rubbed ferociously.

"Is that your baby?" Laura asked as Becky sobbed staring out over the water whispering: "God forgive me," under her breath.

"I'm sorry, Laura," Zach shouted as he averted her eyes, and she pounded his chest.

"I knew it. You piece of shit." Laura slapped Zach's face several times in quick succession. His head crashed against the bookcase, and he made no attempt to block her blows. Emily stood in the doorway crying: "Mommy, stop hitting him."

Tears fell from Becky's chin and landed on her baby bump dampening her blouse as Laura picked up Emily and Zach turned around and faced the bookshelf as Becky whimpered and Zach sobbed as she stared at the back of his head. Slowly Becky walked toward the door and locked it causing Zach to jerk and turn around.

She stood in front of him, wiping her cheeks as he mouthed with tears streaming down his face: "I'm sorry." She fell into his arms; and as his body collapsed onto hers, they hugged as they cried as the baby kicked Zach's stomach repeatedly.

“I love you,” he whispered as she sobbed watching Emily cry in the doorway; “Mommy, stop hitting him,” replaying on the scratched CD in the funnels of her mind.

“I feel so bad” Zach whispered as he cupped her buttocks and she pressed her body into his as the baby kicked him and he giggled. “I should have just told her” he said as tears dropped from his eyes, and Becky backed up and began wiping his tears.

Zach fell to his knees and pressed his wet face into Becky’s inner thighs as Becky’s left hand coddled the back of his head, and he sobbed as she whispered: “It’s my fault, Zach.”

Zach stood and looked into her eyes. Becky stared at the floor as she said: “You knew she couldn’t meet me; I should have left” as a single tear fell from her chin and he kissed her gently, his tongue licking the outer parameters of her lips as his hands reached around her and grabbed each buttock tightly from behind. She felt his erection press into her; and as the baby kicked him and tears soaked his cheeks, she dropped to her knees and fumbled with his button.

He cried as he watched her shimmy his pants to his knees. She swallowed him as his voice trembled: “Did you see Emily’s face?” And as her teeth scraped against him and she suctioned him, he screamed: “Ahhh” as he ejaculated down her throat; and as his tears dropped onto his stomach, he whispered: “I love you, Becky,” as he stroked the back of her head as she suckled.

With her mouth still clutching and suctioning and her teeth clenching his rim, she whispered: “I love you too” as the room filled with the putrid stench of rotten eggs and decaying rotted flesh. She closed her eyes as he shrunk within her mouth and began to gag as the odor suffocated her, consuming her, and she passed out cold at his feet.

“Becky?” Zach said as her head thumped the floor. “Jesus!” he screamed as he pulled up his pants and buttoned them. He looked up; and as his eyes darted, he spotted a water bottle delicately balancing on the edge of the radiator.

As he went to touch the bottle, Charlie picked it up and handed it to him as he smiled and a freezing cold jolt caused Zach's body to quake. Zach watched as the bottle rose by itself from the radiator and implanted into his palm as he mumbled: "What the fuck?" and ran over to Becky's lifeless body.

He began pouring small droplets onto her face and neck; and as her eyes opened, the tang of lilac infiltrated her mucous membranes. Tears cascaded down his face as he slid her head into his lap, and she looked at him before falling back into unconsciousness as she heard: "Charlie, Charlie, Charlie."

"Oh, my God," Zach screamed as he poured water onto her neck as his left hand struggled to unbutton her blouse, allowing the water to drip, slowly saturating her breasts. She opened her eyes and sat up as he whispered: "Becky?" as his iPhone vibrated in his back pocket.

"I think we need to go to the hospital" he said as she stood swaying, and he stood behind her watching her unsteadiness as she leaned into him.

"For what?" she said as her equilibrium returned.

"For what … you just pass out all the time?" he said as she turned around to face him.

"I'm fine. Just it's hot, you know" she whispered as he kissed her and threw his arms around her shoulders: "You scared the shit out of me, you know."

"I'm fine, Zach," she mouthed as his cell vibrated. He backed up and helped her over to the chair and placed the water bottle into her right palm. As she guzzled the Poland Springs, he stared at his touchscreen: "One next text" it displayed, "one missed call: We need to talk now," the message said, "Laura."

Zach flashed his phone toward Becky who continued to sip as Zach sat on the floor Indian style at her feet staring at her face as the color returned to her cheeks. "You okay?" he said as he leaned his forehead into her knees.

“I’m fine,” she said as she finished the water and felt the baby kick.

“I’m gonna get Amanda, okay? I can’t leave you alone right now” he said as she stood.

“I’m fine, Zach,” she said as his left hand stroked her abdomen, and the baby violently kicked it away.

“Marry me?” he said as Becky grew unsteady, and her eyes clouded.

“Zach,” Becky said as she swayed, “I don’t feel so good.”

“I know,” he whispered as he helped Becky to sit in the chair and called Amanda from his cell and began to pace.

By the time Amanda knocked on Becky’s closed door, Becky was fine. Zach sat in the chair across from her staring at her face and smiling whenever their eyes locked.

Amanda knocked and turned the knob to find it was locked: “Zach?” her voice emanated from behind the door. Zach kissed Becky’s left cheek as he walked toward the door and unlocked it and stood with Amanda in the hallway.

“What’s going on?” Amanda shouted as Zach said: “Shhh … Mandy, my wife looked at Becky and looked at me and” --

“She knows, huh?” Zach nodded his head. “Becky just passed out cold on me twice.”

“Seriously?” Amanda said as her mouth dropped open and her brows raised.

“Seriously … and I’ve got to talk to my wife.”

Amanda nodded her head: “Of course you do and?”

“And I want her checked out, can you” --

“Seriously?,” Amanda steamed, “you’re unbelievable. Yeah, I’ll take her to the hospital and take her home. Why don’t you fucking leave her alone?” Amanda screamed as she turned the doorknob, and Zach grabbed her hand on the knob: “I love her.”

“You love her,” Amanda repeated as she pushed Zach’s chest and kept pushing him until his back hit the wall as he grabbed her right wrist and held it in front of his chest: “What’s your problem, Mandy?”

“What’s my problem?” Amanda yelled as Becky listened from behind the door. “My problem … you’re a selfish prick, that’s my problem. She’s six months pregnant and you want me to take her to the hospital?”

“Mandy, what do you want from me?” Zach whispered as tears filled his eyes.

“Go, go smooth it out with your wife … just leave her the fuck alone, will you?” Amanda said as Zach let go of her wrist, and she pushed him violently against the wall. She walked into Becky’s office knocking the door into Becky’s belly.

“Oh, my God,” Amanda shrieked as she stared at Becky who was hunched over clenching her abdomen, “you okay?” Amanda asked noticing her wet blouse.

“Yeah, I’m fine … just really hot, you know.”

“Come on, I’m taking you to Mass. General. Gotta make sure you’re okay … Zach’s freaking.”

“Amanda, I’m fine,” Becky said as she walked around her desk and booted her PC down.

“Becky, something’s wrong … you don’t just pass out cold from being hot or being pregnant. Let’s go.”

As they waited for the cab to pull in front of the Moakley, the blazing sun made Becky dizzy and unable to focus. Amanda stared at Becky as Becky leaned against the brick façade and spun as the color drained from her face.

Amanda walked into the courthouse and exited with Peter just as the yellow cab parked and Amanda waved. Peter and Amanda helped Becky into the cab as Zach exited the Moakley. He ran toward the cab as Amanda stood by the door whispering: "What do you want?"

"Move, Mandy," Zach shouted as he leaned into the cab: "You're gonna be okay, baby" he whispered as Becky smiled and he kissed her gently on the lips and moaned: "Hmmm" as Peter's mouthed dropped open and his eyes bulged as he stared at Amanda who smiled and shrugged.

"You're not coming?" Becky asked as Zach sat down on the seat next to her, and Amanda steamed mumbling as she leaned her right arm on the top of the door: "Coming … selfish prick!"

"I can't." He held his iPhone up to Becky's face. She stared into his dark eyes as she read: "We need to talk; I want a divorce."

"I gotta deal with this. Laura's freaking out and Emily's crying in her room, says Mommy's mad, destroying the house. She's scared, Becky … I'll be there as soon as I can; and if they send you home, I'll be there as soon as I can, okay?" Zach kissed Becky on the lips and made a grimace as he turned his head.

"What?" she said as he smiled and whispered: "I taste myself on your lips."

"Zach?" Becky whispered.

"Yeah," Zach said as he kissed her cheek.

"I'm scared," Becky said as she rubbed her abdomen with her right hand.

"I know, baby," he said as he took her left hand and placed it into his right palm: "You'll be fine … I'll see you in a couple hours." Zach kissed the top of her hand and then kissed her lips as she grabbed the back of his head with her left hand and pushed her tongue into his mouth. Liquid streamed down Becky's inner thighs as Zach's body swayed to her pheromonal release as he whispered: "Take care of my baby," and stood outside the cab as Amanda averted his eyes and stared at the pavement.

Zach whispered: "Thanks, Mandy," as she grunted: "You're a selfish prick," under her breath and hopped into the cab. Zach stood in the middle of Courthouse Way as the cab pulled away, and he ran toward his car in the lot.

Three hours later Amanda helped Becky into her favorite recliner; and as she placed a tall glass of ice water on the table, her Galaxy blazed from her purse:

"There is no pain you are receding, a distant ship smoke on the horizon … you are only coming through in waves, your lips move but I can't hear what you're saying. When I was a child, I had a fever" -- Amanda smiled at Becky as she walked into the kitchen whispering into her cell:

"Where are you?" Amanda said as she stared at the floor and paced in front of the refrigerator.

"She's fine. Baby's fine. They tested her sugar, tested her for, um, toxemia … she's fine; blood pressure's up, that's all."

Tears streamed down Amanda's face as she screamed into her Galaxy: "Prick" and walked back into Becky's living room. Becky was sipping water and stared at Amanda as she approached.

"Zach?" Becky asked as she sipped.

"Hmmm," Amanda moaned as she sat on the ottoman next to Becky's right leg.

“He’s not coming, is he?” Becky said as Amanda nodded her head and bit her bottom lip. “He can’t make it today … you okay?”

“We’ll be fine,” Becky said as her right hand gently rubbed her belly, and she felt the baby kick her sternum as she hunched over and yelled: “Ouch.”

“I gotta go, girlfriend,” Amanda whispered as she stared at her touchscreen, “It’s 5:30; gotta pick ‘em up by 6:30 or pay another 50 bucks … you sure you’re okay?”

“Go,” Becky said as Amanda hugged her whispering: “I love you. Call me;” and as the front door closed and she heard the cab beep by happenstance as it pulled away, tears cascaded down Becky’s cheeks as her iPhone began to vibrate in her pocket. She fumbled to retrieve it as her belly covered her pockets. She stood up and slid the phone out and whimpered as she read: “Can’t make it today. Love you … Z.”

“Can’t make it today,” she repeated as she wiped her tears and sipped her water and started flicking channels until she came upon a little movie called “Unfaithful.” She began to sob as Diane Lane picked up the snow globe she had given as a gift to her lover. Becky bawled as she read Lane’s face struggling to come to the internal realization that her husband, this gentle man, had murdered him.

“What did you do, Edward?” Lane cried as Becky sobbed repeating as she cried: “What did you do, Edward? Tell me what you did.”

As the movie ended and Becky’s eyes grew dim and hazy as her muscles relaxed and her eyes began to close, her iPhone buzzed on the ottoman. She picked it up in her left hand and read: “Missing you … Z.” Becky held the iPhone to her chest and fell fast asleep as the living room diffused with the zesty sweet balm of lilacs in bloom, and she whispered just as she nodded off: “Charlie, Charlie, Charlie.”

Becky awoke at 7:15 as her neck wrenched and seethed in pain and her bladder beckoned her from beyond as the baby squirmed within. She darted into the bathroom unable to open her eyes fully as she saw Emily standing in her office doorway crying: "Mommy, stop hitting him."

Becky crawled into bed and stripped her clothes, throwing them onto the floor haphazardly. She closed her eyes and whispered "Zach" as she fell asleep.

Becky awoke to her iPhone screaming from the living room at 8:30. "Wow," she said as she stared at her alarm clock, "it's 8:30." She yawned and opened her eyes wildly. Smiling she said: "Zach," and threw her terry bathrobe over her nakedness, and ran into the living room excitedly. She stared at her phone as it displayed: "one missed call … Amanda."

Becky strolled into the kitchen yawning, opened the cabinet next to the fridge and set two teabags into a mug and set the Keurig to brew. She sipped her tea from the kitchen table as her iPhone vibrated on the table.

"Hey," Zach whispered, "how's my girl?" Becky's body seismically twitched as she closed her eyes and heard her father say: "How's my girl?, how's my girl?"

"Okay," Becky whispered as she sipped and stared at her iPhone.

"Becky," Zach said as Becky stared at the screen, "I can't leave just yet."

"Yeah?" Becky said as she guzzled her tea.

"Yeah," Zach said, "Laura, she's freaking out." Becky shook her head spasmodically, her mind repeating: "But you love me, remember, Zach, you love me?"

"Stop playing with me, Zach" Becky screamed as her roommate walked into the kitchen and Becky smiled and strolled into her bedroom, holding the phone close to her heart as Zach whispered: "I love you."

"I can't do this anymore," Becky said as tears filled her eyes; "I love you" she whispered as she hit disconnect as Zach screamed: "Becky!"

She sat on the edge of her bed rubbing her belly as her iPhone vibrated. She looked down at the screen displaying: "Zach" and his number … "three missed calls." She placed the iPhone next to her on the bed which caused the mattress to vibrate as she walked to her closet and slipped on a purple lightweight summer dress which accentuated her ballooning abdomen.

She texted two words to Amanda before hitting send: "It's over." Her cell vibrated as it displayed: "Three new voicemails … Zach."

Becky shook her head back and forth as she hit "delete" as the text message displayed: "I'm proud of you … TTYL." Becky hit a smiley face and hit "send" as she smiled as Zach's number displayed across her touchscreen.

Becky hit "ignore" call and walked into the kitchen as her phone vibrated in her right palm. She placed it on the counter and turned it off as she sat at the kitchen table with Sara who sat smiling dousing her blueberry waffles with maple syrup.

"Want some?" Sara asked as she stabbed her waffle with her fork and a tiny dribble of syrup oozed from the left corner of her mouth. Becky grabbed a plate from the cabinet and nodded as she sat down.

Saturday night at 10:30 Becky lied in bed in the dark. She closed her eyes and watched as Zach carried her as she giggled nestled in his arms down the long hallway at the Marriott Longwharf. Her mind flashed backwards in time to every miniscule detail of every intimate physical encounter they'd ever shared.

With tears in her eyes, she turned on the television as the ASPCA commercial began to play. Becky began to cry as she watched the abused and neglected tortured animals on display as she began to sing:

“Spend all your time waiting for that second chance for a break that would make it okay. There's always some reason to feel not good enough, and it's hard at the end of the day.” Becky began to whimper as her tears freely flowed, and she increased the volume and sang loudly with Sara Mclachlan as she wept:

“I need some distraction, oh, a beautiful release, memories seep from my veins. Let me be empty and weightless, and maybe I'll find some peace tonight … in the arms of the angel, fly away from here, from this dark cold hotel room and the endlessness that you fear. You are pulled from the wreckage of your silent reverie, you're in the arms of the angel, may you f-i-i-i-ind some comfort here.”

Zach called 22 times between Saturday morning and Sunday evening. Becky’s iPhone began vibrating Monday morning at 6:55, and Becky smiled as she hit “ignore” and left her apartment; and as she closed the door and her iPhone vibrated in her blazer pocket, she began to hum, pulling a song out from the deep abyss of her mind:

“I will remember you. Will you remember me? Don't let your life pass you by, weep not for the memories … Remember the good times that we had? I let them slip away from us when things got bad. How clearly I first saw you smiling in the sun, wanna feel your warmth upon me, I wanna be the one … I will remember you. Will you remember me? Don't let your life pass you by, weep not for the memories.”

Becky got off the Silver Line across from the courthouse; and as the sun hit her face, she smiled and then sighed “Zach” as her iPhone vibrated inside her pocket as she darted through the parking lot toward the Moakley weaving through vehicles as she sang loudly with tears in her eyes:

“I'm so afraid to love you, but more afraid to lose, clinging to a past that doesn't let me choose.
Once there was a darkness, a deep and endless night; you gave me everything you had; oh, you gave me light … and I will remember

you, will you remember me?"

Becky walked into her office still humming: "Don't let your life pass you by, weep not for the memories" at 8:10 holding a large styrofoam tea in her right hand, her left hand dropping her briefcase on the floor as her mouth dropped open as Zach spun around to face her as he swiveled in her crickety chair.

"Hi" Becky said as she walked toward her desk and placed the tea on the desktop. Zach stared at her as he pounded his right foot on the floor. "We need to talk" he said as he stood and walked toward her.

Becky stood her ground and stared into his eyes as he approached: "There's nothing to talk about, Mr. Woods" Becky said as she stared him down.

"What do you want from me?" Zach said as Becky grinned and opened the rim of her tea and took a sip.

"What do I want from you … I want you to leave me alone, Mr. Woods" she said as Zach walked toward the door, his chin nestled on his chest. As he stood in the doorjamb, he turned around and whispered as he cocked his head to the left: "Okay … see ya" he said as the door closed behind him, and Becky's eyes filled with tears as she slid her iPhone out of her blazer pocket and scrolled down and played a song that she'd recently downloaded, a song all too familiar but sung by a new voice:

"Turn down the lights, turn down the bed," Becky cried as she turned the volume up and sang along and walked toward the harbor using her iPhone as a mic: "Turn down these voices inside my head. Lay down with me, tell me no lies … just hold me closely, don't patronize, don't patronize …'cause I can't make you love me if you don't."

Mascara ran down Becky's cheeks as her tears dropped onto the floor as the sun disappeared from view, and the blue sky turned a deep pale slate of grey as she wept:

“You can't make your heart feel something that it won’t; and here in the dark, in these final hours, I will lay down my heart, and I’ll feel the power, but you won't. No, you won't” … Becky stared into the harbor as tears streaked her cheeks and dribbled down her chin as thunder boomed and lightening light up the sky.

She closed her eyes and sobbed as she sang along with Adele: ‘Cause I can’t make you love me if you don’t, if you don’t. You can’t make your heart feel something it won’t.” Amanda pushed open Becky’s door slowly, and it creaked causing Becky to turn and look into her friend’s eyes.

Amanda began to cry, her left hand covering her mouth as tears saturated her cheeks as she watched her friend wallow in grief as she stared into Amanda’s eyes: “‘Cause I can’t make you love me if you don’t, if you don’t” … Amanda slowly walked toward Becky as Becky’s left arm lied across Amanda’s right shoulder, and they sang loudly as their bodies began to sway to the music and their tears stopped flowing:

“I'll close my eyes, then I won't see the love you don't feel when you're holding me. Morning will come, and I'll do what's right, just give me ‘til then to give up this fight, and I will give up this fight … ‘cause I can't make you love me if you don't, if you don’t.”

Amanda and Becky smiled at each other, and they sang as their voices cracked in perfect harmony with Adele:

“You can’t make your heart feel something it won’t. Here in the dark in these final hours, I will lay down my heart and I’ll feel the power, but you won’t. No, you won’t …. ‘cause I can't make you love me if you don’t, if you don’t.”

Becky and Amanda began giggling which turned into a roaring laughter as the song ended, and Becky and Amanda wiped their wet cheeks with the backs of their hands. Amanda looked into Becky’s eyes and said: “So you ready for the ten o’clock motion hearing?”

Becky giggled from the depths of her soul as Amanda chuckled and said: “I am so proud of you,” and they hugged as the baby kicked Amanda’s stomach and she backed up smiling whispering: “Woe.”

Amanda’s phone began vibrating in her right front pocket. She picked it up and held the screen toward Becky: “Mandy, tell Becky she can handle the motion session on her own … Z.” Becky nodded her head as Amanda said: “So have you looked at the motion?”

Becky sat down at her desk and opened her tea and sipped slowly as Amanda sat down across from her and guzzled her coffee. They communicated without words as Amanda comforted her friend with her presence as she felt the agonizing envelopment of her grief. Becky’s phone vibrated on the desk and before Becky grabbed it with her right hand, Amanda whispered:
“Wonder who that is?”

Becky stared at her iPhone as it displayed: “Can I have a talk with you … Z?” She put her head down on the desk and began lightly thumping her forehead against the desktop as Amanda walked around the desk holding a document in her right hand. She grabbed Becky’s iPhone and texted: “Leave me alone” as Becky stared at the motion entitled: “Motion For Court to Quash Jury Verdict and Indictment.”

“What’s this?” Becky asked as Amanda smiled: “Read, girlfriend” and gently stroked the back of her head before returning to her chair as Becky’s eyes perused …“What the hell is this?” Becky said as she smiled, and Amanda sipped as Becky’s swollen eyes fixated:

“The Defendant hereby moves the Court to set aside the May 12, 2011, verdict and the April 24, 2010, indictment for what amounts to significant, cumulative, and highly prejudicial prosecutorial misconduct” … Becky raised her eyes and said as Amanda grinned: “Seriously?” as she nodded her head and skipped down to the last page of the motion:

“Given the above, there is probable cause to believe that AUSA Zachary Woods in this malicious prosecution was significantly, if not wholly motivated, by private interests and that deliberate pretrial obstructions took place at the United States Attorney's Office, the Massachusetts Attorney General's Office, and the Board of Bar Overseers which unduly prejudiced the Defendant's May 2011 trial.

Given the above, and all things considered, the Court is asked to quash the jury verdict and order the immediate release of the Defendant."

"Amanda, what the hell is this?" Becky asked as Mandy smiled and whispered: "Okay … guy's a nutjob."

"Uh-huh," Becky moaned, "and?"

"Here," Amanda said with a smile throwing a document onto Becky's desktop as Becky nodded her head insanely:

"On May 12, 2005, Clifford was arrested in Scituate, Massachusetts, and that set off a chain of events which eventually resulted in the federal indictment in this case. That day, the Scituate Police Department had received a call from a town resident that Clifford was trespassing on the grounds of her home impersonating a private investigator as he hid in the bushes and snapped photographs of homeowner's residence. The police arrested Clifford for trespassing after he had already left the private residence and charged him with disorderly conduct and impersonating a private investigator.

A jury convicted Clifford of the disorderly conduct count, for which he served six months in state prison, although that conviction was later overturned. (The reason is not in the record.)

He also had admitted that there were sufficient facts to prove his guilt for impersonating an investigator, for which he received a six-month suspended sentence.

In May 2007 Clifford filed a § 1983 lawsuit, pro se, in federal court against the Town of Scituate (Town), two local police officers, the town resident who had accused him of trespassing and that resident's husband, asserting that the arrest had been without probable cause in violation of the Fourth Amendment and pendent common law tort claims. Woods was the AUSA assigned to represent the United States in this case.

On January 9, 2009, AUSA Woods filed a motion for summary judgment arguing that Clifford had no legal basis for his claims. The district court granted summary judgment as to all federal claims on May 22, 2009, declining to exercise jurisdiction over the pendent state law claims.

Again proceeding pro se, on October 27, 2009, Clifford filed another lawsuit in federal court against the Town, the Scituate police officers, and additional defendants, including the United States of America and AUSA Woods; this time Clifford sought damages for "malicious prosecution" and "willful negligence."

The case was assigned to a different federal district court judge. AUSA Woods again represented the government and himself in this second lawsuit. On March 5, 2010, AUSA Woods moved to dismiss the lawsuit as to himself. In response Clifford sent Woods the following email three days later, on March 8, 2010, at 10:25 p.m.:

"Dearest Mr. Woods: I believe you are playing a dangerous game, a very dangerous game. I have every hunch someone is going to get hurt. At this point after years of police/court bullshit and your crap I'm rather hoping someone will, deserving it, of course. Have you ever been punched in the face, Mr. Woods?"

Becky started to giggle as Amanda whispered: "It gets better … keep reading, girlfriend." Becky placed her head on her open right palm supporting it as she read:

"I rather hope you experience that same thrill someday, figuratively or otherwise, maybe even see one of your real 'clients' go to prison, you get disbarred, 'taken to a chop shop on Staten Island,' whatever.

There was never any sufficient facts in my case, and you know it, Mr. Woods, to begin with much less to plea to. You and your people systematically BUTTFUCKED me and you knew it, too. I will say it now, once: one way or another, I will have my day in court or the back alley (hint, hint, veiled threat potential here). You do be careful now, you hear?

You, at this point, I assure you, will get what you deserve. Pow! Bang! Splat! I really truly and sincerely wish you were dead. I am very much looking forward to putting you in your place, Mr. Woods. You disgust me. You are absolute filth (proof positive that a suit and tie ultimately doesn't make a person 'good' or 'respectable')."

"In a separate email sent at 11:22 p.m. Clifford wrote:

'From now on, Mr. Woods, be sure and watch your backside. Mr. Woods, God may step up to the plate at any moment. I don't know; I got this feeling someone's going to get hurt REAL BAD, and it ain't gonna be me. Here's to Law and Order. And, yes, you can expect a full briefing from me in the coming days addressing your truth-twisting, truth-burying masterpiece of a motion. Rationalize all you want but come Judgment Day you've had it ... Jeffrey Clifford.'

Woods read Clifford's email the following morning on March 9th. He testified in this case that he had read the email as a 'personal physical threat.' Clifford moved to dismiss the indictment, arguing in part that the emails are, as a matter of law, protected speech under the First Amendment and do not contain 'true threats,' which are outside the scope of First Amendment protection.

During a three-day trial in May 2011 AUSA Woods testified on behalf of the government and Clifford's emails were submitted as evidence. The defense did not call any witnesses, and Clifford chose not to testify.

At trial Clifford had admitted that: (1), the emails were sent in interstate commerce, traveling from Ohio to Massachusetts; and (2), that he intended to send the emails, so the only issue left for the jury was whether the emails contained a threat to injure someone.

In closing the defense argued that it is not reasonable to construe these emails as literal threats, characterizing Clifford as an 'aggrieved' person who was just blowing off steam because he felt he had been treated unfairly in the state criminal justice system and then by his federal prosecution and was simply frustrated with the progress of his related civil suits.

After deliberating for just under two hours, on May 11, 2011, the jury found Clifford guilty on both counts of sending threats to injure and interstate commerce. Clifford timely appealed."

"Hmmm, no wonder Zach handed this to me today, huh?"

Amanda giggled and she threw the Government's Sentencing Memorandum on top of the Motion to Quash as Becky nodded her head: "I don't even need to read this," she said as she smiled as she shook her head and said "Oy."

"Yeah," Amanda said as she finished her coffee, "Oy!"

Becky and Amanda walked into Courtroom No. 1 at 9:45, and Timmy smiled at Becky as she approached counsel table. He motioned with his right hand for her to come forward as he walked toward her. She met him halfway down the aisle as he whispered: "Take a walk with me a minute, Ms. Lawrence?"

Josh hollered: "Don't disappear, counsel" as Becky waved to him as they sat in the last row.

"Wow, you look so good," Timmy said as Becky tried to sit down.

"Yeah, right," Becky whispered, if you like whales, I guess."

"No, really, you are beautiful," Timmy said as Becky blushed. "Listen, um, Clifford's acting kind of" --

"Nutty?" Becky asked as she grinned.

"Hmmm, I'm glad it's you here this morning; that's all I'm gonna say … you're not married, Becky; are you?"

"No, Tim," Becky said as Tim grabbed her right hand into his left palm. “So your boyfriend must be thrilled about this baby, huh?,” he said as he stared at her baby bump.

“Hmmm … actually, Tim, we broke up” Becky said as she stared at the floor.

“Really, so you’re single?”

“Are you for real?” Becky asked as she grinned, and her right hand rubbed her belly.

“Go out with me,” Tim said as he gently placed his left hand on her abdomen, and the baby kicked his palm.

“You’re serious?” Becky whispered as Tim nodded his head up and down and smiled: “Your boyfriend’s loss … you know what they say?”

Becky nodded her head back and forth: “No, Tim, what do they say?”

Timmy helped Becky to stand as he whispered: “His loss, my gain” and Tim smiled as Becky blushed.

“All rise,” Josh said as he winked at Becky, and the Judge took the bench. “This is the matter of the Sentencing, Day 2, in the U.S. vs. Jeffrey Clifford, Docket No. 10-cr-10244. Would counsel please state your names for the record?

“Day 2?” Becky whispered to Amanda who nodded.

“Good morning, your Honor. Becky Lawrence for the Government.”

Woodbury’s eyes opened widely as he stared at her midriff: “Good morning, Ms. Lawrence.”

“Good morning, your Honor. Timothy O’Brien for the Defendant who is seated at counsel table.”

Woodbury smirked at Becky as he poured a glass of water from his decanter: "Good morning, Mr. O'Brien and Mr. Clifford.

Well, I just had handed up to me this morning a document entitled: Defendant's Motion to Quash Jury Verdict and Indictment. I have read it carefully, and I will deny it. It is in my view not important to the matters before us, which are questions of sentencing the defendant, and this ongoing dispute that the defendant has raised with various persons within the Board of Bar Overseers and the FBI is not material here to my consideration of sentencing.

As this is a continuation from last week, I will ask the defendant if he wishes to address the court before sentence is imposed?"

Clifford stood as Becky sat down: "I just want you, your Honor, to understand who I am, and if you think a person who has written what he has in these last months, geez, you know, is some threat to society and ought to be sent to prison for 77 months, you know, by all means, Judge, Mr. Woodbury, go ahead, give me 77 months, you know. Hallelujah, the system worked or did it, or did it?

So who's respecting or disrespecting the system here? Where on my civil case record, public record, in litigation anywhere that there's any degree of an affront or insult or offense to the reader that says: 'This guy doesn't respect the system.' Where is it?

You don't have it. You have two e-mails. Yes, I'm being prosecuted for them. I'm paying the price and I accept that, but, you know, you're gonna make the toughest decision of all, your Honor. If you believe that I deserve 77 months for writing an email, then so be it."

Woodbury took a sip of his water: "Thank you. I have found this a very challenging case on a variety of levels, and I'll start with the principle factors under Section 3553 that I'm required to consider in evaluating the sentencing guidelines, whether they can be treated as reasonable under the circumstances or not. And that has to do with the nature and the circumstances of the defendant who I've listened to at length today, and I assure you I have read all of the materials that Mr. Clifford has submitted; I've actually read portions of them at certain times, trying to get a sense of this, and I think I do have a sense, but it's one that's been reflected by several different vectors.

What's at issue here is that persons should be secure from threats like this, which any reasonable person would find, and the jury was the core group, to find this to be in violation of federal law.

Now, Mr. Clifford talked in terms of his, I would have to say "budget view," that he used figurative speech, and that he is sometimes spontaneous because of his vocational leanings and background ... I think that essentially understates the matter. This was not a manner or a figure of speech; it was on reflection what anyone would have understood to be disquieting threats.

The spontaneity aspect of it is more important to me. That is to say that it is apparent to me that Mr. Clifford cannot control himself."

Clifford stood and began to scream as Timmy pulled on his right sleeve: "You know what, your Honor" --

Becky stared at Amanda who raised her right finger in the air in a circular motion as she mouthed: "crazy."

Woodbury stared at the defendant as he spoke: "Mr. Clifford" --

"You know what … let's just leave. Let's call this off, I mean fuck it"....

Woodbury began to raise his voice: "Mr. Clifford."

"I mean, really, come on. Mr. Woods wanted this. He wanted those e-mails. I thought the FBI would come to my rescue, and they didn't. He wanted this."

Woodbury scratched his chin: "Mr. Clifford, now just a moment."

The defendant banged counsel table with both fists and attempted to walk around the table as he stared at the Judge angrily. Two CSOs approached the defendant as he wobbled and tripped through his shackles in front of the table. “Sit down, Mr. Clifford” Peter yelled.

“Fuck you,” the defendant screamed, “I just want to talk to him face to face, man to man” … Peter and a CSO that Becky did not recognize jumped the defendant and took him down to the courtroom floor as he screamed: “Ow, ow, goddamn it” as a spectator from the audience began screaming: “Ease up over there, will you?”

Peter held his Motorola in his right hand as he pressed the button and smiled at Becky as their eyes met: “U.S. Marshal, Courtroom No. 1, need assistance Courtroom 1.”

As the defendant began to scream: “Ow, ow … touch me again, I’ll fucking kill you” Woodbury said in a muffled tone: “I'm going to put the court in recess. I'll ask that the marshals provide me with a report of whether or not Mr. Clifford is in a position to continue after the outburst that I just observed here. We’ll be in recess … Becky, can I see you for a minute please in my chambers -- off the record.”

“All rise” Josh said as Becky wobbled over toward the clerk’s bench.

Becky could feel her pulse throbbing in her neck as Josh buzzed her into the back of the house. Woodbury was waiting for her in his robing room looking angry and disheveled. “Can you believe what you just witnessed?” Woodbury asked as he stood and stared at Becky’s midriff.

“Guy’s a nutjob, Judge, guy’s a nutjob,” Becky said as Woodbury grinned, slipped off his robe as with his right hand placed it gently on Becky’s abdomen as the baby violently kicked his palm and he smiled: “Holy!” Woodbury said excitedly as he smiled.

“Come take a walk with me, Ms. Lawrence.”

“Here we go,” Becky thought as she followed the Judge toward his chambers. Woodbury held the door for her as he whispered: “Come with me.”

Becky followed the Judge into his office as he mumbled: “I need coffee" as Becky smiled and sat down in the chair across from his desk. Perspiration beaded down her temples as she dreaded their impending colloquy.

"I'll be right back; make yourself comfortable, Becky," Woodbury said as he smiled and exited.

"I can see the disappointment and disapproval in his eyes," Becky said to herself as she wiped her temples as the baby's foot stuck out of her stomach. She pressed on it and giggled as the baby kicked her.

"So when are we due, Ms. Lawrence?" Woodbury asked as he walked around his desk, spilling his mug as he walked and sat down slurping his brew.

"Um, October 31st, Judge," Becky said as Woodbury's mind flashed back to a brief conversation and humor-filled colloquy in open court: "The final pretrial conference in this case will be October 31st at 4:00 p.m. unless anyone has a scheduling dilemma?" Zach stood: "Your Honor, most respectfully, that's Halloween and" -- "I understand that, Mr. Woods … you have trick-or-treating plans, do you?"

Woodbury shook his head back and forth as he said in the funnels of his mind: "Na, that's ridiculous," and smiled at Becky as he whispered: "You've never looked better you know."

"Thanks," Becky mumbled as her mind reeled, "And here it comes."

"Who's the father?" Woodbury asked as his eyebrows met in the center forming an arch.

Becky squirmed and averted his eyes and stared at the floor. Woodbury walked around his desk and sat on the edge as his left hand picked up her chin, forcing her to confront him. "Talk to me, Becky," the Judge whispered; is it Timmy?"

Becky grinned and nodded her head from side to side: "No, your Honor."

“It’s hard to raise a baby alone, Ms. Lawrence,” Woodbury said as he watched her stomach flutter as he grinned.

“I know, Judge,” Becky whispered as she stared at her feet.

“Becky,” Woodbury whispered, “you’re like a daughter to me.” Becky’s eyes filled as the Judge smiled, and she looked up into his gaze.

“You need anything any time, day or night, all you have to do is call me; I’ll be there.” As her tears exploded, a single tear dropped from the corner of Woodbury’s left eye. He helped her to stand, and he grabbed her into his arms as she wept and soaked his collar.

Becky whispered as she cried: “You’re the father I never had,” and Woodbury wept as Becky hugged and consoled him as the room filled with the aroma of balmy lilacs in bloom, and Charlie cried as the Judge wept.

The Judge’s office line buzzed as the intercom buzzed: “Judge, Line 2 please.” Woodbury wiped his pink cheeks and walked around his desk and pressed Line 2 as Becky walked over toward the curved conoid glass wall overlooking Boston Harbor.

“Okay, thanks,” the Judge whispered as Becky turned her head and inquisitively stared at him as he walked toward her. They stood peering into the ocean as he whispered: “Clifford had to be restrained. Come on, I’ve got to put something on the record.”

Becky followed Woodbury out of his office, down the hallway through the back of the house; and as he held the door open for her at the entrance of his robing room, he whispered: “I love you, Ms. Lawrence” as Becky leaned in and kissed his left cheek. “I love you too, Judge … Judge?”

Woodbury grinned as he blushed.

Becky smiled and whispered: “Baby needs a Godfather, Judge” … Woodbury wiped his cheeks as he walked into the courtroom.

“All rise,” Josh announced as Becky scooted into the courtroom waddling as she tried to run. The Judge waited until she was behind counsel table before he entered as he sniffled. “This is the continuation of the Sentencing, Day 2, in U.S. v Clifford, Docket No. 10-10224.”

Woodbury put his glasses on his nose: “Please be seated. I have been informed that Mr. Clifford after his outburst here in open court had to be physically restrained in lockup as he attacked several United States Marshals. In light of this development, this hearing is suspended until further notice unless counsel has any issue to bring to my attention?”

Timmy smiled at Becky as he stood: “No, your Honor.”

Amanda helped Becky to stand as she struggled: “No, your Honor.”

Woodbury giggled as he mumbled: “Then, we are adjourned … thank you, counsel.”

“All rise” Josh said as he winked at Becky as Timmy walked toward her, and Josh nodded his head as he sat down to detail the clerk’s notes.

“Hey,” Tim whispered, “so go out with me?” Amanda smiled as she said: “I’ll see you later, Becky,” as Becky assembled her legalese spread over the tabletop.

“Well?” Tim said as he grabbed her right forearm.

“All right, all right, all right,” Becky said as she grinned.

“Great. How ‘bout I pick you up here at, say, 5:30?”

“Okay,” Becky said as Tim smiled, “you like pregnant women, huh?”

“I like you,” Timmy said smiling as Becky watched him walk down the center aisle. Timmy abruptly turned around and smiled as Becky's eyes had followed, and he held the heavy door open for her as she exited.

"You're crazy," Becky whispered as Timmy smiled, and they walked out into the sunshine permeating through the conoid wall. Timmy's cell rang as Becky whispered: "You're not some kind of deviant, are ya?" Timmy's right hand touched Becky's abdomen, and he held it gently as the baby squirmed inside as he grinned and answered his blazing cell: "Yep, give me a minute."

Timmy leaned in toward her and whispered into her right ear: "I gotta take this call … 5:30. See ya, beautiful," he said as her face contorted and she whimpered in her mind: "Zach."

Two hours later Amanda walked into Becky's office holding a file folder. "Hi" Amanda said as Becky smiled: "Hi, girlfriend. What's this?"

"Zach wanted me to tell you he needs you to draft a motion to unseal today."

Becky nodded her head from side to side "So this is how we're gonna communicate now, huh?"

Amanda sat down: "He also wanted me to tell you he needs you to draft a motion to get Veloz's Sprint records."

"Seriously?," Becky said as she thought, "Grow up, Zach."

"Not for nothing, Becky, he's out of his mind. After he loses his shit on me, he whispers: "How's Becky?"

"And you said?" Becky said as she opened the file folder and grinned.

"I said she's great" … Amanda smiled as Becky grinned: "Thanks, girlfriend."

Amanda placed her right hand on Becky's desk as she whispered: "Be glad he ain't talking to you," as she smiled; and as she approached the doorjamb, she turned around: "I'm going for coffee … you want?"

"Na," Becky said as she smiled, "but I'll have a tea, though."

"Oh, Zach wants this motion ready by 4 … I'll be back."

Becky tore through the motion at warp speed and had it wrapped by the time Amanda walked in with her tea. She queued it to print as Amanda placed the cardboard tray on her desk and Becky's iPhone vibrated in her blazer pocket.

As Becky walked toward the printer and handed her the completed motion, Amanda's eyes widened: "You're amazing" she said as she sat down and opened the rim and tilted her head back and let the hot coffee pour down her throat.

Becky walked over toward the harbor as she slid her phone into her right palm: "one next text: Miss me? … Z." Becky nodded her head back and forth and closed her eyes and watched as Zach licked her and she exploded.

"Mr. Wonderful?" Amanda asked as she stared at Becky. Becky nodded and placed her cell on her desk as she sat down and opened her tea and sipped as Amanda downed her coffee.

"Timmy asked me out," Becky said smiling as she sipped.

"And?" Amanda said smiling.

"Got a hot date tonight … I asked him: "you like pregnant women, huh?"

Amanda smiled as she stood: "And he said: 'I like you,' right?"

Becky smiled as Amanda nodded: "Proud of you … have a good time." Amanda walked toward the door; and just before she walked through the archway, she turned around and whispered: “Becky, don’t tell him about -- well, you know.”

“I’m not stupid, girlfriend,” Becky said as Amanda went to exit as Becky’s cell vibrated in her pocket and Amanda shook her head and grinned: “See ya, girlfriend.”

At 5:15 Becky’s cell vibrated: “Hi, ready? … Tim.”

Becky smiled as she booted down the PC, left her briefcase on the desk, and closed her office door as she texted: “On my way.”

Just before entering the elevator as she held her iPhone in her right palm, it vibrated: “Waiting in the lobby, beautiful” it read; Becky entered the elevator as she mumbled “Zach” under her breath and closed her eyes and watched as Zach said: “Say it.” Becky’s eyes momentarily filled with tears as she whispered “Zach” and held her cell to her chest.

Timmy smiled as Becky approached. He leaned in and whispered: “Hungry?” as Becky nodded and her right hand touched her abdomen: “Always now,” she said as Tim giggled.

They ate at The Daily Catch right next-door to the Moakley. Becky inhaled her fish as Tim giggled as she ate her last fry. “I’m done” he said with a grin as he turned his plate toward her and Becky finished his fries.

They walked along the Harborwalk along Fan Pier as the sun began to set and the sky lit up in a pink hue. They sat down on a bench, and Becky giggled as Tim rambunctiously chatted about his childhood in Maine and his wild adventures of youth on the Saco.

There was a serene comfortableness between them that allowed Becky to unwind and share memories and moments etched in time she had never shared with anyone before. Tim helped Becky to stand, and he listened intently as they walked along the concrete walk wrapping around the Moakley as Becky whispered: “I’ve never told anyone about this.”

Tim remained silent as Becky recounted the terrors of her childhood, the internal horrors of her mind. He hugged her as he whispered: “You’re not a victim, Becky. You’re a survivor.”

As the night swallowed the day and Becky yawned, Tim whispered: “I’m taking you home.” Becky waited on Courthouse Way as Tim pulled up in his black Jaguar. He threw it into park in the middle of the street as he ran around the car to open the door for Becky and helped her into the passenger’s seat. She smiled as he buckled her seat belt over her protruding hump.

They sat in the parking lot outside of her complex talking and giggling as Becky’s face contorted: “I gotta pee” she whispered as he smiled. She opened the car door and walked around the Jaguar as he opened the door. “Coming?” she said with a grin.

Tim walked Becky to the front door and kissed her left cheek as he whispered: “I want to take you somewhere tomorrow night, okay?”

“Okay,” Becky said with a smile as her brows raised, “you don’t want to come in?”

Tim shook his head back and forth as he kissed her forehead: “See ya tomorrow, Ms. Lawrence.” Becky stood in the foyer clenching her thighs together watching as the Jaguar pulled out of the lot. As she climbed into bed and pulled the sheet and comforter over her head, she closed her eyes as tears cascaded down her cheeks as she whispered: “Zach.”

Tim pulled in front of the Moakley at 5:10 and helped Becky into the front seat. “Hi” he said as he buckled the seat belt around her belly as she kissed his left cheek whispering: “Hi, where we going?”

“Shhh,” he whispered as he ran around the Jag and hopped in and skidded out as the tires spun in the sand. As he pulled into the garage under 60 State Street, Becky said: “You wanted to take me to Faneuil Hall?” as Tim shook his head and smiled as he whispered: “Shhh.”

Tim grabbed Becky's hand as they walked out onto State Street: "Hungry?" he asked as she smiled: "I can wait." They walked hand in hand until they came to a grassy knoll with two large granite monoliths that faced each other squarely.

"What's this, Tim?" Becky whispered as Tim said "Shhh." Becky's eyes were immediately drawn to six large towers of glass with white-etched numbers imbedded into the panes. As they walked along the paved path, Becky raised her right hand to her mouth as she whispered: "The Holocaust?" Tim shook his head up and down as he tightly clenched her left hand. Tears began to fall as her right hand rubbed her belly as she read:

"*Most infants and children were killed immediately upon arrival at the camps. The Nazis murdered as many as one and a half million Jewish children.*"

Becky stared into Tim's eyes as she struggled to understand why he had taken her here. She felt warm air as it rose from the ground. Tim whispered: "It's a grate." As the warm air hit the bottom of her abdomen, she dropped to her knees as a single tear dropped from Tim's left eye. She peered into the grate under the ground into a pit of ragged rocks. Tim knelt down as Becky's face leaned into the grate, and she strained her eyes to see. There were tiny stationary white lights and a singular bright light that illuminated in the darkness.

Tim helped Becky to stand and as her tears streaked her cheeks, he held her against him. "This isn't a story about victims, Becky" he said as she wailed, as a white light illuminated in her mind and she understood why Tim had taken her here.

"I know, Tim," Becky whispered, "it's a story about survivors." Tim held Becky tightly as she blubbered and soaked his blazer right though to his shirt. "Thank you for taking me here" she whispered as Tim wiped her tears with his fingertips. He grabbed her left hand in his clutch as they walked along the path toward a large monolith, and Becky sobbed again as she read:

"They came first for the Communists, and I didn't speak up because I wasn't a Communist. Then they came for the Jews, and I didn't speak up because I wasn't a Jew. Then they came for the trade unionists, and I didn't speak up because I wasn't a trade unionist. Then they came for the Catholics, and I didn't speak up because I was a Protestant. Then they came for me, and by that time no one was left to speak up -- Martin Niemoeller."

Becky's stomach grumbled as Timmy smiled: "Hungry?" They walked holding hands as they entered Regina Pizzeria. Timmy helped Becky into a large booth as she struggled to wiggle in. They ate a large cheese pizza and conversed with their minds without speaking sharing the profound experience they'd shared.

"Tim," Becky whispered as she nervously looked around the bar, "until very recently I thought sex was" --

"Dirty?" Tim asked as Becky's eyes filled with tears, and she shook her head up and down.

"-- something dark, something ugly, something evil," Becky whispered.

"And now, Becky?" Tim asked as he grabbed her right hand in his left palm.

"Now I know different," Becky said as she smiled and Timmy kissed the back of her hand gently as he whispered: "Now you see the beauty, huh?"

"Have you always felt things so deeply?" Becky asked as she finished her third large slice.

Timmy took a sip of Coke and swashed it around his cheeks. "I'm not sure I feel things more deeply than anyone else," Tim replied as he wiped her right cheek with his napkin.

Becky shook her head as she kissed his cheek. "You do," she

whispered as he kissed her on the lips gently, and she slowly pulled away and held back as her mind watched her mouth swallowing Zach.

Six weeks later at 8:30 a.m. Monday morning, September 16th, Amanda sat across from Becky's desk as Becky rambled on and on about Timmy's empathy and the exuberance of his milk of human kindness and the mundane experiences they shared. She smiled as she spoke, and Amanda giggled as Becky recanted their walk through the Boston Museum of Fine Arts, the Aquarium, The Science Museum, and the New England Holocaust Museum.

Amanda guzzled her coffee as Becky sipped her tea: "Timmy's wife died three years ago," Becky said as Amanda placed her coffee on the desk, "breast cancer."

"Ahhh," Amanda said as her smile turned into a frown.

Becky placed her tea on the desktop: "He said with tears: 'she was the love of my life until now.'"

"Becky," Amanda whispered, "he's a great guy. Don't hurt him."

Becky eyes filled with tears: "He asked me to marry him, Mandy."

"Wow," Amanda said as her eyes filled behind their lids, "and you said?"

Becky rubbed her belly trying to quiet the fetus inside as it turned and twisted and protruded though her dress. "He's like my best friend."

"Uh-huh," Amanda said as she stood agitated, "Becky" --

Tears flowed down Becky's cheeks as she spoke: "Amanda, he said as we sat in the car and the sun set: 'I love you. Marry me. I will raise this baby as my own … no man will ever love you or this baby as much as I do.'"

“Oh, my God, Becky,” Amanda said as she wiped her wet cheeks and her tears continued to flow, “and you said?”

“I couldn’t answer him. I just cried and he just held me.”

Amanda walked around Becky’s desk, neither noticing Zach standing in the doorjamb listening or felt his presence as he walked away. “I have to have an ultrasound tomorrow, sugar’s a little high,” Becky whispered as Amanda hugged her, “come with”?

Amanda nodded as she whispered: “What time?”

“1:00 at the Brigham” Becky said as she sat back down in her chair, and Amanda held the back of the seat so it wouldn’t swivel. “I’m gonna put in a leave slip for the rest of the day.”

“Okay,” Amanda said, “what are you gonna do?”

Becky looked deeply into Amanda’s eyes as Amanda leaned the small of her back against Becky’s desk. “I don’t know” Becky said as their eyes locked.

“You’re waiting for Zach, aren’t you?” Amanda said as she stood and walked toward the window and peered into the harbor. Becky stood holding the desk for leverage as she closed her eyes and her cell vibrated in her blazer pocket. “Zach” she whispered in her mind as her cell buzzed.

Becky walked slowly over toward Amanda as her right hand lifted her iPhone from her pocket; she knew intuitively what the message said without looking at the screen; she flashed it in front of Amanda’s eyes. It read: “Miss me, beautiful? … Z.”

Becky studied Amanda’s face searching for empathy or wisdom which didn’t readily display. Amanda became angry as her cheeks reddened as Becky said: “What?”

“You want some advice? Amanda asked as Becky stared out into the water and bobbed her head up and down. “Marry Tim, Becky” she said as Becky began to cry. “If you’re waiting for Zach, you’re gonna be waiting a long time, girlfriend.”

“I love him, Mandy,” Becky said as Amanda placed her right arm over Becky’s left shoulder: “I know” she whispered as Becky sobbed, cradled in her best friend’s arms as the room filled with the vibrant balm of lilac as they embraced.

As they walked out of the Brigham, Amanda stopped short of the exit and whispered: “You’re gonna have a C-Section.”

“Why do you say that?” Becky asked perplexed as she rubbed her stomach unconsciously with her left hand.

“Why? The baby’s ten pounds and you have a month-and-a-half to go, girlfriend.” Becky stared at her massive abdomen as her stomach rumbled, and Amanda giggled: “Hungry?”

They arrived in a cab outside the Moakley at 2:15 and Amanda smiled.

“What?” Becky asked as she waddled out into Courthouse Way.

“Nothing” Amanda said as she chuckled to herself. “Listen, I put a leave slip in for the day. Come on, get your stuff, I’ll take you home.”

As the elevator door closed and they stepped inside, Amanda whispered: “Have sex with Tim yet?”

Becky shook her head back and forth as Amanda smiled: “No, huh … do you want to?”

Becky stared into Amanda’s eyes as Amanda’s smile vacated, and she squinched her face: “No, huh?” Amanda pressed the stop button just as the elevator landed on the ninth: “Becky, talk to me.”

“I love Tim,” Becky said as Amanda smiled, “I really do; he’s like my best friend except for you but we don’t have” --

“A spark?” Amanda interjected.

“Yeah, you know, that like polarized magnetic attraction.”

“Uh-huh, and look where that got you, girlfriend” Amanda said as she broke out into a smile watching as Becky’s abdomen began to rise and fall as the baby hiccupped in the womb.

Amanda’s Galaxy began to play: “There is no pain, you are receding.” Amanda reached into her right front pocket and lifted the Galaxy to her ear as the call disconnected. “Guess who?” she said as she pushed in the stop button and elevator doors opened on the ninth.

“Get your stuff, Becky,” Amanda said as she walked toward the conoid wall and hit “Zach.” Becky booted her PC down and grabbed her briefcase and stuffed her purse within it. Amanda was still on the phone as Becky approached.

“Uh-huh,” Amanda said as Becky smiled at her. “Uh-huh … how, Zach?”

Becky leaned in closer as Amanda held the Galaxy between them: “I don’t know, Mandy, but he’s dead. Somehow there’s a leak and it’s within.”

Becky mouthed to Amanda: “What?” as Amanda nodded her head and raised her left pointer finger toward her mouth in a hush.

“Tell Becky, okay, Mandy?” Zach whispered as his voice cracked. “I don’t have any choice here. If I pursue this, I can’t try him again, you know … I’ll see ya.”

“Zach,” Amanda said as Becky’s brows raised, “you okay?”

“Hmmm, depressed … how’s my baby?” Zach asked as a profound silence set in, and Becky jabbed Amanda’s left arm.

“Good … big, a big boy, Zach.”

“Yeah?,” Zach said as he chuckled, “how big?”

“Ten pounds and growing, sir.”

“Holy shit, Mandy.”

“Zach, I gotta go; I’m off today.”

“I know … tell her I love her, will ya?” A single tear fell from Becky’s right eye, and she wiped it away with her thumb.

“Tell her yourself, Mr. Woods” Amanda said as she hit disconnect and stared into Becky’s eyes.

“What?” Becky asked as Amanda stared at the floor. “What?”

“Hubbard was gunned down this morning as he was getting his haircut … machine gun, killed ten people and injured five.”

Becky’s mouthed dropped open as her right hand raised to her forehead as Amanda whispered: “It’s an inside job, Becky. Someone leaked his whereabouts from within.”

Becky began to pace back and forth nervously as her mind flashed backwards in time: “You’ll be released immediately?” Becky interjected, “today, right now.” She closed her eyes as she saw Hubbard whisper to Timmy as he smiled and said: “He needs protection.”

“Becky, Zach’s gonna dismiss the case against Veloz.”

“What!” Becky screamed as she grabbed her abdomen in contraction.

“You okay?” Amanda whispered as she grabbed Becky’s left arm. “If he goes forward, he won’t be able to prove this case, and he won’t be able to try him again for these crimes; you know that. He has no case.”

Becky began to sweat profusely as she hunched over grabbing her belly as she moaned and then held her breath waiting for relief.

"Oh, my God, Becky," Amanda said as Becky's face turned bright red, "breathe."

"I can't, Mandy," Becky moaned as her contractions began, and she hunched over.

"Shit," Amanda yelled, "I'm calling Zach, Becky."

"Ow," Becky moaned as she attempt to stand: "Please don't, Mandy, please."

"Becky, I don't know what to do" Amanda said as she trembled.

"Call Tim, Mandy," Becky pleaded as Amanda reached into her right blazer pocket and retrieved her iPhone. "Ow," Becky screamed as Amanda hit "T" and connected to Timmy.

"Hey," Timmy said as he answered. "Five-minute recess, just got out of court. Good timing … Becky?"

"Tim, it's Amanda Jenkins."

"What's wrong, Amanda?" Tim asked as he bit his tongue missing his gum and screeched: "Ow."

"We're up on the ninth just outside the office. Becky's having contractions."

"Jesus" Tim screamed, "it's too early. Make her walk."

"She won't" Amanda screamed as Becky began to stand. "Put her on the line" Tim said as he paced nervously in front of Courtroom 19.

"Becky?" Tim asked as Amanda passed the iPhone to Becky as her contractions waned, and she stood upright.

“It’s better; it’s going away, Tim” Becky said as Amanda smiled and wiped the sweat from her brow and mumbled: “Thank God” under her breath.

“Becky, it’s like your body’s getting ready for this. It’s gonna happen again … next time walk it out; if it’s real labor, it won’t stop … understand?”

“Mmm,” Becky said as Amanda smiled and began to cry.

“Let me talk to Amanda, okay?” Timmy said as Becky passed her iPhone to Amanda as she bawled.

“Are you okay, Amanda?” Timmy said as he giggled, and Becky smiled as Amanda shook her head and mumbled: “No, I need a drink.”

“You taking her home?” Tim asked as he smiled as she continued to whimper and cry out loud.

“Yeah, right now,” Amanda said as she passed the phone back to Becky who smiled as she held it to her right ear.

“Becky?” Tim asked as Becky sighed: “Hmmm?”

“I’ll be there right after court today … you okay?”

“Mmm,” Becky said as Amanda wiped her tears and Becky whispered: “Thank you, Timmy” and hit disconnect as Tim said: “I’m late, babe; I’ll see you soon.”

As Amanda helped Becky into the cab parked at the first meter aligning the Moakley, she said: “You know you just scared the shit out of me.”

“Sorry, girlfriend,” Becky said as Amanda smiled and Becky mouthed: “I love you.” As Amanda sat down next to Becky and the cab pulled out into Courthouse Way, Amanda grabbed Becky’s left hand and held it tightly in her right palm as she whispered: “I love you too, Becky.”

As Amanda draped a blanket around Becky’s belly, she whispered: “You still have the AC on? It’s freezing in here.” Becky stared at her stomach as she smiled and said: “I’m hot” and threw the blanket on the floor next to the recliner as Amanda giggled.

“What?” Becky asked as Amanda continued to chuckle.

“Now you know why they call it having one in the oven?” Amanda said smiling coyly as Becky bobbed her head and Amanda sat down on the ottoman next to Becky’s feet.

“You sure you’re okay?” Amanda asked as Becky nodded noticing a perplexed, dumbfounded expression contorting Amanda’s face.

“What?” Becky asked as she rubbed her abdomen gently with her right hand.

“It’s Tim you reached for when you were in trouble, Becky … don’t say anything: just think about it, girlfriend.”

Amanda leaned forward and hugged Becky as the baby kicked Amanda’s breasts and she giggled. “Get some rest” she said as she stood and walked into the kitchen and poured a tall glass of cold water from the Brita. She placed the glass next to Becky on the table as Becky said: “I’m fine, Amanda … go, get outta here.”

Amanda turned to leave and stopped in the doorjamb and turned around and smiled at Becky as Becky said: “What?”

“Nothing,” Amanda replied with a smile, “I love you, girlfriend … call me, ‘k’?”

Becky nodded her head and whispered: “Go” as Amanda left and Becky turned on the television and closed her eyes as the room filled with the aroma of lilac in full bloom, and Becky’s phone vibrated on the table. As the baby kicked her ribs, she rubbed her belly and whispered: "Zach." And as she fell into the land of dreams and entered a garden of blooming purple lilacs, she heard faintly: "Charlie, Charlie, Charlie."

Becky awoke as Tim's voice echoed through the intercom: "Becky?" She opened her eyes and attempted to stand and fell back in her chair giggling. She walked over toward the intercom and buzzed Tim in.

Becky stood in the archway as Tim ran down the hallway. She grabbed him and his body melded into hers as they stood in the doorjamb. "I love you" he whispered as he held her and her body trembled.

"I love you, too, Timmy" she whispered as she led him into her apartment and closed the door. Timmy kissed her gently; and as his tongue entered her mouth, her body swayed and the baby kicked Tim in the gut causing him to back away.

"Woe" he said as she smiled, and he dropped to his knees and pressed his face into her groin.

Becky began to sob as Timmy stood. "No, huh?" he whispered as he led her to the recliner as she wailed: "I can't, Timmy. I love you, but I can't."

Tim sat down on the ottoman and wiped her tears with his right fingertips. "Becky," he whispered, why?"

Becky sobbed as Tim leaned forward and held her in his arms as she cried.

"You think you're not attractive, is that it?" Tim asked as he cupped her face in his hands.

Becky sobbed and shook her head from side to side.

"It's not me you want; is it, Becky?" Tim asked as he stood, and Becky's eyes fixated on his bulge protruding from his slacks.

Tim walked into the bathroom and splashed cold water on his face and neck. He walked back into the living room and stared at Becky who was still sobbing. He sat down on the couch across from her and he whispered: "I'm staying here, right here, tonight." He took his shoes off and whipped his blazer to the floor as he unhinged his tie and lied down on a throw pillow.

"Tim?" Becky said as she wiped her tears with the backs of her hands.

"Yeah?" Tim asked as he looked at her and sat up.

"Just give me a little time?" she said as he smiled and laid back down noticing Becky struggling to rise.

Tim helped Becky up and helped her to the bathroom. He waited with his back leaning against the wall for the door to open. As Becky opened the door, Tim grabbed her by the left arm and walked her back to the recliner as she said: "I'm not an invalid, you know" as he chuckled.

He helped her to sit and whispered: "I'm going get some Chinese … you can't have any." Becky pouted as he giggled: "I'm kidding … what do you want?"

As Becky devoured beef lo mein, her iPhone vibrated on the table in the living room. Becky stared into Timmy's eyes as he put his fork down and walked toward the buzzing cell. He picked it up and read: "one next text: Missing me? … Z."

He walked slowly with his head down into the kitchen and placed the vibrating phone on the kitchen table. She looked at Tim with tears swelling behind her lids.

Tim sat down and pushed his chair next to hers: "Talk to me, Becky" he whispered as he stared at the text displayed. "Are you still seeing him?"

Becky shook her head back and forth and said "no" as tears ran down her face, and she avoided his eyes by staring at the floor.

“Look at me, Becky,” Tim yelled as Becky’s roommate Sara opened the front door. “Hi” she said as she smiled at Tim as she walked past the kitchen. Tim grinned and stared at Becky who stared into the linoleum.

“Okay … call me when you want to talk to me, Becky” Tim yelled as he pushed his chair into the table. He walked into the living room and slipped his black leather dress shoes on, and picked up his blazer and tie from the floor as Becky held her stomach as it contracted. She picked up her iPhone and texted: “Leave me alone, Zach” and the front door swung closed with a thump.

She picked up the phone and stood and left the mess on the table as she waddled toward the recliner. As she sat down “one next text” displayed: “never” she read as she closed her eyes and watched as Zach smiled coyly and said: “Turn over, baby” as he suckled her clit in his mouth and her juice exploded.

Becky dialed Amanda; and as the call connected and Amanda said: “Hey,” Becky sobbed. “What’s wrong, Becky?”

Amanda listened as Becky sobbed unable to form coherent speech, “Tim, I ” --

“Becky, take a sip of water, close your eyes, and talk to me.”

Becky guzzled her now lukewarm water and swished it between her cheeks. She leaned her back against the recliner, and the baby kicked as Becky calmed.

“Talk to me, girlfriend,” Amanda said as Becky whimpered: “Tim wanted to, he wanted to, you know --

“Uh-huh?,” Amanda said as she mumbled, “ ‘bout time.”

“And I, I, I” -- Becky began to cry as Amanda yelled: “You couldn’t, right?”

“Mmm,” Becky sighed, “and then Zach texted me and Tim read it and” --

“Selfish prick,” Amanda yelled as Becky sobbed: “I hurt him; I really hurt him, Mandy.”

“Becky, listen to me: this was bound to happen, better now than later. You’ve got to make a decision here. If you love Tim, either commit to him or” --

“Or let him go, right?” Becky asked as she wiped her tears with her fingers and blew her nose into a tissue.

“Yeah, or let him go,” Amanda said as she whispered: “Zach’s still playing with you.”

The intercom buzzed as Becky’s iPhone blazed and caused an odd reverberation as Amanda shrieked: “Jesus, I’m deaf.”

“Hold on, Mandy” Becky said as she wobbled to her feet and walked over to the intercom holding her iPhone in her left hand cupped to her chest. She pushed the button as she mumbled: “Tim?” as Zach yelled: “Becky!” and Amanda screamed: “Selfish prick. Don’t let him in, Becky.”

Becky pressed the buzzer as Amanda said: “Stand your ground. Call me back,” as Becky placed the iPhone on the ottoman as Amanda shouted: “Becky?” She walked slowly toward the front door as Zach ran down the hallway toward her.

“What do you want?” she said as he fell to his knees and smooshed his face into her groin. Becky closed her eyes as the baby kicked his forehead, and he giggled.

Amanda started screaming: “Becky, don’t do this.” Zach stood and grinned as he walked over toward the ottoman, picked up the iPhone and whispered: “Bye Mandy” as he his disconnect.

Zach grabbed Becky's right hand and led her down the hallway toward her bedroom. He bumped smack into Sara as she walked toward the kitchen. "Hi," Zach said as Sara turned her head smelling the whiskey on his breath.

Zach closed and locked Becky's door as Becky shouted: "I can't do this." Zach kissed her gently on the lips as her body began to sway, and the baby fell fast asleep. She closed her eyes as his right hand rubbed her belly, and she inhaled his unique pheromonal hormonal spice as her juice began to flow.

"Take this off," he said as whiskey flooded her nostrils. "You don't want me, Zach; please don't do this" Becky said as she stumbled back and sat down on the edge of the bed. He wobbled on his knees toward her: "I don't want you … that's what you think?"

He sat down on the floor Indian style at her feet. Becky placed her right hand on her massive abdomen and rubbed in a counterclockwise circle: "Look at me. You don't want me; you don't love me; why are you doing this?"

Zach gently reached his right hand up gingerly caressing her right thigh. "I'm looking at you" he said as both hands reached up and grabbed her baby bump as he looked deeply into her eyes. "You're all I want" he said as his left hand wandered downward and his fingers began to play with her clit through her underwear.

"Take this off," he said as she lifted her dress over her shoulders exposing her braless enormous breasts which now sat on top of her belly. Zach shimmied her underwear toward her knees as he licked her slowly as her right hand pushed his head in deeper.

Her magma erupted down her inner thighs and dropped on his lap as he looked up into her eyes and sighed: "Oooh." Zach stood and watched as her mouth agaped as he unbuttoned his pants and stripped naked in front of her. She stared at his erection as she licked her lips and shimmied away from him toward the headboard. He climbed on top of the bed and smiled at her as she landed her back against the headrest.

"Where you going, baby?" he said as he began to lick the bottom of her left foot which tickled her immensely. She giggled as his tongue licked her ankle; and by the time his tongue reached her knee, she spread her legs apart and began to play with herself as Zach watched and licked his lips. He licked her knee and his tongue began its ascent, meandering up her inner thigh as he watched her clit engorge as she touched herself.

"You do miss me; don't you, baby?" he whispered as he inserted his tongue inside her and attempted to eat her as she drowned him and he gagged.

"I love you," she whispered as he smiled, and she orgasmed inside his mouth as he struggled to swallow her explosion. He wiggled off the bed and pounded the edge with his left hand as he licked his lips. His right hand grabbed his erection as he whispered: "Come here."

Becky tried to wiggle toward the edge of the bed, but she couldn't quite make it and Zach giggled as he pulled her arms and her body toward him. She sat on the edge of the bed and spread her legs as Zach sat on the floor and reached up with his tongue. While staring into her eyes, he tore his tongue from inside and inserted his finger until it was waterlogged. He stuck it deep inside her ass as his mouth suctioned her, and he wiggled her clit wildly with his tongue and watched with his mouth open as cum splashed across the room and dripped from the dresser drawers.

"You do miss me; don't you, baby?" he said as she nodded, and he stood and cocked his head to the side. Becky leaned forward and swallowed him, biting down on him as her teeth scraped against his rim as she vacuumed. Zach closed his eyes and swayed and began to hump her mouth; and just as he felt the ejaculate imminent, he opened his eyes and pulled out and said: "Nope, you're not ready yet, baby."

As she watched his ass walk away toward the head of the bed, she involuntarily reached down and began squeezing her clit between her thumb and forefinger as her juice dripped onto the floor and he whispered: "Come here." She struggled to stand as Zach giggled and watched her lava run down her inner thighs as she approached.

He lied down on the bed and shimmied his back toward the midline and placed a pillow under his head. "Come here, baby" he whispered as he grinned: "Come up on your knees and sit on my face awhile." Becky struggled as her belly was just too big for this position. Zach giggled as he whispered: "On your knees."

She placed herself into his open mouth and leaned back as he drank. He inserted his middle finger deep inside her ass as she climaxed and released. He whispered as he licked her and held her clit gently between his teeth: "What do you want, baby?" as tears streamed down Becky's cheeks as she exploded and submerged the mattress.

"Oh, my God, Zach," she screamed as she humped his tongue, and her sweet clear juice dribbled down his chin soaking his neck and chest. "I gotta lie down," she whispered as he smiled and placed his right hand on her belly up above.

He wiggled out from under her as she leaned forward on her knees moaning. He leaned forward and stuck his tongue inside her ass as the fingers of his left hand wiggled her clit back and forth in gentle strides. She humped as her juice jettisoned, and he smiled as she released. "Oh, God, Zach" she cried as he teased her and slid his tongue deep inside.

"Say it," he whispered as his tongue licked her clit and she moaned and shook her head. "Not ready yet, huh?" he said as he licked her labia, the inner and outer lips of her internal rose and began plunging his middle finger deep within her. She humped him and he giggled as his forearm soaked.

"Say it, baby," he said as she whispered: "I can't. It'll hurt the baby, Zach."

Zach wiggled out from under her and stood erect at the side of her bed as she collapsed onto the waterlogged mattress. "Is that what you're worried about?" he said as he chuckled.

Becky tried to get up but she couldn't as her stomach sunk in. "Help me" she said as he lifted her under her arms into a sitting position as he giggled.

"It won't hurt the baby, Becky," he said as he smiled and stared at her enormous breasts. He reached over and began squeezing both erect hard nipples in each hand; and as her milk dripped down her chest, he said: "Lie on your back, scoot over."

Becky couldn't "scoot" as the enormity of her pregnancy strapped her in place. Zach giggled as he watched her feeble attempts to move. She shimmied over to the right as much as she could as he lied next to her, and she turned onto her right side. He placed her right nipple into his mouth as he reached down between her legs with his left hand and began to diddle. She lied on her back as she saturated the mattress, and Zach's outer thigh dampened as she spread her legs allowing him more access.

She humped his hand; and as he inserted his entire fist inside her while holding her nipple gently between his teeth, she screamed: "Oh, God, Zach."

Zach giggled and whispered: "Say it, baby."

Becky held her breath as she released and shouted: "Fuck me, Zach."

"I'm not sure you're ready yet, baby" he whispered as she deluged the mattress screaming: "Put it in; please, put it in."

"Turn over, baby," he said as he let go of her nipple and his hand slipped out. She tried to turn over, but she couldn't and she watched as he placed his wet fingers inside his mouth and moaned: "Hmmm."

She masturbated as he licked each finger dry and watched her intently play as his cock pressed against her right inner thigh. He sat up and pulled her by both hands onto her knees with her head facing the bureau. He leaned on the mattress on his knees leaning forward and began licking her from behind as she began to cry: "Oh, God,

Zach; put it in."

He continued to lick her ass as she reached down with her right hand and played with herself as he watched and smiled and licked softly and gently. "Say it" he whispered as she screamed: "Fuck me, Zach."

He placed his massive erection against her inner thighs, and her juice dribbled down his balls as he moaned: "What do you want, Becky?"

"Oh, God," she screamed as he shook his member from side to side against each inner sopping thigh as he inserted his middle finger inside her, and she humped him wildly as she pleaded: "Put it in … please, Zach, put it in."

"You're not ready yet," he said as she cried and pulled his cock from between her thighs. He lied back with his head under her and ate her until she sobbed. He lapped and couldn't keep up with her overflow as she cried: "Fuck me … please, Zach, fuck me."

He smiled as he got on his knees and entered her gently as he reached his left hand in front of her vulva and wiggled her clit until she erupted.

"Harder" she screamed as her pelvic floor contracted, and he giggled as he leaned forward and kissed her back: "Nope, you're too far along; can't go harder, baby." As her muscles tightened around him and he played with her clit incessantly, he whispered: "Don't move"; and as he ejaculated inside of her, she seized her pelvic floor as he screamed: "Ahhh!"

As he slid out, he whispered: "Come here. Lay on your side. She turned around and crawled toward the headrest and lied on her left slide as Zach placed a pillow between her legs. He walked around the bed and lied behind her spooning her as she whispered: "Zach, the baby's not moving."

"It's okay, baby," he said as he smiled and placed his right hand on her abdomen. "He's sleeping. He'll wake up as soon as you relax."

“Zach?” Becky asked as she felt his erection press into her ass.

“Yeah?” Zach answered.

“I missed you,” Becky whispered as she closed her eyes.

“Yeah,” Zach mumbled as he whispered, “I missed you too, Becky.”

Becky felt the baby kick, and she began to cry as she screamed: “Why are you doing this?”

“Doing what?” he asked as he sat up and cupped his sack as she leaned her body toward him and fell on her back and stared at his erection.

“Playing with me,” Becky whispered as tears cascaded down her cheeks.

“I’m not playing with you,” he said as he wiped her right cheek with his left thumb. “I filed for divorce last week.”

Becky’s face turned white as her mouth fell open: “Really?” she asked as she licked her top lip.

“Really,” he said as he stood and walked around the bed. He stood erect in front of her as he helped her to the edge by gently pulling her arms forward.

“Staying at the Eliot,” he said and then whispered with an enigmatic grin, “in our room.”

Becky placed her mouth around him, and she suctioned as hard as she could as Zach closed his eyes and allowed her to envelop him. He let her take over his erection; and as he felt the ejaculate rise, he pulled out of her mouth and sat down on the floor at her feet.

“I love you,” he whispered as he placed his head on her left knee, and she slowly opened her legs allowing his face to creep inward. He leaned forward; and as his tongue met her clit, fluid jettisoned across the room and splashed onto the wall. He giggled as he suckled her, and she released. He wiggled his tongue against her labia as Becky humped him, and he whispered: “I love you, Becky.”

Tears flowed as Becky moaned: “Oh, God,” as Zach stuck his middle finger deep inside her while his tongue gently licked her clit. She humped and the bed squeaked as it shook as cum dripped onto the floor.

“Oh, God,” she cried as he plunged his finger in and out, then sticking his tongue deep inside her as his fingers played with her vulva; and just as her orgasm zenithed, he stopped and stood erect in front of her. “Come here,” he whispered as he pulled her to a stand.

“Get on your knees, baby,” he said as she looked at the puddle on the floor.

“Zach, it’s wet,” she said as he smiled and placed her purple dress on top of the flood. Zach helped her to the floor; and as her knees landed on the dress, she spread her arms over the mattress.

“Spread ‘em, baby,” he whispered as he knelt down and licked her clit from underneath, and her juice drenched him. He began whacking his erection against her ass as his right hand reached down and under and played with her until she erupted and pleaded: “Put it in” as he moved back a foot and whispered: “Move back a little and lean against the bed for me.”

She reached her right hand between her legs and masturbated as he inserted himself from behind. Slowly and gently, he mounted her; and as she squeezed her pelvic floor tightly around him as she played with herself, he inserted his wet pointer finger deep inside her ass as she humped him and screamed: “Harder.”

“I can’t, baby,” he whispered as he pulled out abruptly: “what: you’re not ready yet?”

“Oh, God, Zach, don’t,” Becky cried as she masturbated, and he watched as her juice pool on the floor at his knees. He held his cock in his right hand as he held it against her clit and wiggled it back and forth, from side to side, as Becky cried: "Fuck me."

Zach entered her gently and he rode her softly; and as the pointer finger of his left hand rubbed the tip of her clit, she humped him and screamed "harder" as he inserted his finger deep inside her ass. As her muscles seismically contracted and squeezed his ejaculate inside, he screamed: "Ahhh!" as Becky flooded the floor, and he smiled and giggled as his knees soaked as he turned his head to watch her juice spread across the floor.

Zach collapsed leaning into Becky's back as Becky whispered: "Don't leave me" as he giggled and fell out. "I gotta lie down, baby" he said as he stood and helped her to stand. "Stay right there" he said as she swayed and her head spun. He reached for the comforter and spread it over the wet mattress as she watched his ass and smiled as she whispered "Zach."

"Yeah?" he said as he smiled: "Come on, lie down on your left side for me right here, baby."

Becky sat on the edge of the bed and leaned back and fell onto her side as Zach reached for a pillow noticing it was drenched. He slid the pillowcase off and threw it on the floor over the puddle and slid it between her thighs. He walked around the bed and lied beside her with his right hand over her stomach; and as they began to fall asleep, cuddled in each other's warm embrace, the baby kicked Zach's arm as Zach giggled whispering with his eyes closed "woe" finally moving it between her damp thighs as he passed out cold.

On October 10th Becky arrived at the John J. Moakley United States Courthouse at 7:45. She walked through the metal detector and smiled at Peter as he gently placed his right hand against her baby bump.

"Why does everyone touch me?" she thought as she smiled and whispered: "Today's my last day for awhile … I'm gonna miss you, Peter" as Pete pulled her into a bear hug and whispered: "It'll be dark around her without you."

Becky walked into the coffee shop and from 20 feet away, Alan yelled: "Hi, Becky … the usual?" Becky approached the counter as she smiled: "Please, Alan. Listen, I'm on maternity leave after today." Alan stopped pouring the hot water in midstream, placed the styrofoam on the formica, and turned around and grabbed her left hand into his palms: "You're gonna bring the baby in, right?"

"Of course," Becky said as Alan whispered: "I'm gonna miss ya, Becky." Becky walked out of the coffee shop as her cell vibrated in her coat pocket. She placed her briefcase on the elevator floor and stared at her touchscreen.

"One new text" it displayed: "So where are ya, girlfriend?" Becky walked into her office at 7:58 and sat down at her desk as her iPhone began to vibrate once again: "How's my girl?" it read, "Love Z."

Becky's body twitched and trembled as she texted: "Please don't ever say that again." She smiled as she hit "send." She opened the rim of her tea and leaned back in her chair as she slowly sipped as her cell buzzed. She picked it up and smiled as she read: "Sorry, babe. Love you … Z."

Becky placed her tea on the desktop and pulled herself up to a stand by using the edge of the desk as leverage. She held her styrofoam cup in her right hand and walked toward the window and watched as the buoy disappeared under the waves. She sipped her tea and closed her eyes as Amanda snuck into her office, and Becky turned around as her purse thumped into the chair across from her desk.

"Hey," Amanda said as she opened the rim of her coffee and walked toward Becky.

"Hey you," Becky said as she smiled.

Amanda whispered: "Talk to Tim yet?" Becky walked slowly toward her chair, and Amanda followed and helped her to sit down.

Amanda leaned the small of her back against the desk as Becky whispered: “He won’t take my calls … won’t respond to my texts.” Amanda shook her head up and down as Becky’s eyes filled with tears.

“I think I really hurt him,” Becky whispered as Amanda cocked her head back and allowed the coffee to pour down her throat. She coughed as Becky smiled.

“So you think he doesn’t know about” --

“Zach and me … no.”

“Yes, he does, Becky,” Amanda said as she placed her left hand on Becky’s left shoulder and patted gently, “he knows.”

Amanda walked around the desk and threw the empty into the trash can as she sat down and reapplied her strawberry lip gloss and puckered her lips as Becky smiled. Amanda stared into Becky’s eyes and whispered: “And how’s Mr. Wonderful?” as Becky nodded her head up and down smiling.

“Can I ask you something, girlfriend,” Amanda said as Becky grinned: “You love them both, don’t you?” Becky bobbed her head up and down as Amanda smiled.

“Listen, throwing you a shindig at 1 in the caf; Woodbury will be there.” Becky eyes sparkled and she smiled and whispered: “Thanks, girlfriend.”

A serious expression dumbfounded Amanda as she said: “What?”

“Nothing,” Becky said, “just wish Zach could be here today, you know.”

“Yeah, so where is Mr. Wonderful today?” Amanda asked as she twirled her lip gloss between her thumb and pointer finger of her right hand as it oozed all over her fingertips and she said: “Crap,” as she placed the gloss on the desk and began to wipe her hand and fingers on a tissue.

“Noticed he put in a leave slip but he didn’t tell me about it … curious.”

“Last minute prep for trial Monday; he’s at Wyatt interviewing the cast of characters, you know” Becky said with a grin as Amanda chuckled.

“Trial starts tomorrow, babe; jury empanelment, that is … Woodbury wants this trial to start with openings 9 a.m. sharp Monday.”

“Oh,” Becky said as she sipped, “God help Zach, huh?” Amanda chuckled as Becky whispered: “Interesting case, don’t you think?”

“Yeah, I guess, heartbreaking though, you know … poor kid.”

Becky nodded her head as she flung yesterday’s Globe at Amanda that caught the corner of her left eye. “Ow!” Amanda shrieked as Becky said: “Oh, my God; I’m sorry.”

After Amanda’s eye teared, smearing her mascara and blue eyeliner across her cheek, she held the lid down for several minutes; and as her focus adjusted, she stared at the bold headline: “Gay Bashing on Trial.”

She looked up momentarily at Becky as she read:

“Trials where the victim was gay have been in the news a lot lately. These trials raise a host of important sociological (e.g., why does bullying occur, and what can we do about it?), psychological (e.g., what are the mental health causes and consequences of bullying?), and legal questions (e.g., do sexual minorities deserve special legal protection)?

Anti-gay violence is, alas, nothing new; and perhaps no case pending is more compelling or illustrative of the issues at hand than U.S. vs. McLaughlin currently pending in Federal Court for the District of

Massachusetts before Justice Charles P. Woodbury. The trial is slated to begin with jury empanelment Friday morning.

Matthew Thomas McLaughlin was a 19-year-old student at the University of Massachusetts Amherst who was beaten, tortured, and left to die near his dorm on the night of October 6, 2010, and died six days later at Massachusetts General Hospital from severe head injuries as a rock was lodged three-quarters of an inch into the back of his head."

Tears fell from Amanda's eyes as she placed the Globe on the desk. "Sometimes I hate this job" she said as Becky nodded….

Becky arrived home at 4:30 exhausted. Amanda helped Becky into her favorite recliner and turned off the AC as she said: "It's October, Becky. It's freezing in here" as Becky watched the smoke billow from her breath and smiled.

Amanda made several trips to her trunk and created a massive pile of baby paraphernalia in the center of Becky's living room. Becky's iPhone began to buzz and Amanda said: "Sit" and passed Becky her purse. "One next text" it displayed: "Wyatt in lockdown, be home soon … Love Z."

"Mr. Wonderful?" Amanda said as Becky passed her cell.

"Hmmm … in lockdown." Amanda said as Becky leaned forward grasping her abdomen.

"Happened to me one time with Zach; they made us sit there for ten hours." Amanda studied Becky's face intently as she said: "You okay?" as she watched Becky's face contort into a painful wince.

"Ow!" Becky screamed as her contractions began, and Amanda said: "Oh, my God … are you okay?"

Tears streamed down Becky's cheeks as she grumbled: "My back hurts really bad, Mandy … I can't move."

Amanda sat down on the ottoman staring into Becky's face as she held her breath and turned red.

"Come on, let's walk" Amanda said as Becky shook her head no. As she cried, she whispered: "I can't move, Amanda; I can't move."

"Yes, you can, girlfriend," Amanda said as she grabbed Becky's hands and pulled her into a stance. As she stood and straightened her back, her water broke and Amanda stared at the puddle at her feet as she screamed: "Oh, my God."

She picked up Becky's iPhone and texted: "Zach, Becky's water just broke. Get your ass back to Boston."

"I'm scared," Becky said as Amanda hugged her and whispered: "Where's your overnight bag?"

Becky shook her head back and forth: "It's too early, Mandy."

"Okay. I'm calling an ambulance 'cause I'm a nervous wreck; I can't drive." Amanda ran down the hallway as Becky hunched over as her back seized in pain. Amanda assembled a nightgown, a pair of old lady undies, and her bathrobe and ran into the kitchen searching for a trash bag.

She opened every drawer as Becky yelled: "Under the sink." Amanda placed her belongings into a Star Market shopping bag and slid her Galaxy out of her right front pocket. She dialed "911" as she raced around the apartment in a panic screaming: "Woman in labor, 218 Granite, Apartment 322, need assistance."

Amanda walked into the living room and watched as liquid continue to pool under Becky's feet. She dialed her mother and screamed: "Ma, can you get the kids tonight? Becky's in labor …
thanks, Ma."

Zach arrived at Brigham & Women's on Francis Street at 4 a.m. exhausted and disheveled. He was led into a private room decorated in Winnie-the-Pooh motifs, and he smiled at Becky as he approached. Becky's epidural had taken effect, and she was talking and chitchatting away with Amanda as he said: "Hi, beautiful."

He leaned over Becky and kissed her forehead as Amanda looked away and mumbled: "Hi, Zach."

"Hi, Mandy," he said as Amanda stood and pulled on his sleeve. "Can I have a talk with you?"

"I'll be right back, babe; don't go anywhere" he said as she chuckled. Zach followed Amanda into the hall. "What's up?" Zach said as he yawned.

"Um, you look like shit."

"Thanks, Mandy," Zach said as he ran his right hand through his dark hair.

"Listen, they want to do a C-Section."

"Why?" Zach said as his eyes widened.

"Baby's really big and breach and she's tiny. Becky wants to try to push so they're gonna let her try, but you, sir, have trial … so kiss her goodbye, go home, take a shower, and get your ass back here as soon as possible: capish?"

Zach hugged Amanda as he whispered: "Thanks, Mandy," and he walked back into Becky's room as she smiled. He sat on the edge of the bed yawning as Becky whispered: "Get outta here" as a doctor approached bedside.

Zach stood and shook his hand. "Hi, Zach Woods" he said as the doctor smiled: "Hi, Philip Chase," he said as Zach stared at his badge: "Philip A. Chase, M.D."

"You're the father?" Chase asked as Zach smiled and nodded. "Can I have talk with you?" he whispered as Zach followed him into the hallway, and Amanda held Becky's left hand as she sat down on the edge of Becky's cot.

"Listen, Mr. Woods, we ran an ultrasound a couple of hours ago … baby's breach and 13 pounds." Zach turned white as his mouth dropped open: "13 pounds?" Chase smiled and nodded.

"It's really advisable to do a C-Section at this juncture and Becky won't agree, can you" --

Zach stormed into Becky's room as the doctor stood in the doorjamb and Amanda walked toward him. They smiled at each other as Zach screamed: "Are you out of your mind?"

"Zach, what's your problem?" Becky asked with a grin.

"The baby's breach and 13 pounds, that's my problem." He walked toward her and sat down on the bed as Becky whispered: "So?"

"So you need to have a C-Section, baby. It's dangerous for you to push, dangerous for the baby and dangerous for you." Chase and Amanda walked into the room as Becky said: "Okay, let's do this."

Zach stood and turned around and whispered to Chase: "Thanks, Doc … I'm on trial; I'll be back." Chase turned to Amanda and whispered: "he's leaving?" as Amanda and Becky giggled.

Becky awoke groggy; and as her eyes began to focus, she read the clock mounted next to the television high up on the rear wall: "12:55" it read. Becky began hyperventilating and tears free-flowed as her eyes darted searching for a bassinet. Tim sat in the chair next to her bedside and grabbed her left hand as she stirred.

"Tim?," Becky said as she cried, "what happened? Oh, my God, where's my baby?"

Tim kissed her hand and whispered: "He's fine, Becky. He's fine. We almost lost you" he said as tears fell from his eyes. "You remember anything?" he whispered as she whimpered and shook her head from side to side.

Becky looked around the semiprivate room at the bouquets displayed. There were lilies and white roses in large vases on the radiator across from her bed.

"How long was I out, Timmy?"

"You had the baby at six a.m. and went into cardiac arrest … about seven hours." Tim stood and sat down next to Becky as he held her left hand and cradled it in his palms.

"I love you, you know" he said as tears cascaded and dripped from his chin onto the white sheet.

"I love you too, Timmy" she said as Timmy wiped his cheeks, "but I'm not in love with you."

Timmy shook his head up and down as he whispered: "No man will ever love you like I do, Becky." Becky tasted the salt of her tears as Tim kissed the top of her hand and pressed the call button for the nurse. A nurse dashed into the room and smiled as she saw there was no emergency to be had.

Tim backed away as the nurse whispered: "You're fine" and walked around the opposite edge of Becky's hospital bed. She took her pulse as Becky shook and trembled.

"Normal, sweetheart," the nurse said as Timmy bawled and cradled her left hand.

"You want to see your baby, I bet?" the nurse said as Becky bawled and shook her head up and down. As the nurse exited, Zach stood in the doorway. Tears fell from the corners of his eyes as he watched Becky cry.

As he approached her bedside, Tim stood and whispered: "Hi, Zach" as he wiped his cheeks.

"Hi, Tim" Zach said as Tim shook his hand and leaned forward:

“Take care of her” he said as Becky broke down into a wail as she watched Tim walk away.

Zach sat on the edge of her bed and leaned forward and wiped her tears as they embraced. He lifted his head off her neck as he heard an odd scraping of the floor. The nurse wheeled the bassinet to the foot of the bed and smiled at Zach as he stood.

“You want to hold your baby, Daddy?” she said as Zach nodded and Becky cried. She placed the newborn into Zach’s arms as she whispered: “Look at his eyes … he looks just like you.”

Zach cradled the baby as tears landed on the baby’s cheeks. He kissed his forehead as the baby’s dark eyes fixated on his father’s face.

The nurse stood at the foot of the bed as Zach sat down next to Becky and placed the baby into his mother’s arms. The baby stared at Becky as she cried and looked at Zach: “He has your eyes,” she said as tears cascaded, and the nurse slipped quietly into the hallway.

The baby began to cry as Zach reached around Becky’s neck and untied her johnny and shimmied it down exposing her engorged left breast. He nodded as she continued to sob, and she put the baby to the breast as he cried and turned his tiny face away from the nipple.

“What’s his name, Becky?” Zach whispered as he gently squeezed her left nipple and dipped his pointer finger into her oozing colostrum and smeared it gently on the baby’s lips.

“His name is Charlie,” Becky said as the baby latched on for the first time guided by Zach’s gentle hand on his tiny cheek, “Charlie Zachary Lawrence.”

Zach cried so hard he began choking and coughing as he couldn’t catch his breath. He dropped to the floor at Becky’s bedside and slid out a small jewelry box from his blazer and placed it on his open right palm.

“Ow,” she cried as the baby bit down on her nipple, and Zach smiled as he opened the box and she stared at the one carat pearl-shaped diamond in his palm as the baby suckled.

“Marry me?” Zach said as he got off the floor and sat down next to her on the cot. She shook her head up and down as the baby nursed, and Zach hugged them as Becky and Zach wailed.

“Charlie” hugged Zach’s back causing a freezing-cold aura to envelop them in an icicle shroud; and as the room filled with the luscious vibrant scent of lilacs in bloom, Zach whispered: “No, his name is Charlie, Charlie Zachary Woods”….

CPSIA information can be obtained at www.ICGtesting.com
Printed in the USA
LVOW10s0211180216

475523LV00029B/981/P

9 781500 616779